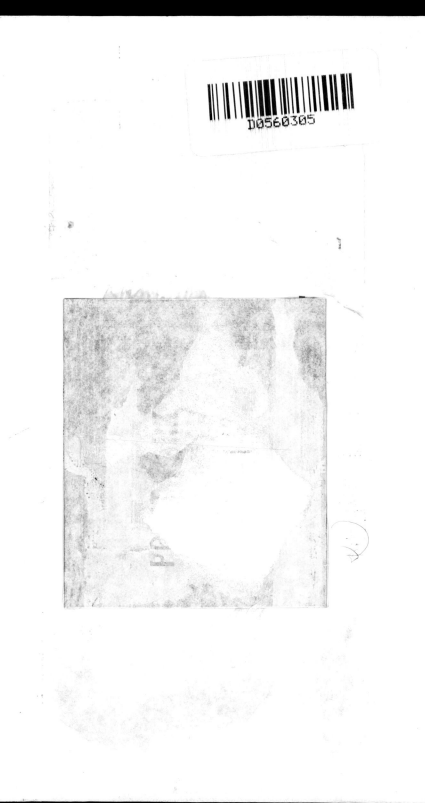

DREAMWATCHER

Other books by Theodore Roszak

Bugs

Person/Planet: The Creative Disintegration of Industrial Society

The Making of a Counter Culture: Reflections on the Technocratic Society and Its Youthful Opposition

Where the Wasteland Ends: Politics and Transcendence in Post-Industrial Society

Pontifex: A Revolutionary Entertainment for the Mind's Eye Theatre

Unfinished Animal: The Aquarian Frontier and the Evolution of Consciousness

Editor and contributor:

The Dissenting Academy

Masculine/Feminine: Readings in Sexual Mythology and the Liberation of Women

Sources

Theodore Roszak

DREAMWATCHER

DOUBLEDAY & COMPANY, INC.
GARDEN CITY, NEW YORK
1985

All characters and events in this book are fictitious.
Any resemblance to actual events or persons living or dead
is strictly coincidental.

Library of Congress Cataloging in Publication Data
Roszak, Theodore, 1933–
Dreamwatcher.
I. Title.
PS3568.08495D7   1985   813'.54
ISBN 0-385-18894-3
Library of Congress Catalog Card Number 84–4109

DREAMWATCHER

1

Blood-red.

Why was her daughter dreaming of a blood-red wolf?

Laney had no taste for predatory beasts. A shy girl, still close enough to childhood to enjoy its playful fictions, her dream habits ran to gentle creatures. Household pets. Songbirds. Barnyard friends and teddy bear toys.

Instinctively, Deirdre moved to dissolve her daughter's dream, then stopped, waiting to see if the danger would deepen.

Magically, a moonlit forest formed about her. Gnarled trees, a traveling ground mist. Through the eerie haze the wolf stalked, coming closer, showing fangs. Its color was the crimson of a fresh kill. Would Laney turn and run, letting the dream slide into a nightmare?

No.

Instead, she dreamed a clearing in the wood and placed herself at its center to confront the beast. Brave girl. The wolf, gliding forward for the attack, reshaped itself, became two-legged. A man. The image was unmistakable. The black cloak, the slicked-back hair, the paste-white face. Count Dracula had entered Laney's dream, the classic movie image. Lord of the Undead, who could be wolf, bat, cloud of smoke. The Vampire King advanced, arms raised to menace Laney. The eyes flared like live coals, the fingers tightened into talons.

Deirdre stepped forward to defend, then stopped short again, hearing her daughter burst into giggles. Looking once more, Deirdre caught the comedy of the situation. Yes, it was a ludicrous display, not frightening at all. No one took this old Hollywood harum-scarum seriously anymore. Kids least of all. She relaxed and drew off, letting the dream continue.

Then Alma, Laney's cousin, was there, taking charge, ordering the vampire to step forward.

"Come here, you sucker!" Alma commanded. The fearless voice of authority.

Obsequiously, the now-chastened monster emerged from the shadowed wood, looking more crumpled and comic by the moment. His clothes sagged. He whimpered and fell to his knees, once more becoming the scarlet wolf but no longer fierce. A *Mother Goose* wolf. Laughing, Alma reached to fasten something around its neck. What was it? A leash to tie the brute? Together the two girls, tittering brightly, inspected Alma's handiwork. Looking more closely, Deirdre saw. It was not a leash but a belt of another kind, one whose use Laney had learned from her cousin only last month.

"Sure it rubs," Alma was explaining self-importantly as she cinched the belt tighter. "But otherwise he'll go leaving a trail of blood. Yuk!"

Deirdre backed farther off. The dream was safe. It was only a playful menstrual fantasy. Laney's pubescent body was coaxing her toward womanhood, filling the picture palace of her sleeping mind with funny-fearful images of the mothering blood. Deirdre thought, *How nicely dreams can deal with the little daily terrors of life.* Last month, she recalled, her daughter had also dreamed of a dangerous crimson. A gory operation. A mad doctor probing the incision with menacing instruments. But that dream too had turned comic-benign. The hideous wound had become—hey, presto!—an ice cream drum and the maniac surgeon became the boy behind the counter at Baskin-Robbins, scooping up drooly gobs of the month's special flavor: Cherry Curse.

There were more girls now in Laney's dream, friends joining in the game. Dracula, riotously shape-shifting—sometimes a bat, sometimes a disheveled Bela Lugosi caricature—frolicked among them, then divided and divided again into two . . . three . . . four of his kind. A punk quartet. Four pelvis-pumping mock-Draculas, corpse-faced, with gaping, black-slashed mouths, each member armed with a wolf-howling guitar. A neon marquee blazed overhead. *The Undead.*

At a signal from Alma (timid Laney often delegated the mischief of her dreams to her older cousin), the girls ganged up on the lead singer, who had become a cadaverous David Bowie look-alike, and roughly stripped him of his leather pants. Carrying on unperturbed, he pranced proudly before his admiring schoolgirl audience, playing the ithyphallic clown. Then a wailing climax in the music and, inhaling mightily to the depths of his pelvis, the Bowie ghoul miraculously sucked the dangling penis inward with a luscious slurp. A vaginal cleft, oversized and brightly engorged, took its place. Laney, pointing and giggling, passed a whispered remark to Alma that sent her cousin into a small convulsion of laughter. The wordplay of dreams had found a more suitable title for the Lord of Menstrual Blood.

"It's Cunt Dracula," Alma squealed and all the girls chorused the pun. It flashed in neon overhead. The music soared.

Deirdre, watching, felt a faint flush of guilt, thinking how unfair it was for her to eavesdrop on her daughter's uncensored dreamlife. *Forgive me, baby*, she thought. Time to leave and restore Laney's privacy.

Turning with a wide-awake part of her mind to the outside, Deirdre noted that the morning was near. She could withdraw now and let the dream run toward diffusion. But before she surrendered her vigil, she made one last deep probe, hunting for what she never wanted to find. Not an image or a word. Not a thing, but Nothing.

The *Nothing*.

The emptiness where the black dreams happened.

The devouring void that had captured Peter's sleep and sucked away his mind.

In the two years she had spent on her secret sentinel duty in Laney's dreams, there had been no sign of that danger. Still, she could not free herself of the fear: that the black dreams would come for her daughter as they had come for her husband, an inherited cancer of the soul, visited father upon child. She searched for the *Nothing* until she was sure it would not appear. The horizons of Laney's dream were clear.

She had guarded her daughter through another night and now she could rest.

2

From where she sat, Deirdre Vale could see the Pacific spread before her like a shield of blue steel flaring beneath the afternoon sun. The longer she gazed into the water's glare, the more human bits and pieces she gleaned from the shimmering surface. Flecks of black that were distant fishing trollers. Sticks on the horizon that were oil rigs toiling many miles across the Santa Barbara Channel. Where the coast swerved away south toward Los Angeles, she could just make out the surfers floating on the rippling skin of the sea like water flies, lazily waiting for the wave that would grant them a giddy ride to the distant shore.

She sat alone in the quiet office, absorbing the ocean's long tranquil swell into herself. Dr. Devane allowed her this moment of meditative calm before their sessions began. She needed it. She was a tautly strung woman, the nerves pressed close to the flesh, the flesh stretched tight to the bone. Lately haggard, she had thinned beyond lean to gaunt. Even relaxed, she kept her narrow shoulders thrust forward like defending arrows. Her essential, fine-crafted beauty might be apparent to a second look, but not to a first. The first would see the lingering fragility of recent illness: a pallor that even generous doses of sunshine and open air had not succeeded in coloring over; a brilliance about her wide, dark eyes that was more feverish than vivacious. She was in her second year at the Clinic, but still not far enough along in her recovery to care about her looks. She wore no makeup; her hair, whipped back and carelessly ribboned, fell across her shoulders more tangled than curled. She was free to wear her own clothes—Dr. Devane encouraged it—but she preferred the baggy gray tunic and string-tied slacks that the Clinic assigned to its new patients: an emblem of dependence she was not yet prepared to surrender.

His usual ten minutes late, Dr. Devane entered briskly. He gave her shoulder a paternal squeeze, then sank into his wheezy leather chair,

notebook in hand, ready at once to talk about the dreams. But first—
she hoped—he would ask about Laney. He did. "Have you been
spending much time with her?"

Yes, she answered. Every night since their last session. She told him
apologetically because Laney was not her assignment. The attention
she gave her daughter's dreams distracted from the patients he expected her to monitor. It also tired her and blunted her perception.
But she knew he would not scold her. He understood her concern and
even shared it. Dr. Devane cared for Laney as much as he cared for
Deirdre.

"Anything we should be concerned about?" he asked.

"At first there was something that worried me. She's been dreaming
about vampires."

"Sounds scary."

"Her dreams have a lot to do with blood. She's anxious about her
period. It's so new for her."

Dr. Devane smiled. "If a twelve-year-old girl weren't a little apprehensive about her period, *that* might be something to worry about. I'd
say what you're finding in Laney's dreams is quite normal."

His voice was low and comforting. It wrapped around her like a
warm blanket. She drew the warmth about herself and let her body
soften. If Deirdre had ever been asked to design a father, he would
have looked—and sounded and acted—like Dr. Devane. He would
have been large, with a large, balding head and a heavy mustache. He
would have had soft, sad eyes and a strong, slightly gruff voice. He
would have been patient, protective, gently domineering. Her own
father had been nothing like that. From the little she could remember
of him before her parents divorced, he had been remote, unconcerned,
perhaps uncaring. And she had needed his care so much, more than he
had ever realized.

Once, two months after she had become Dr. Devane's patient, Deirdre had told him, "My father wasn't what a father should be."

"What should a father be?" he had asked.

The thought had leaped into her mind: *He should be like you.* But she
did not speak the words, fearing they might offend him. Another two
months passed before she found the courage to say, "I wish my father
had been like you." By then, she knew he would not mind. He could be
trusted with her thoughts. She had learned that psychiatrists were
willing to be the fantasy fathers, mothers, lovers, friends of all their

patients. Still, it had thrilled Deirdre to tell him: a small, discreet confession of love.

He had asked, "Why do you think your father should have been like me?"

"Because if he were a doctor like you, he would have known what to do about the dreams. I could have told him and he would have shown me what to do. Maybe he would have made them stop and go away."

"Why go away?"

"They're such a trouble. I'd rather have my own dreams—all to myself. Everybody's dreams should be private."

As often as she dared, Deirdre found ways to remind him how it burdened her to monitor dreams. It was a recurring theme in their sessions, less frequent now than a year ago, or the year before that, but always there, the timid lament that said, "Make this power go away; make me like other people." By now, she knew he could not do that. The power was woven into the texture of her mind, as deeply ingrained as the gift of speech. When she asked, it was only in order to hear his consoling answer, which was always the same.

"But if we stopped the dreams, we wouldn't be able to help people the way we do. Don't you want to use your powers to help people?"

And yes was Deirdre's answer—but not the whole answer. It was really Dr. Devane she wanted to help. He was a famous and important man. People came from all parts of the world to be treated by him. And when they came, Deirdre was his eyes inside their minds. To begin with, she had been one of those troubled people herself. She was still Dr. Devane's patient, a resident of the Clinic, wearing its uniform, following its routines, rarely leaving the grounds. But now she was also his "research assistant." That was how he introduced her to the Clinic's many visitors—though he did not mention the dreamwatching. That was their secret, not to be revealed until Dr. Devane was ready to publish the results of their work. Until she came to the Clinic, Deirdre had spent most of her life bewildered and embarrassed by her uncanny power. "I suppose I'm a sort of freak," she had once told Dr. Devane. That was how she had thought of herself for years: mentally deformed, abnormal, repulsive. "Nonsense," he had insisted. "You must never think of yourself like that. You have a gift." And he had shown her how to make that gift useful. He had let her share his responsibility for healing people.

The dreams let her do that; they were her special way to serve and please him. They allowed her to come to his office two afternoons each week, to be with him alone in the quiet room that stood high and lonely above the ocean like a lighthouse. The dreams made her part of his work. She knew there were other watchers at the Clinic. But they were mere beginners. Those she had met since her arrival were only children, mostly autistic and none of them emotionally stable enough to be of any reliable use. *She* was different. She was the best watcher Dr. Devane had ever discovered. He had told her that many times. She had taken to the training marvelously and her powers were growing sharper all the time. He had great plans for her that would keep them together for many years to come.

By now, after nearly two years at the Clinic, Deirdre was perceptive enough to recognize how Dr. Devane used the promise of his companionship as an enticement for her services. She did not object to his bribery. She understood that he wanted her to exercise and expand her strange talent until she became as excited with it as he was. For all she was worth, Deirdre wanted that too. And she could feel it happening little by little each time they worked together, though she could not always tell if the excitement she experienced arose from the pride she took in her watching or from her deepening love for Dr. Devane.

"Now suppose we get down to work," he said with a wink of encouragement. Deirdre drew herself up in her chair. Very alert, very professional. Waiting.

They monitored patients in groups of five or six, each group for two months at a time. Every night Deirdre went hunting in the dark reaches of the sleeping mind, filling her memory with the dreamlives of others. If Dr. Devane wished it, she could report what each patient dreamed in minute detail. Every image, every word. She was that good. She kept no notes. She did not have to. All she needed to do was settle her mind and let it fill with the sense of friendship or concern she felt for those she monitored. Then, as if she were watching a film running before her eyes, she could recall their dreams and describe them exactly. Many times, Dr. Devane marveled at her powers of observation and retention. In their early days together, when he was still gauging her capacities, he had often invited her total recall. Now he rarely did that. Their work was taking on the rigor and economy of a mature clinical technique. No excess, no time wasted. For each patient, there was a special set of objects—people, words, events—that Dr. Devane wanted to have monitored. "A shopping list," he called it. Deirdre was to watch for just those things. Or, at his direction, she was to insinuate them into the dreams she monitored, then observe the results.

She did not always understand why Dr. Devane chose the items he did. Why was she to look for staircases and turning wheels in Jean O'Malley's dreams? Why burning buildings in John Sturdevant's dreams? What were the tiny, shiny, red circles that fell like snowflakes in little Jimmy Fuller's nightmares? Sometimes it was not the objects themselves that mattered, but their size or color. Sometimes it was not what was said in the dream that Deirdre was to remember, but the tone of voice or the number of times it was repeated. Above all, there was the factor Dr. Devane called "depth." Depth was a special difficulty for Deirdre. It meant the distance the dream happened from the control of the waking mind. Dr. Devane insisted that there had to be an exact way to measure depth because the deeper the dream, the more uncontrolled and therefore the more uncensored. Deirdre was trying hard to develop a reliable sense of depth, but she was still a long way from the precision Dr. Devane wanted. "Pay attention to the light in the dream and the sharpness of the pictures," he insisted. "Evaluate the clarity of the background images." He wanted her to assign numbers to these judgments. "Try to think of yourself as the light meter on a camera," he advised. But that was extremely difficult for her. It was not her way of watching. Instead, she always got distracted by the stories and the feelings she saw before her.

Dr. Devane had a theory about dreams that Deirdre did not fully grasp. He did not seem to want her to. As he put it, he wanted her to be nothing more than a neutral recording device. Eyes and ears without a mind. That was not easy, Deirdre had discovered. It meant stifling her curiosity and sometimes her strong feelings of concern or fear or revulsion. Still, she did understand that by tracing the role the items on the shopping list played in the dream stories people created for themselves, she was helping Dr. Devane chart the progress of his patients. He could tell what preoccupied their minds, what frightened them or soothed them. People never remembered these things as clearly as Deirdre could. Or if they did, they were apt to lie or exaggerate. Now, through Deirdre, Dr. Devane had found a way to read the secrets his patients would not admit to him, sometimes not to themselves. It was like having a microscope of the mind. For the first time, a doctor could see the psychic germs that made his patients sick.

Eager as she was to please Dr. Devane, Deirdre was embarrassed at how little she was offering him today. Meager, blurred reports that gave him little to work with. She could see that he was taking no notes on their session. She had spent too much of her time with Laney during the past several nights. She had not come to her assignments fresh and alert. She knew this was disappointing to him, but she also knew he would not complain. He never complained, but greeted even her failures with good humor. As if to say, "We'll try a little harder next time." And she always vowed to herself that she would.

"What about Pearl?" he asked finally. Pearl was the last of the current group. Deirdre had been careful to make sure she brought something of value to report on Pearl, who was one of Dr. Devane's special cases.

Pearl Johnson was a sensitive and troubled black girl of eighteen. Dr. Devane called her "schizophrenic." That word always puzzled Deirdre. She knew it meant "split," but people could be split in so many different and bewildering ways. Pearl certainly seemed to need a better word than that, something that meant not "split" but "shattered." Young as she was, she had lived through the torments of hell and had arrived at the Clinic as emotional rubble. Throughout her tortured childhood, she had been sexually molested by her father, then by her mother's many lovers, one of whom had turned her into a prostitute at the age of nine. She had spent most of her last four years in mental institutions, withering away, silently despairing, several times attempting suicide. Finally, a year ago, Dr. Devane found her and brought her to the Clinic. She came as part of a new program he had begun on child abuse. "A classic case," he called her, almost as if that made her suffering some form of distinction. He was using Pearl as the centerpiece of his study. And most of what he knew about her, he knew because of Deirdre, who had explored every corner of the girl's dreamlife.

Pearl's dreams were never happy. It seemed impossible for her to visualize herself as anything but a victim, sexually exploited by brutal and domineering men. Night after night, she suffered through dreams of rape and rough seduction, of sexual encounters filled with anguish and humiliation. She skulked through her dreams as if she had no right even to the privacy of her own mind. Patiently, for months now, Dr. Devane had been trying one strategy and another, struggling to restore Pearl's self-esteem. At his instruction, Deirdre spent a part of each day with Pearl, affirming their friendship, gaining a more graceful influence over her dreams. And the effort was beginning to take effect, but in an unforeseen way that had lately begun to trouble Deirdre. As shy and withdrawn as she was in waking life, Pearl was beginning to grow sexually aggressive in her dreams, seeking to force her love upon

Deirdre. At first, the gestures had been timid and hesitant. A tender hug, a brief kiss. Then, last month, things had taken a more dramatic turn.

Deirdre had entered one of Pearl's dreams to plant a suggestion. She and Pearl had walked together, spoken, exchanged endearing words. Pearl, at first little-girlishly, had asked to be held. But when Deirdre complied, seeking to offer a mothering comfort, Pearl had become heatedly passionate, stroking Deirdre's body, kissing her deeply. With startling eagerness, she had torn at Deirdre's blouse. Deirdre, confused and uncertain, had tactfully dissolved the dream. She reported the experience to Dr. Devane with some embarrassment. But he had seized upon it at once with great enthusiasm. "That's the first time we've seen Pearl take the initiative in an encounter. It's because she trusts you. At this point, she may only feel free to act assertively with another woman. That's excellent. Let's watch for that to happen again."

But Deirdre had not liked the idea. For one thing, she could notice that Pearl's newfound erotic attraction was seeping into her waking life. Little unmistakable sexual gestures were coloring their relationship. Deirdre did not care to encourage that. Yet, here was Dr. Devane saying, as he had several times before, "I think we're going to have to do more to draw Pearl out. Try becoming more flirtatious with her in the dreams. Make yourself more sexually available. And this time, let her go as far as she wishes. Just be a passive love object for her. Let's see what happens."

Deirdre recoiled visibly at the suggestion. Dr. Devane could see her shying away from his instruction; he could not have guessed why. Though she had never told him, Deirdre had made love with women many times in dreams. But she was jarred to realize that Dr. Devane believed she could manipulate her sexuality so casually. She did not want him to think of her like that. With him, she wanted to be a woman who needed a man's love—his love.

"I don't think I can do that," she said, playing coy.

Devane smiled, thinking he understood. "Of course, it wouldn't really be a sexual act. You might try to understand it differently. It would be Pearl's way of asserting power and perhaps gaining a bit more confidence in herself."

Still Deirdre hesitated, letting herself look threatened, and he relented. This was not the first time he had surprised her by asking something more than she was ready to give. In recent months, he had more and more frequently urged her to do things in his patients' dreams that frightened or embarrassed her. He seemed to be deliberately pressing her toward new possibilities. But whenever she displayed hesitation, he would back off and say, "Very well. Not yet. We'll let that wait." He was never demanding, never displeased.

"In fact," he went on, "it might be a good idea to taper off on the monitoring for a while—until you feel more secure about Laney. I know you're spending a great deal of time with her dreams—more than you really need to. You're taxing yourself. That's not good."

"I know," Deirdre agreed. "But you see, it's the time of year. Just when school lets out. That's when Peter . . . died. Two years ago. I know Laney remembers. I'm having her take some summer courses—just to keep her thoughts occupied. So she won't have too much time to spend with unhappy memories."

"She hasn't dreamed of Peter for a long while," Dr. Devane reminded her.

"I know. But she's going through so many changes at this age. Sometimes she gets a little broody about things. I can't help it, I remember how it was with Peter when the bad dreams started. And I worry. I'm afraid she might have inherited something from her father. She has so many of his characteristics."

Dr. Devane reached out to take her hand. "No, Deirdre. Believe me. We have absolutely no reason to believe that somnipathy is hereditary."

Somnipathy. A pathology of the sleeping mind. More technically: Acute Compulsive Somnipathy. Dr. Devane had invented that clanking, unfeeling name for the horrors that Deirdre called "black dreams." He had explained to her soon after she arrived at the Clinic for treatment that it was an extremely rare mental condition. It was classified as a "degenerative" disease, meaning that it wasted the mind until it left its victims permanently incapacitated. That was nearly all anybody knew about somnipathy. No one could say how it got started or how to treat it once it struck. But of this much Dr. Devane was certain: the disease was not genetic. There was no possibility Laney would ever be afflicted with it.

"Please," he went on. "Trust me. Once you have Laney settled for the summer, try to spend less time with her dreams. You know, you might do her much more good by giving her all the attention you can during the day when she's awake and with you. At this age, there must be a lot of things she needs your help with."

Smiling, Deirdre agreed. She would follow his advice. She always did. He was pleased.

"You see," he explained, "very soon now, when you feel more confident about Laney, I want to start working quite a bit more intensely."

"You mean with more patients?"

"Not more, but with more difficult cases. The autistic children, for example. You have a gift for dealing with them. Dr. Lichtman thinks you're a gem with the kids. I want to make a thorough survey of their dreamlives. There's no telling how many of them may turn out to be watchers—like you. And then there are the catatonic cases. So much unexplored territory there." Whenever he spoke of his plans, his soft, weary eyes took on a luster that was keen and cold. "Deirdre, we're only skimming the surface. What we're doing with Pearl and the others —it's just standard textbook psychiatry. Traumatic memories, repressed guilt. The same old material, same old techniques. There's so much more to the human mind. We're like pioneers who've landed on an uncharted continent. It's going to be very challenging. You'll have to be well-rested and undistracted. But I'm sure you're ready to begin working at much greater depths."

He was trying to make the prospect sound inviting. But for her, it was also fearful. Deirdre knew that "greater depths" meant darker dreams. And the darkest dreams of all were black dreams. "Was I at a deeper level with Peter—in his dreams?"

"Yes, you were very deep then. That's why I know you're capable of much more than we've done so far. It took great sensitivity and great courage to explore Peter's dreams. And you did that on your own— with no help from me. I want to use that talent to the utmost."

"It was frightening—with Peter."

"That's because you were so close to him. You loved Peter. You were part of his dreams. It won't be that way with others, with strangers. You can be much more neutral, more detached."

"I can't contact the dreams of people I don't care about," she reminded him. The half dozen or so patients she now monitored had become good friends. Caring built the bridge between them, allowing her to cross and enter their sleeping minds.

"Ah, that's one of the things we really must examine," Dr. Devane said. "We want to see if there are other methods of building rapport besides friendship and personal concern. Those emotions are good, but they limit your range and effectiveness as a watcher. On the other hand, a motivation like strong curiosity—now that might allow you to be more objective about your observations. You might not be so squeamish about the things we may have to do. . . ." He could see the trepidation in Deirdre's face. He knew he must be careful not to move her along too quickly. She was still delicate, only just testing out her powers. "Well, we'll talk more about this later," he said, backing off. "Let's let it wait until you feel more settled about Laney. But I want you to know, I have high hopes for you—for us." His hands were on her shoulders, a strong, sure grip raising her from her chair and leading her toward the door. Outside in the corridor, as he sent her on her way, he added, "I want to see you become my most powerful psychiatric instrument. I know you're capable of that."

*　　*　　*

Instrument.

My *instrument.*

Deirdre kept the word with her; later she sat pondering it over coffee while she waited for Laney to come home from school. "Home" was a little white stucco bungalow in a wooded corner of the Clinic grounds, one of a small cluster of modest accommodations set aside for guests and resident staff. It was minimal quarters, but commanded a millionaire's vista of the California coast.

Dr. Devane had never used that word before. She was trying to discover some good, encouraging feel to it. She wasn't certain she could. It touched her mind with a metallic chill.

"What do you think, Smitty? You come into the Devane Clinic as a freak; you leave as an 'instrument.' Is that an improvement?"

Smitty looked up, utterly uncomprehending. He gave no answer. She did not expect one. Smitty never spoke. He was one of the Clinic's aboriginal patients, an autistic child who grew up to be an autistic adult. The cruel silence of the disease had swallowed him once and for all. Now he roamed the grounds like a friendly zombie, assigned menial chores that he left half done. This afternoon he had been sent to clean Deirdre's patio. He had remembered to bring a plastic trash bag, but not a broom. So he busied himself picking up every leaf and twig individually, carrying it to the bag, dropping it in. Clambering about on hands and knees, he looked more than usually doglike. Smitty, the human mascot of the Devane Clinic.

It occurred to Deirdre how much she appreciated Smitty's occasional mindless, speechless company. He listened attentively, understanding almost nothing, incapable of betraying any confidence. The perfect blank presence. He served an important need for her. She talked to Dr. Devane about everything, but she could only talk about Dr. Devane to Smitty.

"He says I'm going to be his best instrument. I guess he means that as a sort of promotion. But I don't know . . . did you ever want an instrument for a friend? Would you take an instrument to a party? Sometimes the way he puts things. . . ."

Smitty was paying strenuous attention, his stiffly deformed face frowning and squinching with the hopeless effort. Deirdre had developed a soft spot for him as soon as she arrived at the Clinic. She knew what it was like to live inside an autistic prison. Whenever she caught sight of Smitty, the thought intruded itself: *There but for the grace of Dr. Devane.* . . .

"Of course, nobody takes a freak out to lunch either, do they? Which do you think has more sex appeal for a big, famous psychiatrist? An instrument or a freak? Not much of a choice, huh?"

The twig Smitty had just picked up turned out to be a bug. He was not sure what to do with that. He brought it across the patio and handed it carefully to Deirdre, who deposited it on the table before her and let it scramble away. She could see Laney's school bus climbing the steep rise that led to the front entrance of the Clinic. She rose and went to meet it, stopping to give the kneeling Smitty a pat and a stroke as she passed.

"But I'll tell you this much. Worse comes to worst, at least people can feel sorry for us freaks. If we're the harmless type, that is."

3

As far back as she could remember, Deirdre Vale had been a dreamwatcher. In her childhood, before she could clearly tell where she left off and others began, she accepted the experience as normal. She simply lived in her family's dreams as if they were her own. Awake and asleep, people were together. It had never been any other way for her.

It was her father who gave the first jarring sign of disapproval. One morning at breakfast, he heard his daughter casually reporting a dream. *His* dream—from last night. Had she done that before? If she had, he had never paid attention. This time he did. Deirdre, in her childish way, was prattling on about Daddy and Juney, the babysitter. Daddy and Juney undressed. Daddy showing Juney his pee-wee. Daddy and Juney tasting bodies. Juney biting Daddy there and there. Daddy spanking Juney, and tying her with a rope, and . . .

It was a garbled and giggly four-year-old version of an adult dream, at once both innocent and impudent. It produced immediate censorship. *Deirdre, be quiet! Deirdre, stop!* Keep your dreams to yourself. Of course Daddy didn't have dreams like that. Those were Deirdre's dreams. Nasty dreams! Where does she pick up ideas like that? A scolding voice. A frowning face.

Later—the same distressed response from her mother and from Meg, her sister. Meg, older by three years, complained how Deirdre teased her in her dreams. Deirdre broke into her sleep and woke her up.

Make Deirdre stop. Make Deirdre stay out of Meg's dreams.

Again, parental displeasure—this time directed at Meg. Don't talk nonsense. Deirdre *couldn't* be in Meg's dreams. Meg's dreams were all her own. But Mother's face, staring at Meg, at Deirdre, was worried, puzzled. The face said, without speaking: *Don't make Mother worried.*

Don't make Mother upset. There are things you must not say—even if they are true.

So Meg stopped saying them. But she was still too young to be reasoned out of what her own startled experience told her. She knew Deirdre had been in her dreams, making mischief, stealing her secrets. And what she knew made her afraid of her uncanny baby sister. With the passing of time, Meg would learn that it was "impossible" for one person to watch another's dreams. She would forget Deirdre's night-time visits to her sleeping mind. But the fear would linger just beneath the surface. It would always stand between the sisters, a barrier of awe and apprehension.

Meg's dream. *Deirdre's* dream.

Your dream. *My* dream.

How bewildering it was for little Deirdre! But in time, she came to understand. Dreams were inside people's heads. Each head was supposed to have its own dreams. Dreams belonged to people—like their own toys. Nobody was supposed to be in another person's dreams. Deirdre must have her own dreams; she mustn't trespass upon others.

But Deirdre had no dreams of her own. She searched for them. She made her mind bright and wakeful in her sleep, only to discover she was in her sister's dream, or her mother's, or her father's. Everything in the dream happened to them, never to her. She could only stand and watch, trying not to be seen. That made her feel jealous and deprived. But mustn't say so. Mustn't talk about the dreams. Watch—and don't tell. Dreams are secret.

Why did they have to be secret? Because people were ashamed of their dreams. That was it. In their dreams, people became all different. In dreams, people did things they told children never to do. They didn't want anybody to see those things. That meant Deirdre had to be careful with people. She had to pretend she only knew their wake-up self, never their dream self. That was hard to do—to act as if she didn't know what she did know. For a time, in her deep confusion, uncertain when to speak and when to keep silent, Deirdre decided she would not speak at all. She would pretend she did not hear when people spoke; she would not answer. She would stay all inside, all by herself. It was like hiding.

Later, her mother would speak of these years as Deirdre's "autistic" period when she was completely out of touch. She took Deirdre to doctors, but they were no help. Once Deirdre came to know them, she could enter their dreams too. She could see them acting funny, acting nasty. And then she had to be careful not to say the "wrong" thing to them. That meant hiding from them too—refusing to hear, refusing to speak.

It helped that during these years her parents divorced. Perhaps it was Deirdre who brought that about—so she often thought. Her father found it impossible to accept his child's strange, intrusive power—especially since he did not want to admit it existed. In Deirdre's presence, he became more and more skittish, afraid of what she might know about his inner life. She developed a peculiarly unsettling stare that he found intensely irritating. She seemed to be trying to look right through people, through their masking flesh at the secrets she knew were there, inside their heads, in the shadowed corners. It was a gaze that was, at once, arrogant, distrustful, and impish. Her father could not stand it. Whenever he caught the look, he would lash out at her. "Stop that! Stop that now!" And once he hit her—very hard. Even when she stopped visiting his dreams, there was no way he could know she was not spying on him. His suspicion, his petulance drove her farther into seclusion. Deirdre's mother, though kinder, felt no less distressed by her mute, retarded child. Everything she did and said let Deirdre know that she was a sick, queer little girl. A freak.

After the divorce, Deirdre's mother turned to her own mother for help, parking Deirdre with her for weeks at a time between visits to doctors and clinics. As it turned out, Deirdre's grandmother was exactly the right choice. A naturally placid old woman, drifting into senility, she treated the troubled child with a benign casualness. She gave little Deirdre a pleasant, unfocused sort of attention, but asked nothing from her. Deirdre spent the most delicate interval of her withdrawal surrounded by an atmosphere of undemanding calm. That lowered the pressure and allowed her an easy return from her autistic retreat. In another home, Dr. Devane later told her when he learned her story, she might have remained caged in by anxious expectations, hidden forever behind a door nobody could open.

Deirdre stayed in hiding for nearly four years—until she was almost ten. But she was a bright child and, all the while she hid, she was learning—what to say, what not to say, where to draw the lines, how to be "normal." Then one day she fell while playing and split her lip. It gushed blood. She ran yowling to her grandmother who—incompetently—tried to mend the gash by holding a damp Kleenex against it. The result would finally be a badly healed wound that left Deirdre with a slight crook in the line of her upper lip—the single blemish (but a prominent one) in what was already taking shape as a very pretty young face. While she sat sniffling in her grandmother's lap having her lip lovingly deformed, Deirdre decided to complain. "Hurts," she said. Her first word in four years. "You're pushing too hard on it."

As if it were nothing special, her grandmother replied without the least surprise, "Oh? I'm sorry, dear. How did you do that?"

"Fell." Deirdre pouted and proceeded to tell the whole sad little story.

In later years, the tiny scar was a reminder—always there to be seen when she looked in the mirror—of the traumatic childhood that lay behind her like a trap she had escaped.

Her mother never ceased to marvel at Deirdre's sudden reentry into normal life. She told the story many times. "All of a sudden one day, she just snapped out of it and started talking again—as if nothing had ever happened. It was a miracle."

Deirdre remembered it another way. She stopped hiding when she learned how to deceive. Gradually, in the course of her four-year silence, it took shape—the realization that nobody in the world wanted to know a dreamwatcher. A dreamwatcher was a monster and a threat. Accordingly, she decided she must stop being a dreamwatcher. At first, she had to struggle to suppress the power. It had always arisen within her automatically and insistently, a natural act of curiosity. But by the time she was halfway through her autistic episode, she was able to thwart the watching impulse for months at a time. That helped her to learn an important lesson: it was better not to know people's dreams. On the inside, people were foolish and weak. There was greed in them, and lechery, and violence. When you knew people from the inside, you could not like them very much.

But not long after her reentry, there came a brief, intense period when Deirdre, almost in spite of herself, drew again upon her peculiar gift. It was the one time she could say she had valued, even enjoyed, being a watcher. That was in her early high school years, when the sexual energies of adolescence began to stir. Outwardly a shy girl with few friends, she began to use her watching power to gratify her insurgent erotic appetite. The temptation to do that was too great to resist, but at first it was far from easy. She was not satisfied simply to watch what people dreamed. She wanted to shape and control. To do that, she had to learn to enter a sleeping mind unobtrusively and delicately guide its images. If she became an alien, unsettling presence, the dream might become a nightmare and the dreamer would be scared awake. Gradually, after months of experimentation, Deirdre discovered ways to touch the dreams of others with her own mind lightly and subtly. It was like reaching into water without creating ripples. She became good at it. She had lots of practice—mainly with the boys she met and lusted for. She devised ways to enter their dreams seductively. She would entice and charm, offering her body coyly—until she had a sure grip on their attention. She would invite them to remove her clothes, to make love to her. For their benefit, she imagined herself wearing the salacious underwear she had seen advertised in magazines. Skimpy upthrust bras, tiny see-through panties with silly frills. It was almost contemptible how easily boys could be mesmerized by these frivolous things—and then made obedient to her wishes. She became the yielding temptress they wanted her to be; then, teased and fascinated, they eagerly surrendered their dreams to her. Upon waking, the boys might censor and forget their fantasies. But for Deirdre, the dreams were as emotionally real, as physically vivid and memorable, as her waking experience. She lived the dreams of others.

Did that make dreams the same as waking life? Did the same rules apply? Deirdre often wondered, but there was no one who could tell her. How responsible was she for what transpired in the dreams she designed? If, for her, dreams were as real as "real" life, then she guessed she had become, in her randy adolescence, the most sexually promiscuous and perverted female who had ever lived. She had imagined herself the lover of nearly every boy she met. She had even—experimentally at first, then with shameless relish—worked her seductions upon any number of girlfriends. Following where the whims of desire led her, she infiltrated the dreams of older men—teachers, family acquaintances, the men she met in shops or who came to make deliveries or repairs. With old and young, male and female alike, she made kinds of love that were physically impossible in waking life. For the appetites of the dreaming mind were bound by no limits of the body or soul.

When she came to the Clinic, she kept most of this secret from Dr. Devane. It was a foolish, shameful episode now far behind her. Still, she knew he would value hearing of it because it proved something important about dreamwatching. He knew she could watch where there was some special emotional rapport between herself and the dreamer: friendship, love, concern. Or hate. Or envy. But she had not yet told him that simple lust would also do the trick, sometimes more effectively than any other feeling. It worked with casual acquaintances where nothing else did. Because, as Deirdre had come to learn, people picked up on one another's sexual vibrations with astonishing ease, almost automatically. People were impulsive lovers. Sex was the immediate—if often unconscious—message that passed between them like an animal heat. And dreams were the natural language of the message.

For that one, turbulent interval of her teenage years, dreamwatching became very nearly an obsession for her. She used the power willfully, selfishly, with a blinding greediness. It amused and gratified her adolescent vanity and served to draw her away from her social timidity. By making their impassioned encounters vivid enough for the boys to remember the morning after, she succeeded in becoming very popular. Having been Deirdre's lovers in their dreams, the boys decided they must indeed desire her—and so they pursued her. It was a baffling development. Much to everybody's surprise, including her teachers', bashful, studious Deirdre had become the dream girl of all the school's most coveted boys.

And then, abruptly, her secret adventure ended. Even before she was out of high school, Deirdre found herself outgrowing the fascination. As her early sexual fevers cooled, the guilt set in. And the disenchantment. She discovered she could not like, did not respect people she had manipulated like puppets. Inevitably, as she toyed with the erotic responses of her friends, sometimes enticing them into unbecoming acts, she found things out about them, things it was unfair and disappointing for her to know. Worst of all, she felt ashamed for behaving like a psychic snoop.

Moreover, sometimes the powers she wielded over the dreams of people produced results she was not able to control. Once, just after she started college, she set about bringing herself to the attention of an instructor by way of a dream seduction. She felt neglected in the large, impersonal lecture section he taught; she wanted him to notice and remember her. Her object was a better grade, but the attention she gained was not what she intended. Instead, there was an awkward sexual encounter, as embarrassing to her as to her teacher. He was a stiff and scholarly man in his sixties, not at all the sort to make a pass at a coed. But something Deirdre had done in the dream and then repeated in his office—an ambiguous signal that was meant to lure and impress—led him to run his hand along her thigh. The gesture was impulsively mindless, like something born out of a posthypnotic suggestion. He watched himself do it with an astonished curiosity, as if the hand were not his own. Then, horrified, he collapsed into flustered apologies. "I don't know what came over me," he stuttered. But Deirdre knew and she suffered the man's shame. She came away from the incident feeling cheap and vile.

Afterward, she moved with greater caution—until she met Peter. That was in her sophomore year (his senior year) at UCLA. Peter was everybody's idea of a campus leader: academically outstanding, a champion debater, athletically talented enough to make the second-string tennis team. He had soft, sleepy-eyed good looks and a gentle virility that guaranteed his popularity with women. Deirdre was drawn to him powerfully after just one dance at a fraternity party. She could not resist entering his dreams that night—though, once again, she more than half feared what they might reveal. She was too bitterly familiar with the juvenile inanity and sexual aberrations that could fill the dreams of "nice boys."

But in Peter's sleeping mind, she encountered no disappointment. He was one of those rare people whose dream self and waking self flowed gracefully into one another. No kinks, no painful psychic detours. In his dreams, he displayed the same confident masculinity, the same decisive self-possession she had sensed in him when they met. Above all, she was delighted to find herself there, affectionately reflected and authentically desired. She watched Peter making strong but delicate love to her dream image and only then merged into his fantasy to enjoy his caresses before they had even kissed once in their waking lives. She entered his dreams several more times, but soon enough, after they had begun to date, the flesh-and-blood reality of their lovemaking made substitutes unnecessary.

Peter, graduating two years before Deirdre, went east to take his master's degree in international finance. For the time they were parted, Deirdre infiltrated his sleep nearly every night, filling his mind with the passionate, remembered images of their love. It was a way of staying close across the miles until he could come back to her for breaks and vacations; it was also a way of keeping Peter hers. Was it wrong to hold him like that? The thought troubled her, but less than her fear of losing him. When he returned, they married and she made a vow to herself. She would respect Peter's privacy and never again eavesdrop upon his sleeping mind.

For the next ten years, Deirdre made sparing use of her powers. Peter would never know how faithful she had been to him. She might have shared the erotic dreams of every man she met. She didn't. She had left such adolescent promiscuity behind her. Her love for Peter was solid and complete; she had no wish to dilute or confuse it. For years at a time, she lived without dreamwatching. It was better that way, she decided. More honest, more normal. Meanwhile, her life with Peter was filled with promise. He enjoyed excellent family connections and prospered brilliantly in his career. Fresh out of the Harvard School of Business, he joined a top brokerage firm in San Francisco and began climbing the corporate ladder swiftly. His responsibilities grew weighty and promotions came in quick time.

Deirdre, comfortably at home in a split-level suburban paradise down the San Francisco peninsula, played the model wife and mother. Laney was born in their first year of marriage. Julia came three years later. Six years after that, Jonathan was born. Judged from the outside, her life might have seemed oppressively ordinary. She might have been the brainless housewife every spot television commercial was designed for. But in her own mind, she took a towering pride in knowing she had scored a great personal victory. She had fought her way out of an autistic dungeon that might have bound her to a lifetime of silence and isolation. Nobody would ever guess how resourcefully she had coped with that secret crisis. But she knew. She remembered it every time she looked in a mirror and saw the little scar on her upper lip. And she was grateful for the life she had salvaged.

It was only after she and Peter were married that Deirdre learned how much her dreamwatching had done to bring them together. To her surprise, she discovered that it was not entirely her influence over his dreams that had drawn him to her. Quite as much, he had been attracted by something the watching had done to Deirdre in her waking life. The power had shaped her in ways she could not always conceal.

"Do you know—you're a very strange person?" Peter once remarked. It was just after Laney had been born. He told her as if it were a secret he had been holding back for a long while.

"How do you mean 'strange'?" she asked.

"I've never found the right words for it. But you have a way of becoming very quiet. Long quiet spells. And when you're like that, your eyes seem to look right through people. Can you?"

"Can I what?"

"Look right through people—as if they didn't have an outside?"

"No, of course not," she answered more than a little defensively. She knew at once what he meant. It was the look that years of dreamwatching had given her, the stare her father had hated so much and for which he had once punished her. Early in life, she had learned there was more to people than their words or faces revealed. That made her want to know who they really were behind the masks they wore. That was what her gaze—piercing, boldly inquisitive, faintly mesmeric—was asking. *Can I trust you? Can I love you?* As she grew older, she took care to restrain the habit, but not always successfully. She sometimes still caught herself studying people with a fixed, almost entranced stare. Or more often she would suddenly become aware that someone she had her eyes upon had flinched under her persistent scrutiny and was looking back uneasily.

"I noticed that about you the first time we met," Peter told her. "I wasn't the only one, either."

"Oh? Who else?"

"Other people we knew at school."

"They thought I was strange?"

"Uh-huh. Brilliant, beautiful . . . but strange."

"Oh, come on!"

"I mean it. Remember Sandy Coleman from my frat house? You dated him, right?"

"A couple of times."

"Once. Just once. He was scared off. Told me he was sure you had second sight, something like that. 'Spooky.' That's what he called you."

"You let him get away with that?"

"Hell no. Strangled the bastard on the spot. He's never been heard from since."

"My hero."

"But he was right. You can be very spooky."

"Well, I'll see what I can do about it."

"Nothing, I hope. Why do you think I'm so crazy about you?"

"Because you've got a thing for spooky girls?"

"Spooky girls with great bodies, that is."

"Did I ever give you any strange, penetrating looks?"

"Constantly."

"And that turned you on?"

"Intrigued me. It made you very special, very mysterious. I wanted to know more about you. And more and more."

"I'm not sure which of us that makes weirder—you or me."

"No kidding, Deir. It's a rare quality. I don't know what to call it. Something . . . enchanted. Are you?"

"Enchanted? No. Probably just nearsighted."

"Well, I can tell you, there are people who'd give a million to have a look like that."

"Oh yes? Who?"

"Lawyers, detectives, spies."

"Oh great! My wife, the spy."

"You know what I mean. People who have to probe beyond the surface. Psychiatrists, for example. You'd make a great shrink, believe me. Just one look from you and . . ."

Peter's remark made her wonder again, as she had many times over the years, if there might be some good use she could make of her dreamwatching. She was not unaware of its possible psychiatric value. But in order to help people, she would have to reveal her ability to help. She would have to let them know she could watch their dreams. And that, she had learned from bitter experience in her childhood, could make her a monster in the eyes of those she cared for. At last, she reached the point where she could almost doubt she had ever possessed the ability to spy upon the dreams of others. It was drifting out of her life and she willingly relinquished it.

Until Peter's bad dreams began.

4

It happened soon after Jonathan was born. At first, Peter's trouble seemed to have nothing to do with dreams. It was simply a run of bad luck, starting with a few problems at work. One problem, then an avalanche of them. The pressures of his job were becoming too great. Peter showed signs of tension. He was often irritable, moody, distracted. He made mistakes, missed appointments, forgot things. At work, his senior officers suggested a vacation. That was not easy to arrange with the new baby at home, still nursing. But Peter insisted, forcing Deirdre to wean Jonathan and come away with him.

They spent two weeks in Hawaii—a tense, unsatisfactory respite. It was then for the first time, while they were away on their own, that Deirdre noticed something new about Peter. He was ogling young men. Again and again, while they sunned themselves on the beach, she caught him staring in the direction of pretty boys with smooth bodies. She could hardly mistake the meaning of the look; she had herself been its object often enough. Finally, one afternoon toward the end of their stay, when he had been staring at a gloriously good-looking surfer for most of an hour, she remarked casually, "He *is* beautiful, isn't he?" She said it the way a woman had a right to say it. Peter returned a look that was both startled and resentful. Then, quite calmly, as if it were meant as a challenge, he answered, "Absolutely gorgeous."

Peter returned to work seemingly well-rested. But in less than a month, the bad temper, the explosive outbursts, the slipshod habits were back. He made a costly error—and then another. He lost a promotion he was banking on. Uncharacteristically, he lashed out at colleagues, accusing them of deceit and betrayal. Another expensive mistake and he was threatened with dismissal. His career was crumbling. Worse, his health began to suffer. He lost weight and complained of headaches. The doctors he consulted could find no cause. He visited a psychiatrist who prescribed an antidepressant. Peter consumed the pills like candy and began to use liquor. Some days he woke so groggy he could not report to work. With Deirdre and the children he became snappish, then abusive, and at last ugly. His eyes changed. They became icy and lightless, filmed over with a suspicious stare. An unyielding depression dragged at him. He was falling, falling into a fathomless despair.

It was in the third month of his illness that Deirdre—quite by accident—discovered the magazines. They were crammed behind some athletic gear at the back of Peter's closet. Page after page of gritty, luridly colored photos. Naked young men—bodybuilders, beach studs —displaying themselves, groping one another. Flipping through, she shuddered with revulsion, then realized. That was exactly Peter's response the last time—it had been weeks ago—she had offered herself to him in bed. Not disinterest. Disgust.

The crisis was far advanced before Deirdre thought of probing Peter's dreams. She had no reason to think of that since Peter never mentioned his dreams. His sleep, if anything, had become deeper, almost drugged—the one calm and relaxed interval in his tortured life. It was only after he had passed into severe depression that his sleep showed any sign of disturbance. Then, for two, three, four nights in a row, he began to mutter and struggle in his sleep, finally waking in a sweat, trembling.

"What were you dreaming?" Deirdre asked, reaching out to comfort him.

He batted her hand away. "Dreaming? Nothing. I never dream anymore."

But Deirdre knew that he did. She could hear his sleep-strangled cries and curses. She could see his body harden, his hands become claws, fists. He struck out in his sleep, once hitting her beside him in bed. In the morning, he did not apologize when she showed him the bruise. "Find someplace safe to sleep," he growled.

At last, Deirdre, though she feared what she might find, willed herself to enter Peter's dreams. It was a simple act, one that still came naturally to her, though she had not drawn upon the power in many years. Anyone watching her in her bed would have said she was deeply asleep. But inwardly she entered a state of wakefulness within sleep— relaxed but alert. Her mind, like a radio receiver, swept across a spectrum of signals, searching for the one telltale vibration that belonged to the person she wished to visit. The action was effortless. If she knew the person well enough, she could reach out across miles. In the realm of sleep, there was no barrier of physical space. There was only emotional distance and that could be crossed instantaneously by a gesture of the mind.

Once she had tuned in to the sleeper's dreams, she woke within her own sleep as if she had opened her eyes in a lighted place. But this time, in Peter's dream, she thought at first her watching power had deserted her. She could see nothing. Yet she knew she was alertly conscious. Looking down, she could see herself—her hands, her body —but that was all. She stood alone, suspended in a pale gray void. On all sides, *nothing.*

She had never experienced a dream like this before. It was the light within the void that was especially queer. Dingy. *Unnatural.* An underground phosphorescence like that given off by rotting matter. It was a negative light. If it made any sense—a *black* light. It lay across her skin like a clammy film. Where it touched, it made her feel as dark and dirty as itself. She thought: *I've grown unfamiliar with watching. When I become accustomed, things will brighten.*

They didn't.

Deirdre had entered her first black dream.

She peered more closely into the emptiness around her. There was movement. She could feel it rather than see it. A slow, turgid churning. She had the feeling of being at the edge of a vast, invisible whirlpool that tunneled down into the yawning vacuum. The space around her seemed to suck at her, drawing her forward and in. She yielded to it . . . and then she was falling, floating almost weightlessly, down and down.

For a long while, as she descended, she saw nothing. Her only distinct sensation was that of sliding slowly through viscous space. Nightmares, she recalled, had the sensation of descent. They worked downward in the mind. This, she decided, was a sort of nightmare, but it was drawing her to a far deeper dimension of consciousness than she realized existed. It troubled her that she saw no figures. That made it difficult for her to orient herself so that she could stay out of sight. Normally, even in a nightmare, she expected to see the dreamer at once, like an actor at center stage. Here, there was only the feeling of endless desolation. The loneliness was so great, it sometimes closed upon her like a giant hand. She felt stifled by too much emptiness. There was nothing to be afraid of, but it was exactly the *Nothing* that made her apprehensive. She longed for contact, for a sense of direction. How many nights of this infinite lostness had Peter endured—

without knowing, as she did, that it *was* a dream and would come to an end?

Dreams, Deirdre had learned long ago, have their own time. In dreams, one can experience the *idea* of time passing. Days, years, centuries pass in no more than a moment. Deirdre found herself wandering in the void of Peter's dream for what seemed like many days. Several times, the oppressive emptiness made her feel sick, made her want to give up and withdraw. She persevered, until, at last, she became aware of sound and movement below her, not much farther down. Something buzzing, buzzing. . . . She made out a distant speck gyrating like an angry fly in the void. She watched it come closer, growing in size, expanding into a noisy bubble as big as a room, then as big as a house. Inside the glassy chamber, there were people thickly jammed together. She could hear voices, shouting, roaring. There was a pounding music, cruelly loud and discordant.

Deirdre moved to enter this strange vehicle. At a certain point, she lost touch with the emptiness. Suddenly, as if the dream had abruptly been turned inside out, the space around her closed in like a prison cell. On all sides, there were feverish bodies crammed together. The dirty light was still here, but now it had curled in upon itself and congealed about the action like some smoldering fluid. It revealed a room filled with dancing men, rubbing against one another, gleaming with sweat. They were bizarrely dressed in tight black vests and jeans; a few were nearly naked, aggressively flaunting their sexual excitement. They caressed hungrily, wiping their hands over one another's flesh. Some embraced and sank to the floor, tearing fiercely at their clothes, locking together, coupling.

Steeling herself, Deirdre squeezed through the crowd, the damp and dirt of bare skin rubbing off on her. The men made her afraid. She knew there was no danger they would see her; they were only figments of Peter's dreaming imagination, performing as the dream made them perform. Still, they filled the room with an atmosphere of sexual violence. She had never been in such a place. Had Peter? When? And why?

She came to a place where the crowd thinned and at last she caught sight of Peter. She moved quickly to keep herself concealed among the dancers. He was on a small stage lit by one searing amber spotlight. He was dressed like the others in tightly cinched leather, cavorting with a young man in a lewd dance. The young man was goading him on; he bent to work his mouth over Peter's face and chest, his hand traveled inside Peter's thigh. Other men gathered and ringed around, watching greedily. The lust in their faces was menacing. Deirdre could tell that Peter took no pleasure in what he did. She could feel his humiliation; it issued from him like a hot wave. He hated being where he was, hated exhibiting himself, but he had no power to break the dream. He was trapped, held by some sick and secret need. Deirdre wanted to help him dispel the dream, but before she could act, he was gone. The young man had pulled him away and led him off.

She moved after them. At the rear of the room, there was a dismal corridor barely wide enough to enter. It ran on and on nightmarishly between high damp walls, leading steeply downward. There was a punishing stench of decay; insects slithered along the dark floor where she stepped. She followed the corridor until she came to a peeling door where she sensed Peter's presence. From inside she could hear the sound of scuffling and a small whimpering voice. Cautiously, she willed herself beyond the door. She emerged in the darkened corner of a reeking, windowless washroom. Overhead there was one bare bulb; the floors were sopping with foul water. At the far end of the room, some figures were knotted together, struggling beside a corroded toilet. The young man, his back turned to Deirdre, was holding some-one—a whining boy. In front of them, Peter was on his knees in the muck. He had wrestled the boy's pants down and was roughly fondling his exposed genitals. Deirdre felt her throat laboring against nausea as she watched her husband mauling the boy. Again, she could feel his shame roaring at her, though his face was that of a zombie, frozen and unfeeling.

The boy was resisting. The young man barked an instruction and Peter struck out viciously. His fists beat and beat at the child in a dull, automatized rhythm. The young man shouted again, a crude com-mand. "Eat the little bastard!" Obediently, Peter bent toward the boy, nuzzling into his groin, offering his mouth.

Just for a moment, the thought flashed upon Deirdre: *This isn't Peter's dream.* But it had to be. What else could it be? She had willed herself into his mind. She saw him before her with all the emotion of the dream fiercely concentrated upon him. Struggling to gain some relief, Deirdre disengaged her attention and drew off. At once, she became aware of something more horrifying than the obscene act she was witnessing. What was it?

The *Nothing.*

The endless emptiness that surrounded the dream—it was still there, shot through with the same leprous light. The realization was totally disorienting. Before her, a vile and hideous act was taking place. A child was being violated. Yet the enveloping nothingness reduced the act to nonentity, a flyspeck in an abyss. Deirdre could feel Peter's mind oscillating between these two dimensions of the dream. There was no way to bring them together. It hurt to try. In the mocking void that engulfed the scene, nothing mattered, nothing existed. Evil did not exist. The shame that tortured Peter did not exist. This was the suffering of hell, an anguish that God had turned his back upon.

Deirdre looked again at Peter. Was this what he had been undergoing night after night? This meaningless horror. Now she understood. This was what he brought back from his dreams each morning, a debasement he could not remember but which lay rotting at the foundations of his mind.

It had to be stopped. Recklessly, Deirdre cried out, trying to shatter the dream. To her surprise, she could hardly hear her own voice. The dirty light closed upon her like a sponge absorbing her cry. She produced only a small eddy of disturbance in the heavy texture of the dream. Bewildered eyes turned in her direction . . . Peter's, the young man's. Did they see her? She could not tell. The light was doing queer things. It was growing thick, becoming a suffocating jelly. Everything was turning the wrong way around like the light and dark in a photographic negative.

What sort of dream was this?

She became panicky. She must escape and waken. It was a terrific labor, like digging her way out of a collapsing pit. She had never been so deeply sunk in dream consciousness before. Finally, she broke the surface of the dream and sat upright in bed, her heart hammering. Beside her, Peter lay asleep. But there were tiny, throttled moans coming from his open mouth. Beside his tensed body, his fisted hands jerked in little spasms. Deirdre slipped from the bed and retreated across the room, her eyes fixed on Peter. Inside the darkness of his sleeping mind, she knew he was still there, in that noisome little room, still engrossed in his obscene task. And this would go on and on through the night. She shuddered, realizing that she was watching a man damn himself.

The next day, when she asked him, Peter snapped at her. "I didn't have any dreams. I don't dream anymore."

On the nights that followed, Deirdre forced herself again and again to enter the bleak underworld of Peter's black dreams. She came to know its squalid imagery well: leather bars and cheap hotel rooms, dark alleys and public toilets, the desolate corners and dead ends of the world where illicit sexual hungers gathered. There she watched as her husband helplessly degraded himself. Most daunting of all, she came upon herself in these dreams, the frequent victim of Peter's twisted desires. One thought sustained her against the loathing she felt for what she saw. She was struck by Peter's rigidly mechanical manner. He moved like a robot, neither willing nor enjoying. *This isn't Peter's dream. He isn't responsible,* she told herself over and over again. She could not say what she meant by that, but the thought kept her from hating Peter for the things he did. It nerved her to return each night and take up her vigil.

She quickly realized that what she confronted in Peter's sleep were not nightmares. Nightmares were something Deirdre knew quite well; she had observed them countless times. Everybody had nightmares, moments when the sleeping mind, ambushed by a traumatic memory or a charged image, veered toward panic. But mercifully, nightmares frightened the sleeper awake; they could then be recognized as unreal and might soon be forgotten. Peter's black dreams were not like that. They were creatures not of fear but of despair—a despair so immense and unyielding that sanity crumbled in its grip. And they did not wake the dreamer; they weighed the mind down and sank it to a level of unconsciousness that was close to coma. Deirdre came to think of the black dreams as something leachlike and parasitic that first narcotized its victim, then proceeded to drain the impulse of life.

It was only after weeks of watching that Deirdre sensed she was making her influence felt in her husband's sleep. In small ways, she was taming and reshaping the dreams, distracting and redirecting Peter's attention. It was hard work; she tired under the strain. She was like a diver descending each night to great oceanic depths, toiling under a crushing weight. There was no place as far from the world of light and life as Peter's black dreams. They happened at the bottom of the universe, stubbornly resisting her most determined efforts. Mornings, she woke from her labors exhausted and had to spend most of the day recouping her energy for the next night. Still, she kept on doggedly, refusing to let Peter slide away from her into the living death of his dreams.

Then came the night that abruptly ended her struggle to save Peter's sanity and nearly cost her own.

From the moment she entered Peter's dream that night, she felt a special apprehension. She had to search for him longer and at greater depths. She had the sense that he was deliberately eluding her. Once again, after a long descent through nothingness, the dream brought her to a cramped, airless place permeated with the odor of decay. She was following Peter at some distance, crawling laboriously over damp, musty earth. Overhead, there was a heavy structure that weighed down ominously. She was underneath what seemed to be the bleacher seats of an immense stadium. There were people above—many people— shouting, cheering. They stamped their feet until the seats trembled. Maniacal faces peered down at her in the blackness, hissing and spitting. They could not see her; still she wanted to hide from their stupid, goggling eyes. The people were dropping things between the seats— clots of dirt and debris. A steady rain of sticky grime descended, coating her. She felt like some sort of vermin.

Then, after what seemed like hours of scrabbling through the fetid darkness, she saw a pale light ahead—a small, low entranceway. Peter was just making his way through it. She approached cautiously and peered out into the light. What she saw jarred her by its very familiarity.

It was her own bedroom, the room where she was lying asleep beside Peter.

But where the ceiling should be overhead, the room had been peeled back; it opened out vastly into the blackness. Shafts of gritty, sulfurous light hammered down. Beyond their glare, she was aware of a multitude of people who were watching like spectators, calling out, howling. Her bedroom had become something like a ballpark lit for a night game. It swelled and shrank in size.

At the center of the arena, where her bed should have been, there was a broad table. Peter was standing over it, his back toward her, blocking her view. He was wearing a tight black jockstrap—nothing more. His body was streaked and clotted with dirt. There was still dirt descending from the blackness overhead, the filth of the world slowly falling through the dense light, filtering down upon Peter and upon the table.

Deirdre strained to see what Peter was doing. She made her way a few steps into the room. There was someone on the table, a naked form. It was a woman with ugly bloated breasts and a cavernous sex organ. She was tied there, struggling. Peter was working over her with a queerly shaped instrument. It was a curled blade. He was moving it across the woman's body with a slow ritualistic precision. Each time he applied the blade, the roaring of the crowd swelled, cheering him on. Deirdre craned forward. And then she saw.

Peter was flaying the woman inch by living inch.

The sight struck her like a fist. She flinched back and bumped into someone in the doorway behind her. She turned. It was a man, a young man with a head of wild black hair and one oddly cocked eye. His gaze was riveted to her, hard and hate-filled. Before she could think, he pushed her backward. She stumbled into the room, colliding with Peter. An ear-splitting cheer went up from the spectators. Somebody— it was the young man—had taken hold of her. He was thrusting her on the table, down toward the woman—toward what was left of her. Deirdre turned and saw . . . *herself*, her own tortured face frozen in a spasm of pain. *She* was the woman on the table.

Then Peter was looming above her, staring down bewilderedly with great blank eyes. Close behind him, the young man was shouting in his ear, but his voice was lost in the growing uproar. Peter's hands were on her. He was forcing her down alongside her own dream form, forcing her *into* that form. Deirdre felt the woman's ruined flesh closing over her like a damp garment. She felt the pain of that flesh becoming her own. The sensation jarred her, suddenly and sharply focusing her attention.

This can't be happening. Nothing like this has ever happened. The thought sprang up in her mind, a frail barrier against the frenzy that was rising up to overwhelm her. She clutched at it, held fast to it like a timber in a raging sea. *This can't happen if I don't want it to.* She concentrated her powers around that conviction and began forcing the dream back from her, refusing to become the woman on the table. Slowly, Peter's hands went slack, freeing her. But the dream would not break. Instead, it began to deform, warping like a scene projected across a bending surface. Deirdre had the sense of sliding away across that surface, losing touch. The sound of the crowd was distorting into a high-pitched whine.

Distantly, she could still see Peter and the young man as the plane of the dream tilted steeply. Peter held the knife high. It glinted. With infinite slowness, he was bringing it down and down, slicing into the dream Deirdre beneath him. Then the light thickened and turned inside out. Deirdre slipped down and away . . . and woke, just in time to see Peter—the real Peter—stumble from the bed groaning, holding his hand to his mouth. He lurched away—toward the bathroom, she assumed. Then she heard him in another part of the house . . . in the kitchen, rummaging.

Deirdre was free of the dream, but its terror was still with her. It writhed in her chest like something alive and trapped. Her head still swimming, she made her way across the hall to the room Julia and Jonathan shared. An instinctive concern drew her to the children. She found them fast asleep, then groped toward Laney's room down the hall. She bent above the calmly sleeping child, waiting for her composure to return. It didn't. There was something in the air around her, an imperceptible sense of tautness like a shrill note just out of the range of hearing. She remembered the high whining sound from the dream. It was still there in her ears, lingering. Suddenly, there was a howling in the house—Peter's voice, twisted into an animal roar. She heard him in the hall rushing by, thudding drunkenly against the walls. In the next room, there was a violent commotion and through it one small, sharp cry. Julia's voice, screaming, then cut off, severed by a cleaver of silence.

At the sound, Laney woke and sat up. Deirdre rushed out of the room and threw the light switch, just as Peter stepped back into the hall. She saw his eyes first, stretched wide open and glazed. It was the zombie stare she had seen in the dreams. His mouth worked, emitting low, rasping sounds. There was blood across his chest. In one hand he held a stained kitchen knife. In the other, limp as a broken doll, was the torn body of their infant son.

The dream hasn't ended, Deirdre told herself. *This is still the dream.*

But she knew that was not so. She was fully awake—shocked awake— and the man who stared at her from the end of the hall was real, the knife was real, the remnant of her baby in his hand was real.

Behind her, Laney called out in fear. Deirdre whipped back into the room, slamming and locking the door. Then, sweeping Laney awkwardly into her arms, she fled, stumbling, toward the sliding glass door that opened into the yard. It was locked. She bent to struggle with the catch, breaking her nails on the stubborn metal. In the hall outside the door, Peter was pounding, kicking. His foot crashed through the thin wood. Deirdre unlatched the sliding door and yanked it to one side. With Laney clutched to her chest, she raced blindly into the yard, screaming now for help. She ran with her daughter across the lawn and out through the back gate. In the alley outside, she fell to one knee. By the time she rose, Peter was not far behind. She turned and saw him at the gate, still carrying the shapeless rag of flesh in his hand.

At the end of the alley, a car turned in and stopped as its headlights fell upon the scene. The lights shot past Deirdre and caught Peter like a spotlight against the garage door. The car's horn suddenly sounded, harsh and blaring. Startled, Peter stood frozen, his eyes blinking. He was a sleepwalker awaking. He squinted into the light, then down along his arm to see what it was that weighed so heavily in his hand. For a long moment, he stared uncomprehendingly at what he held. Then, realizing, he threw it from him. His head went back and he gave a choked wail of grief. The headlights were still on him when he put the knife to his own throat.

5

The discreet brass plaque on the door read:

ROBERT G. COSTELLO
CHIEF OF ADMINISTRATION

Nobody at the Devane Clinic could have explained with any certainty what the Chief of Administration was there to do. The title, while imposing, was deliberately vague. Besides Devane himself, the medical staff rarely had occasion to meet Costello. He was generally understood to have a background in clinical psychology, but he was not a physician. The accounting and clerical personnel knew little more than that about him. The patients never saw him.

Still, nobody doubted that Costello was important. He looked important and talked important: crisp, sober, abrupt. He had been with the Clinic since it was founded twelve years ago; in that time, whenever a weighty matter was brought before Devane—especially questions of money—his stock response was "I'll take it up with Costello."

It was just after five-thirty in the afternoon when Devane knocked at Costello's door and entered, not waiting to be invited. Costello was on his terrace, a mixed drink already in his hand. He glanced over his shoulder and nodded as Devane came in. Grunting an equally minimal greeting, Devane moved to the wet bar to pour his own drink. He had fortified himself with a double Scotch in his own office; he estimated that the meeting coming up merited another three fingers on top of that, with perhaps a slosh more. He joined Costello at the railing outside. The terrace commanded an imperial vista of the coast running north. On a clear day, the Channel Islands were visible well out to sea and, toward evening, the winking beacon at Point Conception. The sun was streaking the low clouds with crimson as it drew a flaming sky behind it down over the edge of the world. Along the horizon, the offshore oil rigs were just lighting up like a row of Christmas trees.

"I've always thought this view was wasted on you," Devane remarked after he and Costello had stood several minutes in chilly silence. "You don't go in for that sort of thing, do you?"

"What sort of thing?"

"Views. Sunsets. Beauties of nature."

"I value the privacy." Costello gestured upward, drawing a circle in the air above the terrace. "No overlooking hills on this side."

"Yes, I know. The high ground. Still, I think it's wasted. You're sure you aren't willing to let me move over here?"

"You have a rather sensational view from your office."

"Southern exposure. Too much afternoon sun."

"But your side has the hills," Costello reminded him.

"Yes, troublesome things. Well, I could take over here and we could move you into one of the storage rooms in the basement. Very dungeony. You might like that. Solid concrete, no windows. No chance of eavesdropping there."

Costello, unamused, gave a straight-faced answer. "I prefer this. You get your best sound insulation from open air, with no direct sight lines."

"Is that so? I thought we had all sorts of state-of-the-art long-range technology these days for listening in from outer space. Are you sure you can trust the sea gulls?" To Devane's surprise, his drink was almost gone. He studied the remaining drops, then drank them down. "I wonder how long it will be before we start exchanging our precious secrets by sense of smell—like the lower animals. Sniffing under one another's tails and so on." He turned back to the bar, seeking more drink. He knew Costello's disapproving eyes were on him as he poured. "No need to worry," he said without looking around. "It all works out very neatly. I only drink to excess when life become unbearable. And since life is only unbearable when you and I get together"— he turned to offer a sardonic toast to Costello—"there's no danger of me spilling any beans with strangers around."

"Just try to stay clear enough to follow what Alex has to tell you," Costello admonished.

"Of course. I'm sure it's monumentally important. I'll give him all the attention he deserves." Devane noticed the glass-top table on the terrace elaborately set for three. "Dinner *intime* again, I see. I thought we might be dining out this time."

"Alex has decided we have only two kinds of four-star restaurants in Santa Barbara. Those that are so noisy you have to shout to be heard.

And those that are so quiet you can be heard across the room whispering."

Devane shrugged. "Can't you talk him into just sending out for pizza? If he shows up again with sweetbreads . . ."

"You know Alex."

"Unfortunately."

Another cold silence. Devane, pacing the terrace, studied Costello from behind. The mile-wide shoulders, the bull neck. The man had once played college football. Now in his late forties, he still kept his athletic bulk tautly packaged. He remained vain about his body, working hard to keep trim. Mornings, he could be seen jogging the grounds of the Clinic, including the rough terrain over the crest of the hill.

"What was it you played at Navy?" Devane asked wryly. "Some kind of guard."

"The line. I've told you—I played the line," Costello murmured into the air beyond the terrace, hardly audible.

"Yes, I know. But you said it was some kind of guard. I can't remember."

"The defensive line, that's all."

"No, some kind of guard. The . . . what was it? The crotch guard, something like that."

"Nose guard," Costello half whispered.

"Ah yes. Nose guard. All-American nose guard."

"I was never All-American."

"Pity. I'm sure you deserved it. Must have been a dirty Communist plot you didn't make All-American. I can see you there in the middle of the defensive line—like the Rock of Gibraltar. Rocky Costello. You must have had a name like that. Crusher, perhaps. Crusher Costello, that's it. Nobody gets through. Nobody gets past. Am I right, Crusher? The look alone was enough to flatten them."

Costello turned to give him a studied glare. He had a disconcertingly smooth face and cherub-plump cheeks. But the eyes behind his heavy-rimmed glasses were calmly predatory. A baby face with shark's eyes. "You *will* stay sober, I hope," he said—instructing, not requesting.

". . . as a judge. Better yet, sober as a nose guard." Devane deliberately slurred his words. He held his liquor extremely well, better than he let Costello know. He was not the least bit woozy. But pretending to be irresponsibly drunk was his way of teasing. He enjoyed making Costello play nursemaid. Costello had his own ways of teasing back.

Just after six o'clock, Alex Shawsing bustled in, followed by a white-coated delivery boy carrying a large wicker basket. "Aaron," he called out to Devane and offered an exaggerated two-handed shake. "So pleased." He directed the boy to place the basket on the table and sent him away with a ten-dollar tip. With an air of housewifely fussiness, he began to unpack the hamper, drawing out various small plastic containers and neatly wrapped packages. He was a lean, hawk-faced man with a pencil-thin mustache and sandy-gray hair that was artfully arranged to disguise his balding top. His linen suit was wedding-cake white and razor-creased, the trousers cracking at exactly the correct angle over his white canvas shoes. A mauve silk handkerchief blossomed from his breast pocket. The man's style had more than once made Devane wonder if he might not be gay. But in his line of work, that could not be so.

Shawsing visited from Washington only once or twice a year, never for more than an overnight stop. He liked to treat his excursions to Santa Barbara—inevitably he referred to it as "Lotusland"—as a sybaritic holiday. When pricey restaurants could not be used, he would personally select a spread of delicacies at Androuet's, the town's most elegant charcuterie, and have them packed in a hamper. The Clinic was Devane's, the terrace was Costello's, but on these occasions, Shawsing held forth like the gourmet host.

"One of these is lobster quiche," Shawsing explained as he unwrapped and served. "The other is squab. I can't tell which is which. Ah, these are the truffles. And this, I believe, Androuet said was eel. Eel in something. Now I know you hate sweetbreads, Aaron, so you can leave those for us—if you can find them. Bob, will you do the honors with the wine? The California first, will you? We'll save the French for dinner. I wouldn't have thought I could find a Pouilly-Fumé out here. And let me get the coffee perking for afters."

Devane, surveying the food without appetite, could not identify any of the saucy, frothy dishes for what they were. Everything looked exotic to the point of being alien. "That's the trouble with take out from these fancy delis. You can't tell what anything is until you taste it. And even then . . ."

"Take-out?" Shawsing winced. "I'd rather hoped you'd think of it as personally catered."

Devane dug into something pink and oily. He dangled it to his plate on a dripping fork. Once it was there, he gave it a long uncertain stare. "Pasta?" he asked.

"Tripe," Shawsing answered. "Marinated in honey. One of Androuet's specialties. Don't be squeamish. It's good for your pH. Settles the digestion."

It would go on like this for the first hour or so—Shawsing prattling on about the wine, the food, the liqueur. He relished playing the bon vivant. It lent a sickly note of decadence to the real purpose of their meeting.

When the meal had straggled into its last elegant course, Costello went to his desk and punched a button. Within seconds, the office door opened and a white-jacketed man appeared, listening for instructions. Smitty had obviously been waiting in the outer office. Under one arm, he carried a large plastic basin. Costello curtly waved him toward the table on the terrace. He shuffled slowly across the room, seeming to test each step, and began to bus the dishes. Catching sight of him, Devane gave an overloud greeting, as if he were speaking to a deaf man.

"Hello, Smitty!" he called out and walked over to apply a friendly pat on the shoulder.

Smitty looked up, frowning with confusion. His face was sullen to the point of being vaguely hostile. His hair had recently been cut to a ridiculous stubble that gave him the look of a pinhead. Smitty's face worked and squinted powerfully as he studied Devane for a long, uncomprehending moment. Then his eyes gave the barest glint of recognition and his heavy features relaxed.

"Go ahead," Devane said. "Clean up. That's the boy." He loitered to watch Smitty at his task, welcoming the break from Shawsing and Costello.

"One of Aaron's experiments in occupational therapy," Costello explained, settling into a deck chair beside Shawsing. "Also makes for cheap help—but not terribly efficient."

"Ah yes," Shawsing said. He had encountered working patients at the Clinic on previous visits. He understood that it was safe to talk in front of those chosen for Costello's office. Still, Smitty's mute, pathetic presence made him uneasy. "Perhaps we should wait until he clears away," he suggested.

"No risk," Costello assured him. "Smitty's one of our old-reliable hands. If he tries very hard, he seems to be able to pick up every other monosyllable. It's all he can do to find his way back to the kitchen. The other day he delivered my lunch to the laundry."

"Very well then," Shawsing said and called Devane to join them as he poured coffee. Reluctantly, Devane returned and took a seat.

"Something very big this time, Aaron," Shawsing announced as the conversation finally turned serious over cognac and coffee. He offered a crooked black Havana to Devane, who refused it. Costello disappeared for a moment into a metal storage closet in his office; he returned with a large envelope. He drew a magazine from it and passed it to Devane. It was a copy of *Time* that dated back a month. The cover bore the picture of a woman. Her skin was dark and deeply haggard, but the eyes burned with a riveting energy.

The magazine was clipped to open at the article that went with the cover. The woman was Mother Constancia. Devane recognized the name; it had appeared several times in the news over the past year. But he could not have said with certainty who she was. Devane's grasp of current events outside his own profession was shamelessly minimal. Quickly, he skimmed the article. It told him that Mother Constancia was Guatemalan . . . a Catholic nun . . . now in the United States . . . living in exile . . . politically controversial. His racing eyes collected the words "revolutionary" . . . "Marxist" . . . "Church" . . . "terrorism" . . . "human rights" . . . "peasants" . . . "saint." He looked up, searching Shawsing's face.

"They're calling her 'the Red Madonna,' " Shawsing said with an owlish stare. He waited for Devane's response. Deliberately, Devane remained flaccid, playing more than a little drunk. "She's a bit of trouble," Shawsing remarked.

"Oh? The article says she's a saint," Devane commented. He proceeded to quote from the copy before him. " 'Possibly the closest thing any of us will know of saintliness in our time.' "

"Unhappily, that is not how our Guatemalan allies see it," Shawsing answered. "They would describe her as the devil's own."

"What's she done that's so terrible?"

Costello picked up the question impatiently. "She's fronting for revolutionary elements throughout Central America. Lending them religious respectability." The answer was terse; the tone implied it was more than Devane had any business expecting to be told. "That's why she got forced out of the country."

"Well then, she's off their hands," Devane concluded. "It says she's living in L.A.—in exile."

"She's living in what they call . . ." Shawsing groped for the word, glancing to Costello for help.

"The *barrio*. In east L.A."

"Yes, the *barrio*. Which is, I gather, a Mexican-speaking slum. She has a sort of storefront center there. *Casa Libertad.* She sleeps on the floor, lives on a crust, wears rags. The whole mortifying, ascetic bit. She does 'community work' among the Latinos, or Chicanos, or whatever the vogue word is these days. Feeds the hungry, takes in battered wives, leads rent strikes—that sort of thing. Not much to be objected to in that. But, unfortunately, she's kept up her activity on the Central American front. Shelters a lot of political exiles, does some rather impressive agitating for human rights. Free all political prisoners, no arms for the dictators, bring the troops home, redistribute the land. The usual left-wing agenda. But, you see, she lends it a certain prophetical luster. Very troublesome." He paused to study Devane's obviously bored response. "I don't suppose you keep up with these things, do you, Aaron?"

Devane shrugged. "Vaguely, vaguely."

"Well, you should know we're dealing with a formidable lady. Last year she headed up major demonstrations against Administration policy. New York, San Francisco, Los Angeles. A half-million people in Central Park." He spread open the issue of *Time* to a half-page aerial photo of a demonstrating crowd. "She's got something even bigger scheduled for Washington this Christmas. One has to admit she cuts a dramatic figure in front of a mob. Very impassioned. Very charismatic. Especially for Catholics. Probably don't understand a word of what she says, but they turn out by the battalions to bask in the blessed aura. Needless to say, the world press simply eats it up. We now have Mother Constancia quoted like an oracle on all and sundry. Foreign affairs, divorce, abortion, the arms race, toxic wastes. The Guatemalan authorities thought running her out of the country would put a crimp in her work. Instead, it's turned her into an international celebrity. She enjoys far more of the limelight here than she ever did in the banana fields."

Devane shrugged. "Still, she can't do the Guatemalans too much damage at this distance. I don't see the problem."

"The problem," Shawsing answered, dropping his voice and leaning across the table to dip his cigar in the cognac, "is that the wretched woman is going to win the Nobel Prize."

"The Peace Prize," Costello explained.

That impressed Devane. "How do you know?"

"Reliable sources," Shawsing said. "Inside the Nobel Committee. There are five votes. She has two, with two more leaning. We can count on one sure negative. Not enough to block her out."

"Well then, congratulations to her." Devane raised his glass and drained the last of the Hennessy it held, then reached out to pour more.

"Would that I could join you in your toast." Shawsing pulled a mock sad face. "But we have foreign friends who would rather not see the day. You may know what an embarrassment the Guatemalan government already is to our State Department. She's bound to use the occasion of the award to give the regime more unflattering publicity than it needs. And that may only be the beginning. As it is, the Latin American governments are under more than enough pressure from their clergy. The Church is simply riddled through with radical elements. The last thing the Guatemalans can afford is to see the Red Madonna gain a world platform. It would make what they are pleased to call 'intelligent reform' impossible."

Devane knew where the discussion was headed. A dismal loathing began to fill his mind. Still, he would play dumb as long as he could. Make the bastards spell it out in capitals. Meanwhile, down all the alcohol in sight. "I don't see what we can do about it."

Costello was eager to volunteer instant clarification. "We can snuff her."

Shawsing winced at the words—or rather at the volume of the remark. He glanced across the terrace at Smitty, who had been clearing the table at an incompetent slow pace. The man was just finishing and heading for the door. When he got there, he stopped and stood puzzled; both hands were taken up gripping the plastic basin. Devane, noticing his dilemma, rose to help him through the door with an encouraging squeeze of the arm. It was only a few seconds of escape, but Devane welcomed it. When he returned, Shawsing resumed by tactfully adjusting Costello's remark. "Bob means, of course, snuff her reputation. As Head Office has been at great pains explaining to our rather overzealous Guatemalan friends, assassination—anything as crude as that, especially on American turf—would be counterproductive. You recall what the execution of Archbishop Romero did for the revolutionaries in El Salvador. Also, these days, anything so indelicate leads to awkward investigations. The good Mother has loyal supporters in the Congress. No no, we have to strike at the woman's mystique. The immediate objective is really only to sway a few votes on the Nobel Committee. I suspect all we need for that is a disgraced, possibly psychotic saint. Totally neutralized, totally out of commission. It's right up your alley, Aaron. A perfect assignment for one of your watchers, don't you think?"

"A suicide would be ideal," Costello noted with clinical objectivity. "That'd have a devastating impact on her Catholic following."

Shawsing did not disagree. He weighed the suggestion judiciously. "Possibly, possibly. If we have the time. Let's see . . . the Nobel Committee usually announces by mid-October. That would give us about four months."

"We've done suicides in as little as ten weeks," Costello observed. "Of course, those were especially vulnerable targets."

"Here, as you know, we're dealing with a somewhat tougher assignment. Let's say we allow some two months to prepare the good Mother, another month or so to arrange a few high-visibility instances of psychotic imbalance, and then the act itself. . . . That might be cutting it a bit thin. There is the possibility of arranging some stubborn infighting on the Nobel Committee. That could eke out a few more weeks for us—say, into November. I'd say we have some four and a half months at the outside."

"That's tight, but not impossible," Costello judged.

"We actually could make do, you know, with any sort of unbecoming public act or statement on the woman's part. For example, if we could have her openly declare for Marxism or simply disparage the Pope. The Nobel Committee could never side with that. For that matter, even a high-profile, well-reported display of profanity might do the trick. Anything to give her feet of clay."

"I say go for the suicide and settle for the best we can get short of that," Costello said. "That's how we went after Kesselring. Remember, Aaron?"

Devane, glaring across the table, refused to respond.

"Kesselring?" Shawsing searched his memory. He coordinated too many operations to remember all the names. "That was the German Socialist leader, wasn't it? Wasn't that a suicide?"

"Eventually, yes," Costello reminded him. "But that was several months after we were finished with him. We got through our part of the assignment without having to push that far. We just unbalanced him enough to slap his wife in public."

"And he lost the election," Shawsing recalled. "Yes, very neat. Zublocki—that was the suicide, wasn't it?"

"Zublocki was a suicide. Also Kobayashi and Jelinek."

"Now, let's see . . . somewhere I recall an ugly outburst in a church that nicely blackened a reputation. Who was that?"

"Dominguez—in Venezuela," Costello laughed. "But that was tricky. Some of his peon followers thought he might be speaking in tongues. We almost succeeded in turning him into a rhapsodic prophet. We don't want anything like that with Mother Constancia."

Devane pushed himself away from the table and wandered to the end of the terrace, staring out at the darkening sea. Behind him, his colleagues went on comparing notes. They had a rich file to draw upon— the many ingenious applications of Devane's research that had nothing to do with healing sick minds. Though the medical profession still knew nothing of dreamwatching and dream manipulation, Devane's techniques had proved of great service in other quarters over the past twenty years. There were the diplomats who had been burdened with unaccountable depression until they gave up their secret instructions, the intelligence operatives who had been driven crazy enough with Sleep Terror to defect, the troublesome political leaders who had been secretly stressed to the point of public disgrace or suicide. There was no need to review this grim record of psychic espionage; but, for Devane's benefit, Costello loitered over the choice examples. That was his way of teasing.

"Well," Shawsing concluded, "it seems we have lots of options, then. I'm sure we can find something that suits Mother Constancia."

Costello gave a nasty laugh. "How about getting her to offer the Pope a blow job? What do you think, Aaron?"

Devane returned to the table, no longer playing drunk. He spoke to Shawsing, cold and absolute. "No more dirty work for me, Alex. You know that. I'm done with it."

"Ah, but the dirty work pays the bills, doesn't it? And there are still bills to be paid. I understand you're budgeting in excess of five million for the Clinic next year."

"Five million, six and a quarter." Costello supplied the exact figures.

"And how much of that from classified sources?" Shawsing asked.

"Nearly half."

"Well, there you are, Aaron. One pays the piper—even in pure science."

"I've paid with my life's blood," Devane burst out. "That's enough. Listen to me, Alex. Do you realize that right here in this Clinic, we are doing the most significant research in the history of modern psychiatry? Ground-breaking. Absolutely revolutionary. We're charting the deep-sea bottoms of the unconscious mind. Do you know what that means?"

"Of course I do, Aaron." Shawsing looked hurt. "What sort of a philistine do you take me for? My own background is in psychology, though of course it's been a good many years since . . ."

"Direct empirical observation of the unconscious," Devane underscored it. "No more guesswork. No more theoretical muddling. Freud said that dreams were the royal road to the unconscious. What he never guessed was that the dreams could be observed—actually observed. This is like being the first person to study the living cell . . . or to see a galaxy."

Shawsing gave an indulgent sigh. "You think we don't appreciate the importance of that back in Washington? We've been the major beneficiaries of your work. I shouldn't have to remind you who built your clinic."

Devane slapped the table hard enough to rattle the glasses it held. "Jesus, Alex! That's the trouble. I'm working for you . . . exclusively. I haven't been able to publish more than a fraction of my research. You've got me trapped in a ghetto of classified material. I'll be dead and buried before anybody besides you and Bob is permitted to read my papers. Do you know how my books are treated by the psychiatric community? 'Inspired but idle speculation.' 'Rootless theory.' By the time you get finished censoring my stuff, there's no evidence left. It's as if Pasteur couldn't make mention of the microscope. Where does it end, Alex?"

Again, Shawsing affected hurt feelings. "Be fair, Aaron. Everything you've done along this line has come out of military intelligence funding. Since the early days, it's all been defense-related. Where else would something as bizarre as dreamwatching have been taken seriously all these years? I don't need to tell you how expensive it's been. Is it unreasonable for Head Office to expect something back on its investment?"

"But how long does it go on? Is that all I have in front of me for the rest of my years—one filthy little security assignment after another? When do I go public?"

Costello observed what was for him the obvious point. "Dreamwatching is an exclusive—thanks to you, Aaron. As long as our side has got it and the opposition hasn't, it stays under wraps. Nobody gives away an advantage like this."

"So that's what I'm waiting for? East-West parity," Devane said bitterly. "I stay classified until my Russian opposite number—if there is one—gets lucky enough to reproduce my findings. Maybe I should simply defect, in the interests of science. That would speed things up."

It was as if Devane had uttered an obscenity in church. There was a crisp silence. He could hear it crackle. Shawsing's eyes turned on him, leaden with seriousness. "I'd be careful about remarks like that, Aaron. They have a way of getting back to Head Office without the sarcastic nuance."

Devane backed off hurriedly. "Sorry. Bad joke. After twenty years, the frustration gets to you." Deflated, he resigned the argument. "All right, have it your way. You've got Moray to work with. He's the best watcher I can give you. I'm sure he can rape the good Mother's psyche for you. He'll enjoy doing it. Just leave me out of it. I don't want to hear . . ."

Shawsing was wagging his head slowly from side to side. "No good."

"What do you mean 'no good'?"

"Moray. We've tried him. Very disappointing."

"You've been using Moray with the nun?" He stared severely into their faces. "I wasn't told."

Costello sniffed. "As you just said—you wanted to be left out of it. I put Moray on the project six months ago."

"Yes," Shawsing added. "That was our understanding at Head Office. Bob has full charge of Moray. We've had excellent results from him with other, more routine targets. But with Constancia, well, he seems to be out of his depth. Hence my visit. I'm afraid Head Office wants your help on this, Aaron."

Repelled as he was by the use Costello and Shawsing made of his work, Devane was hotly curious to know what had come of Moray's efforts. There were always things to be learned, even from these obnoxious little intelligence projects. Hesitantly, he asked, "What have your results been with her?"

Costello greeted his interest with a quick, smug smile. He drew a file of notes from an envelope he held and passed it across the table to Devane. "We've been at an impasse for the past month at least. Part of the problem is Moray. He's always been a bit insubordinate. Now he's much worse—erratic, moody, stubborn. That's pretty much your fault, Aaron. Since you turned him over to me, he misses your paternal attentions. He broods a lot about that—like a sulky little boy. He was totally dependent on you. You can't break off a relationship like that overnight."

"How old is Moray?" Shawsing asked.

"Twenty-seven. But like all these watchers who come out of an autistic background, his emotional age is much younger. It's even more difficult with Moray. He's an orphan. When we took him into the Clinic, he had nobody in the world—except Aaron. He was pretty delicate. But he developed quickly—maybe too quickly. For four or five years, he was our star pupil, the best watcher Aaron ever trained. You remember the Senator Preston assignment. Moray handled that for us. He was only in his teens at the time."

"Ah yes," Shawsing remarked admiringly. "Very well done, very neat. How did you get Moray close enough to Preston to establish rapport?"

"We sent him in as a congressional page," Costello explained. "It didn't take long. He was into Preston's dreams in less than a month. By the end of the year, we had Preston displaying himself all over Washington as a raving homosexual. Moray was good, very good. A precision instrument."

Devane interrupted impatiently. "Yes, and that's what ruined him. He was too young for these assignments. They take their toll. The violence, the perversion . . . you can't confabulate with psychological materials like that without paying a price. Moray's useless now for research. He's . . . warped."

"Be that as it may," Costello went on, "it wasn't wise to dump him the way you did. That's what really damaged him. It's been . . . how long since you last talked with him? Over a year. You might have guessed how that would affect him. He's reverted. Just like that, he'll turn into a bratty, mischievous child. Oh, he knows how to disturb Constancia's sleep with low-grade nightmares. He likes playing bogeyman. He scares her, wakes her up. She loses some sleep, gets nasty headaches. But that's not enough to cripple her. Working with nothing more than physical fatigue, there's no telling how long it might take to break her down. The old girl's got lots of stamina. Moray's just not producing significant depression. Without that, we don't stand a chance of manipulating her."

In spite of himself, Devane offered a word of advice. "It may be that Moray hasn't worked up sufficient rapport. You know how he is with women. It can be hard for him at times to work around his misogyny."

Costello dismissed the idea. "I allowed for that. Before we started the probes, I planted him in Constancia's community center, let him work around the place for some three months. He met her almost daily

—except when she was traveling. At one point, I was even concerned he might get too fond of her. She's the maternal type. The truth is: we've spent more time developing rapport with Constancia than with any target in the last eight years."

Shawsing had a suggestion. "Perhaps if Aaron were to have a talk with Moray. He may simply need a little reassurance that he hasn't lost favor."

"That wouldn't do much good," Costello answered. "It's more likely to rattle Moray so much he'll become totally useless. There are too many hurt feelings between him and Aaron to sort out in the time we have. For another thing, Constancia is a special case. The woman seems to do incredibly little dreaming. Night after night, Moray makes no contact. And when he does, she requires more skill than he's got. We've tried everything we can think of. All the standard probes. So far with no better result than chronic headaches. Trouble is: Moray can't find anything he can use against her. No morbid fears. No sadistic fantasies. No sexual hang-ups."

"You have to find something of that sort, do you?" Shawsing asked.

"That's the method we've always used. Acute Compulsive Somnipathy. The patented Devane technique. Dredge up some emotionally charged item from the unconscious mind, work it down underneath the waking reflex, and establish a permanent linkage. That allows us to produce prolonged Sleep Terror—all night long if we want. Normally, that will give us the state of depression we need within a month's time and we can begin controlling. In Constancia's case, it isn't taking. I confess, I thought she'd be a soft touch. You always expect these religious types to be a bundle of hair-trigger repressions. Maybe she really is a saint." He eyed Devane quizzically. "I think you might find her interesting, Aaron. It's as if the woman has no unconscious at all. No guilty secrets, no hidden terrors."

Costello was tempting effectively; Devane would have loved to probe Mother Constancia's mind. But he knew that the price of satisfying his curiosity would be cooperation. He shrugged. "Then I guess you're out of luck on this one. Moray is the best I have to give you."

There was a heavy silence. Then Shawsing spoke. "What about the Vale woman?" Devane recoiled sharply. He had not expected that. "Bob tells me she's exceptional," Shawsing went on. "Possibly better than Moray. Steadier, more sensitive, more mature."

"Oh no," Devane protested at once, refusing to consider the matter. "She's out of it. She's strictly for research. That's been agreed upon."

"Yes, so I understand," Shawsing continued. "Bob gets Moray and you get Mrs. Vale. But I wonder if you might not see this case as a sort of research project. Aren't you the least bit eager to investigate Constancia? She seems rather a juicy specimen."

"This isn't research," Devane snapped contemptuously. "You're out to kill this woman."

"Oh come now!" Shawsing hastened to soothe his anger. "That's being extreme, don't you think? We have no reason to believe the matter will go that far."

"And suppose it does," Costello added bluntly. "It wouldn't be the first time."

"Yes, Aaron," Shawsing joined in. "I must admit I'm puzzled by this virginal blushing. Why such scruples now?"

Devane's mind labored. What explanation could he offer that would be negotiable in this company? That he had reached the point of moral saturation? That he wanted to stop feeling dirty and wasted? "The work would be too much for Deirdre," he said. "She's delicate. I've been bringing her along very carefully. I don't want to see her damaged the way all my other instruments have been damaged. For God's sake, Alex, we've messed this woman around enough. It's a miracle she's survived at all."

"That's a measure of how resilient she is," Costello remarked. "You've told me she's one of the best you've ever seen. It won't hurt her to do a few exploratory probes on the nun."

"Yes, that's it," Shawsing added. "Just enough to give Moray something to work with. That's not much to ask, Aaron."

"Deirdre doesn't even know Constancia," Devane protested. "There's no rapport."

"That can be arranged," Shawsing assured him. "Constancia is in need of medical care. Sleepless nights, bad dreams. We have contacts that will make her willing to be examined at the Clinic. Mrs. Vale could meet her here."

Devane felt boxed in, hounded. "No," he insisted. "Deirdre is mine. I have the right to save something for. . . ." He rose abruptly from the table, his chair scraping loudly on the stone floor. It was like turning his back on a man holding a gun. Hopeless, perhaps, but there was a sudden, giddy sense of freedom.

"Aaron," Shawsing called after him. His voice had the sound of a whip in it. "This is quite important. You really don't have any choice."

Devane stopped. He could feel their eyes—Costello's, Shawsing's—

boring into his back. He did not want to see them. Not turning, he said, "I can refuse. There's no way you can make use of her without me. I've trained her. I have her trust."

Shawsing's voice was deeply modulated with the authority of his office. "You're requesting over two million dollars from Head Office for next year. Is this worth two million dollars to you?"

There had been moments like this before, when Devane had determined to become his own master, regardless of the money. They had never passed beyond the privacy of his own thoughts. It had always been one more compromise—and then another. Was this the moment, finally, to take the step, to cut loose and run? Trembling, he moved to the bar, seeking a steadying drink. "I don't think Head Office would sink the Clinic over a matter like this. You have an interest in this place —as much as I."

"Yes, that's true," Shawsing agreed. "The funds will be here next year. No doubt of that. Also the dreamwatch program will be here. But *you* may not be. You're valuable, Aaron. But not indispensable. There are plenty of bright young men who would be madly eager to step into a position like this."

Even so . . . even so . . . Devane was saying to himself. Was it so bad, what Shawsing was threatening? To be discarded, cast out? He could almost wish it. No more Costello. No more dirty work. Again, he felt the dizziness of the moment—the anxious elation of an escaping prisoner dashing toward open ground. What could they do? What could they really do to hold him if he decided now to bolt, taking Deirdre with him? The refusal was on his lips, almost spoken.

Then Costello said, "I wonder what would happen if Mrs. Vale found out about her husband's death."

Devane, racing in his mind toward freedom, jolted to a stop. The words were like a rockslide falling across his path. Yes, *that* was what they had to hold him. He turned and searched Costello's face. The blank stare barely concealed the vindictiveness behind his eyes. Trust the Crusher to bring him down. Nobody gets through. Nobody gets past.

Mutely acquiescent, he sagged into the nearest chair, hunching over the bottle he held in his hand.

After a long, merciful pause, Shawsing said, "What a magnificent evening it is. Lotusland—I tell you, you're living in Lotusland."

6

It was just after the Korean War that Aaron Devane discovered his first watcher. In those days, the military was spending lavishly on psychological research. Chinese brainwashing—the real practice inflated by extravagant rumors that hinted of diabolical ingenuity—had become a priority item on the Pentagon agenda. How effective was it? Could the techniques be resisted? Could they be duplicated and improved? Devane, freshly graduated with highest honors from Johns Hopkins, was working with former prisoners of war in a high-level rehabilitation program at the Bethesda Naval Hospital. Among his patients, there was a Marine captain named Goldschmidt. He was one of the few who had held out well against the psychological abuse of his captors. How had he done it? The captain had an unusual story to tell.

"I started dreaming of my son Arty back home. Almost every night. I guess I must have dreamed about Arty before that, but this was different. Arty would show up in my dreams, really vividly. And we'd spend the night talking. Just talking. Like a real father-and-son conversation. He'd tell me about things back home. It gave me something to hang on to, knowing the kid would be there every night. I didn't want to let him down. Wanted him to be proud of me, you know? But the funny thing was: the things he told me, they all really happened. Like my sister having a baby and the garage burning down. When I got back stateside, it was all true, everything Arty told me. Like some kind of second sight. And what was especially weird: in those dreams, that's the only time I ever talked to Arty in my life, I mean like a normal human being."

Arty, Devane discovered, was an autistic child. He had not spoken since his baby-talk years.

Most psychiatrists, hearing the captain's story, would have assumed some form of delusional compensation at work. The stress of imprisonment, the constant threat of torture had given rise to wishful thinking. The mind, especially in dreams, is quick to invent consolations. But Devane's intuition told him the captain was not the delusional type. He asked, "And since then? Do you dream of your son anymore?"

"Yes. Now and then. That's how I found out last summer he broke his wrist. Told me in a dream. Sure enough, it was true."

From the outset of his career, Devane had regarded himself as an innovator. Imagination was his strong suit. He took pride in his speculative originality and had learned to give it free reign. At once, he formed a bold conjecture. Could there be some form of telepathic communication between Captain Goldschmidt and his son? The question came naturally to Devane; since his undergraduate days, he had read extensively in parapsychology. He was professionally astute enough not to advertise the fact, but his hunch was that the way forward in psychiatry was through responsible psychic research. He was an ambitious young man, looking for breakthroughs, willing to gamble, and in a position to do so. On his own initiative, he sought out Arty Goldschmidt, then a twelve-year-old under care in a Cleveland psychiatric clinic that specialized in autism.

"Yes, it's strange about Arty," the boy's doctor told Devane. "He sometimes pops up in my dreams, too. Always thoroughly normal— and very talkative. At least one other staff member has dreamed of him in the same way. It's as if there were two different Arties: the real one we're treating—who is frankly as close to hopeless as they come—and the one we dream about, the boy I guess we'd like to see him be."

"Do you dream that way about your other patients?"

"Now that you ask, I recall a girl we had here. I dreamed of her very often. So did others on the staff—just like Arty. That was years back. I suppose some of the kids have a special charm for us; they get into our subconscious."

For the next half year, as often as three times a month, Devane visited with Arty, offering to work with the boy's doctors. It made for a backbreaking schedule of air commutes between Bethesda and Cleveland, but he was riding the crest of an intoxicating hypothesis. The clinic staff regarded his fascination with Arty as bizarre, even a little suspicious. He offered feeble excuses for the unsolicited—and unpaid —attention he was giving the boy. "It's helping me deal with his father," he explained, though no one could quite see how. Finally, Arty began to appear in Devane's own dreams—just as normal and chatty as Captain Goldschmidt had described him. That was when Devane prevailed upon the captain to have the boy transferred to the Bethesda area. There Devane took him into his own private care.

Hesitantly, he mentioned his new interest to his superiors. "I think the boy may have certain . . . well . . . paranormal powers. I can't be sure. It's only a far-out hunch, but I'd like to follow up on it. It might help with the rehabilitation work."

But there was no need for his reticence. One of his bosses at Bethesda was heading up a classified Army intelligence project on telepathy. He welcomed Devane—already singled out as an enterprising talent—into his group and set him up with a generous budget. The military, hearing reports of Russian work in psychic phenomena, was lavishing money on a number of wild possibilities. Even if very little came of the research, it was the military's way of buying up promising brains.

Singlemindedly pursued and richly funded, Devane's project flowered. He was able to establish that Arty's dreamwatching was an objective fact. Whatever Devane told Arty in his dreams, the boy could recall the next day. His dreamwatching, Devane speculated, was the cause of his autism. Unable to discriminate the overlapping mental worlds he experienced in his waking and dream lives, the boy retreated into a fortress of silence. But his intelligence and perception remained abnormally high, his alertness exceptionally keen. These qualities, once recognized, marked his autism as a special type. Using Arty as a model, Devane devised a battery of tests and began to search for other cases. He found them institutionalized around the country. In the course of the next two years, he located a dozen children and a few adults gifted with Arty's powers. All of them had been written off by the doctors who treated them as beyond hope of recovery. Most of them were. All but two or three proved too emotionally fragile to be salvaged. But the few who could be coaxed out of their protective shell took on confidence and, like Arty, blossomed under Devane's patient tutelage. They were still crude, erratic instruments, but they were his first generation of trained watchers, the first to explore the secret world of dreams and bring back reports.

At the end of five years of steady work, Devane was ready to publish. He presented his results to the superior who had been overseeing his project. "You realize what we have here," Devane explained proudly. "It's direct, empirical access to the unconscious mind. If we can bring these watchers a little farther along, we'll be able to . . ."

"Yes, of course," his boss agreed. "It's extremely exciting. But let's not rush into print just yet. There may be some valuable applications we can make before we go public."

"Such as?"

"Well, you do realize this is a classified project?"

Within a few months, Devane received his first "assignment." It was described as a routine security check—investigating the rumored homosexuality of an aerospace engineer working on a top-secret project. And then there was a British embassy official whose loyalty needed some probing. And then a member of a Soviet trade delegation whom Devane was supposed to embarrass—just a little, just enough so that he might defect.

Devane took the assignments in stride as practical demonstrations of his research findings. He was pleased to see his watchers perform as impressively as they did, though not always with complete success. To his surprise, the result of his first run of experiments was not permission to publish, but a higher, more restrictive security classification. With it, however, came a breathtaking increase in his budget and a new West Coast research facility, which would eventually grow into—so he was promised—the Devane Clinic. The new budget and facility brought with them a new administrative superior, a young clinical psychologist named Costello who did not dissolve his connection with naval intelligence when he took over the position. It did not take Devane long to realize that Costello's competence in psychology was mediocre and woefully out of date. His grasp of the field was stalled back in the days of the reflex arc and the Skinner box. In Costello's view, the mind was the brain and the brain was a sort of meat machine that ran on a crude fuel of rewards and punishments. Dreamwatching was merely a way of fast-injecting that fuel in a completely unobtrusive way. The man was an intellectual barbarian, but, as Devane recognized, he was not on hand to provide professional expertise. He was there to pace an ambitious agenda of ever-more-demanding assignments through the Clinic. And to keep tabs on Devane. He did both with great skill. He was a cool, relentless, low-key bully.

It took another dozen years before Devane's experiments with dreamwatching matured into a reliable psychological research instrument. By then, his work—more tightly classified than ever—had also become a weapon, deadly enough in its application to destroy (among others) a well-regarded and rising young financier named Peter Vale.

The assignment was one of the Clinic's lesser projects. Devane had long since forgotten the details of the operation, if he ever knew them.

He rarely interested himself in the purposes his work served. He invited no explanations; as often as not, none were given. Or if they were, he had learned to mistrust what he was told by Costello. Defensively, for the sake of his professional pride, Devane preferred to function in a purely technical capacity. A target was named; Devane's job was to soften it up. Head Office found ways to establish rapport between the target and the watcher assigned to the project. Meetings were arranged, relationships orchestrated. When the watcher had succeeded in contacting the target's dreams, a series of preliminary probes was made under Devane's direction. He analyzed the watcher's reports and selected suitable points of psychological leverage. A morbid fear, a buried childhood obsession, a hot spot of sexual anxiety. The choices were always much the same, a matter of routine.

A small, repressed residue of homosexuality showed up in Peter Vale's dreams. Nothing extraordinary; a few minor erotic excitations that would easily pass for normal, probably never finding overt expression. But played upon in just the right way, it was the sort of psychic instability that would do nicely to unnerve an ambitious young executive in a highly conservative brokerage house. The watcher bore down upon the forbidden fascination, teasing, toying, shaping it into an enticing bait. Ordinarily, within a few weeks, a month at most, the titillating fantasies could be exaggerated into nightmarish anxieties and worked down below the level of waking recollection. Through the daylight hours, only an amorphous guilt lingered in the dreamer's memory, festering and deepening until an unaccountable depression took hold. Finally, the target's will began to fracture under the strain. At the right moment, when resistance sagged and moral disorientation mounted, instructions were planted—sometimes by the watcher within the dream, sometimes by a waking contact—and the target, obedient as a sleepwalker, began to act as directed.

Peter Vale's case had something to do with transferring clandestine funds for Head Office. It was a run-of-the-mill operation. The firms and personnel involved in such assignments were selected almost at random. Devane had handled a score of similar projects; in his mind, they all ran together into one blurred stain which he filed away at the fringe of his awareness under the heading: "Dirty Work with Money." Money to be finessed in and out of various accounts, laundered and sequestered. Somewhere along the line, Peter Vale's role in the matter would drift into the general area of embezzlement. That was part of the design, a way of distracting attention when the funds were missed. He would be left to make whatever excuses he could for himself from the little he could remember about his own actions and motives. He might come out of the exercise with enough mental competence to talk himself out of serious punishment—though that was not likely.

But before the project got that far along, things bogged down. Devane's watcher ran into unusual resistance. The resistance was Deirdre exploring her husband's troubled dreams, laboring to save his sanity. It was an unprecedented problem, the first time two watchers had crossed paths in a dream. Devane had many times sought to achieve that result, one watcher verifying the reports of another, but he had never succeeded.

Learning that Peter's wife was a gifted if untrained watcher, Devane at once pressed to call off the operation. He wanted to meet Deirdre and investigate her powers. Costello overruled him. Things had gone too far for that. Instead, the intensity of the watcher's efforts was increased to maximum. Peter, thrust too rapidly into psychic chaos, became erratic. His actions escaped control. Against Devane's protests, the watcher was instructed to take any measures necessary to block Deirdre's intervention. Peter was to abuse her, disgust her, drive her off. Finally, she was turned into the object of a murderous rage that was intended to frighten or force her out of Peter's dreams. But when Peter reached the point of waking violence, the effort misfired. He struck out blindly at his children, then at himself.

Within a week of Peter's death, the newspapers had what passed for the whole story. Peter Vale, a bright and promising junior member of his firm, had diverted nearly three million dollars from the accounts he managed. Breaking under the pressure of suspicion, he had gone off his head, killed his son and daughter, and then taken his own life. The money could not be traced.

Deirdre held together long enough after the tragedy to talk to the police, the reporters, the federal investigators. With a calm born of numbness, she answered the same questions over and over, telling nothing of what she knew about Peter's dreams. It was her concern for Laney that kept her afloat until she found a new home with her sister Meg in Santa Monica. Then, with Laney off her hands, she quietly slid beneath the waters. Something like the autism of her childhood returned mercifully to envelop her shattered mind, a period of sullen withdrawal.

For a month and most of another, Meg did her sisterly duty, caring for Deirdre attentively but with a reluctance she was less and less able to hide. Deirdre, moving through her sister's home in brooding silence, brought back memories of her strange and troubled childhood. She was again becoming an object of awe and dread in Meg's life, someone whose insistent, alien stare made the blood chill. Over the past several months, Meg had followed Deirdre's blurred reports of Peter's deteriorating sanity; she had learned something—not much—about his sleep disorders. And then the shattering news: Peter—sweet, gentle Peter—had become a murderous sleepwalker, the destroyer of himself and his family. Once more, in Deirdre's presence, the dreamlives of people had turned unnatural. Meg could not fathom the matter; she did not want to. As soon as she could make the arrangements, she placed Deirdre in a rest home in the high desert behind San Diego.

That was where Devane found her, a ghost of a woman who spent her days staring unseeing from windows. He came in person to explain his interest in Deirdre to her astonished physician. "I've been searching out cases like hers—advanced attention deficit disorders. Part of a special study we're handling for NIMH. With your consent, I'd like to take over her treatment. Full residential care at my Clinic. The charges will be nominal. If necessary, we can provide a subsidy."

Deirdre's doctor snapped at the offer. "It's the finest care you can expect to find anywhere in the country," he dutifully informed Meg. "Devane is the most distinguished man working in the field. You've heard of his clinic, of course. World-famous. I cannot recommend too strongly . . ." Meg needed no persuasion. This was her chance to distance herself still farther from Deirdre and yet to salve her conscience, knowing her sister was in the best of medical hands.

Less than four months after her husband's suicide, Deirdre was installed at the Devane Clinic under Aaron Devane's personal care.

7

"A nun. A sort of social reformer."

There was an unaccustomed snappishness in Devane's voice that discouraged questions. Deirdre, listening closely, struggled to understand about the unusual new patient he was announcing with such irritated urgency. The nuns she recalled from her Catholic school days had no connections with politics. She remembered them as somewhat prissy teachers, often painfully timid, sometimes severe, but having little to do with the world outside the walls of the schoolroom or the church.

"You might look at this," Devane added as he sent her away from his office. He handed her the copy of *Time* Costello had left with him. "You don't have to spend any time on the politics. That's not relevant. Just pick up what you can on the woman. Her life, her character, that sort of thing. And, oh yes . . . I'd appreciate it if you'd try a change of costume when she comes. Blouse, skirt, stockings. You might wear this, too. Just to look a bit more . . . professional." He handed her a white jacket, the sort the Clinic staff wore.

Deirdre took the jacket and the magazine. The connection between the two items seemed to hint at a clear increase in status for her. "She's important . . . ?" Deirdre asked, deducing the obvious from the cover picture.

"Some people are calling her a saint," Devane answered grudgingly. "Whatever that may mean."

There Deirdre drew a blank. Saints—it was the only picture she could conjure up from her Catholic girlhood—were robed figures with sweetly smiling faces, beatifically aglow and bleeding from various wounds. That left her no idea what to expect of Mother Constancia.

A week later, when the woman herself stood before her—a tiny, hunched, and sunken figure, bent over a cane and swaddled to the ankles in a black gown—she looked like nothing so much as Deirdre's childhood image of a fairy-tale witch. There was the comically over-sized nose and jutting chin framing a nearly toothless mouth, even a few warts on the brow. She might have been made up for a Halloween party. But the eyes that shone out of her lined and leathery face were a different matter. Deirdre had never seen (or been seen by) eyes like these. The cover picture on *Time* had been greatly idealized. It led her to expect someone benign and grandmotherly. But Mother Constancia's eyes were catlike: hard, piercing, and unblinking. They might have been the eyes of a watchful savage on the lookout for prey.

From the moment she entered Devane's office, Mother Constancia had singled Deirdre out, and had fixed her with an unsettling gaze. What was this look? Not hostile, not fierce. But not welcoming either. Perhaps Devane would have called it "objective," though it was not a scientist's objectivity. These were eyes that took the world for what it was, without sentimentality or illusion, ready to see the evil and folly of things without flinching. Eyes that saw you for what you were, not judging, but never to be deceived. Under Mother Constancia's candid gaze, Deirdre felt herself wilt inwardly. Devane had instructed her to say nothing about the dreamwatching; but the old nun's eyes seemed to be searching for that one hidden fact, asking: *Who are you? Why are you here?*

Two tall men, one on either side, accompanied the little woman, making her seem even tinier than she was. Devane introduced the older, more distinguished man first—even before he introduced Mother Constancia. He wore a suit of clerical black, subdued but elegantly tailored. "Deirdre, I want you to meet Archbishop McCaffrey. He has brought Mother Constancia to us. Your Excellency, this is Mrs. Vale. She will be assisting me with Mother Constancia."

The Archbishop's hand was cool and limp in Deirdre's. He smiled minimally, offering a small, formal nod. His long face beneath a high white dune of hair was a smooth and pale slab. More to Devane than to Deirdre, he said, "A woman's touch. I'm sure Mother will welcome that. She was most reluctant to come. Her work—there is so much of it. We could hardly tear her away." His voice had a silky authority, rich and intimidating.

Deirdre's hand passed into Mother Constancia's surprisingly tight grip. The old woman's skin was coarse as shoe leather, her arthritic fingers knobbed and kinked. Unspeaking, she continued to search Deirdre's face. Then she asked, "*¿Una médica?*"

The man at her other side repeated the question. "You're a physician?"

Devane answered for her. "One of my clinicians. Invaluable in my work. She has a great deal of experience with the sort of sleep disturbance Mother Constancia seems to be suffering."

The man began to translate, but Mother Constancia waved him to silence. "I understand. Not a doctor. Good. Señora . . ."

"Vale," Deirdre answered.

"Señora Vale. We will be good friends." Her grip, still rock-solid, tightened.

"Mother prefers nonmedical people," the man at her side explained. "In her home country, she always uses a native healer." He was dark and moody-faced, with jutting black brows and a ragged beard. His hair was a tangle of curls, sooty black and streaked with gray. He wore a rumpled denim jacket and faded jeans frayed at the cuff. His plaid shirt, open at the neck, showed the wiry stubble of his chest. He was introduced by the Archbishop as Father Ripley. "Father Ripley has been working very closely with Mother for several years—both in Guatemala and now at *Casa Libertad.* Mother's right-hand man, isn't that so, Father?"

Devane, giving the priest a minimally formal nod and handshake, offered a curt correction. "I hope you won't be disappointed to learn that we have no native healers on our staff. Mrs. Vale, while not a physician, is very 'medical'—as are all my assistants."

Ripley, making no apologies, returned a coolly quizzical look. "Yes, of course," he said. "What else could we expect?"

The remainder of Mother Constancia's entourage was made up of three women who were introduced as members of her community center. The two who looked like nuns spoke no English. The third, who looked nothing like a nun, was a young American named Sister Charlotte. Her appearance was as unclerical as Father Ripley's: a snug T-shirt and peasant skirt, her hair done in a long braid. The shirt carried a poorly sketched image of four heads, apparently women's faces. Devane squinted to make them out, then turned abruptly when he realized he was staring too intently at the young nun's chest. But before she left, he had picked up the phrase: "*¡Viva las monjas!*" As far as he could see, the only concession Sister Charlotte's costume made to her calling was the short white-rimmed veil she wore pinned, not very securely, at the back of her head. It had been agreed with the Archbishop that the priest and the three nuns would be included in

Mother Constancia's party for the length of her stay. "She will not travel without them," McCaffrey had told Devane. "You should allow for a good deal of coming and going on the part of her staff while she's at the Clinic. Messages from the front. The last thing you can expect is for the good Mother to rest. Almost no one seems to have seen her sleep—ever."

When introductions had been made all around, Devane asked to have some time alone with Mother Constancia—"just to get acquainted." He kept Deirdre by him. On her side, Mother Constancia refused to let Ripley depart. She held his hand tightly to keep him close by. There was a sense of two teams squaring off against one another.

"Tell me your dreams," Devane asked when the others were gone. He decided, under pressure from Costello, to move quickly, even indelicately, frankly not caring what results he produced. "I understand your sleep has been disturbed by unpleasant dreams."

"Since Easter, yes. Very often."

"These are frightening dreams? Nightmares?"

"Not frightening, no. *Desalentador.*" She looked to Ripley for the translation. They exchanged a mixture of Spanish and English.

"Disheartening," Ripley reported. "Saddening. Frequently, she has dreams that startle her and wake her. She loses sleep."

"Isn't that the same as frightening?" Devane asked.

"No. She feels no fear. But sudden, surprising things happen."

"Such as . . ."

Ripley continued to speak for her. This seemed to be a well-established pattern. "She sees people she knows attacked or struck down, killed."

"By what? By whom?"

"Political violence, mainly. She dreams of the Death Squads."

"Death Squads?"

"Government terrorists. Guatemalan politics is pretty ugly. Many of our coworkers have been murdered. It's a daily occurrence in the outlying villages."

Constancia made a sour face. "Of this I have seen enough. When it enters my dreams, I prefer to be awake—to work, to pray."

"Are you ever attacked or injured yourself in these dreams?" Devane went on.

Ripley, quite automatically, answered for Constancia. "She's told me of a few dreams where she has been the target of the attack. These seem much less a source of anxiety for her. You see, she's lived through a good deal of violence in her time. That seems to give her some degree of fortitude."

Devane was annoyed by Ripley's intervention. "I gather you've talked with Mother Constancia about her dreams a good deal."

"I should explain," Ripley answered. "I'm Mother's confessor. I have been for the last seven years."

"I didn't know that involved discussing dreams."

"It can involve a great deal. Confession, when it's properly done, can be a lot like psychiatry, maybe even a bit more serious. I suppose I'm Mother's spiritual counselor—in so far as she needs one. My background, incidentally, is in psychiatric social work." He was unflinching under the doctor's obviously haughty gaze.

Devane turned back to Mother Constancia. "There's nothing else that makes you wakeful in the dreams? Nothing . . . sexual?" He handled the term gingerly.

For the first time Mother Constancia's face unfolded into a broad gap-toothed grin. "Oh *sí.* But such silly dreams."

"Yes?" Devane asked.

Ripley began to reply for her, but Devane cut him short. "Please. I'd like Mother Constancia to answer."

"There is sometime a young man. He undresses. He brings with him women, dressed like sisters. They . . . *tienen relationes.*" She looked to Ripley for the English she wanted, then remembering, she supplied it herself. "*Sí.* Fuck. Very much fucking. On and on." She used the word innocently, an amusing bit of American street talk she had recently acquired. "This is very silly. I have no interest in watching."

"It makes you uncomfortable?"

"It is unpleasant when there is so much for so long. These people—the man, the women—they do not enjoy what they do. They make me very weary, very sad."

"Not . . . guilty perhaps? Ashamed?"

Mother Constancia answered casually. "How ashamed? These are not my dreams."

Devane stared at her, obviously thrown off-balance. "What do you mean by that?"

Mother Constancia shrugged and pursed her lips in puzzlement. Ripley said, "She often speaks of the dreams that way—as not being hers."

"But whose dreams could they be but yours?"

Again, Constancia shrugged, gesturing *Who knows?* with her hands. "These things are not inside of me. Who can say how they come?"

Devane shifted uncomfortably in his chair. "But they must be your dreams, Mother. Where else could they come from?" He flinched inwardly, fearing that the priest might notice this heavy-handed violation of standard professional procedure. He was disputing the patient's statement, rather than working with it. But his curiosity had the better of him. He had to know what she took to be the source of her dreams.

"The devil, perhaps." Her answer was offhanded but utterly sober.

Devane started a scoffing laugh, then quickly choked it back. Deirdre had never seen him lose this much of his composure. "Well, assuming we aren't dealing with the supernatural . . ."

"But why not?" Constancia continued in the same flat, matter-of-fact tone. "Dreams are many times from the devil. Also from God and the blessed angels. These are the most important dreams. All the others are . . . *barbujas.*" Again, she looked to Ripley for the English. He supplied it. "Yes, bubbles. Bubbles in the head. But from God we receive messages. Even among the *campesinos* of my homeland, this is well-known. You do not care also about these dreams, Doctor?"

"I care about all the dreams my patients bring me," Devane answered. "Have you had any dreams that came from God?"

Her reply had the precision of total conviction. "Three times God has sent me dreams. It was in these dreams that my vocation came to me."

"These were recent dreams?" Devane asked.

She shook her head. "Many, many years ago. The last was on the night before I took my vows. I was nineteen years old. Afterward, there was no need for God to trouble with me again."

For the first time, Deirdre spoke. Devane had asked her to participate so that she might begin establishing rapport with Constancia, but she had held back until her curiosity was aroused. "How many times have you had dreams from the devil?"

Constancia studied her closely, as if she wondered why Deirdre had asked this question. Her look said: *This interests you? Why?* She answered, "This happens more often. Many times there are temptations."

More eagerly, Deirdre asked again, "What are they like—these temptations?"

"My faith is tempted."

"Your faith in God?"

"No no. Never that. My faith in people. This is very clever, you see. The devil is very clever. He makes me doubt my vocation."

"How do the dreams do that?"

"When I see the evil of people, the weakness, the *fealdad* . . ." Ripley gave her the word. "Ugliness."

"*Sí.* The ugliness. Then I have doubts. I think perhaps my work is wasted. But this is only while I sleep. When I wake, I pray—and God is there to restore my strength. Then the devil goes away—maybe for many years. But now, since Easter, he does not go away. He comes many nights. Each time I dream. I do not understand this. You think my prayers have grown weak?" Her eyes stayed on Deirdre's face, as if she expected an answer to her question. Deirdre flushed and looked away.

Devane started another question, but broke off when Constancia rose unsteadily from her chair and reached for her cane. "Now we will stop. It is time." Ripley moved quickly to her side.

Devane studied his watch ostentatiously. "It's not quite five-thirty. Dinner isn't for nearly an hour."

"Mother won't be taking dinner," Ripley explained. "She begins her prayers soon after six."

"So soon?" Devane asked.

"Mother intends to use her time here as a sort of retreat. That was part of her agreement with Archbishop McCaffrey. She'd like to hold her sessions with you to about a half hour—in the midafternoon."

Devane, bristling, let the annoyance sound in his voice. "I thought we might have a bit more time than that. Ordinarily, I spend fifty-minute intervals with my patients."

"Am I your patient, Doctor?" Constancia asked. "I thought perhaps your guest."

"Yes, of course," Devane yielded gracefully, seeking to keep her trust. "We must try not to disrupt your routine."

On her way to the door, Constancia paused before Deirdre and once again took her hand. "You will be here when I come again?"

"Yes."

"Good." She turned to Ripley. "*Una curandera. Una curandera dotada.*" Then, running her gnarled fingers across Deirdre's brow, just above the eyes, she said, "But in here there is too much fear. The fear comes in the way of the healing. You must place yourself in God's hands."

*   *   *

"I hope you won't mind me saying so, Your Excellency," Devane complained, "but I'm not particularly happy having the priest here."

Costello was driving, slowly looping the car around the steep, switchback curves that led away from the Clinic into town. The three men were heading for dinner at the beachfront hotel where the Archbishop would be spending the night before returning to Los Angeles.

From the back seat, Archbishop McCaffrey said, "I'm afraid we didn't have much choice about that, Doctor. Father Ripley accompanies Mother Constancia everywhere. She never would have come without him. You realize I had to place her under orders of holy obedience to leave off at *Casa Libertad* and come here. That's as strong a command as I can give."

"But will he be sitting in on all my sessions with Mother Constancia?"

"Unless you can persuade Mother to come on her own."

"Could we keep him occupied with other matters?" Costello wondered. "Liaison with Los Angeles, maybe?"

"I believe Sister Charlotte is on hand for that."

"Sister Charlotte." Devane gave a bewildered wag of the head, remembering the tight T-shirt, the skirt, the bare legs, and sandals. "She doesn't look like any nun I've ever seen."

The Archbishop gave an amused, commiserating sigh. "I quite sympathize, Doctor. Even I have trouble adjusting to the new clerical image." Then, giving a small, discrete chuckle, "I'll tell you a little story. When I was a boy—it was in the third grade, I believe—I recall having an argument with a group of my friends in the schoolyard one day. The subject of the dispute was whether nuns had legs. One of my friends was certain they didn't and that it was blasphemous to say they did. Well, I was a nervy child, so I decided to ask one of the sisters. 'Do nuns have legs?' I asked. And do you know what she answered? She looked down thoughtfully and then said she really couldn't remember. That was the Church I grew up in."

"Ripley, too, for that matter," Devane answered. "He could pass for a longshoreman."

"Ah, but that's exactly the idea," the Archbishop explained. "They're a new breed in the Church—the Father Ripleys and Sister Charlottes. Vatican II was responsible for many changes, the least of them being clerical dress. All such minor, harmless reforms—so it seemed at the time. I supported many of them myself. Skirts for the sisters. The Mass in the vernacular. Hymns for the congregation. Meat on Fridays. But drop by drop, they add up to a tidal wave. You'll find, among Mother Constancia's followers, that very few of the old traditions survive. She is one of the champions of the new clergy. You should be careful, Doctor, about the assumptions you make in dealing with her. She may look quaint and old-fashioned, but you may find yourself discussing more politics with her than religion."

"Theology of liberation," Costello commented.

"Yes, that's right, Mr. Costello. That's what you'll find if you look behind the T-shirts and blue denim."

"Theology of liberation?" Devane asked. He had never heard the phrase.

"Religion mixed with revolution," Costello explained. "An explosive mixture, especially in Latin America, wouldn't you say, Your Excellency?"

"Explosive—and possibly heretical. Christ in dialogue with Marx. It's never clear, when you're dealing with men like Ripley, who's getting the best of the encounter: Our Lord or Saint Karl. The Church goes through these phases periodically. In the thirties and forties, we had the worker-priests in the factories. Now we have the guerrilla clergy. It costs the faith deeply, these paroxysms of ethical enthusiasm. But you can't talk these people out of such commitments."

"Ripley tells me that he's a psychiatric social worker," Devane observed. "He seems to feel that gives him some professional expertise."

"He was, yes," Archbishop McCaffrey said. "Like a great many of his order—he's a Jesuit—he was drawn off into secular affairs. Very deeply so. It's a short step from the slums of Newark to the jungles of Central America. He was with the Sandinistas in Nicaragua—we hope not in a fighting capacity. That's how he found his way to Mother Constancia."

"I don't care about his politics," Devane said. "It's his 'spiritual counseling' that concerns me. Am I going to have to compete with him for Mother Constancia's attention? There's nothing worse than having an amateur therapist watching over your shoulder."

The Archbishop had a suggestion. "It occurs to me that if Mother hits it off well with your assistant . . . the woman, what was her name?"

"Mrs. Vale?"

"Yes, Mrs. Vale. If Mother gets on well with her, she might not feel she needs Father Ripley with her. At least, not each time you meet. And if Father Ripley comes to trust Mrs. Vale as well, he might be willing to stay away. Of course, that places Mrs. Vale in a rather critical position."

"We more or less suspected that might be the case," Costello observed.

After a pause, Devane asked, "What are *monjas?*" He inserted a hard American *j* in the word.

"Hm?" The Archbishop could not follow.

"Sister Charlotte's T-shirt. It said '¡*Viva las monjas!*' "

"*Monjas.*" The Archbishop supplied the correct Spanish. "It means 'nuns': 'Hurrah for the nuns.' Something like that."

"Oh." The phrase meant nothing to Devane.

"The four nuns," the Archbishop explained. "The four American churchwomen—who got themselves raped and killed in El Salvador."

"They *got themselves* raped . . . ?"

"Poking around where they had no business. Apparently, they tried to run a roadblock. You must have read the story. It kicked up a devil of a row. Made lots of trouble for the Salvadoran authorities."

Devane remembered nothing of the incident. "They were raped for running a roadblock?"

"The response of the Salvadoran troops was excessive. No doubt they recognized the women as agitators."

"The country's in a revolution," Costello reminded Devane. "In a touchy situation, you don't provoke the troops like that."

"Or you get raped," Devane added with clear sarcasm.

"In any case," the Archbishop continued, "the four nuns have become quite the heroes for some of our radical Brides of Christ—like Sister Charlotte. Such is the material from which our liberated clergy would make its martyrs. Alas."

8

Laney was astonished. She had never heard anything like it. "You mean Mother Constancia prays *all night?*" she asked. "Without stopping?"

"As far as I know," Ripley answered.

"Wow! That's really religious," Laney observed with honest admiration. "That's the most religious thing I ever heard."

She was sitting with Ripley on the patio of the small bungalow she shared with her mother. On the far side of the house, a towering stand of eucalyptus filtered the sunlight that fell across them into a cool, lacy pattern. Where the trees ended, the crest of the hill dropped away sharply toward the town below. Beyond, the early evening sea spread to meet the sky like an undulating green blanket.

An hour earlier, Mother Constancia had finished her first week of sessions with Dr. Devane and, as abruptly as on the day she arrived, had retired to her rooms, taking the three nuns with her. That left Ripley once again with time weighing heavy on his hands. It was what he had feared when the visit to Santa Barbara was arranged: long, empty hours subtracted from his life, lost in the service of loyal attendance. At Devane's suggestion, Deirdre had invited him to have dinner with her and Laney. Devane had been trying to bring her together with Ripley as often as possible. "Find out all you can about Mother Constancia," he had instructed her, clearly unhappy with the meager progress he was making on his own.

Deirdre, alone with Ripley, found it difficult to question him. There was an angularity about the man, even a hint of surliness that held her at a distance. Not so Laney. She was proving to be fascinated with the mysterious figure of Mother Constancia, all the more so since Deirdre had shown her the *Time* magazine cover story. Laney had struggled through the thickly political article, picking up only fragments of information; but the face on the cover meant real status to her, a glamour she associated with film stars and presidents.

"But what's she praying *for* so much?" Laney wanted to know.

Ripley, amused by Laney's aggressive curiosity, tried to explain. "She isn't praying *for* something—the way most people do. For Mother, praying is a form of communion with God. It's more like listening than speaking. Do you know what a contemplative is?"

Laney didn't, but the word caught at her imagination. She was a bright girl with a taste for the exotic. She had already learned from the *Time* article that Mother Constancia had reportedly experienced her first vision of God when she was about Laney's own age. She could not help but wonder what such an experience was like.

"In the Church," Ripley explained, "there are certain nuns and monks we call 'contemplatives.' That means they try to spend a great deal of each day simply thinking about God. They have special times set aside for that, even at night—with special names. Vespers, matins, lauds. Well, Mother sort of runs all the nighttime hours together. You might call her a nonstop marathon contemplative."

"But when does she sleep?" Laney asked.

"That's hard to say. Very few people have actually seen Mother sleep. She's always the last to bed and the first up in the morning."

"But she's got to sleep sometime."

"I'm sure she does. But I gather not much—especially lately. Sister Charlotte—who's with her now—tells me Mother tries to spend a good part of the night in a sort of trance."

Deirdre, returning to the patio with coffee and dessert, picked up on his answer. "Trance?"

"An ecstasy, I suppose it might be called. They say Saint John of the Cross could pass days in a state much like that. Very likely, it's the true meaning of prayer."

The word "ecstasy" sounded faintly salacious to Laney. She associated it with advertisements for adults-only movies. What did that have to do with religion? Mother Constancia was becoming more and more intriguing.

"Why aren't you praying with her?" Laney wanted to know.

Ripley threw off a small dismissive laugh, but Deirdre could hear the underlying note of bitterness in it. "I don't do much praying these days," he said.

"How come?" Laney asked. "I thought religious people *had* to pray."

Ripley's eyes darkened and his throat worked as if he were swallowing away the answer that arose. Deirdre had seen that happen before when the conversation got around to matters he did not wish to discuss. Tactfully, he asked Laney, "Well, do *you* pray?"

"Me? Well, gee, no. I mean not much. I mean I don't do any *official* praying."

"Well, unofficial praying is the best kind anyway."

"But I'm not religious. My mother says we're sort of nothing."

"Oh. But just 'sort of,' eh?"

"I mean—you're a priest. I thought praying is what you got paid for."

Deirdre decided to intercept the remark with offers of cake all around and the matter was forgotten. But Laney had more to ask about.

"Is Mother Constancia really a saint, like it says in the magazine?"

Ripley parried the question. "I suppose that depends on what you think a saint is."

It might only have been a way of deflecting her inquiry, but Laney took the challenge seriously. She pondered it, hoping Ripley would notice how thoughtfully. "Somebody who can do miracles," she said.

Ripley parried again. "And what do you mean by miracles?"

Under this sober gaze Laney felt embarrassed by the things that first leaped into her mind. Obvious kid's stuff. With someone like Father Ripley, she felt she must give a passably grown-up answer. "I mean something wonderful that makes the world better . . . and that only a saint can do . . . I guess."

Ripley gave her a kind smile. "If that's what you mean, then I'd have to say Mother Constancia is a saint. Do you recall how many times the article said she's been arrested?"

"You mean put in jail?" Laney looked away, squinted, tried to remember. "Not exactly. I think it said a couple times."

"A couple times, yes. More likely a couple hundred times. I doubt there's a jail in Guatemala Mother hasn't been in. And they aren't very nice jails. One miracle is certainly that she's survived at all."

"Why does she keep getting put in jail so much?"

"For trying to do 'something wonderful that makes the world better.' Leading demonstrations. Speaking out against the government. Getting people together to take over the land they work on. *Time* wasn't too accurate about all that. When it talks about a saint, it doesn't quite have a jailbird in mind."

"What *does* it have in mind?"

"Most likely somebody whose picture on the cover will sell a lot of copies that week."

"They could do that with a movie star."

"Right. One week a movie star, the next week a saint. The week after that a millionaire or a gangster. Just remember, saints aren't what magazines tell you they are. They're a lot more trouble than the world cares to have on its hands."

Ripley's abrasive manner seemed to soften and relax in Laney's presence. That made things easier for Deirdre. Later, when Laney, with a good deal of protest, had been sent off to do her homework, Deirdre resumed the conversation. "You say you've been with Mother Constancia for seven years."

"As her confessor," Ripley corrected, "seven years, yes. But I started working with her in Guatemala a few years before that."

"What sort of work was it?"

He looked at her keenly, his expression balanced between amusement and irritated disbelief. " 'And what sort of things do you write, Mr. Shakespeare?' "

Deirdre flushed with embarrassment. "I'm sorry. I'm not very well-informed."

"There *is* the article in *Time,* which everybody around here seems to have read like the gospel—including your daughter. Haven't you?"

"Yes, but there was so much I couldn't follow. I mean the political things."

"It was hardly a deep analysis. The basic stuff is there. About the poverty, the repression, the violations of human rights—all, of course, symmetrically balanced off against the usual anti-Communist shibboleths. I thought everybody knew that much about 'the Red Madonna.' " He repeated the phrase to himself with a sour chuckle. "The Red Madonna! Don't you read the papers?"

"Not much," Deirdre confessed. "I guess we're sort of cut off here."

"Life on the Magic Mountain," Ripley sighed. "The Pope's visit to Central America—you must have heard about that."

Deirdre vaguely recalled a report on the television news. Images of the Pope threading his way through cheering throngs, waving, reaching out to touch and bless. Had that been months ago or years ago? She could not be certain. Mother Constancia had risen to prominence in the United States during Deirdre's long, isolated convalescence. While the revolutionary upheaval in Central America was catching fire on the front pages, Deirdre had been fighting her own secret war against shock and grief. Instinctively, she had exiled herself from the world outside during those torturous months. The last time she had paid attention to newspapers and television, they had constantly threatened to ambush her with lurid reports of Peter's death, his crimes, her own suffering and humiliation. She had learned to fear the news and to hide from it. "Yes," she answered. "I remember about the Pope. Did that have to do with your work?"

"Unfortunately, yes," Ripley sighed. "We—Mother and her followers—were the erring clergy he came all that way to scold. The rumor is he made the trip primarily to see Mother—his prize headache in Latin America."

"Headache? I don't understand. I thought she was . . . Isn't she doing a great deal of good?"

Could she be teasing? he half-wondered. "And you're the people who are going to heal her?" He shook his head and gave a low, sardonic laugh.

Deirdre hastened to apologize, "I'm sorry. I'm sure Dr. Devane knows all about these things."

"Does he?" Ripley was clearly skeptical. If anything, Devane's practiced professional detachment was proving more annoying to him than Deirdre's sincere ignorance.

"Oh yes, I'm sure," she insisted. "It's just that I don't keep up with the news. Dr. Devane thinks it could be too disruptive for me."

Ripley studied her closely. "Sometimes you sound more like a patient than a . . . psychologist."

Deirdre was quick to correct. "Oh, I'm not a psychologist. I *am* a patient. I mean I used to be. I came here for treatment—about two years ago. Now I assist Dr. Devane."

"Oh? How?"

Her instructions were to tell no one about the dreamwatching. That left her with no idea how to answer. "Dr. Devane thinks I'm helpful with certain kinds of people. In an intuitive way."

She was trying not to sound evasive, but Ripley could feel her drawing off, looking for cover. He let her, although he was naggingly curious about her role at the Clinic. Her strangeness and vulnerability had several times held his thoughts. The other day he had caught sight of her on the grounds looking unkempt and scraggly, wearing the drab uniform the Clinic's patients wore. She had been helping the mute, retarded servant called Smitty serve cookies and milk to a small, unruly group of autistic kids. Yet, at other times—with Constancia—she wore the same white jacket as the professional staff. Tonight, he noted, she had taken some trouble with her appearance. The usually tousled hair had been neatly combed and fluffed; she wore no lipstick, but there was the hint of makeup around the eyes. The effect of that was to lend her a more startled look than she must have intended. She was also wearing a rather elegant dress that was meant to show her off to advantage. It did.

He could tell she was painfully sensitive to questions; he decided not to press her. There was no need to. It was enough that Constancia had warmed to Deirdre as she had. Ripley had learned to trust her judgment about people, especially when it was immediate and certain.

"Well, I give Devane credit for bringing you in on Constancia's treatment—in whatever capacity. So far, in your own odd way, you're the one right note that's been struck in this foolish exercise."

"How do you mean?"

"You're one small breach of medical orthodoxy. That's good. Because Devane won't be able to help Mother in the least if he isn't willing to bend the rules."

"In what way?"

There was genuine curiosity in her face. More than that: concern. He wondered if he could use her to reach Devane with his advice. He knew the doctor would pay no attention to him otherwise. "For one thing, he's going to have to take Mother's politics into account. The problem she's having—the bad dreams—aren't simply neurotic symptoms. They stem from political realities in her life. These have to be understood."

"What do you mean?"

"I mean, beginning with the fact that she's here, in California, not in Guatemala, where she belongs—in her own country, among her own people. If you pulled a fish out of the sea, you wouldn't need a doctor to tell you why it was gasping for breath. That's what Mother is—a fish out of water. Of course she's disturbed. That's because she's been driven out of her element and into exile. That isn't so hard to understand, is it?"

"She can't go back?"

"She'd go back tomorrow if it was up to her. It's not that she's afraid. But . . . she's a nun. *Still* a nun, I should say. And when the Pope gives direct, personal orders to a nun, she obeys, even if it tears her apart."

"The Pope made her leave?" Deirdre was trying to piece together the picture Ripley was drawing for her.

"Not in so many words—though it would have been a lot cleaner if he had simply instructed her to pack up and get out. What he did was to threaten her with excommunication if she continued having friendly contact with the revolutionary forces in Guatemala. That was like waving her death warrant in front of her. The Church is all she's had to lean on. It's been little enough, God knows. If she stopped being a nun, she'd be as good as dead. Even so, it was all we could do to make her leave the country."

"Would he really have excommunicated her?" Deirdre recalled the word from her Catholic girlhood. *Excommunicated.* Cast out, like Satan from heaven. Hopelessly damned, like the heretics and the unbelievers. The word still carried a small, secret charge for her.

"It's a good question. Maybe we should have dared him to do it. If he did, it could fan a lot of burning questions into a great blaze, a greater blaze than he might be able to control. I think it could split the Church. It wouldn't be the first time a Pope went up against a saint and paid dearly for it."

"But why is the Pope so upset with her?"

"Upset!" He laughed at her school-teacherish choice of words. "It's not just the Pope who's 'upset' with her; it's the entire, decrepit Vatican hierarchy. Maybe it's everything the Church has become since Jesus that's 'upset' with Mother. You see, she takes Christianity seriously. She believes the Church belongs to the real world—where people work and struggle and live and die. That means revolution, a religion of true redemption here and now." He paused, watching the bewilderment and fascination that passed across her face. "I gather all this sounds pretty mysterious to you. You're not a Catholic, are you?"

"Not for a long time. I was raised as one. But I'm afraid I've drifted away. I've forgotten so much . . ."

The brooding, impatient look returned to his eyes "You needn't apologize to me for that. I'm drifting myself—or rather being swept away. Hanging on by my fingernails. Constancia is all the Church there is for me. If it weren't for her, I wouldn't be . . ." He went silent, giving Deirdre a resentful stare, as if he objected to the way she had drawn him out. Tersely, he muttered, "I'm not the one who's here to have the demons cast out."

"You don't want to be here, do you?"

"God! I hope that's clear to all concerned—including Mother. I don't have the time to waste." Then, relenting, he wearily rubbed the heels of his hands into his eyes. "Maybe I'm being unfair. She does need the rest, even if I don't. She's very run down. It's these dreams— they've taken away the little peace and quiet she allows herself. We all work her too hard. I suppose this is as good a place as any for her to get away—provided you don't treat her like one of your run-of-the-mill nut cases." There was anger in his voice, but also an appeal for understanding. "You've got to see that. She's special. That's what I'm afraid Devane won't understand. Maybe you can get through to him with that message. He's got to know he's dealing with a woman who needs her work the way she needs food and air. Take that away from her for too long and she'll become difficult. And that's *not* a neurotic symptom for him to analyze. It's a sign of her health. Her work is what matters to her, more than her comfort or her health. After all, she's spent years gambling her life for what she believes in. A lot she cares for losing a night's sleep now and then. You should let Devane know that. She won't sit still for long."

*   *   *

When he was leaving, Laney, now in her bathrobe and slippers, rushed to catch him at the door. "Look," she said proudly, holding out a heavy schoolbook. It was her history text, opened to a chapter on the Counter-Reformation. "See what I found."

She was pointing to a picture: a photograph of Bernini's famous Vatican sculpture, *The Ecstasy of Saint Teresa*. The delicious young virgin melting under the darts of a valentine-sweet angel. "It says that's 'ecstasy.' Is that what happens to Mother Constancia?"

Ripley paused in the entranceway to muse over the picture. "To tell you the truth, Laney, I wouldn't know." After a few moments of serious thought, he added, "Looks a bit sensational, actually. But who can tell what goes on in the heart of a saint? Would we want to know if we could?"

"Oh, I would," Laney remarked at once.

"Would you?" To Deirdre, he remarked, "Innocence is very brave, isn't it? I'm sure most of us would find it simply shattering. Do you know that poem by T. S. Eliot about humankind not being able to stand too much reality? He was right, I think."

9

Ripley could not remember when he had last met anyone as politically illiterate as Deirdre. To judge by the questions she asked about Central America, she might have been locked away in solitary confinement for the past two years. Yet she inquired eagerly and listened when he answered as hungrily as an amnesiac struggling to recapture a forgotten life. Perhaps that was why her naïveté was not more abrasive to him. Her interest was desperately sincere; she had made him want to teach her.

Even so, he had not expected to spend most of his time at the Clinic lecturing on the facts of life in Guatemala to an audience of one. At first, he had answered her questions grudgingly, as if to shame her for her ignorance. Until one day when she asked about the violence he had personally witnessed. Automatically, he tossed off the graphic particulars as he had often done in the past for journalists and visiting observers in Guatemala, the commonplace barbarity of a nation torn by revolutionary strife. He was telling her about an incident. A village he had seen terrorized by government forces for sheltering rebels. He had watched helplessly from the jungle while the men of the village were herded into the marketplace, beaten by interrogators, a few of them castrated before the eyes of their wives and children, then shot. After that, the young women were hustled off into nearby houses and . . .

He had intended to shock her. Since he had returned to the United States, he had fallen into the habit of wanting to shock those who asked about Central American politics. Shocking was a way of punishing the complacent. With Deirdre, he succeeded more dramatically than he could have expected. Before he had finished his account of the atrocity, he felt a pressure on his sleeve. He turned and saw it was her hand on his arm. "Please," she said. Only that. Her face had gone white and her eyes flared with alarm. She looked away, then stood and walked off unsteadily in no direction.

He stopped at once, in the middle of a sentence, feeling a wave of remorse wash over him. He rose to go to her. "I'm sorry," he said. The apology was not only for distressing her; he was suddenly appalled by his own insensitivity. He had recited the story—that story and others just as ugly—too often. Such memories had begun to unfold from him like a rehearsed script, glib to the point of unfeeling. For the first time, he realized how the brutality he had lived with for the past ten years had hardened him. He was capable of using the human misery he had witnessed like a weapon—to strike and wound. How long had it been since he had responded as she did to these horrors—with genuine and unguarded vulnerability?

Her fragility, he could see, was that of illness, the hurt and anxiety of someone still delicately close to great personal suffering. She had told him she was at the Clinic under care. What right did he have to unsettle her as he had? He was playing for cheap effects.

Still, a day later, assuring him that she was prepared for his words, she asked to hear more. She wanted to know everything he had seen. She seemed to be testing herself, asking for his help to guide her back into the world that lay beyond the protecting solitude of the Clinic. He hesitated before doing what she asked. He discovered it was not easy for him to get a sure fix on her responses when they talked together. She had the odd habit of going silent for long intervals, leaving a question unanswered, a fragment of conversation balanced inconclusively. This was not merely a matter of absentmindedness; at the center of that silence, her eyes would take on a riveting concentration, as if she were searching his words to the roots for their hidden meaning. The first few times, he found the characteristic unsettling, but then it became unaccountably attractive, a reflection of deep attentiveness. There was a muted, emotional intensity about her that had to be handled with care, like live explosives.

With great caution, weighing each word and watching for its effect, he told her of the violence he had seen. As he did so, he realized he was, within the spell of her earnest attention, reexperiencing the terror of the events himself. He had built a wall against it, a barrier of anger and recrimination. The bloodshed, the torture had ceased to be real; they had become mere lifeless evidence supporting an indictment against political enemies. Now this woman was bringing that wall down; she was teaching him, without knowing she did so, that there was more than vindictiveness in him, more than ideological rhetoric and the dry appeal for justice. He could remember now what it was like when his own political innocence had been violated—before the rage took over and froze him into a vengeful instrument prepared to strike out, to kill. Talking with her, he was finding his way back to that moment of moral purity when he was simply a human being suffering with other human beings.

And there was something else that was happening between them, this a more troubling development.

What he told her of his experiences made him seem courageous in her eyes. There was no way to avoid that. The plain truth was: he had taken risks, more than once gambling his life. He tried to relate the fact coldly, with all the detachment he could muster. But in spite of himself, he was winning her admiration.

He knew it.

And he liked it.

10

Deirdre lay awake and alert behind her sleeping eyes. Her mind was a beacon slowly scanning the night, searching for Mother Constancia.

Each night since Constancia's arrival, she had carried out the same exercise until she tired and sleep overtook her. Her search had come to nothing. She could not find Constancia's dreams. She felt the emotional link between them was strong enough to bring their minds together. It had formed quickly at their first meeting, an irresistibly spontaneous bond that drew her to this old woman about whom she knew so little. She could not say she *liked* Constancia; it was nothing as simple as affection that linked them. If anything, Deirdre felt a distinct unease, an intimidating awe in the woman's presence. Constancia's gaze possessed a relentless candor. It demanded more honesty than Deirdre felt free to give. But Constancia had called her a *curandera*, a healer, had trusted her and thereby made a claim upon her. More forcefully than Dr. Devane, Constancia had summoned up something in Deirdre that wanted to grow and flourish—a power to serve that had been buried for too long. It was at that moment, when Constancia had seemed to say "Cure me," that the bond between them had locked into place. Deirdre knew the feeling of that connection—two lives suddenly fusing, a sharing of the mind and will.

But when in sleep she reached out for Constancia, she could not find the signal she looked for. Perhaps it was because the old woman slept so little. Deirdre thought she might be missing the brief intervals in which she dreamed.

Searching, finding nothing, Deirdre recalled something Ripley had mentioned that evening. He had said that Constancia often spent part of each night in a trance—neither awake nor asleep. Deirdre wondered: had she been looking for the wrong signal? She decided to experiment. She allowed her attention to spread across a wider band of consciousness. She discovered an intoxicating sense of buoyancy, a desire to ascend. Cautiously, she cultivated an image of rising, reaching higher, stretching upward. She found herself drifting into levels of sleep she had never explored before and at last reached a zone of the mind where she detected a slightly dizzying, hypnotic pulse. She now felt so close to wakefulness that she thought for a moment she could hear the outside world—the pulse becoming an airy rumble that sounded like a deep, guttural voice speaking nearby, in her room. She was on the point of opening her eyes to look around, when she found her attention sucked back powerfully into the darkness.

Toward what?

An elusive flicker. Points of radiance that came and vanished. Deirdre reached out; several tiny bright sparks played across her palm. She cupped her hand and gathered the luminous fragments closer. In their glow, she saw intricate shapes that formed, dissolved, and formed again. A crystalline geometry never the same from one moment to the next. She had a memory—something from her childhood. Catching a snowflake, taking it on the tip of her tongue. She bent forward, licked cautiously. The taste: not cold but stinging sharp, like a needle. Inside her head there was a sweeping vapor. Her eyes were assaulted by a rough wave of heat that brought a stunning clarity to her vision. The points of light bunched and congealed, exploded silently into an image.

There was a figure—a young girl, perhaps Laney's age, seated on the ground. She was dark-skinned, with large, slanting eyes—so piercing they seemed frozen in a state of amazement. She was barefoot, wearing a drab patched dress. Her hair was long and scraggly. Around her neck there was a necklace of brown wooden beads or nuts. The necklace held Deirdre's eye. Where had she seen it before? Mother Constancia wore a necklace like this. She often ran the beads between her fingers when she spoke with Dr. Devane.

The girl was hunkering down beside a small pond or river. She swayed on her heels rhythmically over the water back and forward Washing something. Rubbing something, an article of clothing, kneading it against a flat stone. The scene took on definition. There were trees all about and high brush, a dense forest deeply shadowed. Overhead, the sun struck down fiercely where the girl sat, a sword of noonday fire. Deirdre, watching, saw the girl stop, freeze motionless. Her face became tensely concentrated, staring down into the water. A spangling light danced there. The girl, curious, reached to touch it. But no, the light was not there. It was above her, a flutter of eye-stinging brightness reflecting off the pond. The child turned, startled. A bird, was it? Something—*there,* just above her head, hovering in a blinding hot flare of sunlight, wings beating frantically.

Then this happened.

The sound Deirdre had heard, the not-quite-voice, became a voice, as vast as the wind, and uttered one rasping word. At the command, spears of light flashed down from the fire-haloed flying thing striking the girl at the forehead and breast. Where the darts of flame touched, points of blood broke the flesh, streamed.

And the scene froze. Nothing moved. The voice had swept by. Silence. The silence locked everything in like a glacier.

Slowly, almost imperceptibly, the girl, kneeling, gazing up wide-eyed, was lifted in the shafts of light like a speared animal, rigid with fear. The surrounding scene faded and, for a moment, there was only a radiant void, the girl suspended in it on two tethers of light. Deirdre, now entering fully into the dream, could uneasily feel the floating sensation. It left her drunken, disoriented. Hard to hold her balance . . . yet she knew there was no danger of falling. Here, nothing fell. The pull of hard matter did not exist.

As if the light were infusing her, the dark little girl took on a vibrant clarity. Around her, the scene re-formed, but now as an iridescent garden whose colors were lost in the luster of their own glow. Everywhere there was a brightness too bright for the eye—for Deirdre's eye. The child sank slowly to the ground released from the shafts of light, eyes still wide and fixed on the blazing cloud above her and the . . . bird (was it?) that hid within it, its wings spread like sails.

But what sort of bird? Deirdre squinted against the light to see. Then wished she hadn't.

Within the glowing cloud, she could make out two still more radiant points of fire. Eyes, fiercely burning. Then, an open beak. In it, spikes of teeth. Saber-sharp fangs.

Not a bird, despite its wings. Something she did not want to see more closely.

How did it hang there, so still in the air—like an image etched upon space?

Deirdre turned her gaze away from the bird-thing back to the glowing garden. *How very beautiful this is,* she thought. But it was an eerie beauty, glassy and lifeless in its perfection. She reached out toward the leaves of a nearby bush, expecting them to be brittle to the touch. Instead, they were soft and warm, like living crystal. Surprised, she bent to study the leaf that lay upon her fingers. Its brightness swam in her vision, shifting and scintillating. On the leaf, a tiny stick-thin insect busied itself exploring the fine-veined surface. It too shone glass-clear. Deirdre examined it long and fixedly, realizing as she did so that she might spend as much time gazing at every leaf, every blade of grass. *How much time?* she asked herself. A great deal of time seemed to have passed. Or had it?

Then it occurred to her, as casually as she might notice the day turning warm or cool, that the question had no meaning. *There is no time here,* Deirdre said. The girl, the garden, the suspended bird-thing on its outspread wings were as free of time as figures in a painting. Things shaped of light. Ageless.

And realizing that, she woke.

Daylight was in the room.

11

Costello was growing impatient. "You've been working with the woman for four weeks," he reminded Devane. "When do we begin getting results?"

They were in Costello's office, the first time they had met in several days. Once again, Devane was using drink to conceal his evasiveness. He felt more secure confronting Costello across a moat of alcohol.

"Be reasonable," he protested, making no apologies. "This isn't some laboratory rat we're dealing with here. Constancia, if you recall, believes we're trying to help her, not dissect her like a clinical specimen. I gather you want me to maintain that illusion."

There was a note of defensive pride in Devane's muzzy voice. As usual, he was being treated like a mechanic assigned to tear down a mental carburetor. Costello worked from a brutally crude psychology. When the human mind failed to perform to specifications, you sent it in for an overnight fix.

"Remember," Devane went on, "I've only just managed to get the priest off my back in the last week. Constancia has finally worked up enough trust to see me alone. Well, not *me,* actually. Deirdre. She treats the sessions as if Deirdre were running them. I provide the questions, but the interchange takes place between them."

"And what's Mrs. Vale finding out for us?" Costello asked.

"Not much so far. You see, Constancia sleeps very little—not more than a few hours each night. Some nights, not at all. That's why Moray has had such limited success with her. No sleep, no dreams."

"The woman doesn't sleep?" That caught Costello off-balance. He was determined to treat Mother Constancia as another routine assignment. No privileged status, no special powers. But in spite of himself, he was impressed. "How does she spend her nights?"

"Ah, that's where things get interesting. She prays." Devane paused over a long sip of Scotch to see what effect this bit of unlikely information produced. Nothing. A stolid, poker-faced stare. It was the face he knew Costello used to mask severe disapproval. "And then," Devane continued, "for several hours of the night, she may fall into some form of autohypnotic trance. Not awake, not asleep. And not at all relaxed, as she might be in advanced meditation, but very high, very tense. A condition of superalertness. Fascinating. It's an exotic state of consciousness. Moray missed that entirely, you see—as you might expect he would. God, I'd love to get encephalographic readings on her."

Costello did not share his enthusiasm. "This isn't a piece of NIMH research, Aaron. What happens in this trance? Is there anything we can use?"

"Too early to say," Devane lied. Deirdre had been observing Constancia's trances for several nights and making detailed reports. But Devane had no intention of telling Costello more than he had to. Information about Constancia was the only card of any value he held; he had to play it skillfully.

"No images? Nothing we can work with?"

"Sorry, not yet. There may be some psychologically significant content we can use, but it hasn't come through with any clarity. Deirdre is just beginning to fine-tune her observations."

Costello, half-suspecting deception, returned a long, frigid stare. Tactfully, Devane offered a small measure of advice. "I can tell you this much. What you and Moray have been trying will get you exactly nowhere. You can't scare the woman into submission. Constancia's a brave lady. A will of steel. She's lived through worse than anything Moray can invent in her dreams. Images of physical violence are totally unproductive with her. She'll just wake up and brush them aside. Also, you can't shame her. I can tell you for certain she's not repressing any sexual hang-ups. She finds Moray's little obscenities ludicrous."

Costello showed no signs of appreciating the help. Devane was telling him again that Constancia was exceptional. He did not want to hear that. Resentfully, as if he were defending an article of religious faith, he said, "Everybody's got a button to push somewhere. What about her virginity—if she is a virgin? Can we threaten that?"

Son of a bitch, Devane thought. He let the contempt of the unspoken words show in his face. Aloud, he said, "I'm sure you and Moray have tried that. I have the impression from what Constancia says about her dreams over the last four months that the two of you have tried every kinky kind of sexual hijinx in the book." He gave Costello a paternal, disapproving frown. "Constancia isn't exactly a blushing schoolgirl,

you know. Really, she finds such things laughable—if not boring."
Noting Costello's annoyance, he was perversely encouraged to elabo-
rate. "Chastity, Bob. I don't suppose any of us really understand its
true meaning any longer. But that's the only way I can describe Constancia. Not repressed, not insecurely sublimated, but chaste. I don't
know if that means asexual, nonsexual, transsexual. But all this juvenile ass-grabbing you've been dumping into her dreams just doesn't
carry any charge for her."

Costello blew out an exasperated breath. "So where does that leave
us?"

Devane weighed his choices carefully. Constancia had become a
significant study for him. He wanted as much time with her as he could
get before he reported anything useful to Costello. Once she was
turned over to Moray, she would be lost to him; she might not survive
what followed. Still, he must not seem to be totally stymied. That might
drive Costello toward something as reckless as outright violence. He
had to offer at least a glimmer of progress. "I think we might be able to
do something with sacrilege."

"Sacrilege?" Costello lit up at once.

It was only a scrap, but enough, Devane hoped, to take the edge off
Costello's appetite. "Yes, you know, insulting the symbols of her
faith."

"That gets to her?"

"Well, there's some indication . . ." Devane was playing for time,
but he was not wholly improvising. He was thinking of a dream Constancia had mentioned a few days before, one of Moray's obscene
frolics that still lodged in her memory. She had dreamed of herself in a
church. Moray, intervening with one of his desperate orgies, had assembled a collection of young nuns. He imagined them kneeling before him for oral sex, a lineup of eager mouths lusting for him along
the altar rail. He had gone from one to the other, providing. Constancia's reaction was odd. It was not the sex itself that had shaken her,
but the crude parody of the eucharistic service. Had Moray intended
that? Then, when he was finished, he had used the tabernacle cloth to
wipe his organ clean and had flung it aside. That, as much as anything
else he had done, left her torn between outrage and embarrassment.
When she recounted the dream to Deirdre, her voice still throbbed
with fury. Anger, Devane knew, was not the best emotion to use for
Costello's purposes, but it was the best token he could offer. "Constancia may be a saintly woman," he explained, "but there's still a lot of

good, old-fashioned peasant superstition in her. It wounds her to see holy objects desecrated."

Costello wanted more. "What objects? Candles, crosses?"

Devane backed off gingerly. "I haven't worked that out yet. As you might guess, it's painful for her to talk about such things. But I think there may be just a trace of shame and dread there for us to explore."

Costello would not easily be put off. "You must have more than that to report. What in particular sets her off?"

"Well, things involving the altar, for example."

"Like what? Pissing on the altar? Abusing the statues? The Black Mass . . . things of that sort?"

"I can't be certain yet."

"Come on, Aaron, what have you got?"

"I told you, it's just an indication. We have to work on it. I've asked Deirdre to take it up with Constancia in our next few sessions." He could see Costello's mind busily at work on the little he had told him, racing ahead—possibly too fast.

"What do you mean by the altar?" Costello pressed him. "The whole altar or some part of it? The crucifix . . . ?"

"We have to proceed carefully here," Devane quickly cautioned. "We have to isolate exactly the right images to work with. Otherwise, we could make a serious mistake, push the *wrong* button. We don't want to do that. Give me another few weeks . . . a month, say."

"A month!" Costello glared at him. "We don't have months to work with here. The Nobel Committee could announce its selection anytime in early fall. That's a month and a half off. That means, if we're going to make this look realistic, then the committee has got to begin registering some kind of serious deviance from Constancia in the next six weeks."

Devane shrugged helplessly. "I can't make up what I don't know. And I advise you not to resort to guesswork. Be reasonable. I'm working in the dark here. The woman is practically an enigma."

"You have our complete file on her."

Devane scoffed. "An intelligence file! What good is that to me? I'm not interested in her political associations or her arrest record. I need to know about her psyche. When it comes to that, the woman is an unknown quantity to both of us."

12

But Mother Constancia was not quite the enigma Devane pretended she was. He had learned more about her than he was ready to share with Costello.

He had learned about the girl in the garden and the sunburst bird.

He had learned about the caves of the Cuchumatánes and the rainbow fire.

He had learned about the Sainted Children who left the soul drunken and singing.

He had learned what Deirdre had discovered for him—that there were two Mother Constancias. There was the Red Madonna whom Devane was under orders to destroy. But hidden away within that now-world-famous figure, like a nesting doll inside its double, there was the enchanted child whom Deirdre had found in the dream trance. The story of that Constancia read like a chapter out of medieval folklore, an intoxicating mixture of superstition and sublime faith. This was nothing the woman herself would speak of; she had long since left that part of herself behind, an identity that clashed too discordantly with the world of revolutionary cadres that had become the principal audience for her political work.

Ripley was equally unwilling to talk about that distant stage of Constancia's life. There was no room in his loyalty for a peasant faith so remote from his own revolutionary Christianity that he visibly winced whenever it was mentioned. Where Constancia was concerned, he had had his fill of sensational and sentimental hagiography. His Constancia was the champion of the *campesinos*, just that and nothing more.

But Deirdre had found someone else to turn to. Sister Charlotte, who, as the days passed, began to spend a few idle hours of each evening with her and Ripley, away from Constancia's retreat. Sister Charlotte was more than willing to talk about Constancia the saint; she was eager.

She was a pleasant, chatty young woman, with wide owlish eyes that swam in and out of focus behind thick, blurry glasses. Her manner, like her dress, was studiously nonclerical. It was no easier for Deirdre to think of her as a nun than to think of Ripley as a priest and harder still to think of her as a militant revolutionary. But behind her smiling, pie-shaped face, Charlotte was an even queerer mix than Ripley. While her political passions were every bit as intense as his, she had found her way to Mother Constancia along a very different route. Ripley was the battle-tempered Jesuit theologian who had become a streetwise radical in the black slums of Newark before he had gone to Central America in search of revolutionary service. Sister Charlotte had begun as a scholar. She had moved directly from her seminary to the university, pursuing a degree in anthropology, then to Guatemala to study the native cultures. There, by way of a demure political conversion, she had left her fieldwork behind and joined Constancia's circle.

Her new career at Mother Constancia's side brought her trials of the flesh as well as the spirit. She was twice imprisoned for taking part in land reform demonstrations; once, when she refused to separate herself from her coworkers by identifying herself as an American and a nun, she was beaten and threatened with execution by government patrols. The experience left her with one visible reminder: a jagged white slash mark along her left cheek and jaw. But if there were any emotional scars, she did not let the bitterness darken her perpetually cheery disposition. Instead, her politics remained tinged with a quaintly academic flavor, almost as if her association with Constancia were a continuation of the research she had come to Central America to pursue. From the outset, assuming the role of Constancia's biographer-to-be, she had busied herself assembling notes on Mother's life and teachings. Similarly, she looked upon the peasants, whose cause had nearly cost her life, not simply as political victims, but as an absorbing cultural study. She accepted the fact, as Ripley could not, that Constancia's Catholicism, like that of the villages from which she came, was saturated through with the ancient religion of the rain forest, the myths that were older than the myths of Christ or the saints of the Church. She saw that heritage as an essential ingredient of Constancia's influence. "It's *all* Constancia," she insisted, though she saw Ripley cringe to hear her say it. "It's the way her people know her. Who are we to pretend we know better than the people who made her what she is?"

Ripley warned Deirdre with an only half-humorous laugh, "Be careful of Charlotte. She's gone native."

Charlotte, unabashed, retorted, "But we have to see the world the way her people do. That's the only way we can share her power."

As Sister Charlotte told the story one warm evening over coffee on the patio of Deirdre's bungalow, the life of Constancia the saint began with an incident in the jungle more than sixty years ago. A girl of eleven, not yet called Constancia—she still answered to the Indian nickname Ixta, still spoke the Kanjobal dialect—was sent to wash clothes at the riverbank outside her village. Hours later, she was found in the forest lying stunned and speechless, her brow and breast marked with wounds that streamed blood. She was carried home where, for weeks afterward, weakened and bewildered, she lay like an invalid in her parents' hut. It was only after many days that the frightened child managed to tell her mother what she remembered. Blinding light in the trees. A strange, brilliant bird. A voice. A crystal garden. It was a kaleidoscope of images. But the mother recognized the experience at once. A visitation, a sign of divine appointment.

Soon, as the word got around, the *campesinos* from the surrounding countryside came, bearing gifts, asking to see the child. They wanted marvels and, expecting them, received them. Crippled limbs straightened. Pains of the flesh soothed. A lost cow located. A disaster foreseen. Now, sixty years later, stories were still told in the villages of *la santa pequeña,* the little saint whose touch could cast out demons, whose wounds would bleed in the presence of evil.

"Something extremely important happened during that interval of her life," Sister Charlotte explained with scholarly relish. "At home, little Constancia fell under the care of her mother's aunt. Her mother insisted on that and she got her way. You have to understand about this aunt. This was a formidable lady. A *sabia*—that's how her family thought of her. A wise woman and a healer in her own right. Others, of course, regarded her as a *hechicera*—a witch and an idolator. Of which there are far more throughout the banana forests than the Church likes to admit. In any case, the aunt—her name was Doña Rosaura—was a woman of great reputation in her time. In the villages of northwest Quiché, she was treated with that mixture of reverence and dread that frequently surrounds sorcerers in peasant communities. The more educated natives—that included Constancia's father—apparently saw her as plain crazy . . . and not harmlessly so. Still, nobody cared to cross her. Cranky or not, she was understood to be a woman of power.

"From Doña Rosaura's point of view, Constancia's vision was an affirmation of the family calling. It was a visitation from Kulkulcan, the great Mayan deity who had bestowed her own vocation upon her. The child's wounds, she insisted, were divination spots. She had some of her own. They bled in the presence of hostile spirits or in anticipation of disaster. Earthquakes, droughts, and so on. Incidentally, that's probably the historical origin of Christian stigmata; it's a universal religious phenomenon. Well, Doña Rosaura was convinced that she had special rights with respect to her niece's vocation. The child was to become her *escogida,* her apprentice. She was to learn the knowledge of the craft and carry on the family tradition.

"But that was too much for Constancia's father. He was proud of his *Ladino* connections, especially in the Church. He was also a devout Catholic, fearful of seeing his daughter diverted from the true faith. Against his wife's wishes, he implored the Church authorities to take a hand in the matter. By this time, the child saint of Quiché had attracted quite a following in the region; the Church knew all about her and about the healing sessions. But then as now, the policy was to handle these things tactfully. Wait for the matter to subside naturally. Or, if it continued, spread some respectable Christian veneer over it. But there was a certain concern about Doña Rosaura's role in the situation. She was a notorious *piruja,* an unreconstructed pagan. The Church had to be worried about the use she was making of her niece to resurrect old rites and to inflate her own reputation.

"Well, the bishop came up with an idea. He proposed having Constancia taken into a convent to be taught by the sisters. That was considered quite an honor, a great chance in life for an ignorant little *india.* And after lots of family debate, the mother agreed.

"But not the aunt. On the night before Constancia was to be sent away, the aunt abducted her. And that was the beginning of a true ordeal. For six months, through an entire rainy season, Constancia and her aunt hid out in the Cuchumatán Mountains. That's the wild, volcanic range to the west. Very rugged country, some of the worst in Central America. They lived in caves and survived on whatever they could pick or trap. It was a real reversion to the primitive ways. When the father finally caught up with them the next spring, Constancia was in pretty bad shape. Half-starved, nearly catatonic, and almost feral after half a year in the wilderness. I'd give my right eye to find out what went on between Constancia and her aunt in the Cuchumatánes that long, rainy season. It could be a treasure trove of old religious lore."

Ripley shifted in his seat impatiently. "Really, Charlotte," he objected, "that's morbid. The whole episode must have been a nightmare for the child. Trapped in those caves with a mad old woman."

"Maybe so. But whatever happened, it helped make Constancia what she is today. It certainly has given her a special rapport with the Indian population."

Ripley dissented vigorously. "It isn't this sad old superstition that connects her with the *campesinos*. It's her politics." Deirdre could see that this was part of a long-standing argument between them. They seemed to have fought the issue to a draw countless times before. "Besides, these things took place sixty years ago. She was only a kid at the time. It has no relevance."

"Does Constancia remember any of it?" Deirdre asked.

"No," Ripley answered firmly.

"I'm not so sure," Sister Charlotte countered. "She *says* she's forgotten it all. Which is entirely possible. She might very well have spent most of the period in a semistupor, too sick to register anything clearly. And too strung out. You see, the aunt was cramming her full of everything she knew, including the knowledge of the Sainted Children."

"The Sainted Children?" Deirdre asked.

"The sacred mushroom. *Psilocybe mexicana.* It goes by many names in the various localities. *Teonanácatl* is the traditional Mayan term: 'the flesh of the gods.' All the *brujos* and *curanderos* of Central America are skilled in hallucinogenic rites. It's strong medicine and always hazardous under the best of circumstances. It takes years to learn the proper use of the drugs. But here was Doña Rosaura on the run, desperate and no doubt bordering on psychosis, dumping all she knew into her eleven-year-old niece in a matter of weeks. It's a wonder Constancia survived the experience. It would only have been natural for her to blank out the whole incident. But I suspect she remembers a lot more than she lets on."

"Why do you say that?" Deirdre asked.

"Well, for one thing—there are the beads."

"The beads?"

"Haven't you noticed them? She's always playing with them—especially when she's tense or troubled."

"The rosary, you mean?"

"It *isn't* a rosary. Not originally. Oh, she's pinned a crucifix on them, but Doña Rosaura gave her those beads, a not very Christian christening gift. She's never given them up, never takes them off. She won't let anybody see them."

Ripley protested, "Come on, Charlotte, it's an old family trinket, that's all."

"Have you seen how she clings to them when there's some crisis? If there's real aggravation in her life, that's what she grabs for. I'm sure there're memories in those beads. But that's not all. It goes a lot deeper." Here she dropped her voice into a hush. "Once, about five years ago, when we were traveling through the villages above Ixtahua-cán—a really remote region in the northwest—I sat in with Mother at a *velada*, a seance, held by the local *curanderos*. She didn't take any of the drugs, but I saw her help prepare them. She knew all the moves. Afterward, there was a lot of talk about the Sainted Children—most of it in dialect or pidgin Spanish—and there was Mother holding forth like a member of the guild. I tell you, the group was very impressed. Though, of course, she was trying to persuade them to see the eucha-ristic supper as the *true* 'flesh of the gods.' That was Constancia the nun talking. But it was really Constancia the *sabia* who commanded their respect. You see, that's what Mother is able to do. Speak the people's language. She's not just another university-trained cleric sent out from the city to catechize the peons. She belongs to the culture.

"I remember there was a phrase the *curanderos* used that night. *Un arco iris encendido*. 'Like the rainbow on fire.' That's how they described the experience of the mushrooms. Later on, I asked Mother if it was really like that. And she nodded: *Yes yes yes, the rainbow on fire. A rainbow vast as all the sky, setting the earth on fire with wild colors, and every color a living spirit.* She *knew!* She really knew. That was one of the few times she would ever talk about it to me. 'It sounds beautiful,' I said. I was that close to asking her to initiate me. 'Yes, beautiful,' she said, 'but a beauty that blinds the soul. The devil uses such beauty.' And she gave me this strict, scolding look. Well, that was Constancia the nun talking again. And that's as far as we got on that occasion."

All the while Sister Charlotte talked to her, Deirdre was aware of Ripley's restiveness and distraction. He listened, not wanting to hear, a veil of troubled thoughts across his eyes.

"What happened to the aunt?" Deirdre wanted to know.

"Came to a bad end. She was taken into custody after Constancia's father and the provincial police caught up with her. She died in prison that spring. Poor woman."

"And Constancia?"

"She went into the convent, as planned. A Dominican house in Guatemala City. Very rigid, very conservative. Which was perhaps what she needed at that point. Anyway, that's when she became 'Constancia.' A new name, a new life. And things settled down to dull normality. The sisters set about giving her a good Catholic education. In those days, that meant they ran her through the catechism like a parrot and made a proper little Hispanic lady out of her. Or so they thought."

"And when did she get involved in politics?" Deirdre asked.

"That came much later, a world of time later, when the period called the Repression started in the fifties. You see, there was what you might call a latency period in Constancia's life. Twenty-some years in Guatemala City, cut off from her roots. Isolated. Insulated. A very ordinary, very obedient nun. Nobody special. Just another self-effacing Bride of Christ doing the shitwork of the Church. But then she was sent back to her own district, the Quiché, to take charge of a small convent school. And that was the turning point. Or rather the *re*turning point. Because, remember, she was Ixta the child saint. Maybe she had forgotten all about that herself, forced it out of her mind. But not so her family. Not her village. Especially not her mother, who never stopped speaking of her child as a *sabia*, the pupil of the renowned Doña Rosaura. She had kept the legend alive throughout the district and of course had freely embroidered it. You see, that's what I think built the bridge for Constancia back to her people, just as the Repression was beginning.

"When she returned to Quiché, she was received as someone special, with a special authority. She had an aura. Whether she liked it or not, her people empowered her. In their eyes, she was a native *sabia*, *and* a Catholic saint, *and* a miracle worker who connected up with traditions older than the Conquistadors. I don't think Mother has ever been able to sort it out herself and tell what source she really draws her authority from. I think she's given up trying.

"Her childhood vision, for example. People speak of it in very different ways. Among Catholics, it's referred to as a visitation from the Holy Spirit—in the classic form of the white dove. But the *campesinos* understand it to have been a vision of the quetzal bird, which is the symbol of the old sun god. Mother blithely accepts either description, depending on the company she's keeping at the time. Maybe at this point she can't remember what kind of bird it was."

"But it wasn't a bird. It was a snake." The words leaped from Deirdre's lips before she thought. Her own remembered impression from Constancia's trance. She had seen the image several times now, never without cringing. It was always the same, a fierce emblem cruelly fanged, with unpitying eyes.

Both Charlotte and Ripley fixed their gaze upon her. "Oh?" Charlotte said, wanting more.

Flustered, Deirdre tried to explain herself. She turned to Ripley. "I mean . . . didn't she describe it that way?"

"Not any time I was around. I've never heard from Mother about this."

"Oh. Well, it must have come up this past week, after you . . ."

"She said her vision was a *serpent?*" Sister Charlotte pressed hard for more. "You're sure?"

"Well, yes. I think so. A snake with wings. Brightly colored wings."

"You mean she actually described the visitation? That would be the first time in living memory." Sister Charlotte was aggressively interested. "What did she say—exactly?"

Deirdre retreated awkwardly. "That was all, really. I don't remember anything else. I shouldn't have mentioned it, I suppose. Please don't tell her I did."

"The plumed serpent," Charlotte mused. "Kulkulcan himself. That would be the first time she's admitted to pagan inspiration. Wow! Doña Rosaura must be cheering."

"You won't mention it to her," Deirdre pleaded.

Ripley was becoming uneasy with Charlotte's enthusiasm. "Look, before we get carried away, I really think we should regard this as confidential. Mother's here under extraordinary circumstances. She's been severely stressed, she's hardly sleeping, she's undergoing a form of treatment that's new and wholly alien to her. We can't be certain about anything Devane draws out of her."

Charlotte explained Ripley's concern to Deirdre. "This could be used to discredit her. Devout Catholics could set it down as idolatry—if they wished to. Mother does have enemies, in the Church as well as the government."

Deirdre labored to undo the remark. "Really, I might have heard her wrong."

"There's quite a difference between saying you've seen a bird and saying you've seen a snake," Ripley observed.

After a moment of pondering, Sister Charlotte said, "But that really makes such perfect sense, John—that it should be a vision out of the native tradition. Because, you see, once she was back among her own people—and once the Repression began—that's when Mother found the courage to reclaim her own heritage. The vision she had been granted as a child—it came to her as a vocation to serve her people. It was the wounds that did it, after all. And the wounds were from Kulkulcan. It fits perfectly."

"The wounds?" Deirdre asked.

"Yes. Whatever Constancia's visitation was—dove or serpent or what have you—the sisters at the convent did their best to erase it from her memory. After all, what use would the Church have in those days for a peasant saint? A barefoot child, no less, who couldn't even speak Spanish. No doubt they thought they were doing the ignorant, little *campesina* a great benefit to help her forget all about it. But the wounds were still there. On the brow and the breast. The sisters couldn't do anything about those. They never healed. They never went away." Sister Charlotte's eyes widened behind her fishbowl lenses and her voice dropped to a whisper. "They're *still* there. They *still* bleed."

That was too much for Ripley. His impatience crested. Throwing up his hands, he wandered off abruptly with a groan of exasperation.

"John won't believe it," Charlotte continued, her tone both hurt and annoyed. "He won't hear anything about it. But Sister Veronica has seen it. And Sister Concepcion. And others. Beginning in 1962, when the violence came to Quiché, the night the village of Santo Tomás was massacred by government security forces, *Mother's wounds bled.* She was at her school in Nebaj—sixty miles away. But she had a premonition. The wounds opened and bled. And they have many times since. When the earthquake struck in 1976. Whenever an atrocity takes place. When these bad dreams started at the beginning of the year, the first night, she bled. She senses the evil."

"Have you seen it?" Deirdre asked.

"No," Charlotte replied stiffly, as if she were being challenged. "But there's no doubt it's true. The sisters around Mother aren't gullible *peons.* They don't make things up."

"I'm sure they don't."

"Anyway, that's when Mother made the transition—after the atrocity at Santo Tomás. That's when she became *our* Constancia. The premonition showed her. She had no choice but to take the side of the *campesinos.*"

Deirdre was puzzled. "The winged serpent—it's one of the ancient gods?"

"Yes. Kulkulcan. The Aztecs called him Quetzalcoatl."

"Doesn't it bother you that it might have been a pagan god Constancia saw?"

Charlotte's face lit up in a wide, generous smile, as if she was delighted to have the question asked. "God wears many masks," she said, an answer that sounded almost rehearsed. "Who are we to say what face or what name He might choose to assume in another culture?"

"So it would be all right, then—if Constancia's vision was of a winged serpent? Even it if looked . . . fierce, cruel?"

"The religious sensibilities of the Meso-American cultures were very different from our own. Much more ferocious. These were a jungle people. They experienced another aspect of the divine, one that perhaps we've been too squeamish to accept." Sister Charlotte's tone had become crisply professional, a specialist talking to a freshman student. "But, you see, it's still possible for someone like Constancia to emerge from that background and to use it to bring an authentically Christian witness to her people. It's important not to let symbols stand in the way."

Deirdre was watching Ripley. He was far across the lawn, pacing slowly at the crest of the hill, his eyes scanning the sea. Even at this distance she could see the shadow that lay across his features.

"Does John believe that?" she asked.

Sister Charlotte's reply came slowly, a note of more than annoyance in her voice. "Frankly, I don't think we're at all sure what John believes anymore."

13

Devane was frankly amazed with himself. He would never have predicted it. He was falling under Mother Constancia's spell. It was neither her politics nor her moral conviction that fascinated him, but her dreams. *Were* they dreams? He was not even sure how to classify the trance state into which she passed at night. Perhaps it was an entirely new psychological domain. In the speculative literature of his profession, he sometimes came across references to a "superconsciousness" that supposedly lifted the mind above the neurotic fears and passions of ordinary life. He was familiar too with the concept of "high dreaming," which was said to verge upon religious experience. But he had never had the occasion to study these matters; he was generally skeptical about their very existence.

Now, in Mother Constancia, he began to feel that he had found such a rare new level of the psyche. He was more authentically excited than he had been at any time since he had discovered his first watcher. Working from what Deirdre reported to him, he was now prepared to believe that there was a dimension of "height" as well as "depth" to dreams. Deirdre always experienced Constancia's trance as an elevated condition of the mind that resolved all tensions and brought an unshakable tranquillity. He was feverishly eager to know more about this exotic state of consciousness. How was it induced? How might it be reproduced and manipulated for therapeutic purposes? As a scientist, he could not accept the notion that Constancia enjoyed some privileged form of inspiration. Instead, he envisioned himself claiming her trance state as a major contribution to his extensive writing on the psychology of dreams. Aaron Devane, the man who had first explored what Deirdre called "black dreams,"—dreams that arose from the deepest, most repressed foundations of the psyche—had now discovered their opposite extreme. Dreams of light- and life-giving power.

Dreams that gave wings to the mind and raised it above the shadowed vale of disease.

He realized he might only have a few more weeks to work with Constancia before she became Costello's property. That made him all the more greedy to learn what he could about her in the brief time remaining. He became steadily more demanding with Deirdre. She had never known him to be so insistent. She was to monitor Mother Constancia every minute of the night, for as long as she could fend off sleep. If Constancia dreamed, she was to report the dream in precise detail. If there was only the trance, she was to watch for the slightest variations. Stay with her. Make the most of every opportunity. Don't miss a thing.

Obedient to his instructions, Deirdre's night mind once again homed in upon Constancia's peculiar trance signal and hovered at the edge of the now-familiar scene. Still there, the glowing garden. Still there, the child Ixta transfixed beneath the radiant cloud. Still there, the bird that was not only bird but serpent and savage god. It never altered. It had nowhere to go, nothing to become. It was whole. An image outside of time, shaped from changeless crystal.

On other nights, Constancia's epiphany had never failed to hold Deirdre with hypnotic force. It was a rare, sweet experience. It left the mind calmly intoxicated. She valued imprinting it upon her deep memory, a resource of the spirit. But this night, she would not stay with it, despite her promise to Devane. Something else plucked at her attention. Another, more urgent concern. A need of her own, pressing to be satisfied.

She sank back and down into the shadowed pool of sleep, searching for another signal, sweeping the night. Then found a shaft of light—like a tunnel opening in a wall of smoke. She stepped through into:

Tumult. A dream of terrific activity. Men racing back and forth. A surge of bodies, oppressive heat, maximum exertion.

Thunk. Thunk. Thunk.

A thudding rhythm.

Thunk. Thunk.

It was a bouncing ball. Rubber against cement. The men were playing a game. Basketball. Passing, dribbling the ball at great speed. Bodies colliding. The slap of flesh. Uplifted voices. Shouts. Groans. The shuddering wheeze of hard breathing.

Then she saw him. At the center, catching the ball, holding it away from a defender, curling around, throwing, dancing to the action.

Ripley.

For the first time, she had dared to enter his dreams.

The game was being played in a concrete yard, rimmed by a chain-metal fence. Beyond it, high buildings, the grim streets of a crowded city. Traffic.

Most of the players were black and young. They moved nimbly, played with ferocious intensity. She saw Ripley ram into another player, go down hard. "Shit!" he hissed, but shot back to his feet, smiling. Resumed play. Shouting to him, the players called him "Father" . . . "Fadder" . . . Rough voices, hard city accents. "Pass it here, Fadder." "Put it up, Fadder." "Dat's de way, Fadder." Ripley, grinning, sweating. Leaped. Swatted at the ball. A score. Cheers. He clapped his arms around a large black boy, congratulating him. They slapped hands, palm upon palm. The boy laughed back, a great savage grin, flashing teeth.

Suddenly, the boy's face twisted with pain. He crumpled and slid to the ground. Others dropped with him. Ripley wheeled about, staring, frightened. Beyond the fence, movement. A line of uniformed men. Blue shirts. Leather boots. Police? Hard faces. Helmets. Dark goggles. A voice, flattened mechanically by a bullhorn, barked an announcement: "All games of freedom are prohibited." The police were armed. Guns raised. The dry cough of rifle fire. More players fell. The others, trying to escape, charged the fence on all sides like maddened animals. Struggled to climb. Ripley too. He leaped, clawed into the chain-link barrier, hauled himself upward, away from the bullets.

His hands reached for the top of the fence, but the fence was extending. It grew higher, higher than he could climb. From below, the firing continued. Black bodies fell from the fence like swatted flies. Others stuck spread-eagled where they were shot. Ripley's eyes, sweeping the scene, saw them on all sides, crucified on the cruel metal.

He climbed to a dizzy height. His muscles ached with the labor, but the fence was always higher. It stretched to the sky. Trapped. He shouted to warn the others, but there were none to hear. *"It's a cage, all the way up to heaven."*

Then, high above him, there were planes. Helicopters circling, swooping like roaring birds of prey. More police. No. Men in green fatigues and crushed-down caps. Soldiers. They were firing at him. The buildings beyond the fence were gone now, replaced by trees. A surrounding wall of jungle. Ripley, high up on the endless fence, grew weak. Surrendering, he released his grip. Waited to fall. Didn't. Instead, he was gently, gently floating, sailing out across the matted forests below, the cool air streaming past him.

Free. Safe. His body was naked now in the caressing wind. Exhilarated, he laughed, shouted. He was shouting in Spanish. A long, glad oration to the sky and the jungle. He spread his arms. His shadow was a drifting cross on the emerald treetops.

Below, in a clearing, there were people, a small huddled group of men and women. Dark-skinned. Ragged. Carrying weapons. They were shouting up to him in Spanish, *"Padre! Padre!"* They waved at him to come faster, come faster. Instead, gleefully, he spun and somersaulted in the bracing air. Free. Safe. He laughed. Why did the people below seem so frightened? He gestured to them, called out, *"Wait, compañeros!"* But they were gone, scattered. There was another shadow across the trees, darting this way and that. The helicopter, still pursuing, firing at him. He struggled to fall faster, but couldn't. He had no weight. The air buoyed him up like a bit of milkweed. A thought crossed his mind: *The fall of man must have been faster than this.*

The helicopter was catching up. Bullets bit into his hovering body, cruel bites. A great hook swished by, once, twice, then caught him in the air, just below the jaw. He could see the faces of the hostile soldiers as they reeled him in across the sky. A final hard tug.

"I will make you fishers of men . . ."

He screamed. His scream scorched the air about him. The scene blurred, was gone. The darkness of sleep closed upon him. Then brightened.

Again, the jungle was there, the tropic sweet-sour air. The wind flowing past his falling body had become water. He was floating in a broad river. On the bank, a figure in khaki appeared and began to undress. He called out in Spanish. A name . . . Cristina? The figure shed its clothes, became a young woman, dark-skinned, with full breasts, well-rounded flanks. She smiled at him, shook her long hair free, waded out toward him, her shining body taking the bright sun. The scene blurred.

He was scrambling upward, hands clawing at rough stone and dirt. Breathless. Driven. Was it the fence again? No. Stairs, ascending steeply skyward. Ancient stone, crumbling away under his desperate grip. The staircase was almost perpendicular. It led endlessly nowhere into the air. So steep he could almost fall backward. Emptiness gaped to either side, sucked at him from behind. Below, there were pursuing cries. Gunfire. His body was like lead, refusing motion, weighing against his aching muscles. He was slowing, moving as if underwater. Hopeless.

And then hands were on him. He was on his back. Bound down on cold stone. A great square temple loomed against the bright sky, richly carved with Aztec emblems. Helmeted soldiers hovered over him, berating him in Spanish, cursing him. Black goggles stared down pitilessly. A figure—fabulously dressed, crowned with bright feathers—leaned above. His face was masked. A snake face, like Constancia's bird serpent. In English, the figure said, "It's all right. We are priests together, Father. We kill for God."

Powerful hands reached down, surgically parted the flesh of his breast. There was no pain. The movement was quick and expert. The snake-faced priest gave a quick twist and brought forth Ripley's quivering heart, a child-shaped red lump fighting to live. It gasped and cried.

His heart, an aborted birth.

The serpent priest held it out to Ripley's lips to kiss. Deirdre caught something in Latin that she recognized. *"Hoc est meum corpus."* Ripley, watching his heart lifted, cried out, "It can't live without me! Put it back! Don't let it die!" The scene melted and went dim.

Other hands were on him, calming him, moving soothingly across his bare chest, knitting the raw wound. The heart had been returned. He grew calm. The young woman from the river knelt beside him, her body gleaming moist in the dull light. He reached for her eagerly. "Taking the heart is the worst abortion," he said. "It wasn't ready to be born. Not yet." She did not understand. He repeated in Spanish, his hand covering her breast at the heart, then cupping it, bringing it to his lips, sucking at the soft tip. She bent, kissed him heatedly. Their bodies stretched along one another, clinging. He rolled atop her, stroked the length of her torso, reaching for her sex, knotting his grip in her coiled hair. His fingers moved in her secret flesh, exploring. He spoke her name. "Cristina, Cristina."

Covering her, he worked his thigh between her legs, muscling hard against the rough thatch that covered her cleft. Deirdre watched the woman opening to his desire. They moved, not hurriedly. Stretching time, holding it back. Their lovemaking grew languid, prolonged in dream time. Unreal. Ecstatic.

Deirdre, watching, became aware of her heart racing. Her throat worked. An appetite had taken hold, swiftly and despotically. Not to be resisted. A sudden wave of desire. She wanted to be this woman. Needed to be this woman. It had been years since she had stolen another's dream. She was uncertain the skill was still there. Eagerly but with caution, she let herself merge with Ripley's lover. She eased into the garment of the woman's image until she could feel his sexual rhythm within her, insistent but gentle. She had become moist fire where he moved inside, the first time a man had been there since Peter, years away now. Her body, tight with disuse, gripped roughly at his organ. Even so, she squeezed more firmly, trying to slow him, to still and preserve the moment.

She reached to touch his face beside her own, feeling the sweat on her fingertips. Under her, there was warm earth that smelled of harsh fertility. Above, a ragged roof of dried grass. Trees, stars showed through. At her ear, he was whispering urgently in Spanish. Several times, the name "Cristina." But she had displaced Cristina, intercepting his love, stealing it to meet her own need. The act brought no guilt. Instead, she felt strong, decisive. For the first time since Peter's death, she had acted in her own behalf, asking nobody's permission. The pleasure Ripley brought her mingled richly with pride.

She kept his face against her cheek, not letting him see her until his love had crested. His body pumped, then buckled in fatigue. Inside, she felt the spread of his juices mixing with her own. Then, sweetly tired, they lay beside one another, their breathing filling the small hut. She did not withdraw from the dream but waited for him to turn to her, to recognize her. She saw the bewilderment that briefly filled his eyes. At once, she moved to kiss him, now in her own right. There was no protest. He took her into his arms, accepting her love, offering his.

14

It was the end of her second month at the Clinic and Mother Constancia was growing restless. She was spending less time at her self-imposed retreat—and more with Ripley and Sister Charlotte, reviewing the reports that were phoned to her daily from *Casa Libertad*. Her attention was slipping away from her afternoon sessions with Devane, though he did his best to keep that fact from Costello. Constancia looked as worn and frail as the day she arrived; she was as much in need of rest. Yet she was already scheduling events for the month ahead. As far as Deirdre could tell, besides her trance visions, Constancia had dreamed not more than three or four times since she had come to the Clinic. They were ordinary, fleeting dreams that revealed nothing of value for Costello's purposes. But "the devil"—meaning Moray—had not been in those dreams. To Constancia's way of thinking, that meant the temptations were passing. She needed no further care and could make ready to leave. Devane began to fear he was close to failing in his assignment. His concern was for Constancia, whose earthiness and rough candor had won his respect, quite as much as the strangeness of her psychic life had drawn his curiosity. Devane had hoped to find some promising psychological strategy that would satisfy Costello, but do her minimum damage. If nothing of that sort turned up as an option before she insisted on leaving, Costello and Shawsing were likely to resort to less subtle methods. He did not want that to happen.

Working from what Deirdre had learned about Constancia's childhood, Devane was now focusing intently on her experiences with her aunt. The grueling months spent hiding out in the Cuchumatán Mountains, the pagan lore that had been forced upon her, the hallucinogenic adventures of that distant time—surely, remnants of that ordeal survived in Constancia's deep memory, little buried childish anxieties that could be used to unsettle her just enough. Urgently, Devane searched for soft spots in her psyche that would yield quickly to a sharp, well-placed thrust. He had carefully scrutinized Moray's file on Constancia. There his expert eye could pick out dream fragments which he was certain reflected those memories. A stern old woman who threatened and punished: that was Doña Rosaura. Associated with her: experiences of smoke, fire, dizzy disorientation, flight, and falling. There were dim recollections of shadowed caves and tunnels, always wrapped in a sense of the ominous. A remembered need to hide. A thwarted desire to escape.

Moray, hastily looking for more conventional anxieties that were no part of Constancia's character, had missed this elusive material. He had not known how to read the scattered images he came upon in the few dreams he had managed to infiltrate. He did not have the key Devane now held. Here—somewhere—was the button Costello wanted. But Devane had told Costello nothing of all this. He was giving nothing away cheaply. When the time came, he wanted to be in the position to manipulate Constancia with surgical precision and the least psychic harm. "Watch carefully," Devane instructed Deirdre. "Watch for anything you can use to draw her back to the caves. Try to use the aunt—if she appears."

"But we don't want to make her afraid," Deirdre protested, already suspecting the unsettling powers these memories held for Constancia.

"Of course not," Devane hastened to assure her. "It's simply a matter of analyzing her phobias so that we can reconcile her to them and put an end to these disturbing dreams. That's what we're here to do." He reminded her that they had undertaken similar treatment with other patients, efforts at a form of psychological inoculation. He tried to make his deception seem like clinical routine.

Deirdre listened and agreed. He was pleased, convinced that she would soon find the secret dread at the bottom of Constancia's mind. He did not know how unreliable an instrument she had become. Deirdre lied when she assured him that she was spending all her time with Constancia. She lied without guilt, taking a strangely gratifying strength from her ability to deceive Devane. Day by day, she could feel his authority over her weakening as she grew away from her need to please him and obey. She was sharing Ripley's dreams each night now, willfully embarked upon an assignment of her own. She would become his lover, if only while he slept, when her image and that of the woman named Cristina mixed and blended in his thoughts. It was a stolen love, but already, after only a few nights, her intervention in his dreams was having its effect. When they were together, Ripley looked at her

with different eyes; she could detect in them a hesitant affection, puzzled but marked. How vividly was he remembering his dreams with
her? Enough to draw them closer. She could tell he wanted that.

It was the fifth and hottest day of a late-summer heat wave. The hills
above Santa Barbara had become scorched bronze; the sun raised a
glare from the sea that stunned the eye. In the garden of the Clinic,
Deirdre sat with Constancia and her entourage beneath the dense
wisteria arbor. A courier had come from *Casa Libertad* with a bulging
parcel of mail. He waited while Ripley and Sister Charlotte sorted
through, skimming the more important items. Constancia listened,
asked for advice, made rapid choices of dates and events. Vaguely, at
the edge of her mind, Deirdre registered plans that were being laid for
a major activity: a series of demonstrations in support of human rights
in Central America, culminating in a Christmas vigil at the White
House to be led by Constancia and attended by clergy of many denom-
inations.

Deirdre was distinctly an outsider in these discussions; at times, she
felt almost like an intruder. She had nothing to offer, no clear understanding of the importance of what was being planned. Her attention
wandered. Smitty, as mute and wooden as ever, had brought out a
pitcher of iced tea. He shuffled from person to person, waiting patiently while each poured and spooned out sugar. Deirdre, filling her
glass, smiled up at him. As usual, there was no response. Smitty's eyes
rarely made contact; when they did, they were eyes of stone, dead and
unreflecting. He might have been a life-sized mechanical doll moving
among them.

Her gaze drifted toward Constancia, idly observing her while the
others busied themselves sifting through the correspondence. She was
the only one to see Constancia's face going slack with surprise, then
drawing back tightly into a mask of panic, the eyes widening painfully.
Deirdre followed her fixed gaze, down across her lap toward the
ground. She saw nothing. A sheaf of letters slipped from Constancia's
grip; her hand went to the wooden beads under her habit; her body
cringed back, angled and stiff in her chair. There was a hideous sound,
a blade-sharp hiss: Constancia's breath flying from her like an arrow
sent to kill. What was it? Deirdre searched, but saw nothing.

The others turned at the sound of Constancia's gasp. Ripley, moving
swiftly, came around behind her chair. He took hold of her shoulders
to steady her. "What is it?" he asked. But Constancia's voice had

turned to dust in her throat; she choked on her words. Only her eyes
could tell what she saw.

And then Deirdre noticed. Darting from a fold in the old woman's
robe just below the knee, scarcely visible against the dark cloth—a tiny
black shape. It was visible for a split second, racing jerkily out of sight
into another crease of the garment. A spider. Constancia hissed again
like a terrified cat, her jaw shuddering violently. The spider reap-
peared, scrambling higher. Deirdre, puzzled, started to rise from her
chair, but it was Smitty who acted. He stepped forward quickly, balancing the pitcher of tea in one hand, bent, and swatted the tiny pest away.
Deirdre had never seen him move so decisively. For one flash of a
moment, his eyes seemed to come alive with comprehension. But just
as rapidly, his features dimmed again to their cadaverous stolidity.
Then he stood by, sullen and stupid as ever.

Constancia, recovering her voice, rasped, "¿Dónde es?" As soon as
the spasm of fear unlocked, she began to cross herself over and over.
She stared this way and that, trying to see where the spider had fallen,
struggling to hold her feet and robe away from the ground. The tiny
intruder was lost in the grass. It had been a harmless garden spider;
one saw them all the time. But Constancia had flinched from it as if it
were a rattlesnake. Shaken with fright, she excused herself and the
morning session ended abruptly. Two of the sisters led her away to her
room, consoling her at every step. Constancia followed beside them,
walking gingerly over the lawn, as if the spider might spring from
ambush. Her hand never left the beads under her robe. She took the
shortest route toward the cinder path, looking for safe ground. Smitty
shambled after her, trying to keep up as best he could. Pathetically, he
held out an unsteady hand as if to offer protection to Constancia along
the way. At the path, she paused to give him a grateful smile and to
squeeze his arm. He watched after her, falling into his sad slouch. After
a long moment of indecision, he turned and shuffled off toward the
Clinic, his face knotted with its usual bewilderment.

"Faustino," Sister Charlotte said when Constancia was out of hearing.

Deirdre looked to her for an explanation.

"You remember Doña Rosaura. Like many sabias, she had a rival. A
diablero, as she called him. The devil's man. Between the two of them
there was a family vendetta that went back generations. That's the dark
side of the native tradition. Hexes, curses, bad medicine. That's how
the indios usually interpret misfortune or disease. Black magic. They

live in a condition of cosmic paranoia. Doña Rosaura's rival was named Faustino Mendez. He lived in a village several miles away, but they had been hexing one another's families all their lives. That was why Doña Rosaura was so maniacal about making Constancia her apprentice. She wanted young blood to defend her.

"Faustino claimed that he could transform himself into a spider—or at least that's what Doña Rosaura came to believe of him. All these sorcerers are supposedly shape-shifters. Doña Rosaura, for example, claimed she could change herself into a quetzal bird. She was convinced that Faustino came to spy on her in the form of a spider. That's how he stole her secrets and did his mischief. That rainy season in the Cuchumatánes, she did a damned effective job of passing her fear of Faustino along to little Constancia. God knows how she made the lesson so real, but no doubt the caves were full of spiders. In any event, it stuck. Sixty years later, whenever Mother travels, the rooms have to be swept clean and paper has to be wedged in the cracks under the doors to keep the spiders out. She can't bear the thought of one touching her. She's quite embarrassed about it. At one level of her mind, she knows she's being superstitious. But you see how real the fear is. Somewhere in her subconscious, Faustino the old spider-wizard seems to have become Constancia's vision of all Satanic evil. That's why our center in L.A. is so immaculate. Not a cobweb to be found. Swept morning and night."

Later Sister Charlotte recalled one thing more. "There was a rumor —I can't recall who passed it on to me—that Faustino was responsible for Doña Rosaura's death. Of course, that's the way all sorcerers supposedly die. Never of natural causes. Doña Rosaura died in prison that spring, after Constancia's father and the police brought her out of the mountains. A stroke. A seizure. Something like that. But the place must have had plenty of spiders around to take the blame."

*   *   *

That afternoon Constancia canceled her session with Devane. But Deirdre had something to tell him that more than made up for the loss. She told him about the incident in the garden. "Laney used to be scared of rats and mice," she recalled. "I mean screaming scared. But this was worse than that by far. Constancia was paralyzed. Couldn't speak or move. I was certain she was having a heart attack."

Devane brightened with interest. "Spiders. It's not an uncommon phobia. Of course, we'll have to find out what it means to Constancia."

But Deirdre already knew. She told him about Faustino. "Doña Rosaura was convinced the old man was the devil himself. Do you think this is important?"

The aunt. The caves. The rival sorcerer. It all clicked into place for Devane. Restraining his eagerness, he said, "Possibly. Yes, it might be of use."

15

"Who is Cristina?" Deirdre asked. She let the question drop casually, as if she might be asking about the weather.

It was just after dinner, the early hours of an unusually humid evening. She had driven into town with Ripley to run some errands before the stores closed. She intended the question to sound casual, but it stopped him in his tracks as they crossed the parking lot. He studied her closely, as if he were trying to piece what she had asked him into a private jigsaw puzzle of recollections that were part dream, part real.

"How do you know about Cristina?" he asked.

"Oh . . . Mother mentioned her. The other day." Not a smart lie, she realized. How could she be certain Constancia knew anything about Cristina?

Still lost in thought, he resumed walking. "She's a woman who worked with us in Guatemala. Why should Mother . . . ?" He shrugged, bewildered.

"One of the sisters?"

"No." He did not say more until they were back in the car. "Cristina was a member of the CUC. Committee for Peasant Unity. Guerrillas. One of the more militant organizations. She was Nicaraguan. She fought with the Sandinistas. That's where I met her."

Is she your lover? Deirdre wanted to ask. *Is there anything more than dreams between the two of you?* After a silence, she asked, "Did you know her well?"

"Yes. We did a lot of organizing together in the Quiché. Land reform." They had driven out of town and were climbing steeply toward the Clinic before he added, "She was taken by government troops. Killed. Tortured. Killed." His jaw tightened on the words. His hands, clamped to the steering wheel, went dead white at the knuckles.

"I'm so sorry," she said.

Then a long pause until they had pulled into the Clinic grounds and parked.

"She was twenty-two years old," he noted as they left the car. His eyes held her fast. He might have been trying to map Cristina's face upon hers, looking for a fit, a match—all the while pondering why he should be trying to do that.

*   *   *

More than ever she wanted to be with him that night. She might never know if Cristina, when she was alive, had been anything more to him than a longing he experienced in dreams. But Cristina was dead, forever part of his real or imagined past. And now Deirdre wanted Ripley to bring her own image back from sleep, vivid and strong. When the dream had passed with the night, she wanted to be remembered in Cristina's place. His lover.

She reflected on how she had lied to Devane, how she had infiltrated Ripley's dreams to steal another woman's love. She was surprised to find that she was not more troubled by these acts of deception and willfulness. Instinctively, she knew that the selfishness of what she did was a sign of assertion, of health returning. She was regaining something Devane had never planned to offer. Independence.

But that afternoon, Devane had made her promise with unusual urgency that she would monitor Constancia more closely than ever. If Constancia dreamed, some trace of the incident in the garden might surface. If it did, they must not miss it.

Reluctantly, that night she sacrificed Ripley's dreams and searched the darkness for Constancia. Once again, she found herself in the midst of the trance scene. But this time there was something different. The vision seemed shadowed. Again and again, holes opened in the image, darkness showed through. Constancia's concentration was weak. Then, for one split second, Deirdre caught sight of an intruding form. The blurred, remembered figure of Smitty, stepping forward, flailing with one arm. A few moments later, the same image, the identical movement. It was the gesture he had made in the garden that afternoon, swiping at the spider on Constancia's robe. The shock of that experience still reverberated in her mind, distracting her attention. Deirdre could feel the strain of great fatigue heavy upon her.

And then, like a picture drawn on air, the crystal garden disintegrated. A wave of darkness scattered it. Constancia lost her little girl's identity, became herself, whirlpooling down and down into troubled sleep. Deirdre followed the descent of her mind, catching streams and eddies of watery consciousness as they came and went in the surrounding emptiness. Dreams. Fragments of dreams cascading past. Then nothing. A long descent through vacuous gray space, until . . .

. . . Constancia, dreaming, stood in a cavernous space. She turned, bewildered, taking her bearings. Deirdre shrank back into the shadows. Her hands behind her encountered a wall. Rough natural stone, damp and chilly. She fingered cool moss. A cave? *The* cave? No. Slender oblongs of colored light appeared. A row of pointed windows high up. The space was reshaping into a church. Or rather, the ruin of a church. On all sides there were marks of damage. The windows broken out. Statues smashed. Dust and debris everywhere. The sickening odor of decay.

Something, Deirdre realized, was odd. Odd because familiar. What could she be recognizing in Constancia's dream? Not the scene; this was new. Then *what?*

Constancia was no longer alone. Three robed figures were leading her forward, one at each side, one crowding her from behind. Toward . . . ? An altar that was as much a moldering wreck as the rest of the cathedral. From somewhere impossibly high above, thin voices sounded like a choir of bats, squealing more than singing. Long, raw, discordant strains braiding through one another.

There were people, more and more of them, condensing out of the shadows. A restive, thickly packed crowd, kneeling, standing in lines at the side. Deirdre, merging with the dream congregation, edged forward to observe. She saw Constancia, bowed with effort, struggling forward. Her robe stretched out far behind her and on it, weighing her down, there were . . . what were they? Children? Deirdre looked more closely, then winced. They were tiny men with old, mushy faces. Dwarves. Weasely-looking, snouted, with hot eager eyes. Constancia, creeping forward up the center aisle, had to drag them after her, an unwelcome cargo.

It was an ugly dream, the menace of nightmare bleeding into its texture. And then Deirdre grasped it. The sense of familiarity that had been teasing her mind . . . *it was the light,* something about the feel of the light that leaked in from the high windows. Dense and fetid like stagnant water, staining what it touched. She could feel it on her skin, a sticky, oily film. She knew this vile light. She remembered it. It was the sign of a black dream, the dreams she had found in Peter's sleep. There was the same sense of immense desolation on all sides, not yet as far advanced, but unmistakably the nothingness of a black dream, pressing in, trying to close upon the scene, to consume.

At the altar, Constancia knelt, leaning heavily on the rail, laboring to regain her breath. Two of the robed figures who had led her forward were kneeling beside her, crowding close. The third was at the altar offering up a chalice, raising it high, lowering it. Then, bending, he spit into the cup, poked his finger in and stirred. Deirdre felt, then heard Constancia's shocked response. Two or three of the little men rushed forward, jostling each other, to do the same, each spitting, then dancing away. Misshapen, toothless mouths, gaping, cackling. Evil clowns. One, mounting the altar rail, balancing precariously, tugged a lumpy, oversized penis from his trousers and proceeded to masturbate into the chalice. Constancia, horrified, struggled to turn away. Deirdre could see the heat in her face, a pained mixture of fury and chagrin. But also great weariness. Though she exerted herself, she did not have the strength to control the dream. The hooded priest thrust a hand under her chin and turned her face back toward him. Then, fishing into the cup, he brought out not a communion wafer, but something gleaming wet and furred. He pressed it upon her lips, into her mouth. She jerked away and spat it out, then bent in a hard cough. With wicked glee, the dwarves scrambled to retrieve the morsel where it lay, squirming on the altar steps, alive. The priest had thrown them the gold-threaded altar cloth from the tabernacle. The little men used it to mop at the object, leaving a muddy red smear. There was a whining sound, like a baby crying.

Wake up! Deirdre wanted to shout. But her voice would not carry. The dirty light sponged away the sound and it died. She could feel Constancia fighting to thrust the scene away, but she seemed feeble, overtaxed. About her, the dream was thickening, holding her trapped.

Deirdre scanned the church in all directions. Her eyes moved along a row of worshipers at the far side. Again, the sense of familiarity. She saw the same imbecilic faces she had so often seen in Peter's sleep, faces whose blankness mocked the suffering before them, making it meaningless. Her gaze tracked back to the altar where the priest stood, looming above the wilted Constancia. There was something very wrong. What? It took a moment for her to fix on the fact. She looked twice. Yes, it was so. The priest's eyes. They were not directed at Constancia. They were looking at Deirdre. *Someone in Constancia's dream was watching her.* Deirdre stared back, as if a hard look might deflect the man's gaze and adjust the dream. It didn't. His eyes held steady.

Some mistake, Deirdre thought. But no. The priest had left the altar rail. He was moving forward, toward her. Toward *her.* Instinctively, Deirdre tried to shrink back, to hide in the crowd. But the man moved more quickly in her direction. And then he was directly in front of her. She could see his mouth curved in a smug smile.

"Hello, Mrs. Vale," the priest said. He reached up to drop the hood that surrounded his face. Deirdre stared at him, fixed in her place, until his hand reached out, touched her cheek—a soft, tickling caress that moved down her neck, between her breasts. His lips were moving, saying something more. She could not hear. The whining voices high above had grown too loud, were growing louder, a shrill, insect chorus that made the air throb.

Deirdre, a wave of frenzy building within her, wanted to close the scene out and fight free of the dream. But Constancia still held one crumbling edge of her attention. She must not abandon Constancia. Her eyes still fixed on the priest's face, on his tight, nasty smile, Deirdre backed off, then turned, ran. The little men were gleefully dismantling the altar before Constancia's helpless gaze, manhandling and mangling each part. Deirdre, seizing the old woman's shoulders, spun her away from the sight. "Wake up!" she called, forcing the words out. It was like speaking underwater. Constancia, her face filled with confusion, saw and heard. For an instant, her eyes brightened to see Deirdre. And then the dream began to crack and splinter.

Deirdre surfaced into wakefulness like someone drowning. She drew herself up on the bed into a tight knot, the covers wrapped around her. The night was not cold, but she quivered with a violent chill. *Only a dream,* she wanted to say. But not her dream. Constancia's. Deirdre was a watcher. She had no dreams of her own. Yet, there, along her neck, across her breast, she could feel, where the priest's finger had touched her, the track of something unclean on her flesh.

16

"It was Constancia's dream, but he was looking at *me*. He spoke to *me*. That never happened before. How could it happen?"

Once awake, Deirdre had not slept again that night. She had wanted to phone Devane at once, then, restraining herself, had waited, spending the early morning hours reliving the experience, picking through it again and again. At the first sign of light, she called Devane. When they met an hour later in his office, her voice was still tense and trembling as she recounted the dream—once, twice, still again. "Here. He touched me here. I can still feel it."

Devane tried lamely to calm her, but his own anxiety was too obvious. His words only contributed to her distress. Deirdre did not like seeing him disturbed and uncertain. She looked to him for steadiness. She wanted to collapse into his care, to become small and soft and helpless. He was not letting that happen.

"I'm sure this can't be true," he said. But behind his words, she could tell his mind was racing, searching for explanations. "You must be mistaken."

"No no! It was a dream *just like Peter's*. I know the feeling. The emptiness. The light. I couldn't forget."

"I should have known this would be too great a strain for you," he said. "I should never have agreed . . ."

He wasn't taking it in. He was refusing to register how shaken she was. She moved close to him, forcing herself into his embrace. It was a bold move and caught him off guard. Once, when she had first come to the Clinic, she had needed to be held and he had held her, only for a moment to steady her. It was his practice not to touch his patients. Now, awkwardly, he pressed her against him, only then realizing how much he too wanted the contact. When she was closed in his arms, she was at last able to tell him what most frightened her.

"I knew him."

"Knew him?"

"The man who spoke to me. It was the man in Peter's dreams, the man who was there on the last night." She felt Devane's body stiffen. She could not know it was anger exploding inside him.

"No no. I'm certain that's not so. It's been a long time since you saw him."

"It was *him!* I could tell. There's something about his eye . . . a cast or something. It's the same man I saw with Peter, the man who was forcing Peter to attack me in his dreams. He smiled at me—as if he had been waiting for me. Why was he there?"

Devane led her to a chair and sat her down. "Listen to me carefully, Deirdre. I don't want you to monitor any more of Constancia's dreams —not until I tell you it's all right. We must reevaluate the matter. And you're not to mention this to anyone. I want us both to be very careful now—about what we say and do."

"He's another watcher, isn't he? But it wouldn't be anyone you knew. Are there watchers you don't know? Where do they come from?"

Devane gave no answer. He did not want to lie to her. He would never lie to her again. He said, "Deirdre, I don't want to talk about this now. I need to think." But his silence was as good as an answer. Her mind was working on it. It was frightening to think that there might be watchers Dr. Devane did not know about. But there was something even more fearful: that he did know *this* watcher.

*   *   *

Without waiting to be announced, Devane marched past Costello's secretary and pushed open the office door. If he expected to create a dramatic entrance, he failed. Costello, writing at his desk, barely lifted his eyes. He gave no greeting.

"I understood we had an agreement," Devane announced, his throat as tight as a fist.

Costello, almost inaudible, asked, "What agreement is that, Aaron?"

"Deirdre and Moray were never to meet."

"Have they met?"

"I think you know they have."

"As far as I know, Moray is still at La Jolla."

"You know what I mean. They met last night in Constancia's dream."

"Well, that must have been quite an encounter." He was absolutely cool. But Devane knew Costello. He knew this studied calm. It was the calm of a cat watching its prey.

"What about the agreement?"

"We had an agreement to break Constancia. We did not agree to fart around with this operation as if it were a piece of personal research. You were warned. Time is running out. We used what we had."

"Yes? And with what results?"

Costello shrugged. "Remains to be seen. Moray thinks we've found exactly the right tactic. Sacrilege. I can't think why we didn't hit on it sooner. Maybe because we didn't take her religion seriously. Such a secular age."

"Moray *thinks!* What's his judgment worth?"

"At least he wants to get on with the job. He's very good, you know —once he really gets into an assignment. He's developed quite a bit since you last worked with him. More imaginative, more daring. Snottier too. Still, I think you'd be proud. You should give him another try sometime. Teamed with the right psychiatrist, he could be a magnificent instrument."

"A sadistic nut," Devane fumed. "That's what he's developed into. I hope you realize he *likes* to destroy. He's not neutral. He likes it."

"Maybe that's what makes him so inventive. Feeding the nun the aborted fetus. That was his idea. Worked it out himself."

"You won't break Constancia that way. There's too much anger in her response to desecration. Not fear—anger. Anger's positive. It's assertive. You can't work it into depression."

Costello was taking his criticism seriously. "We were going on your recommendation. 'Sacrilege,' you said. Have you got anything better to suggest?"

"No. Nothing else." What he had learned yesterday afternoon about the spider went unmentioned. It might become the one thing he had to bargain with.

"We'll take the anger into account," Costello went on. "You might have mentioned that before."

"I told you not to move too fast."

"And I told you time is short. We have to work from what we've got. Moray thinks he can go with this. We'll have to try. At the very least, we can grind her down physically, ruin her health. Moray broke off too early last night. We're displeased about that. He couldn't pass up the temptation of giving Mrs. Vale a scare. That was his own idea. It wasn't part of the assignment. In fact, he was told specifically to steer clear of her. But there's a lot of jealousy there. Moray believes Mrs. Vale has alienated your affections. He hates that. And, as you've observed, he can be hard to control. Anyway, the little run-in with Mrs. Vale was a sideshow. Unnecessary. Sorry it happened." He gave a small sniff. It was as close to an apology as Costello had ever come.

Solemnly, Devane said, "This finishes it, you realize. I can't continue here." He wanted the statement to sting. A whiplash of punishment for broken promises. But there was no point. Costello's hide was leather-tough and an inch thick.

"I think it's been finished for some time now," Costello answered. "Pity. It's not too late for you to reconsider." But he said it as if he knew the answer. Devane was already wagging his head: *No no no!*

"All I want is a clean break. For myself and Deirdre."

"You must think about this, Aaron. Clean breaks are very hard to arrange. You can't walk out of the Clinic and set up independently. You must realize that. You couldn't simply take your research and your reputation out of here and put them on the auction block. They're not your property."

"What about Deirdre? Is she free to leave?"

Costello fetched up an impatient sigh. "I hope she's not thinking of an early departure. It might be best to wait until we're finished with Mother Constancia."

"She's not a prisoner," Devane insisted.

Costello gave no response. "We'll talk about this more."

"We are talking."

"We'll talk again, after you've thought it through. Incidentally, what does she make of last night's encounter?"

This was delicate. What Deirdre knew—or rather what Costello thought she knew—had everything to do with her future.

"She's confused," Devane answered. "I'll try to keep her that way."

"Did she recognize Moray?"

"No," Devane lied.

"We don't want her to know about Moray. After all, that connects with Peter Vale."

"I have as great an interest in keeping that connection a secret as you do."

"Yes, that's true, isn't it?" He stopped Devane on his way to the door. "One thing. Do make certain Mrs. Vale stays out of Mother Constancia's dreams. That's Moray's territory now. You can consider your part of the assignment wrapped up." Devane nodded agreement. "Do be persuasive with her. It wouldn't be wise for her to cross paths with Moray again. She's an amateur, after all. And Moray . . . well, you know how mean our boy can get."

17

When she came to Ripley that night, his dreams were a maelstrom of anger and despair. Ragged episodes of violence surged across his sleeping mind, tossing him close to the surface of wakefulness, then sucking him down into fitful unconsciousness. Cristina was in his dreams. Deirdre too. Two women now blending into one shape. But mainly his thoughts were of Constancia. The many fears he harbored for her had been brought to a head and now tumbled wildly through his brain.

All that day, Constancia had stayed in her quarters, fasting and lost in prayer, haunted by the obscene fantasy Moray had inflicted upon her the night before. She would speak to no one, but she did not have to. When Sister Charlotte found her in the morning already deep in anxious prayer, her expression was eloquent with grief. It was unmistakable that she had suffered a severe setback. Later that afternoon, she called Ripley to her and confessed the dream to him. She understood it to be a renewed temptation, but now mixed with something worse. She had no words to describe it, except one phrase. *"La nada."* The *Nothing*. Her voice fell into a whisper as she told him of the annihilating void that had enveloped her dream. She reported the experience like a secret too terrible for the world to know. "It was as if God has turned His face from me. I suffer, but He does not care, He does not know. Can there be such a place, where God has never been? Only the *Nothing?"*

Why did God see fit to test her in this way? Ripley had no answer he dared to make known to her. If he spoke his true thoughts, they would assail her faith, not strengthen it. He listened silently, thinking how useless he had become to her as a confessor. He felt his spirit sink and that night descended into troubled sleep, carrying the burden of her anguish.

There he saw her persecuted by her enemies, subjected to fragmented scenes of atrocity and degradation. Deirdre, entering and watching his dreams, struggled in vain to soothe his fears. Through much of the night she waited, fighting down her impatience, watching for the interval of calm that would allow her to shape his thoughts. The dream they shared that night must be one he would remember. That was doubly urgent. She wanted him to know of her love. But she also wanted him to know she possessed the power to watch. By morning, he must believe that with no trace of doubt. Because, as she now realized, only her watching could save Constancia.

In the world outside, the darkness had begun to give way to morning. But inside Ripley's sleeping head, it was still the depth of an interminable jungle night. For what seemed like days in dream time, he had been leading the way through the brooding rain forest. Behind him, Constancia followed with Sister Charlotte and a small contingent of *compañeros*. The darkness around them pulsed with menace. The cries of pursuers. Gunfire. From the sky above, the searching beams of the predatory helicopters sliced across the night like white rapiers.

The group came to a clearing and paused. At its center, there stood a weathered monolith, dark against the dark jungle. A gigantic, time-worn Olmec head, its face austere, ominous. Constancia, suddenly fearful, flinched back.

"No," Ripley commanded, "don't be afraid. It's dead like all the other gods."

He stepped forward and struck the stone colossus with the butt of the rifle he carried. Where he hit it, a piece of the cheek crumbled away. Behind it, there were strange markings, barely visible in the gloom of the night. Writing. An ancient script.

Seeing it, Sister Charlotte strode forward and began tearing away the surface stone that covered it. It came away like papier-mâché. "You see," she told Ripley, "the real god is underneath. Only the mask is dead." The others voiced agreement and joined her. Soon the entire face had been peeled away; a vast wall of hieroglyphs loomed above them.

Constancia turned to Ripley, suddenly severe and challenging. "These are the instructions of our salvation. Only John can read them." Ripley stared at the cryptic writing. He could make out not one word. "It's too dark to see," he protested. Sister Charlotte was running her hands over the wall. "You have to read with your fingers," she said. "Hurry! There's not much time."

Ripley pressed his hands against the stone inscription, then jerked them back suddenly. The hieroglyphs were razor-sharp; they cut into his flesh. "Hurry!" Sister Charlotte shouted. "Before they find us!" Hesitantly, Ripley returned his wounded fingers to the wall. Again, the stone cut where he touched. "I can't," he protested.

"Read!" Constancia shouted. She had become an imperious presence towering over Ripley. In her hands she carried a stick . . . a ruler. She tapped it threateningly against her palm. Before her, Ripley had grown smaller. He looked like a cowering schoolboy.

"Sister, please, I can't," he whined. "It hurts."

"Love always hurts," Constancia said. But she was not Constancia now. She was a strange, glowering old nun. "God makes His love hurt."

Ripley's little-boy face glowed with anger. "That's nonsense. I don't believe that." The punishing sister reached out to rap his injured hands with the ruler.

"Unbeliever!" she shouted. "He has become an unbeliever."

"Hurry, John!" Sister Charlotte cried. "They're coming!"

"Our salvation depends upon an unbeliever," Constancia wailed, as Ripley, now a little boy in short pants, began to scale the hieroglyphic wall like a fly, struggling to understand the inscription it carried. "I don't know this language," he explained. "Nobody knows this language anymore."

"Then we are finished," Constancia announced. "And it is *his* fault."

"*Your* fault," the others chorused.

"John has failed!" Constancia shouted after him, now high up on the wall. "Ten demerits for John. Report to Archbishop McCaffrey after class."

At the edge of the clearing, armed men gathered.

"Watch out!" Ripley called.

Constancia, once again herself, turned and stretched out her arms toward the enemy. In the palms of her hands, eyes appeared. They shone like lights, glaring through the darkness at the men as they came closer. Gunfire tore through the night. Ripley watched helplessly, clinging to the wall, too far off to defend his companions. He saw them fall. Constancia lay spread-eagled on the ground. But the eyes in her hands were still open and alive, staring up reproachfully at Ripley, unblinking.

The enemy troops rushed toward her body and, with quick machete strokes, cut away the hands. Ripley, shaking with rage, leaped from the wall. He swung his gun into position as he fell. It stuttered bullets. He

roared down like a diving airplane strafing the ground. On all sides
troops crumpled and went down. *Good!* he told himself. *Good, good,
good! I have a right to kill!* He exulted in his vengeance. Killing. Killing.

On the ground at the center of the clearing, lay Constancia's muti-
lated hands, the eyes they bore still open, staring. Unspeaking, they
accused him. He swept them up, two damp leaves fallen to the earth,
and ran with them to the forest. He came to a riverbank, stopped short,
panting, exhausted. Then, one after the other, he sailed the hands out
over the water, as if to escape their gaze once and for all. But they did
not sink. They floated upon the river, then rose slowly to become two
watching lights like low stars in the night. Their expression was one of
pity. Beneath them, Ripley felt strangely comforted. He sank down,
seeking rest, wrapped in a warm sense of forgiveness. The two stars
continued to rise; with great and curious fascination, he noticed that
they had given the heavens a new pattern. All the lights in the sky had
been rearranged into one great constellation, the vast visible emblem
of that force ". . . *which moves the sun and other stars.*"

He reached to embrace this thought . . . and then his mind went
slack with weariness. He lay, battered and trembling, in the poor jungle
hut to which his dreams often brought him. A remembered place,
always experienced as safe. The place inside his head where he turned
to find Cristina. And again she was there, though mixed fluidly with
Deirdre. A woman, two women. Finally, Deirdre entered the double
woman, invested her with her own image, and took him in her arms.
Cradling him, caressing his torn body, she allowed time for his
strength to gather after the frenzy of the night.

Then she began.

On another night, she would have been content to hold him, comfort him, nothing more. But there was more that had to be done. There
had to be a dream that stayed alive in his memory until morning. It was
a labor for her to be both caring and calculating in the love she offered
him. Calculation brought with it a sense of artificiality. She did not
want that. But she must make certain he would remember her. Her
decision was that he should not act but remain passive—absolutely so.
What happened must be all hers. She did not want her actions confused or displaced by his. When he reached to take hold of her, she
stopped and gestured no, waited and relaxed him. Then started again.
Caressing, arousing. This was bound to seem like teasing. It *was* teasing. But it was a way to prolong and heighten the experience. At last,

he understood and obeyed. He lay back, excited but actionless, accepting what she did to tune his body to a high, fine pitch.

She leaned down to ask, "What do you want me to do? Tell me." She asked again and again. She wanted the words to come from him, his own desire spoken. He whispered to her. She kissed him and moved along his body, offering what he wanted, but loitering over him, keeping him balanced at the keen edge of completion, holding off his climax.

And then she was over him, straddling him and staring down steadily into his eyes while she worked his body beneath her. Gently, she rocked him within her, telling him over and over again, "Remember this, John. Remember this." Before she was finished, she was certain he would not forget.

18

"I watch dreams." She began bluntly, knowing he would not understand. "Other people's dreams. That's why I'm here. That's my work. *I watch dreams.*"

She waited for her words to provoke bewilderment before she went on. It was morning. She had come to his room early, before breakfast, while his mind was still fresh and undistracted. She asked him to walk with her where they could be alone, a secluded corner of the Clinic grounds where the hill sloped away into a deep arroyo. The heat wave had broken. The morning brought clouds and a crisp breeze off the sea.

"Last night, I was in your dreams," she went on when they were out of sight of the Clinic. "Do you remember?"

He gave no answer. He did not have to. She could tell by the way he had greeted her when she came to his door that he remembered. But his face also said that what she was telling him was crazy. If he answered yes, what was he agreeing to? He gave only a vague nod which might mean nothing more than "Go on."

She could have recounted every detail of his dreams from first to last. But there was no point in that. He would have forgotten most of what he dreamed through the early hours of the night. She had learned how spendthrift the waking mind is with dreams, casting them away as soon as the morning comes and the world takes hold of the attention. All this he would recollect only as she mentioned it. That would be unconvincing. He might think she was planting suggestions. She moved at once to tell him about the dreams she knew were still vivid in his memory.

"Your dream took place somewhere hot and forested. A jungle, I suppose. Guatemala. I've watched you there before. That's how I knew about Cristina. I watched you with her. Last night, you and I were together in a cabin or hut where you come to meet her. You could see through the roof. Stars. Trees. We made love. Or rather I made love to you. I took a very long time.''

She was speaking in a dry, flat voice, struggling for a totally dispassionate tone. All the while, she willed herself to look directly into his eyes, challenging him to believe her. "I asked you what you wanted me to do. And I did it. I did things so you would remember. I *told* you to remember. I said, 'Remember this, John.' And when we were finished, I leaned down and bit you. Here. Very hard.'' She touched his right shoulder. "If it hadn't been a dream, there would be a mark. There isn't, of course. But you felt that. And then, do you remember what I did?''

He was staring at her, too astonished to speak. She kept steady under his gaze.

"I was leaning over you. You were . . . inside of me. And I made a mark with my finger. I made you watch while I drew this.'' She found a small stick and used it to scratch an image in the dirt where they were standing. She drew a circle, then stopped and looked at him. "It was bright red in the dream. Like fire. It doesn't mean anything. It was just for you to remember. Do you remember? I made this circle. And then I took your hand . . . and then what?'' She pressed the stick into his hand. "Please, it's important.''

Slowly, wondering at his own action, he took the stick and drew two crossed lines, quartering the circle.

"That's right,'' she said. "I used your finger to draw that. And do you remember where I drew it? You can only do things like that in dreams.'' She took his hand and pressed it against her chest. "Here. I drew it here. You watched me. And then . . .'' She drew herself up and kissed him, as she had in the dream.

She had finished. She shuddered slightly and went soft. An ordeal completed. "Don't be angry. It was only a dream.''

Only a dream. People used that phrase, not knowing the power of dreams, the reality that could kill.

For a long while he stared at the little drawing in the dust. He remembered everything she had described with fierce clarity. He remembered the circle as she drew it between her breasts, the sort of unreal moment that you accept in a dream. But now she was recounting it as an event observed, stolen from the privacy of his mind.

"What sort of place is this?'' he asked finally. "What kind of person are you?''

"A sort of freak,'' she answered candidly. "I've been able to dream other people's dreams all my life. Since I was a child. I can't say how I do it. I can watch their dreams—anybody's dreams—if I know them well enough. I can shape their dreams any way I wish. I'm not supposed to tell you that. It's my secret with Dr. Devane. He says I'm an 'instrument'—his instrument. Like a microscope. He uses me to monitor his patients' dreams. It's meant to help them get well. But I guess I'm really just freakish. There shouldn't be people like me. Dreams are meant to be private."

"Yes," Ripley said. "I think I agree with that." For the first time she heard a hint of reproach in his voice, the disapproval of someone spied upon.

"But you must understand why I did it last night. It wasn't a prank or just taking advantage. Please believe that. I wanted you to know that I could watch."

"I'd say you proved your point. Of course, you might have chosen other ways to do that." This time the tone was not disapproving but frankly curious.

"Yes, I could have. But I wanted it to be that way."

His eyes were searching her. After a pause, he asked, "Are you a mind reader as well? Can you tell what I'm thinking?"

"No."

"Good. I'm relieved to know I have some secrets. That means, if I choose, I can pretend to be very priestlike. Insulted and outraged and so forth."

"But you aren't," she said, asking.

He gave no answer. "This power of yours—you say it's a secret between you and Devane. Why? Why keep it secret?"

"Dr. Devane says we're only at the beginning of the research he wants to do. He's not ready to tell what he's learned."

"But here you are, telling me."

"Yes."

"Disobeying orders."

"Yes." She said it with an air of distinct defiance. Since they had begun talking that morning, he had noticed something different about her. Nervous as she had been, there was a strength he had not seen in her before. Perhaps for the first time in a long while, she was making her own decisions, breaking with Devane's authority. She brought that act of rebellion to him, a more precious gift than the kiss she had offered.

"Why?" he asked.

"There's another watcher. *I think* there's another watcher." This meant nothing to him. "He's someone . . . bad," she went on. "He's in Constancia's dreams."

She told him about her meeting with Moray the night before. Her description of Constancia's dream checked closely enough with the little Constancia had told him in the course of her confession. She had mentioned especially how Deirdre had intervened to end the nightmare.

"This other watcher—is it someone Devane knows?"

"Oh no." The suggestion jarred her. She rejected it at once.

"No one from here, working at the Clinic?"

"No no. He wouldn't know someone like that."

"And you? Do you know him?"

"Yes, I do. I've seen him before. But I didn't know then that he was a watcher. He was the man who destroyed my husband. And my children."

And she told him about Peter's black dreams—as much as she could bring herself to recount. "That's why I'm here, you see. After Peter's death, I needed help. Dr. Devane brought me to the Clinic. I would have gone crazy otherwise."

He pondered the story somberly. "This was two years ago—these 'black dreams' of Peter's, as you call them?"

"Yes."

"And now you've encountered the same man in Constancia's dreams? You're sure—the same man?"

"Yes. I couldn't be mistaken."

"Describe him," he said challengingly. She did, in detail, noting especially the cast in one eye. He was convinced. "Listen to me, Deirdre. No more secrets now. Exactly what has Devane told you about this power of yours? How unique are you? Has he ever talked to you about other watchers?"

"I've never met another real watcher. Dr. Devane says he's worked with others, but never with anybody who can do what I do. He thinks there's the possibility that watchers like me might be found and trained. That's one of the things we've been trying to do together. But the people I work with are just children—mainly the autistic children. Some of them can watch a little, but they're unreliable. Of course, with enough training, a few of them might develop into useful . . . instruments." Devane's word left a small, unpleasant taste on her lips.

"And that's why Devane is keeping your work under wraps—until he's trained other watchers and done more research? Is that what he's told you?"

"Yes."

"That's the only reason?"

"Yes."

"But there is this other watcher. You've encountered him twice now. You don't know who he is; neither does Devane."

"That's right." She could see the suspicion in his face. Something wrong. "What is it?"

"Maybe you don't know him. And maybe Devane doesn't know him. But I do. I've met him—awake and walking. I even know his name."

19

Ripley knew him simply as "Howard." Maybe he had once mentioned a last name; if he had, Ripley could not recall. He was one of scores of young people who drifted through Constancia's life at *Casa Libertad*. They came wanting to help or needing more help themselves than they could ever offer. Some—a few—would stay and become permanent members of Constancia's circle, dedicated volunteers willing to make sacrifices and endure the discipline. The greater number would melt away after a few days or weeks when it became clear how much Constancia demanded of them.

The first time Ripley took notice of Howard, he spotted him as one of the transients. A dark, angular young man, with fragile good looks and quick, nervous eyes. He was amiable enough. Too amiable, too eager to please. The sort who rushed to open doors or pick up fallen objects, but volunteered for nothing that demanded as much as an hour's hard work. He could be charmingly boyish, but his ways of ingratiation seemed to be learned from a book. Ripley could tell: he had no staying power.

He claimed to be in his mid-twenties. He was bright enough to be that old, but looked and often behaved younger. There was an air of emotional retardation about him. He was jittery in a way that made his presence disquieting. Constancia's people had plenty of experience dealing with these needy and erratic types. They were given work—clean-up chores, kitchen crew, day-care duties. Their assignments started small, then gradually grew in importance. Either they settled into their responsibilities and shaped up or—more likely—when things became too burdensome, they gave up and went their way. They were welcomed with kindness, but never coddled or indulged. They were given to understand that *Casa Libertad* did not exist for their benefit, unless the answer to their needs happened to be a life of service and political action.

Howard had shown early on that he was not much of a worker. For weeks, he spent whole days at *Casa Libertad,* but carried out his assignments grudgingly and minimally. No one knew where he came from or where he lived. He was a loner, always moving along the outer edges, observing—at times with a certain barely disguised arrogance. He made no friends, for all his friendly chatter. He had only one real interest, an obsessive one. Constancia. That was common enough among the oddballs who drifted through. They came to bask in her charisma, possibly looking to be mothered as well as edified. Whenever Constancia was at the House, Howard dogged her constantly, offering help that was seldom needed. He took his meals as close to her as he could sit. When she assembled the members of the House and spoke, he shouldered his way up front to listen, hanging gravely on every word. She noticed him. She could not help but notice him. He bullied her attention. Once or twice, when she reached out to pat him as she might pat a demanding pet, he caught hold of her hand and held it—too tight—staring wantingly into her eyes. She recognized his strangeness, but in no special manner. There were many troubled souls who came her way—more than she could expect to help. She offered them a characteristically impersonal concern: patience, gentleness, occasional gestures of attention. She knew better than to baby them.

Three months after he first appeared at *Casa Libertad,* Howard was gone without a word of farewell. That in itself was not remarkable. It was what one expected of such fragile hangers-on. No one at the House would have remembered him for very long afterward, least of all Ripley, if it had not been for one ugly incident.

At the very end of his stay, Howard had a run-in with Sister Monica, one of the young American nuns, then in charge of the kitchen crew. Following instructions, she had begun stepping up Howard's responsibilities, demanding more of him each week. But the work was getting beyond him. He left assignments undone. She responded by taking minor disciplinary action: an extra clean-up job that kept him away from one of Constancia's morning talks. Howard was furious when he learned what he had missed. Passing Sister Monica in the hall, he called her (she thought) "Bitch" under his breath. A few days later, her parakeet was found dead in its cage: its head was missing. She had no proof, but she was convinced Howard had killed the bird. She confronted him, trying to be friendly but firm. He gave her no answer, but when she was finished, he asked, smirking, "Isn't it a sin for a nun to dream about fucking?"

"He's a sickie," Sister Monica complained at a staff meeting and asked Ripley to speak to him. Ripley hated such chores, but he did it, quietly and gently. Howard answered not a word but listened, still as a manikin. Ripley would have remembered the interview if for no other reason than the young man's unsettling stare. His right eye bore a cast that lent his expression a sense of crazy imbalance. The cockeyed look might have been a comic imperfection; but Howard's ice-cold anger deprived it of humor. Finally, Ripley ran out of patience and broke off, letting Howard know that he was no longer welcome at *Casa Libertad.* Ripley assumed that was the end of the meeting, but Howard had something to add. With a nasty twist to his words, he said, "Tell Sister Monica I'm very, very sorry. Here's a little gift for her to make it up."

He handed Ripley a wadded ball of paper. Inside was the parakeet's head.

That was the last time anybody at *Casa Libertad* saw Howard. Except for Constancia. Less than a month later—just before Easter—her bad dreams began. Howard was in them.

She did not remember him at once. Her dreams were few and widely spaced. But at last she recognized him as the obnoxious youth who was always there when her dreams turned violent or obscene. When she told Ripley in the course of a confessional session, he remarked, "He's a bad memory for all of us." He assumed that Constancia had stored away some intuitive perception of Howard's psychotic cruelty, an unconscious impression that emerged in her troubled dreams. At the time, that seemed like a neat psychological interpretation.

"But now we have another explanation," Ripley explained as Deirdre and Constancia listened, half eagerly, half fearfully. "Howard is really there—in your dreams. He's *put* himself there. He can do what Deirdre can do. He's a watcher."

It was the early afternoon. Ripley had decided to lay everything Deirdre had told him that morning before Constancia. As proof of Deirdre's powers, he had her recount in excruciating detail all that had happened in Constancia's black dream. The ruined church, the dwarves, the mock-eucharistic rites. Constancia herself remembered vividly how Deirdre had awakened her at the end of the nightmare. It was a convincing display. Constancia accepted its validity. She fixed her catlike eyes on Deirdre and nodded gravely. *"Es una sabia,"* she said. *"Una sabia verdadera."* Deirdre, recalling the role Doña Rosaura had played in Constancia's life, felt the full weight of the words. *A true sabia.* She both thrilled and cringed at the judgment Constancia was making. It was as if she had proved herself and had passed an initiation.

"But why does he wish me harm, this boy?" Constancia asked, turning back to Ripley.

Ripley returned the question. "Why did he wish Deirdre's husband any harm? Maybe he's a psychotic who strikes at random. Either that or there's some pattern to his malice that we don't see."

"But how can there be?" Deirdre asked. "There's no connection at all between Peter and Mother."

"There's *you.* And there's this Clinic."

"But this man Howard has nothing to do with the Clinic."

Ripley totaled it up. "Howard turned your husband into a homicidal maniac; he drove him to murder and to suicide. He very nearly managed to get you killed. In the course of doing his mischief, he meets you in Peter's dreams. After Peter's death, Devane appears out of thin air and, for no reason you can think of, he brings you to his Clinic free of charge. There he uses you as a dreamwatcher. Mother comes to the Clinic and you meet Howard again, this time in her dreams. Does this sound like a run of coincidences?"

"But I asked Dr. Devane about this man yesterday morning."

"And what did he say? Did he actually deny knowing him?"

"He didn't say anything. But I know he couldn't be involved with someone like that."

"You may want to ask him again. And this time make sure he gives you an answer."

Constancia, looking to Ripley for guidance, asked, "John, what does this mean?"

"It means you should leave here. We should all leave here. You won't be made well by Devane."

Constancia shook her head. "No no. I have given my promise of holy obedience to the Archbishop. I will stay until Dr. Devane permits me to leave. We have no reason to condemn him."

Ripley argued with her, but she was firm. Even his anger could not dent her resolution. It had not been easy for the Archbishop to extract a promise from her. Once given, she would not go back on it. "He has asked for my obedience," she insisted. She seemed to treat that promise as a penance properly imposed upon her.

"Then we'll get him to release you from your promise," Ripley announced, unable to disguise his heated displeasure. "We'll do that today. I'll call McCaffrey. I want you away from here, Mother, as soon as possible."

But his phone call to McCaffrey did not gain Constancia's freedom. "From what you tell me, John," the Archbishop said, "I gather Constancia has suffered a relapse. Isn't that all the more reason to continue treatment?"

"I'm not making the situation clear," Ripley said. "I believe she's in danger. There are people here at the Clinic, possibly Devane himself, who are trying to unbalance her."

The Archbishop's voice came back coolly incredulous. "John, these are serious accusations. How exactly do you know this?"

Ripley realized he would have to explain about Deirdre and the dreamwatching. It was more than he felt comfortable discussing on the phone. He agreed to drive to Los Angeles that afternoon for a personal meeting.

Before he left, Ripley saved a moment for Deirdre. "You wanted to know if I was outraged by what happened in my dream—in *our* dream—last night."

"I thought perhaps—well, you *are* a priest."

"You mustn't take that more seriously than I do. No, I wasn't outraged. Surprised to know how it came about, yes. But not insulted. Quite the opposite. And"—he added as he turned toward the car—"I don't think this dream was *only* a dream."

20

Laney thought: *If I had more to cover up, boy, would this be a daring bathing suit.*

As it was, the string bikini she was wearing looked modestly right for a smallish twelve-year-old whose body was still stubbornly straight where she would have liked it to curve. Only a few hundred yards farther south of where she sat, there was a stretch of nude beach, minimally concealed by a shallow cleft in the sea cliffs. Her slightly better-endowed companions, Becky and Jan, had been lost from sight there for nearly an hour now. Laney, cruelly abandoned, peered after them with a mixture of resentment and self-pity. Some friends! Probably showing off for all they were worth. Laney, having so little to show, had stayed behind. No fun being a brazen woman when you were still being mistaken from ten feet off for a boy.

As usual, Deirdre had made her promise if she went to the beach after school, she had to get some homework done. Laney did give it a try. But here she was, starting to read the same words over again for the tenth time. The sun blazing off the shiny page made it impossible to concentrate. Besides, the books got all thumbed up with suntan lotion. Nobody could do geometry at the beach. Or history. Or lit. What a dumb idea, lugging all these heavy volumes with her. Bad enough when your body had all the sex appeal of a toothpick. What if somebody—meaning some boy—came along and got the idea you were a brain as well!

She stacked the book on top of the others and stared out toward the horizon. More fun to watch the surfers careening off the high waves, and to let the sun toast your pigments, and to just go limp. . . .

"Got an interesting proposition for me today?"

Laney shook herself out of the light sun stupor she had slipped into. She looked around. It was Richard, kneeling beside her, flipping through her geometry text.

"Oh, hi," she said, brightening up to have some company.

"Brought your personal library with you again, I see," he said.

"Yeah. My mother makes me. It's real unfair. The whole idea of summer school sucks."

"How come you have to go? Are you flunking?"

"Hey, no! I got a three-point-two average. I'm advanced honors. That's why I gotta do dumb geometry so soon."

"So? How come summer school?"

"My mother says it'll keep my mind occupied. God! Who wants their mind occupied at the beach?"

"How's the geometry coming? What proposition are you on?"

"Number twenty-nine already. Something about the Python . . . Python-agoran . . ."

"Pythagorean," Richard corrected. "Yeah, that's a bitch. Need help?" He was skimming the assignment.

"Well, yeah, I suppose. But who wants to do geometry at the beach, you know?"

"Geometry is the best thing to study at the beach."

"Yeah? Why?"

"Because you can draw the proofs on the sand. That's how the ancient Greeks used to do it. See?" With his finger, he began etching a triangle into the bright, grainy surface. "Of course, it works better on the wet sand. But you get the idea."

"Yeah, well . . . I guess my brain doesn't work in the sunshine."

"Tell you what," Richard said. "I'll give you a choice. A geometry lesson. Or a Fudgsicle. Which?"

"Three guesses," Laney answered.

"All right. Don't go away." He jogged off toward the refreshment stand beside the highway.

Richard was nice, but odd. Odd enough so you didn't want to introduce him to your friends. Laney had met him on the beach at the beginning of the summer. He was behind her in line at the refreshment stand. They exchanged a few words, then met again, and again—about a half-dozen times since, always when she was by herself, like now. On a beach this big and crowded, that had to be more than a coincidence. But what "more" was it? He was too old to be interested in her as a girlfriend; Laney knew that much. He said he was in college. Nor did he seem to be a weirdo. Sure, he had bought her a few ice creams and Cokes, but he never asked her for a date, never tried to sit close or touch. If he did, that would be the end of it, right there. She'd begin running when she saw him. Laney had been amply warned about men like that—old or young.

But Richard never did more than talk, mostly about school, and never for more than a half hour or so. He was smart. He had guided her through some fierce geometry lessons she could never have handled on her own. Laney was terrible at mathematics, so she appreciated the help. Also, she didn't entirely mind receiving the attentions of a good-looking man on the beach, even if he was too old for her. She tried to think of him as an older brother type. That kept things casual and relaxed. Still, it was odd—how he seemed to appear whenever she was sitting alone, as if he were just waiting for the chance. If he actually were looking out for her, that would be more than odd.

He was trotting back now, holding two dripping snow cones. "Sorry, no Fudgsicles," he announced and plopped down beside her in the sand. "Great day," he said after a pause, while they watched the surfers.

"Yeah."

"This is probably the best surfing beach in California. Do you do any surfing?"

"Me? God, I can't even swim."

"I thought maybe you did. You've got the body for it."

"I have?"

"Sure. Trim, strong, agile. Athletic, you know."

"Yeah? Well, I don't. Do you?"

"What?"

"Surf."

He laughed. "Well, to tell you the truth, I can't swim either."

"Are you back at school now?"

"School?"

"The university. I thought you said you went to the university."

"Oh yes. But not here in Santa Barbara. Down at La Jolla."

"You study there? Or teach?"

"Well, neither. Research. I'm in research."

"Oh? What kind?"

"Psychology."

"Oh." After a pause. "My mother is sort of into psychology."

"Is she? At the university?"

"No. At the Devane Clinic. Up there." Laney pointed behind them into the steep hills behind Santa Barbara.

"Oh, well, the Devane Clinic. That's a very famous place."

"I guess so. You know about it?"

"Everybody in psychology knows about the Devane Clinic. What's it like living there?"

"I didn't say I lived there."

"Didn't you? Oh."

"Well, actually I do. Live there."

"Oh."

"I mean I don't live there like one of the patients."

"Of course not."

"My mother and I are guests."

"I see. And have you met the great man himself?"

"Huh?"

"Dr. Devane. Dr. Aaron Devane. The world's greatest. Have you met him?"

"Oh sure. My mother works with him."

"You mean as a nurse or something like that?"

"No, that's *not* what I mean. Women don't have to be just nurses, you know."

"Of course not. I was kidding."

"She does research too, as a matter of fact. She's one of Dr. Devane's most important assistants. She sees him every day. He'd be practically lost without her."

"Assistant? That's very impressive. Assistant to the famous Dr. Devane. Maybe someday she'll be famous too."

"Could be. I wouldn't be surprised. At college, she was Phi Beta Kappa. You know what that is?"

"Sure. Right up there, top of her class."

"She's really, really smart."

"Is your father a psychologist too?"

Laney didn't answer. The question hung in the air weightily. Finally, "My father's dead."

"Oh, I'm sorry." Then, changing the pace, "Say, here's something you'd like." He pulled a paperback book from the backpack he carried. "Lots more fun to read on the beach than old Python-agoras there." He held it out, then mockingly drew it back. "You *are* old enough to read scary things, aren't you?"

"Oh, come on!"

"No, I'm serious. This is a real industrial-strength chiller. I don't want to be responsible for giving you nightmares."

"I can handle it," Laney answered, giving her lip a curl of heavy annoyance. He passed her the book. It was a pulp horror thriller with a lurid cover. "Vampires, huh?"

"Yeah. Are you into vampires?"

"Oh, sort of. Kind of." In fact, vampires were currently a consuming fascination with Laney. So much so that Deirdre had expressed concern. Supposedly, the subject had been placed off-limits—in the form of both books and movies. But Laney was still smuggling home the occasional paperback.

"Well, me—I'm a real vampire freak," Richard confessed. "Ever since I was a kid. But this isn't the old creaky stuff. This book's got a twist. These are high-fashion bloodsuckers. Spend their days in designer coffins. What they do is run a sort of Playboy Key Club . . . You know what that is?"

"Yeah, I know."

"Anyway, it's a cute idea. Also"—he dropped into a stage whisper—"very sexy."

"Yeah, it looks it," Laney said. She had been studying the cover picture with some care. The upper torso of a bare-breasted girl in a filmy gown bent backward across what looked like a waterbed, her arched throat punctured by two trickling wounds. Around her stood a ring of elegantly dressed men and women, each equipped with fangs.

"You think your mother'd let you read something like that?" Richard asked.

Laney shot him a fiercely disconcerted look. "Hey, listen, that's really insulting, you know? I don't have to clear what I read with my mother."

"Sure you don't. Just kidding."

"I'm not a kid, okay?"

"Honest, I wouldn't be loaning you the book if I didn't think you could handle it. Actually, it's not all that scary. It gets pretty ridiculous after a while. Except for how they get rid of the bodies. Yuck!"

"Yeah? How?"

"Down in the basement. The sewer babies."

"The what?"

"Real gross."

"Tell me."

"Uh-uh. I don't want to ruin it for you. You don't ever have nightmares, do you?"

"Oh, when I was a kid sometimes. But not anymore. You're sure I can have this?"

"Sure. I'm finished with it. Keep it."

"Well, thanks."

"Tell you what. I'll sign it for you. Memento of the summer. Why not?" Turning to the front of the book, he quickly scribbled a few lines.

Laney inspected the inscription. "How'd you know my initials?"

"From your book wrappers."

"Oh." But she was puzzled. Her textbooks carried covers marked "Laney Vale." He had written "E.V." in the paperback.

"That's what Laney stands for, doesn't it? Elaine?"

"Yeah. And your initials . . . What do they . . . ?"

"Hi! Hope we're interrupting something real intimate." The voice burst in suddenly from behind them. Becky and Jan returning, plumping down in the sand. Richard, more startled than Laney, leaped to his feet and spun around. He stared at the two girls who had stolen up in back of them. "Christ!" he snapped. "That's a hell of a trick!" His lips made a shape like "Bitches" under his breath.

"Sorry," Becky said, flinching at his reaction. "Didn't mean to give you a heart attack." She glanced toward Laney for an introduction.

"This is Richard . . ." Laney said almost apologetically. "He . . ."

"He was just going," Richard announced, now smiling a rigid, too-strenuous smile. "Have fun with old Python-agoras," he said to Laney as he hurriedly retrieved his backpack and began retreating across the beach. Laney waved him off, not eager to have him stay.

The three girls watched after him. "Well, well," Becky said. "Leave you alone for a minute and you're making out already."

"That's right," Laney retorted smartly. "Not all of us have to flash our boobs to pick up a man."

"Isn't he a little old for you?"

"Not at all. He admires my sophistication," Laney said, playing smug. "Some of us know how to handle older men."

"Come on, who is he?" Jan demanded.

"Oh, just a guy I met on the beach. He's good at mathematics."

"Yeah? Can I hire him to tutor me? He's cute. Nervous maybe, but cute."

Becky wasn't so sure. "Looks kind of dorky to me. Those eyes . . ."

"Cut it out!" Laney protested. "Don't make fun. I like his eyes. They're distinctive."

"Sure," Becky said. "If you like your men cockeyed. You can't tell if he's looking at you or over your shoulder."

"I mean it. Cut it out! He's a nice guy." But Laney had other things on her mind. "Hey, did you two do it? Did you really go bare?"

"It's the only way to get an even tan," Becky answered, very blasé.

"With guys around? Tell the truth. Right in front of guys?"

"You should have seen her," Jan reported, teasing Becky. "Couldn't wait till we got there. She dropped her top before we even got to the lifeguard station."

"Really? She did? Really? God!"

And Richard was quickly forgotten in the bubbly girl talk that followed. Laney did not think of him again until she got home. Then she found the book he had given her.

The Blood Club by Kevin Queen.

The cover blurb asked: "Are You Ready for the New Vampires?"

On the title page was his inscription:

> TO E.V.
> FROM R.M.
> PLEASANT DREAMS.

She carefully hid the book in the closet.

21

"It's an excellent sherry, don't you think? Do have some more, John."
The Archbishop leaned across to fill Ripley's glass for the third time.
Ripley, toiling to control his impatience, accepted. "It's Spanish. Really too much of an indulgence. My worst vice—so I flatter myself to
believe. Or perhaps you would prefer something stronger?"

"No. Really. Thank you," Ripley answered. He had been with Mc-
Caffrey in his office for over an hour, groping his way awkwardly
through a convoluted conversation that kept returning to the subject
of sherry and similar trivia. "Archbishop, I did want to get back to
Santa Barbara this evening and begin arrangements for Mother Constancia to leave." He had reminded McCaffrey of that at least twice
since they had sat down to talk.

"Yes, but John, I'm not at all certain we really want her to leave."

"*I'm* certain."

"Then I must say I don't understand your urgency. It seems wholly
premature. You say Mother experienced a terrible nightmare last
night. Doesn't that mean that she's as much in need of care now as
ever?"

"Not the sort of care Devane is offering her."

"But really, John, are you the person to decide about that? Am I?"
McCaffrey's tone was smooth but challenging. "You realize what Dr.
Devane's reputation is."

"I do. But I also know Devane is wrong for her. There are things
going on at the Clinic that Mother should not be exposed to."

McCaffrey held his sherry to the light and studied its amber radiance. "Yes, this idea about the dreams . . . I don't believe I fully
grasp that as yet. You claim Devane is somehow manipulating Mother
Constancia's dreams."

"I don't know if it's Devane. It may be people who work with him,
people who monitor dreams."

"Monitor dreams." McCaffrey mused upon the phrase. "But is that really possible, John? I'm not aware I've ever come across such a thing."

"Nor have I—until this morning."

"Just this morning. This woman—Mrs. Vale—told you about it. And you believe her." Tactfully, McCaffrey was giving his words a skeptical coloring.

"Yes."

"You know, John, as I recall, Mrs. Vale has been under care herself at the Clinic. Has it occurred to you that she may be a bit . . . well . . . unstable?"

"As I told you, she offered me a convincing demonstration of her powers."

"Yes, but I'm not at all clear about this demonstration. Do you think you might go over that once more?"

"Mrs. Vale was able to describe a dream that I had. She was also able to describe Mother's dream. Both in exact detail. More clearly than we could have recalled them ourselves."

"Ah, now *that's* where I begin to have a problem. She recalled the dreams *more* clearly than you did. Might there not have been some form of suggestion at work here? She may have talked you into believing things you hadn't dreamed at all. Do you see what I mean?"

Wearily, Ripley rejected the idea. "I'm certain I had the dream. And Mrs. Vale was in it—observing it."

"Did you discuss this with Dr. Devane? Did he participate in this demonstration?"

"No."

"Has he ever mentioned this monitoring of dreams?"

"Obviously not. He wants to keep his dreamwatching research secret."

"Mrs. Vale told you that?"

"Yes."

"You realize it would be quite insulting to remove Mother Constancia from Dr. Devane's care simply on the basis of some rather strange things you've been told by one of his patients."

Ripley showed a touch of temper. "Mrs. Vale is no longer a patient. In any case, it's not Dr. Devane's feelings I'm thinking about. It's Mother's well-being."

"And I too, John," the Archbishop rushed to assure him. "By all means, let us keep Mother Constancia's well-being paramount. Now

what effect might it have on her to be taken out of care so precipitously
—against her doctor's wishes? You know how unwilling she was to go
to Santa Barbara in the first place. I finally had to order her there for
her own good. If she leaves, she won't be any more willing to go
elsewhere. And I confess, I would have no idea where to send her. Now
I think we all agree she's in need of care."

"Yes, but the right kind of care."

"And where is she to find that? You have someone else in mind?"

"No. Not immediately. But I am convinced that she needs to be kept
close to her work at *Casa Libertad*. The work gives her strength."

The Archbishop studied Ripley for a long moment. Ripley, looking
back steadily, reflected how perfectly the man suited the title "a Prince
of the Church." There was aristocracy in his every gesture, in the
graceful arch of his brow, the velvet calm of his voice. With one long
finger, he was lazily circling the rim of his sherry glass, sending out a
faint musical shimmer. After a long interval, McCaffrey rose and
walked slowly to a window, adjusted the blind, and gazed out across
the city. He spoke in measured tones, without turning to look at Ripley.
"John, I ask you to weigh your own motivations in this matter. I realize
how eager you are to resume your work at *Casa Libertad*. From the
outset, you resisted having Mother sent away for rest because it would
interfere with that work. Now you want her to return to Los Angeles,
even though she shows no sign of improvement. Are you quite sure
you aren't being selfish about this? Suppose Mother were to return and
suffer a nervous collapse. Are you willing to be responsible for that?"

"Of course not."

"Nor am I." McCaffrey allowed a long silence to settle. "You know,
John, these problems you are so involved with—these political issues—
they do have to be kept in perspective, especially by those of us in the
Church. There has always been injustice in the world. There always
will be. You are exaggerating the Church's power to alter that tragic
fact. Even if we were to let Mother Constancia return to her work and
burn herself out, how much good would it do? For all we can say,
Mother's efforts have only made things worse for the very people she
wishes to help. Please take this possibility seriously. Consider the
cruelty of raising expectations that can never be fulfilled—and which
may only serve to undermine delicate structures of authority that safe-
guard these poor people from far worse than they have ever suffered.
They are, after all, such very simple people, these unfortunate peasants
she speaks for. Many of them are not even fully converted to our faith.

Are they ready to be entrusted with the freedom Mother means to give them? Would they really be 'free'? For how long—before some new, utterly godless despotism was imposed upon them? These are great questions, John. Not easily answered."

The response that crowded into Ripley's head, crying out to be voiced, was far too much to be spoken now. A lifetime of moral anguish welled up within him, the worst of it spelled out in the blood he could all too vividly imagine spread across a young woman's body, the body of Cristina, whom he had held and loved. What could this elegantly corrupted prelate understand of a politics so personal that it belonged as much to the love of the flesh as to the love of an ideal? Ripley settled for "As I think you know, Archbishop, we have very different views on these matters."

"I realize that," McCaffrey answered, turning from the window. "I don't ask you to agree with me—except in one small respect. Patience. Let us have enough patience to see Mother rested and healed. Surely we can take the time necessary for that. Meanwhile, perhaps if I had a word with Dr. Devane . . ."

"How long are you thinking of keeping Mother in retreat?"

"I'm prepared to leave that wholly in her physician's hands, as I believe you should. If it should require some months more, can we afford to take less time?"

"Months! It's September now. I don't believe she expected her treatment to last beyond the summer."

McCaffrey, pacing the room, gave an indulgent laugh. "Mother is as impetuous as you are. And quite capable of martyring herself. Fortunately for her health, I don't share that impetuosity. I don't expect to see the world saved by the week after next, least of all by the sort of revolutionary violence to which Mother has been willing to lend her tolerance. I know that sounds complacent to you. But our faith teaches that the poor must always be with us. We are not permitted to expect the fulfillment of all our hopes in this life."

Barely concealing his contempt, Ripley replied, "We are also not permitted to despair."

"True. But realistic expectation is as far from despair as from pride. It simply accepts the fact of human imperfection. It is the enemy's snare to make us forget that the kingdom we serve is not of *this* world."

The Archbishop's tones were as silky and disarming as ever. But one word touched a nerve. "The enemy?" Ripley asked.

"There *is* an enemy, John."

"Oh yes. I know that. I only wondered whom *you* had in mind."

"No doubt on that, too, we would disagree."

Ripley fixed him with a severe gaze. "Is it your conclusion that Mother is on 'the enemy's' side?"

McCaffrey returned to his chair and sank down deep in its cushions. "That would be a harsh thing to say. Most unkind and bound to be misunderstood. Mother is an extraordinary woman. I respect her sincerity. I might question her judgment—she is, after all, only a nun . . . and not all that well-trained—but I would never doubt her sincerity. Of course, clarity of judgment is essential to moral virtue. Sincerity by itself is capable of great error."

"You speak as if you were ready to see Constancia's work suspended indefinitely."

"No, I don't say that. No no. But for as long as she is mentally unbalanced . . ."

"Unbalanced!"

"How else would you describe her condition? These dreams are obviously . . ."

"These dreams are being forced upon her—somehow."

"Ah, but we don't *know* that, John. We have only Mrs. Vale's word for that. Do you think I can hold that against Dr. Devane's authority?"

A long while back in the conversation, Ripley knew he had reached a dead end. His journey to Los Angeles was futile; McCaffrey was not going to give Mother Constancia permission to leave the Clinic. But he was trying to satisfy himself about the Archbishop's motives. He wanted something to bring back to Constancia, some expression of hostility, a hint of betrayal that would undermine McCaffrey's authority in her eyes. He needed that because he saw no alternative now to outright defiance. That would be no problem for him. Even now, as he sat in the Archbishop's presence, he knew his service in the priesthood was over. There was no Church that could hold both himself and McCaffrey. But Mother Constancia would not lightly break the promise she had given. For another half hour, Ripley probed tactfully, but all he could elicit were subtle nuances of McCaffrey's profound disdain for all that Constancia represented. There was nothing clearly stated. The Archbishop's politics hid behind a façade of tone and gesture. His capacity for deception was absolutely masterful and absolutely deadly. There was no hope of making him say that he numbered Constancia among the enemies of the Church. Nevertheless, as he rose to leave,

Ripley had no doubt who Constancia's enemies were. And he feared she was in their hands.

*   *   *

After Ripley departed, McCaffrey sat for a long, quiet time over his sherry. His features remained composed—an impassive and regal mask. But behind it, he was pondering how deeply he loathed Ripley. The man was no proper priest; he did not even wear the garb of his vocation. He dressed like a hoodlum. Denim. Ridiculous work shoes. His hair and his beard were scruffy. He let the dirt accumulate under his fingernails. There was no dignity to his appearance, nor to his bearing in life. How long had it been since he had performed the Mass? Did he even believe in the office of the priesthood any longer?

For years now, the Archbishop had observed the activities of these rabble-rousers who called themselves nuns and priests. He had been forced by the permissiveness of the times to stand by and watch while they more and more boldly proclaimed their presence in the Church, endorsing every trendy cause of the day, borrowing the cheap rhetoric of secular ideologues. How they disgusted him. Wherever their influence made itself felt, they were turning the Church into a mere organ of Marxist propaganda. Before him on his desk lay files he had been sent on Ripley and on Constancia's other followers. What he had read there filled him with abhorrence. It drew an unmistakable picture of clergy who had violated every oath of their calling. They trampled on chastity. They preached rebellion. They took up arms in battle against lawful authority. Ripley himself was known to have served in the ranks of guerrilla insurgents. He had taken one of their women as his lover. He was a killer, proud to have killed.

Bad enough when these perversions were hidden from view in faraway jungles. But now the fanatics themselves were suddenly quartered in his diocese, seeking to rally people to this ignorant old nun, exploiting her charismatic image, presuming to call her a saint. Ripley had asked him if he believed Constancia was on the enemy's side. Nothing so dramatic. Who was she to "take sides"? She was the enemy's mindless tool, a puppet of rags and straw. There were reports that she could not even clearly distinguish her own faith from the heathen superstition that still permeated her backward homeland. Yet several times now, since she had come to America, he had had to lower himself to dispute with her over her activities. Each time, she—a mere nun!—had presumed to question his judgment, had bridled at his orders. There was no womanly subservience in her. Therefore, let Devane do what he could to discredit her. If she were fortunate, she might learn humility from the experience and save herself yet. If not, if there were no other way, then let her be brought down pitilessly. And let it happen *soon*.

At the corner of his desk, the light on his telephone flashed. He picked it up. His secretary's voice said, "Your call to Washington, Your Excellency."

"Thank you," he answered, waiting for the connection.

Another voice came on the line. "Hello, James?"

"Yes, hello," McCaffrey said.

"So good to hear from you, James. Before we begin, do you remember how to use the little toy?"

"Yes, I think so," McCaffrey answered. He reached across the desk to switch on the scrambler that had recently been attached to his phone.

Now he and Shawsing would be able to talk in private.

22

Drinking time had started earlier than usual for Devane. He had a great deal to nerve himself for in the next few hours and he knew the insulating numbness he was after would not begin to set in until he was on the far side of his fourth double Scotch. Over the years, the state of alcoholic calm he needed to punctuate the end of each day had become more elusive: it took longer and longer to get there, sometimes the better part of an evening. The sooner he started embalming his metabolism, the better.

The words still echoed in his head from that afternoon. Himself standing up to Costello, declaring he was finished, ready to resign. If only he could simply stop his brain long enough—no second thoughts, no doubts—he could make that decision stick. That was what tonight was for.

It would cost him dearly to break with Head Office. He would lose the Clinic and—with it—most of his professional standing. He would have to leave his most important research behind. It would amount to giving up a life's work. But he had to view the matter squarely. He had already paid more than he could afford for his reputation. His marriage . . . that had gone years ago—and not painlessly. He had had to nurse his troubled wife through years of alcoholism and through more than one attempted suicide. He had never known the professional freedom to publish, to converse and exchange with peers. His self-respect—he had surrendered that when he had given in to Costello's demand for what his superiors cutely called "applied research." He had morally bankrupted himself to create the Clinic. And the exquisite irony was: the Clinic had never really been his. It bore his name, but it belonged to Costello and to Shawsing—and beyond them to a remote intelligence agency whose members remained as faceless and nameless to him as the day he became their servant. The Clinic was their facility, their weapon. In it, he was little more than a hired technician.

His failure was no one's fault but his own. Somewhere along the line
—no, at the very *beginning* of the line—he had agreed to play by their
rules, always consoling himself that he could shelter his science in a
separate compartment, pure and principled. It had been a Faustian
bargain and he had been a fool to make it. But now they were the fools
for having snatched away his last fragile shred of scientific respectability: Deirdre, the one watcher whom he had insisted on keeping wholly
under his own influence. She was still in the early stages of her development. She lacked the precision and manipulative skill of Moray. She
might never have the objectivity Devane had achieved with other
watchers. But she had an extraordinary power, one that held great
promise. Above all, she had the instincts of a healer. She cared with
great sensitivity for her patients and, where their needs were involved,
she was capable of remarkable courage. As long as Deirdre was his—
exclusively—he had the hope or the illusion of reaching the world with
original research.

But now he saw. They would take her too, use her, blunt her talents
as they had all the others. Demanding her help with Mother Constancia
was only the first concession. It would not end there. It would go on
and on, until both Deirdre and himself were depleted. For years,
Devane had felt like a man trapped in a swamp, sinking deeper and
deeper in the slime. Though she did not know it, Deirdre had become
the one thing left that kept his head above the muck. Around her, his
last energies of assertion and rebellion gathered. It was not only that
she was a gifted watcher; she had become someone special to Devane
in her own right as a person, as a woman. Perhaps he loved her—if for
no other reason than that she so genuinely saw him as the savior and
the mentor he wanted to be. Her naïve admiration, her dependence
made her dear to him. If Deirdre became what Moray had become—a
moral monstrosity—he would go under once and for all.

He had only one way to prevent that from happening. He must tell
her the truth—everything, no matter what the result. Costello had
threatened to let Deirdre know about her husband's death. That was
how he had coerced Devane's assistance with Constancia. But Devane
had the same threat to wield. He could also let the truth be known.
Deirdre might then be lost to him, but she would certainly be lost to
Costello as well. She would never become an instrument for Head
Office.

It was past nine o'clock when Deirdre arrived at Devane's home. He
had invited her to meet him there, away from the Clinic. He led her at

once into his study. The room, she noticed, was uncomfortably close; acrid wisps of smoke hung in the still air. Despite the warmth of the evening, Devane had started a fire, a smudgy little blaze that was fighting to stay alive beneath a charring mound of papers that looked like files, notebooks, manuscripts. Devane, moving to the fireplace, took a moment to poke the flames to a healthy roar. In his mind, he had scripted a conversation, the sort of talk he was used to having with Deirdre. He would lead her from point to point, winning as much of her sympathy as possible, displaying his fatherly concern and authority so that his actions appeared in the best light. But no sooner had he turned from the fire than she surprised him by speaking first—and not timidly. "I want to know about the man in Constancia's dream," she said.

That was not where Devane had planned to begin. He intended to review his career at a leisurely pace, describing how he had become involved with men like Costello, how his best ideals had been betrayed and his trust abused. "We'll talk about that in due course," he answered stiltedly. He tried to summon up his usual paternalistic tone, gentle but intimidating, but the liquor was in the way, making him insecure. Perhaps he needed a bit more. "You've been put through a great strain, something you weren't ready for. I want to . . ."

"*Now*, Aaron," she said. "I want to know *now*." It was not a request, it was a demand. It caught Devane off guard. There was something discordant in her manner, an unfamiliar self-possession. "There are other watchers, aren't there? Like me. Not children, but fully developed. The man in Constancia's dreams is a watcher. He was in Peter's dreams. You must know who he is. Tell me."

He was jarred by her aggressiveness. He preferred to have her vulnerable, in need of domination. He wished now his head were clear, not fogged with drink. He must not say the wrong thing. But what was the *right* thing? He struggled to remember the conversation he had planned. One more drink would steady him. He went for it.

"Deirdre, I do want to explain all this to you. It's time for that, I agree. But you must let me tell you in my own way. You see, I want you to . . ."

"Tell me about the man in the dream. You know who he is. I know you do."

"Yes!" He shouted the answer, as if that might silence her. Father bawling out his little girl. Then, relenting, he repeated softly, "Yes."

"Who is he?"

"His name is Richard Moray. You're right. He's a watcher, like you. An extremely talented watcher. Talented and ruthless."

"Is he here—at the Clinic?"

"No no. Not any longer. I haven't had anything to do with him—not for a long while."

"Where is he?"

"I don't keep track of his movements. The last I heard—La Jolla. At a government facility there. Naval intelligence . . . something like that."

"But he was once here? He was one of your watchers? He did things for you, the way I do?"

"No, not the way you do. He's a very different kind of watcher. I discovered him several years ago. He was only a boy, an orphan. One of the autistic children. Unusually gifted. Intelligence of a genius. He responded marvelously to treatment. He became the best watcher I ever trained. He was eager and quite daring, willing to try things, risky things. And once I drew him out of his autism, he was clever beyond his years. My star pupil. Better than you, Deirdre. Better even than you. More resilient, more objective. Tougher. He developed astonishing manipulative powers. Anything—he could do anything with people's dreams."

"But Peter didn't know this man. How could he control Peter's dreams?"

"Oh, Peter knew him. You didn't, but Peter did. Just well enough to get things started. They met at Peter's club. He was working there—in the gym. Handing out towels, as I recall. All quite casual. But enough to establish rapport."

"But how could he have been at Peter's club if he worked here, with you?"

"That was arranged. These things are always arranged. The chance meeting, the casual conversation. A cocktail party, a golf date. Often it's done on a plane trip. Oh, that's the easiest part of it all, getting the watcher and the target together."

"Target?"

"Peter was the target. We call them 'targets,' not victims. Sounds more sporting, I suppose. Moray and Peter met several times. The rapport developed quickly. Moray's good at that. He can be very charming—if he wants to be. Often he works with a book. A trick I showed him. He passes a book or a magazine with something in it that's likely to stick in the mind of the target. Something arousing or sensational that's apt to show up in dreams. It helps get the same images going in both minds. He passed a book or magazine to Peter, I believe. Something homosexual. Bait. Peter took it."

Deirdre recalled magazines and picture books. Salacious trash that had to do with bodybuilding. She had come across several examples in Peter's closet soon after the dreams began. They had surprised her. When she had asked about it, he gave her an ugly reply about "snooping." Later there were more books and magazines that he did not bother to hide.

"What happened to him—to Moray? Where is he now?"

"He went bad. I sent him away."

"Bad?"

Devane crossed the room for another drink. It would not steady him. He knew that. But it would let the talk come easier. It would lubricate the path, letting the unlovely truth slide out. On his way back to the chair, he paused to poke the smoldering fire and to cast another handful of papers upon it. Deirdre was beginning to find the heat oppressive, but Devane did not seem to notice. He was saying, "There were things he did as a watcher that weren't good for him. Things that made him sick."

"You mean the sort of things that he experienced with Peter? The black dreams?"

"Yes. Acute Compulsive Somnipathy. It's an ugly psychic condition. Ugly, unnatural. And contaminating. Like radioactive material. Watchers who spend too much time with it become warped. They burn out. Most of them break down hopelessly. Eventually, that will happen to Moray. He's stronger than the others. Amazing willpower. He keeps going. But he's become pathologically brutal, morbid. A destroyer— harder and harder to control."

Deirdre thought she understood. Her eyes filled with reproach. "You let him become contaminated with the black dreams, doing your research—on Peter and others. Was it that important for you—to know about this disease? Was it worth doing that to him? That's so selfish."

It took him a moment to realize. She had gotten things the wrong way around. How marvelously innocent she was! Devane was almost tempted to seize upon her misunderstanding and wrap himself in it. But there was no point in that. She was bound to see the truth. As if he were opening his own veins, he corrected her mistake. "No no, you don't have it yet. The somnipathy isn't there to begin with; it doesn't just come into existence like some neurotic state. It has to be *created*.

Watchers like Moray infect people with it. They *make* it happen. They *use* it. Your husband had black dreams, as you call them, because Moray *made* him have black dreams. There was nothing wrong with Peter, not until Moray got hold of him."

She stared back, still more baffled than horrified. "But why would he do that?"

Now he was at the edge, the annihilating boundary. Answering that question for her, especially for *her,* would take him across a line he had never wanted to cross. He pushed the words out through his teeth. *"Because that's what we do here.* That's why this Clinic exists. Oh, we do a little good for the world around the edges. The sort of thing you and I have been doing with our patients—that's good. But it's just window dressing. The Clinic wasn't built for that. It was built to perfect black dreams."

Learning that, Deirdre knew less than ever. She could not even think of the question she wanted to ask. Devane, tossing down another drink, yielding to the liberating spin of the alcohol, answered what she had not asked. Obliquely—but clearly enough—he told her about Head Office and why it had established the Clinic. He told her how his dreamwatchers had been used and what had happened to their various targets. Listening to himself, he seemed to hear another person speaking. Not the Aaron Devane who had once been young and brilliant and inspired. Instead, he heard someone old, besotten, brimming with self-pity, a voice that had only one sad, obscene story to tell.

And finally he told her about Peter.

"It wasn't even that important with Peter. A matter of money. Secret funding for . . . something, I forget what. Probably I never knew. But it was small potatoes. They often used brokers or bankers for such operations—new men, junior partners usually. Somebody who could shuffle accounts around without too much visibility. The trouble was: your Peter turned out to be a difficult target. Because of you. If you hadn't turned up, we might have gotten through the assignment quite neatly, with minimal damage. Peter might have recovered; he might even have been clever enough to cover up the embezzlement. Maybe. I don't know. But *you* became a problem. You nearly stopped things cold. I wanted to abandon the operation there and then. Believe me, I did. But I was overruled. And Moray . . . Moray was getting beyond my control. He was determined to prove himself. That meant over-powering you. He has this hostility for women, you see. And you were thwarting him—very effectively. It was something quite new. Two watchers pitted against one another. Moray took it as a challenge. He refused to be called off. The way he turned Peter against you—that was his own idea—his and Costello's. They wanted Peter to kill you. Everything Peter did in his black dreams was because of Moray."

"And because of *you*," she said. She was shaken, but clearly focused now on the meaning of his words.

"Not the violence. Not the killing. That had nothing to do with me. I didn't want to see Peter destroyed . . . or your children."

"But you said there were others. Other 'targets'—you allowed them to be driven to murder, suicide, the way Peter was."

"I . . . I went along. I didn't want it. I allowed it."

"You *caused* it."

He was floundering now, out of his moral depth. For the first time, she detected a pleading whine in his voice. "These were political matters. None of my business. I was told it was necessary. National security. What do I know about that? It was what I had to do to keep the Clinic operating. My only interest was . . . science." His voice slid from the word like the hand of a man clinging for his life, losing his grip on a rotted ledge, falling.

A hundred questions about Peter crowded into Deirdre's mind. She swept them aside in behalf of something more urgent. "Mother Constancia—why is she here?"

"She's a target."

"Why?"

"Also a political matter. Something about her activities in Guatemala. Land reform, human rights . . . I don't know about these things. They want to cripple her psychologically—if possible, discredit her. They want her stopped."

"They?"

"People. People who disapprove of her work. I don't know who. I never ask questions about that. Head Office takes care of the politics. Somewhere higher up there are people who don't like troublesome nuns. Not just political people. What's his name . . . the Archbishop. He's in on it. That's why he forced her to come here. He wants her stopped."

"Constancia's dreams—they're like Peter's dreams? Moray makes them happen?"

"Yes. But he hasn't made much progress with Constancia. She's unique. The usual things—violence, sexual perversion, repressed aggression—they don't work with her. Moray couldn't get the necessary state of somnipathy started. He needed help."

"From you."

"From me. And from you."

"*Me?*"

"That's what we've been trying to find, you and I. Something Moray can use. A soft spot. A weakness. Fear, shame, guilt. A magic bullet, just for Constancia."

Her face went white as if he had slapped her. "My God, you've told them what I've found out about Constancia?"

"No, nothing about the caves or the spiders. And I won't. Believe me, I won't. I've broken with them. I'm finished. They can have the Clinic. No more watchers, no more dirty work." He made his way to his desk, as if he were negotiating the deck of a ship in a rugged sea. Awkwardly, he filled both hands with papers. Notebooks, loose-leaf binders, file folders. He trudged to the dying fire and began to feed what he held into the flames. "My private files. Go back years. To the beginning. Things I've never told them. About finding watchers, training them. Things about Moray, about you. Costello doesn't know any of this exists. Secret. Now he'll never know. You see? Ashes. All ashes."

He returned to the desk where a small heap of materials remained, some notebooks and a small stack of tape cassettes. "Mother Constancia . . . these are the things we don't want them to know about her. Take them. Take them all. Make sure they don't . . ." He gestured vaguely toward the desk, then dropped like a dead weight into his chair. By now his thoughts were like flotsam bobbing away over the fogbound ocean, scattering, losing coherence. He was achingly tired. He sagged down into a chair. "Oh, Deirdre, Deirdre. I wanted so much . . . Leave here. Take Constancia with you. Go away. Hide. If you stay, they'll use you the way they use Moray."

"I'll never do that."

"No, of course not. But they'll try. They have ways. They might try to make use of Laney."

The words jarred her. "Laney? How?"

"I don't know. Somehow—to strike at you, to force you . . ."

"They wouldn't." But she sensed the feebleness of what she said. These were the people who had killed her husband and her children.

"You see," Devane was explaining, his voice growing more slurred by the moment, "there's just you and Moray now. All the others . . . burned out, unreliable. Costello was so greedy he used them up. And I wouldn't train any others. Just pretended. Dragging my feet. Me too, unreliable. They're sick to death of me. If they had their way . . . but they always have their way—in the end." He was somewhere so consolingly close to oblivion he could reach out and take hold of it like a soft blanket. But from across the room, he could feel her eyes burning into him, a steady, hating gaze. For a long while—many minutes—they said nothing. He knew these quiet spells she fell into, long concentrated intervals of searching silence, the habit her years of dreamwatching had left with her. But this was different. This silence was hostile. It was a weapon, as keen as a razor slicing into him. He could not endure these eyes, but he knew of no way to shield himself. He had no right to fend her off. Unspeaking, he let her take him in for what he was, the crumbling façade of a man she had once admired. Finally, he said, "Tell Ripley to get Constancia away from here. You go too. You can save Constancia. Guard her, the way you guarded Peter. Just a little longer. Moray won't be able to break her—not in time. Not soon enough. They'll lose, lose . . ."

"In time for what?" Deirdre asked, but he gave no answer. He had slipped away, wrapped in a last comforting thought: Costello losing, because of him. Gently, he let his mind go dim.

Still gazing at him, she let the silence thicken in the room. Her feelings for him were a whirling confusion, more than she could sort through and understand. There was rage, even hatred. But underlying these, still stubbornly surviving, there was some thread of the bond that had held her to him as a patient, the bond he had used to draw her back from isolation and madness. What was she to think of a man who had shattered her life and then saved it, someone she had clung to when there was no one else?

In the fireplace behind the desk, the flames were choking under the load Devane had dumped upon them. With a deliberation born of numbness, she went to the fire and stirred it back to life, focusing all her attention on that one mindless task until the last scrap of Devane's papers had turned to black, curled cinders.

His work, his science becoming nothing. She was purging the world of the evil he had brought into it.

When the fire died away, the only sound in the quiet room was Devane's turgid breathing. For a long while she studied him where he sat in his stupor, imprinting this loathsome image of him on her memory. This, she realized, was the worst revenge she could have upon him: to carry away this picture of the dissolute and pathetic creature he really was, someone too contemptible to merit pity, too weak to be worth hating.

It was nearly an hour later before she left, satisfied that she was finished with Aaron Devane.

23

It was past midnight when Ripley returned from Los Angeles. On the drive back, he had sifted through every word of his talk with McCaffrey. There was no doubt in his mind that the Archbishop, if he had his way, would close *Casa Libertad*. McCaffrey's political conservatism was well-known in the Church and came as no surprise. He had been frank in stating his points of disagreement with Ripley; still, in all he had said, there was nothing that cast doubt on his honest concern for Constancia's health. The questions he had raised were reasonable enough. In fact, the way he had reacted to the idea of dreamwatching—patiently curious, but politely incredulous—nearly shook Ripley's own conviction in what Deirdre had told him. Was there the chance that he was being taken in by some form of psychotic cunning, believing her because he wanted to believe? Or because she had used some powerful sexual bait to draw him in?

He found Deirdre waiting for him in his room. She was poised on the edge of his bed, wound up tense as a spring. "They killed Peter. Jonathan . . . Julia . . . they killed them." She had been holding the words back for hours, until he returned. Once they were spoken, the rest came like a flood, everything she had learned from Devane. And with it, the tears, the horror, the physical revulsion of taking a truth so vile into her life.

Ripley held her, comforted her, all the while burning with questions he had to have answered before the night was over. It took the better part of an hour for him to reconstruct Deirdre's conversation with Devane from her scrambled recollection. There were scores of things that needed to be explained, but in the torrent of Deirdre's words, he seized on the one scrap of information that mattered most just now.

"You're sure he said McCaffrey was part of the plan?"

"Yes."

"Tell me exactly what he said. I've got to be able to convince Mother of this. She won't leave otherwise."

"It's here," Deirdre said, drawing out one of Devane's notebooks. "What's this?"

"His notebooks. He told me to take them. He said they mustn't get hold of them." Deirdre could not have explained who "they" were—beyond Costello. But Ripley seemed to need no clarification. He began leafing through the books at once. What he found there might as well have been in cipher. Devane's notes written in a crabbed, choppy script, the references crudely abbreviated and telescoped into a kind of personal shorthand. Without Deirdre's help, Ripley could have made nothing of what he found in the notebooks. She pointed out the passages for him, explaining, " 'C' is for Constancia. 'RC' must be for Robert Costello. Remember? You met him at the sherry party. He's important here, though I don't know exactly why. I don't know who 'AS' is. 'McC' must be . . ."

"McCaffrey." Ripley read where she showed him.

> July 2: Met with AS, RC, McC. Discussed time factor for C. McC says C can be kept at Clinic indefinitely. Under orders, will obey. AS says C must break by mid-Sept. NP is mid-October latest. Stressed that the priest will slow us down, must find way to remove him from sessions.

"I'm the priest," Ripley commented. "But who's 'NP'? And what happens in October?" He asked, but she could not answer.

> July 3: Met with RC and McC re: C. Stressed need for more intimate details on C. Family, childhood, school? Traumas, anxieties? McC is no help. Only talks Church politics. Sees C as backward peasant and communist. C has no personal reality for him—only a political symbol. Contempt and hatred. Too biased. Smug SOB. Let RC deal with him. Birds of a feather.

That was all Ripley needed. By the time dawn arrived, with Deirdre's help, he had prevailed upon Mother Constancia to leave the Clinic with him. "This place is a trap. McCaffrey sent you here to be driven mad. He knows what they're up to."

Constancia accepted what he told her without resistance, without a hint of surprise. But the sorrow in her face was worse to see than shock. She did not inspect Devane's notebooks when Ripley offered to show them to her. She did not question his judgment in the matter. Constancia had encountered many opponents like McCaffrey in the Church. She understood the politics of the situation. She also knew that breaking her promise now and leaving the Clinic would provoke a showdown with McCaffrey and possibly with greater authorities in the Church. It was a decisive step. More than merely leaving, it was defying.

Before the sun was up, Ripley and the nuns had loaded their van to leave. Deirdre and Laney would come with them, bringing a few hastily packed suitcases. They rushed with their preparations, hoping to leave unseen. But nobody stopped them when their activities were noticed. "We have Dr. Devane's permission to leave—if we need that," Ripley answered abruptly when one of the clinicians asked what was happening. The ease of their departure puzzled him. As he pulled away from the Clinic and started down the long, crooked road into Santa Barbara, he remarked with a note of elation, "We made it. No one interfered. We're lucky."

Deirdre, beside him in the front seat, knew better. She knew there was no need to stop them. When the mind dreams, distance means nothing. It did not matter how far they drove, Constancia would never be beyond Moray's reach.

*   *   *

Deirdre was free—and she was lost.

For nearly two years, the Clinic had been her entire life, a castle on a hilltop where Devane's protective presence was always close and wholly hers to draw upon. Within the haven of his expert care, she had begun to piece together a new life out of the ruins of personal tragedy. She had recovered her sanity; she had found a purpose in living.

Now, abruptly, all this was gone. Nothing she had believed about Devane or the Clinic survived. She found herself with new people in a new place. The drive from Santa Barbara had taken only two hours, but she seemed to have traveled across whole continents. At *Casa Libertad*, deep within the *Latino* section of east Los Angeles, the language and the culture were strange to her. She was surrounded by nuns and priests who practiced a Catholicism she did not remotely recognize. The issues they debated so passionately among themselves and with the people of the surrounding community meant nothing to her. Deirdre was not a political person; she had not come to *Casa Libertad* to serve the causes to which these people devoted their lives. She had only come to escape, to hide.

Most troubling of all, she could not explain to Laney why they had come away from the Clinic in such desperate haste. The lies and evasions she invented were a poor disguise for her own fear. But there was no way to explain to Laney the danger they had fled. She was not ready to hear about the dreamwatchers or about Devane's treachery. When Deirdre's sister Meg came to take Laney off her hands, she welcomed being free of her daughter's questions—if only for a little while. But for how long, before they would be back together? Weeks? Months? She could not say.

Ripley had become the one fixed point in her life. She told herself she was here because this was his place, the only home he could offer her. She needed to be with him. Perhaps the love that had sprung up between them would draw her into his work. She knew he wanted that, but she made no promises. *Casa Libertad* was permeated by a steamy ethical intensity and a sacrificial air that filled her with unease. People demanded too much of themselves and of one another. Deirdre was not ready for that. Knowing as much, Ripley tried to shield her from the political militancy of the House, but she could not avoid feeling intimidated by her own lack of involvement. It did not really help that he and Sister Charlotte went out of their way to make her seem special. That only led people to mistake her for a doctor or a therapist, somebody vaguely connected with Constancia's recent illness. When it became clear this was not exactly the case, she was left with only one other claim to importance: she kept close company with Ripley. As she quickly discovered, this did not always guarantee her a friendly reception. *Casa Libertad* was a heatedly intimate little community; everybody knew about everybody. It was no secret that Deirdre was sharing Ripley's apartment, that she was somehow connected with his break with the Church. He had returned with Deirdre as his lover, unwilling any longer to be called "Father." That sudden transformation disturbed some of his coworkers. A few of the sisters clearly resented the change and held Deirdre responsible for luring him from his vocation.

But not Constancia. She had known for years how fragile Ripley's tie to the priesthood was. In part, that was why she had made him her confessor; she hoped it would bind him to her and, through her, to his faith. But now, knowing what she did about Archbishop McCaffrey, she understood his decision. She feared her own days in the Church might be numbered. How much longer would she be able to accept the authority of those who believed she was in league with the devil?

* * *

There was one remnant of her life at the Clinic that Deirdre would not surrender. Devane's notebooks. Their fascination grew with each new reading. Not because of what she found recorded there about Mother Constancia, but because of what they revealed about Devane. Hidden in their pages were cryptic references to a man she had only begun to know the last time they had met. Someone vulnerable, devious, cowardly. Reading in the light of what she now knew about Devane, she could detect his fear of Costello, his unbecoming intimidation by the mysterious agency he called "Head Office." Next to the entry that noted what she had found out about Mother Constancia's fear of spiders, she found the words:

> Top secret. Hold this back from RC. Avoid him. Stall. No confrontations.

Then, farther along:

> Nasty session with RC. Threatening and abusive. Suspects deception. Must not anger. Pretend ignorance.

Gradually, she came to see that it was a measure of her newly found strength that she could open herself to this jarring image of Devane as a squeamish tool in the hands of more powerful forces. A year ago, perhaps as recently as a month ago, she could not have permitted herself to admit his weakness. She had needed somebody to protect and anchor her. She had turned to Devane for that—a father, a defender, a champion. Even more significantly, she realized that Devane —knowing he was none of these—had nevertheless allowed her to make him a figure of superhuman strength and wisdom. He needed her admiration and dependence as much as she had needed his support. This also came through to her as she studied the notebooks: the crucial part she had unwittingly come to play in his moral struggles. She read:

> D's loyalty paramount now. Must keep her trust. How? What happens if I tell her all?

And again:

> Must not lose D! Confront RC on this. Stand firm. No concessions.

Punctuating another passage:

> No more lies. Tell D now. Face what comes. Possible to
> win her back afterward? No future without her.

It was unmistakably clear; she had become Devane's rebellious conscience, his better self fighting to survive. Not wanting to betray and
lose her, he had begun to take courage, had finally asserted himself
against Costello. She had never imagined herself cast in such a role. It
was flattering and deeply gratifying to see herself assuming that stature
in Devane's life.

There was more. The notebooks revealed honest amazement at
Deirdre's powers. They recorded greater praise than Devane had ever
offered her in the course of their relationship. Where their sessions
with Constancia began, he had noted:

> D more perceptive than ever. C is drawing out D's best
> powers of insight. Remarkable rapport between the two
> women. C regards her as a gifted healer. Must agree.

Later, where she began to tell him of Constancia's trance visions:

> Major breakthrough! First direct observation of high-
> dreaming. D's reports are of ideal precision. Astonishing
> clarity. Her range seems limitless.

She thrilled to read the words. But when she brought them to
Ripley's attention, he was curtly dismissive. Not of her, but of Devane.
He would allow himself to take no interest in Devane's judgments or in
his moral anguish. His contempt for the man was total and unyielding.
In his eyes, Devane stood condemned beyond forgiveness, one of the
enemy. His concern was limited to what the notebooks might have to
say that would help protect Constancia. "I don't understand their
urgency in wanting to strike at Mother," he said many times. "Why
now? Unless they're out to derail the Christmas Mobilization."

It was all he could think of and it did not really make sense. The
mobilization was an important event, but it was nothing unique. Constancia had organized a score of similar efforts in behalf of human
rights since coming to the United States. This one looked to be no
more effective. Not once did the Peace Prize cross his mind as an
explanation for Devane's attack on Constancia's sanity. He had heard
the same rumors others had picked up about the Nobel award. He
understood there was a faction on the committee that had made a

serious attempt to nominate Constancia the previous year. He had no reason to believe they would be any more successful in the near future.

There was one more theme in Devane's notes that drew Deirdre's attention. It began obscurely with an entry that seemed to date back to the middle of the summer. It read:

> Last night—RM? Check for this. Careful of the liquor. It distorts.

At first, the words meant nothing to her. But then, in the notes for a few days farther along, she came upon:

> Dream of lecture at Menninger Clinic. Unruly audience. Much disruption. Hostile questions. Dim light—could not see lecture notes. Much fumbling, anxiety, embarrassment. Sensed RM in audience? How? Must be more alert.

She could not remember that Constancia had reported any dream like this. It only dawned upon her as she read further that this and other unfamiliar passages she came across referred to Devane's own dreams. They were little scribbled messages to himself, often paralleling his notes on Constancia. Once she grasped this, the final pages of the notebooks assumed a frightening pattern.

> RM in dreams? Have RC check this. Must be stopped. Insist!
> Last night—RM again. Could not wake. Why?
> RC pretends ignorance about RM. Lying. What are they after?
> Dream of D. Making love. Unfamiliar location. RM watching. Could not defend. Extreme anxiety.

And then the last entry of all:

> Certain now—RM is watching. *Must stop!*

"RM." Richard Moray. He had broken through Devane's defenses, had found a way to enter and watch. The phrases were terse, but in them Deirdre could feel the force of Devane's fear. He had become a target. Was that why he had wanted her to take the notebooks away? They were his cry for help.

24

Devane was third in line now, moving steadily forward. In a few more minutes, he would have his ticket and be on his way. He glanced around nervously. He knew he was being followed, but the airport was thronging with people. He felt certain nobody could see him in this crowd. The line shuffled forward; he reached down to inch his heavy suitcase along the floor. He wished now he had not packed so much. The suitcase would barely move.

"You're going to have to pay extra for that," a voice said. It was the man behind him in line. He was tall, wearing a cowboy hat. He looked like someone Devane should know. A movie star. That was it. Someone he had seen many times. But what was his name?

"Yes, I suppose so," Devane said apologetically, tugging at the suitcase. "But, you see, this is my life's work. I have to bring it with me."

The airport was growing oppressively muggy. It had a glass ceiling; the sun beat down fiercely through it. In the sky overhead, he saw airplanes drifting past, carrying people to distant places, to safety.

"Next!" the attendant at the ticket counter called out. Devane stepped forward, laboriously dragging the leaden suitcase after him. It was scratching the shiny tile floor, making a hideously loud noise. People were staring disapprovingly.

"Look what he's doing to the floor," the man in the cowboy hat said. He flicked his jacket open and revealed a large tin star. "If I was a real sheriff, I'd arrest you for that."

Now Devane recognized him. Gary Cooper. But how could it be Gary Cooper? With an embarrassed laugh, Devane said, "I'm sorry, I thought you were dead."

"You must be thinking of my stand-in," Gary Cooper answered. The people in line broke out in raucous laughter.

Devane, struggling with the suitcase, said, "This would be easier if you'd help me."

Winking cutely, Gary Cooper said, "That's not in the script." Again a roar of laughter went up. Everybody in the airport seemed to enjoy the joke. Except Devane. On his own, he could not get the suitcase nearly close enough to the counter. Not wishing to lose his chance to buy a ticket, he placed one foot on the suitcase and stretched himself awkwardly across the floor, until one hand just barely touched the base of the counter. "Will this do?" he called up to the ticket agent, who was craning over to see him. "Can I buy a ticket from here? It's the best I can manage."

The agent came around and squatted down beside him where he lay. He looked dubiously at the enormous suitcase. "Have you considered leaving it behind?" he asked.

"It's my life's work," Devane explained.

"If you leave it behind, you'll be able to travel free."

"I will? I didn't know that."

"People who leave their luggage behind are always allowed to travel free—unless they are fleeing from the scene of a crime."

"Well, I'm certainly not doing that. I'm a doctor, after all."

"Even doctors can be criminals," the man said haughtily. "Some of the worst criminals in history have been doctors. Jack the Ripper, for example."

Devane had never heard that Jack the Ripper was a doctor, but he thought it best not to argue the point. Studying his troublesome suitcase, he said, "Perhaps I could just take the best parts with me and leave behind the things I'm ashamed of."

"Then you'd wind up throwing most of it away," the agent remarked with a smug grin.

"Yes, that's true," Devane admitted. "But I'm sure I could find a few items to keep."

"Sorry, there's no time for that," the man said, suddenly tugging at Devane's arm. "Your plane is departing now. Hurry!"

The next thing he knew, Devane was following the ticket agent up a flight of stairs toward a departure gate. The man ushered him through a door and suddenly he was inside a plushly appointed airplane. It seemed to be as vast as a hotel lobby. There were several elevators that ran up and out of sight. A stewardess came forward to meet him. She was tall and lovely, wearing no clothes except for a tiny peaked cap and high-heeled shoes. Her breasts were extraordinarily large and shaped into hard-pointed cones like machine-tooled objects.

"Doctor Devane?" she asked, smiling. "I have your seat right here."

She led him down a broad central aisle. Following her, Devane admired her well-shaped body. When he reached his seat, he continued to study her. He said, "It's perfectly all right for me to look at you like this. I'm a doctor."

"It's what I expect," she said. "You may examine me whenever you wish. Just press this button right here."

"Of course," he admitted, "I'm really a psychiatrist."

The stewardess smiled more broadly, making dimples in her cheeks. "A woman is even more naked in the eyes of her psychiatrist."

Devane took his seat. The plane was now airborne, floating silently across the sky. He was on his way. He felt exuberant. He leaned to speak to the man next to him. "I don't even know where this plane is going. Do you?"

"It's an escape plane," the man answered. "It uses all available routes."

"What are you escaping from?" Devane asked in a whisper.

"The scene of the crime." The man did not seem at all apologetic.

"Did they make you pay for your ticket?"

"I paid twelve million dollars."

Sagely Devane said, "It can be worth that much to escape."

"It was all the money I could raise," the man said. "I had to sell everything I owned." He bent forward and began to sob quietly into his cupped hands.

The stewardess was back. Very businesslike, she settled herself in Devane's lap and offered him her ample breasts, hefting one in each hand, her oversized nipples thrusting between spread fingers.

"Is this an examination?" Devane asked, jokingly.

"No. This is snack."

He placed his mouth greedily against her left breast and began to suck. To his delight, he tasted milk, sweet and warm. *How does she make milk?* he wondered. *She looks too young to be a mother. Probably it's artificial.* Taking his mouth from her nipple, he turned to the man next to him, who was still sobbing. "You can have her when I'm finished," he said consolingly. "I'll save her other breast for you."

"There's enough for everyone," the young woman said. "Otherwise the company wouldn't hire us."

After a long, comforting feed, Devane, satisfied, passed the girl to the other man. He felt refreshed and exhilarated. "It was worth leaving my life's work behind," he decided.

But the other man, he saw, did not choose to feed at the stewardess's breasts. He had stretched her across Devane's lap and had buried his face between her thighs. The stewardess lay back, languid and acquiescing, gazing up at Devane. Her eyes fluttered. Pleasure showed in her face.

"I didn't know we were allowed to do that," Devane said. He looked enviously at the man who was mouthing the stewardess hungrily. Her pubic hair formed a beard around his cheeks.

"Oh yes," she said. "It's even encouraged. It's much more nourishing for long trips."

"If I had known, I would have done the same thing. But you didn't tell me." He let her know he was hurt.

She looked deeply concerned. "I'm so very sorry. Please don't report me. I'll make it up to you." She reached to unzip his trousers. Then, arching gracefully backward, she took his erected penis in her mouth, smiling all the while.

Devane sat back luxuriously, enjoying her attentions. It was an excellent flight. There was only one problem. There was a disturbing draft at his back. It made him feel vulnerable—as if he were being watched. Cautiously, he turned to look up the aisle behind him. What he saw was astounding. The plane had no rear end. The fuselage broke off just behind the seat. Beyond, there was open sky rushing by, tearing objects out of the plane with a shattering roar.

Devane turned back to the stewardess. His penis was now buried deep between her lips, completely out of sight. He labored to extricate himself, but the suction of her clinging mouth was too great. "The plane has no tail," he told her urgently. "You have to let me go. We're in great danger."

Still smiling dreamily, she released him. "You should report any defect in the equipment to the captain."

"Why don't you?" he asked, fighting down his panic.

"I can't until all the passengers are fed."

Devane noticed that the man next to him was still gorging between her sprawled legs, paying no attention to the danger. *Ridiculous,* he thought. He struggled out of his seat and began to make his way up the aisle to the pilot's cabin. All at once, his body became terrifically inert and slow. The open end of the plane was like a vacuum drawing at him. It was all he could do to keep himself from slipping backward and falling out into empty space. The door of the cockpit seemed to be miles away, but someone had opened it and was looking through, beckoning. It was Alex Shawsing, calling to him down the length of the plane. "Hurry, Aaron. If you can make it in time, I'll put you in touch with the President. He'll know what to do."

Devane clawed his way up the aisle. In each seat along the way, there was a stewardess in a contorted sexual position with people feeding on her body. *They're too busy to care,* Devane said to himself. *They don't realize that we're in danger.*

Then he was at the cockpit door. Shawsing pulled him through and helped him into a seat. Embarrassed, Devane realized he had lost his clothes on the way. They had been sucked out the rear of the plane. *But that doesn't matter now,* he thought. "We're going to crash," he announced to the pilot. "The plane has no tail. It's completely open."

"That's serious," the pilot said. "I can feel the plane going down."

"What can we do?" Devane asked, suddenly growing extremely frightened.

"We need secrets," Shawsing said. "This plane runs on secrets. It belongs to the Secret Service. If we feed enough classified information into the computer, we'll stay in the air."

"He's right," the pilot affirmed. "The computer is almost empty."

Devane studied the pilot. *I know him,* he thought. *If he weren't wearing those glasses, I'd recognize him.*

"Did you enjoy your snack?" the pilot asked, smirking. The question distracted Devane's train of thought. He suddenly remembered the stewardess.

"Yes, very much," he said.

"The service was satisfactory?"

"Perfect."

"Then you should give us some secrets to run on. It's only fair."

"Yes, a psychiatrist knows lots of secrets," Shawsing insisted.

"But it would violate my medical ethics to tell them," Devane explained.

"Then we'll crash!" the pilot shouted. His voice thundered. Devane could feel the plane plummeting down, the wind screeching at the windows.

"Since you're already naked, you may as well tell us your secrets," Shawsing commented.

He's right about that, Devane thought. "But what about you? You know lots of secrets. Spies know more secrets than psychiatrists."

"Sorry," Shawsing answered. "I've used all my secrets up. That's how we got as far as Guatemala."

"I see. Well, what secret shall I tell you?"

"Something you can tell us quickly." The pilot, fighting to keep the plane under control, sounded urgent. "We don't have much time left."

"Like what?" Devane asked.

"Like—what is Mother Constancia afraid of?"

"That's a good choice," Devane said. "Spiders. See how quickly I told you that?"

At once the plane began to level off.

"Excellent!" Shawsing cried. "You saved us."

"But why is she afraid of spiders?" the pilot asked.

"That's all in my notes," Devane answered.

"But you gave your notes away," Shawsing reminded him.

"That's right. Deirdre has them."

"You'll have to tell us, then."

"But Deirdre's escaping too. She must be on the plane. You can ask her."

"She's one of the stewardesses," Shawsing said. "She's busy now. Snacktime."

"Oh yes. That's right." Devane was scrutinizing the pilot again, trying to find a name.

"Don't you wish Deirdre had been your stewardess?" the pilot asked, once more distracting his attention.

"Yes, very much."

"That can be arranged," the pilot said. "Look here."

Deirdre entered the cockpit, smiling and unclothed like the other stewardesses. Her body was magnificent, as Devane always imagined it in his dreams. She eased herself into Devane's lap. He was pleased to see her. In the deep cleft of her chest, a tiny phrase was tattooed. He looked close. It read: PERSONAL ANGEL.

"Tell them about the spiders," she said, holding his cheek against her breasts.

"Do you think it's all right?" he asked.

"Otherwise we'll crash."

"Will you feed me if I tell them?"

"Of course." She was already bending backward against the control panel to make herself generously available.

"It's really very simple," Devane said. "Constancia believes there is an evil sorcerer who takes the form of a spider. Spiders are associated for her with the devil. It's all quite superstitious."

"That's brilliant!" Shawsing cheered. "What a secret! We could fly all the way to the moon on a secret like that."

Devane felt proud. He had saved the airplane. Everybody would escape. He deserved his reward. He lowered his head to feed on Deirdre. She received his mouth gratefully.

25

"That's the third time we've come up with spiders," Costello observed. "Sound reliable to you?"

Across the room, the young man with the cast in his right eye reflected with bitterness on the dream he had just reported. "He wants her because she's a woman. Only for that. Bitch!"

"Don't let that bother you," Costello said.

"I want her *dead*," Moray announced. The judgment was quiet and cold.

"The first order of business is to make sure about Constancia," Costello emphasized. "Do you feel confident about the spiders? Can we go with that?"

"Yes," Moray snapped. "I don't understand about the sorcerer, but I'm sure about the spiders."

"Devane never mentioned that," Costello mused. "He was holding out. There's no possibility he's deceiving you?"

"I could tell if he was. He isn't. He's wide open."

"We're keeping him heavily dosed on Thorazine. Feeding him the stuff around the clock in all his food. Do you think there's any chance that's distorting his dreams?"

"He's like all the others," Moray said contemptuously. "Just as easy to fool. Show him a piece of ass and his brain stops working. He's a pushover." He sniffed in disgust. "I used to think he was God, you know that? I used to think he was so great."

"Richard, were you ever in Devane's dreams before these last few months?" Costello asked.

"Sure. At the beginning, when I was a kid. That's how he drew me out. In his dreams. He starts with all the watchers that way. But after that—strictly forbidden. Forbidden! Who was *he* to forbid? The rule was: no watchers in doctor's dreams. Because doctor would be displeased."

"How would he know if you were watching his dreams?"

"He knew. He was very sensitive. He trained himself to be. No matter how careful you were, he could tell you were there and he'd wake up. Right away. Next day, he'd give you hell. He'd threaten to send you away forever. Son of a bitch!"

"But that's not happening now? He's not waking up now when you watch? You can tell: he has no idea you're there?"

"I told you—he's as easy as all the others. A pushover."

"It must be the Thorazine. Also, he's drinking a lot. We're encouraging that. He can't be too alert."

"His mind is heavy."

"What do you mean?"

"Heavy. Coarse. Burned-out. He's not even trying to resist. He's ready for it—anything I want to do. He saw me and he didn't even recognize me."

"Saw you?" Costello flashed.

"I was the pilot," Moray giggled. "He looked right at me, the stupid shit."

"I told you not to run any risks."

"It was no risk. He's nothing special. He's *nothing*. I could give him any dream I wanted. I could rub his nose in it."

"You're sure of that?"

"Any dream."

"All right, then. That's good. Now, what about Mrs. Vale . . . ?"

"Cunt!"

"Will she have any trouble entering his dreams? Assuming we can entice her into trying?"

"She won't have any trouble. Not if he's like this."

"Or even more heavily sedated?"

"She won't have any trouble. A beginner could get into a head like that. He's wide open. Unless, of course, she's afraid of disobeying doctor."

"We'll make sure she isn't. We'll use some pretty strong bait."

Moray's face lit up with a hungry glow. "I'm gonna love scaring the shit out of her. Scare her to death."

"You'll have your chance. Be ready. It could be tomorrow night."

"I'm ready. Don't worry about me," Moray snapped. He rose impatiently to leave Costello's office.

"Where are you off to?" Costello tried to make the question sound casually curious.

"Why ask? You always have me followed. You think I don't know that?"

Moray was right. Costello had become steadily more concerned about his movements. Moray was restless and footloose. He wandered. Long walks. Long drives. In La Jolla, he had been known to drop out of sight across the Mexican border for two or three days at a time. Twice he wound up arrested, most recently in Tijuana for starting a fight in a brothel. He had gotten rough with one of the hookers, took a razor to her, and produced a minor riot. After that, Costello had arranged to keep him under surveillance whenever he went out. Since he had come to Santa Barbara to monitor Devane's dreams, he was spending much of his time in the local porno film theaters, with occasional visits to a few whorehouses in the area.

"I'd like you to stay close," Costello said placatingly.

"This town is worse than La Jolla," Moray complained. "It's a mortuary. Boring. I get bored."

"You can get the cablevision where you are, can't you?"

The day he arrived in Santa Barbara, Moray had thrown a tantrum when he discovered that the hotel where Costello had reserved his room did not take the local X-rated cable channel. He was becoming a prima donna. Costello had him moved to another hotel.

"Big deal!" Moray sneered. "What they stick on the TV is kid's stuff. Boring."

"Things will get more interesting around here. That's why you should try to get some rest. We have a few long, hard nights ahead of us."

"Ahead of *me,* you mean," Moray corrected. "I do the shitwork, right? All you do is take notes and give orders, Costello. Well, don't worry about me. I'm ready. I won't screw up. I told you: Devane is nothing. Zero. And what's this girlfriend of his? An amateur. I'll mangle her. And her kid."

"Not the kid. Understand?"

Moray waited before he answered. If Costello could have read the pause, he would have learned that Moray's interest was with Deirdre, not Constancia. Constancia was part of Costello's politics, but Deirdre was a personal grudge. Moray could not help thinking of Laney as a way of punishing the woman who had replaced him in Devane's affections.

"Did you hear me?" Costello asked.

"Yeah, I heard."

"I don't want to tip our hand about the daughter. I just want her prepared. She's our backup. If this move doesn't work, we may have to use the kid against the mother."

"She's prepared."

"You gave her the book?"

"Yeah."

"Which one? Nothing hard-core, I hope. In case the mother comes across it."

"Spook stuff," Moray answered. "It'll scare the pants off her." He laughed as he opened the door. "I even autographed it for her," he boasted.

Costello glared at him. Moray's bravado was becoming a major problem.

"Don't worry, Mr. Costello. Just initials."

Costello was used to giving orders and having them obeyed. When he wasn't obeyed, he was used to punishing—surely and swiftly. None of that worked with Moray. Moray enjoyed defiance, knowing there was no way Costello could bully him. The power Costello needed was locked inside his watcher's head. It could only be tapped if Moray permitted it. Costello had no choice but to pamper him and to indulge his sick wishes. Devane had been right: Moray's mind was cracking along a hundred hairline fissures; he was becoming more difficult to control by the day. He had always been erratic; now, since Devane had turned from him, a bitter fury had seeped into his character. He liked to pick fights; worst of all, he began to improvise on his instructions, pushing farther, taking risks. All the more so now because Moray's personal feelings had gotten tangled up in the assignment. He was driven by a hot grudge against Devane, by wild jealousy of Deirdre. That worried Costello, but he judged he could ride things out. Moray had become an expert destroyer. And just now, destruction was all Costello wanted of him.

26

"Aaron certainly wouldn't approve of my coming here, but I felt I had to do something. He's in rotten shape. I thought you could help us understand why."

Deirdre had always liked Dr. Lichtman. He was a gentle, high-spirited little man, boyishly good-looking, with wide blue eyes and an easy smile. His New York accent was thick enough to be comic. Next to Devane, he was the staff member she had worked with most at the Clinic. He supervised the autistic children. She admired his way with them, kind and infinitely patient.

"Has Aaron been sleeping well?" Deirdre asked.

"No, he hasn't, as a matter of fact," Lichtman answered. "He's been fighting it, taking uppers on the sly. If anything, he needs sedation."

"Bad dreams?"

"Yeah. He won't talk about them, but they keep him restless through the night. Why do you ask?"

She shuddered inwardly at the answer, but only said, "I'm sure he needs all the rest he can get."

Lichtman had arrived toward the middle of Deirdre's second week at *Casa Libertad*. He did not call ahead; he simply appeared one afternoon at the door and asked to see her. He brought word that Devane had suffered a nervous breakdown. It had happened a day or so after her departure. Lichtman wondered if the collapse had anything to do with Mother Constancia's treatment.

"Frankly, it left us all in a spin—the way you took off. So hasty and mysterious. We thought there might have been some unpleasant incident. A misunderstanding . . . ?"

Ripley insisted on sitting in while Deirdre talked to Lichtman. He answered for her. "Mother Constancia's treatment at the Clinic was concluded. Dr. Devane decided she was free to leave. She keeps a busy schedule. We had to get away quickly."

"I see," Lichtman said. "I hope the treatment was successful."

"She's better—now."

"I'm pleased to hear that. She was a distinguished guest for us. Glad we could help. Aaron gave us no explanation for her departure. In fact, we heard nothing at all from him—not until two days after you left. When we did, well . . . he was in a very bad way. I don't know if you ever realized it, Deirdre, but Aaron has a drinking problem. It's been getting worse over the last few years—but nothing as bad as this. It's never kept him from his work. Anyway, when you and the others left, that seems to have launched him on one hell of a binge. It was Bob Costello who found him—at his home, really smashed. We dried him out, but then he just fell apart right before our eyes. It's tragic to see that happen. A man of his stature. We had no idea things had gone that far. We're all stymied about what to do. As for the Clinic, it's at a standstill. After all, he's the captain of the ship."

"How did you know Deirdre would be here?" Ripley asked.

The question puzzled Lichtman. "Well, where else would she be? She left with you. We knew she was helping with Mother Constancia's treatment. I simply assumed . . ." He smiled and shrugged.

"You're sure it wasn't Devane's idea for you to come here?"

"Just now, Father Ripley, Aaron isn't having very many ideas. Mostly we're keeping him tranquilized to the point of stupor. He certainly didn't send me here—if that's what you mean. It was my idea to look you up, Deirdre. Mainly because . . . well . . . you seem to be what's on his mind. When he talks, mostly he talks about you. You and Laney. He seems anxious about your well-being. He wants to make some provision for you now that you've left the Clinic."

"Provision?" Deirdre could not follow his meaning.

"Money, I guess. A job maybe. Something for you to live on. And medical care—if you need it. He rambles a good deal, but he keeps coming back to you and Laney. How grateful he is to you, how concerned he is for your future. He wants to make sure you're looked after. I thought maybe this was something you and he had worked out between yourselves. Anyway, there's such a strong attachment. It made me wonder if his breakdown was somehow connected with you. Was there an argument? Something like that?"

Lichtman was the only other person at the Clinic with whom Deirdre had been permitted to discuss the dreamwatching research. Under Devane's direction, they were collaborating in trying to develop watchers among the autistic children. He was also aware—though she had no idea in how much detail—of her monitoring activities with Devane's patients. But what did he know about the black dreams? Perhaps as little as she had known before Devane told her. She hoped that was so. She would have liked to believe in Lichtman's innocence. In any case, she dare not raise the point with him. That made it difficult for her to explain anything about her last days at the Clinic. She settled for saying, "No, there was no argument. We simply decided that I should leave the Clinic. He wanted me to. He thought it was time."

"But so abruptly?" Lichtman asked, persisting. He made it clear he knew she was holding a good deal back. "I don't have to tell you, Deirdre, how important you had become to Aaron. He was building some pretty ambitious plans around you—and around your talents." He dropped his voice rather too obviously as he made this reference to her watching—as if he should make some effort to keep Ripley from hearing. "I don't think this was a wholly professional matter with Aaron either. If you don't mind my saying so, I believe there were some very strong personal feelings involved in his plans for you. Aaron could put up a cold-blooded front, but, in your case, I think there was a lot of genuine care."

Deirdre, backing away under Lichtman's pressure, tried to cut things short. "I don't know how I can be of any help."

"She's not going back to the Clinic," Ripley announced sharply. The remark was touched with vehemence. It caught Lichtman off-balance. His eyes went back and forth between Ripley and Deirdre, showing hurt bewilderment at their response.

"I think there may be undercurrents here I don't quite grasp. Do understand: I'm not prying. Only trying to find something that might assist in Aaron's recovery. A man doesn't just collapse like this for no good reason. I mean Aaron's a strong-minded individual. There must have been something pretty jolting to bring this on. In any case, I assumed you'd want to know what happened."

"Yes, thank you," Deirdre said. "I'm glad you came."

Awkwardly, Lichtman prepared to leave, making his dissatisfaction with the meeting tactfully apparent. "If you think of anything that might help us, do get in touch with me."

On their way to the door, Lichtman managed to lead Deirdre to one side. "Incidentally, Aaron's secretary seems to be missing some material from the files. Some tapes and notes regarding Mother Constancia. Did Aaron mention anything about this to you?"

Deirdre was not good at lying. She mumbled a no that was barely convincing. Still out of Ripley's hearing, Lichtman said, "Aaron needs you, Deirdre. I think you owe him something. You just can't let things break off like this. Please—if there's any help you can offer . . . if it did nothing more than give the man one good night's sleep, that would mean a lot." He squeezed her hand and gave her a pleading smile.

When he was gone, Ripley said, "They're trying to get you back. You're not going. Promise me you won't think about leaving."

"No, I won't leave," she assured him. But she made the promise knowing that the mind is a phantom traveler, with its own ways of staying and leaving.

*　　　　　*　　　　　*

Before he started back for Santa Barbara, Lichtman stopped for a sandwich along the beach. As instructed, he placed a phone call to Costello.

"I wrung her heart all I could," he reported. "Yeah, I think it'll work. There's a lot of feeling there. She's a softy, believe me."

27

She lay beside Ripley in the night, darkly pondering a paradox only she could appreciate.

When they were little more than strangers, they had found in Ripley's dreams an intimacy closer than the flesh could mimic. Now, in waking life, they were lovers. She shared his bed; an hour earlier, their bodies had been braided skin to skin. But soon, though she lay close enough to count his every breath, her mind would journey vast star distances beyond his reach. Somewhere in the gulf of the night, Aaron Devane was silently calling for help, a broken man suffering a pathetic fate. She would hunt for the signal his dream sent out and, finding it, she would enter another universe where Ripley could never follow.

She clung close to him, burying her face in his shoulder. His nearness would be no help, but it nerved her for what the night might bring. ". . . love you," her lips said soundlessly, but already her voyaging mind was slipping from his world.

After Lichtman left, Ripley had thought it necessary to lecture her at great length. It was his bad, though sometimes comforting habit to be overbearing with her. He warned that she must not be taken in by the appeal Lichtman made to her. She owed Devane nothing. "Stay away from them," he had nearly ordered her. She heard him out, pretending compliance but thinking resentfully: *How naïve I must seem to him.* Did he think that the bitter experience of the Clinic had been lost on her? It hadn't. She had learned to ration her trust—even with Lichtman. Gentle, comic little man, so kind with children—she knew in her heart that he was a deceiver and traitor like all the others. She did not need the benefit of Ripley's cynical eye to see that Lichtman had been sent to tug on her conscience, to tempt her into Devane's dreams. He and Costello believed she could be manipulated like a child. They wanted to divert and sidetrack her, to preoccupy her with Devane's suffering. No doubt they thought if they could tax and fatigue her enough, she would not be able to guard Constancia. Well, she would accept their challenge—but not out of concern for Devane. There they had miscalculated badly.

It was not her loyalty to Devane—or what was left of it—that drew her toward his dreams. It was Moray she was after. She knew she would find him in Devane's dreams. Find him, punish him, defeat him.

She was ashamed—and furious—to think how she had allowed Moray to bully her when they had met in Constancia's dream. What contempt he must have for her! She had fled from him like a child running from a Halloween ghost. And yet, in the dream, he was a figure of air, a cerebral illusion, nothing more. He could try to scare or disgust, but he could do her no damage. She must let him know she would not turn and run again. If the only way she could do that was to seek him in Devane's dreams, then she would meet him there—and this time she would stand her ground.

In her years of watching, she had endured nightmares; she had stood up to Peter's black dreams, fought Moray and almost thwarted him, not even knowing who he was or what he intended. Why had Devane been so convinced that Moray was "better" than she was? It had stung her to hear him make that judgment. Moray was only a miserable, psychotic boy, playing cruel tricks. He acted from the same hurt and anger she had dealt with in all the autistic children she knew—sad little creatures. She was certain she could face the worst his twisted imagination could conceive—if she were ready for it. She was *good* at watching. She knew she was. It was her one proud achievement in life. She was the only watcher who had ever shown how the power could heal and save. She was not going to back down and surrender before an overgrown, mischievous child like Moray.

But there was more than this in her thoughts. One remark from her last meeting with Devane nagged at her relentlessly. Devane had hinted at the possibility of danger to Laney. Was there some chance Costello and Moray would strike at her daughter? Before that happened, she would let them know the strength of her will. She would never scare off again, never again let them harm someone she loved.

She had no difficulty homing in on Devane's dream. It swam up out of the darkness, a dirty, dancing blur of light that opened out and out into a vast, interstellar emptiness. She entered and at once felt the clammy atmosphere of a black dream swirling turgidly around and down into the void. Even for a black dream, the quality of light around her was unusually dense. She recognized from her work with patients at the Clinic the characteristic texture of drugged sleep, a mind muffled by tranquilizers, dimmed and slowed. Devane had been heavily dosed on sedatives. There was no resistance; she entered his mind like an open door . . .

. . . and found herself on a gigantic staircase, so broad that the edges to left and right could not be seen. She could feel the dream continuing to descend. The stairs were traveling massively downward, like an escalator running into a low tunnel. Ahead and behind, the staircase spiraled out of sight in the gloomy vacuum. The sense of lostness was oppressive, almost tangible.

There were people massed on the stairs, standing or seated in small groups. At the center of one of these, she sighted Devane. He sat dejectedly on the stairs, his features bloated and cheerless. His clothes were rumpled, he needed a shave. He was clinging for all he was worth to an enormous coffin-shaped suitcase beside him.

Deirdre at once looked around for Moray. She could not find him. She moved closer to Devane, not in the least fearful that he would see her. She could tell that his senses were clouded, his mind almost paralyzed. He looked drunk—like the last time she had seen him. Worse than that. Heavier, more dismal. The people around him were teasing: pointing, laughing. Helplessly, Devane was trying to defend himself. "I'm a very famous doctor," she heard him whine. "And this is my life's work." The suitcase he hugged close was now larger than himself, but he held it as if someone might steal it from him. His hands shook.

"They won't let you take that into Bedlam!" a fat, stupid-looking woman yelled at him. "They wouldn't let me take Saint Mary's Holy Book." Deirdre recognized her as one of the patients at the Clinic. Now she saw that many of the people were patients.

"I'm not going to Bedlam," Devane protested. "You can't put a psychiatrist in Bedlam. Psychiatrists are in charge of Bedlam."

The people laughed knowingly. The fat woman jeered, "When you get to the end of the line, everything is inside out."

"I'm on my way to win the Nobel Prize," Devane blurted out. "Mother Constancia is going to recommend me. She has great influence."

"This is the only flight there is," a mocking voice said, "and it goes to Bedlam. After that, it goes to hell. And after that, someplace worse." Deirdre recognized the voice. It was Moray. But she could not see him.

Devane, suddenly panicked, began to struggle up the stairs, dragging his ponderous suitcase after him. The task was impossible. He was barely able to lever his burden up one step before he collapsed, exhausted. The suitcase bumped down several stairs, dragging him behind it. All around him, the people stood, teasing cruelly. Their faces were full of wicked glee. Deirdre was close enough to hear Devane cry out with childish petulance, "It isn't fair. Every step I go up, the plane goes down a hundred."

Moray's voice cried out, *"Down* is the only direction there is. *Up* has been canceled forever." This time Deirdre caught sight of him, peering out at her from behind a small knot of spectators. She started to move toward him and at once the dream reshaped itself.

A vast hall formed on the great descending staircase. The steps became rows of seats rising steeply. An auditorium like a medical amphitheater. It was filled with formally dressed men, their faces stiff and severe. A spotlight searched for Devane like a skeletal finger, found him and fixed him where he lay, battered and weary, still clinging to his suitcase. Someone in the audience rose and spoke, a distinguished-looking man. "Dr. Devane, we've been waiting all day to view your life's work. How much longer do you intend to keep us here?"

Devane looked frantically around, as if he wished to escape. He struggled to elude the spotlight, but the suitcase anchored him where he stood. He was handcuffed to it.

"I'm not ready," Devane moaned. He was burning with shame at his shabby appearance. His clothes were torn and gaping everywhere. The seat of his pants was out.

"We're waiting, Dr. Devane," the man called. "Do you realize that we are traveling toward Bedlam at one hundred miles an hour? Will you please begin your presentation?"

Devane's misery was extreme. "I didn't know there was a presentation," he pleaded. "I didn't bring my notes. I don't have anything . . ." He squirmed with anguish while the audience booed and flung catcalls.

His humiliation was grinding Devane to pieces. Deirdre would have tried to disrupt the dream out of pity for him, but she had not come to save Devane. She was here to confront Moray. She searched the crowd and found him again, seated in the audience now, grinning down at her. She made her way toward him. Her resolution grew with each step. She was not going to be bluffed. He waited until she stood before him. "I'm not afraid of you," she said. "Do you hear me? You won't drive me off again. There's nothing you can do to hurt me."

His eyes were fixed on her, a savage grin frozen on his face. Her words seemed to have no effect. He was doing something behind the row of seats, just out of her view. She stepped closer and saw. He was masturbating while she spoke, his congested penis filling his hand. When she saw, he laughed and worked at himself more vigorously. He was testing her, she knew. He was trying to disgust her. It would not work. "You're just a nasty, sick little boy," she said quietly.

Moray answered by miming an exaggerated orgasm, panting and gurgling. He flicked his seed at her; it landed on her arm and throat—large, hot gobs. She did not even move to wipe them away.

"I know your tricks," she said, still very calm. "You won't make me go away. *You*—you're the one to leave. You can't have this dream. You can't have any dream I don't want you to have."

But by then, he had climaxed and sat, eyes closed, paying no attention. Very well, she would dissolve the dream. She turned to where Devane sat in a terrified stupor, staring at her and Moray. He had been watching their confrontation, becoming more miserable by the moment. She willed him to awaken, but the dream held; its fabric was tougher than she realized.

As if he had read her thoughts, Moray said, "He can't wake up. I don't want him to wake up. You have no power here, you ugly, ignorant cunt! Look!" He gestured toward Devane. Members of the audience were surrounding him, attacking. They had wrenched the suitcase from him and were prying up the top. Devane cried out as it opened. The case tipped and dozens, hundreds of small, round objects bounced out, rolled across the steps. They looked like tennis balls.

They weren't.

"Look!" Moray ordered her, as he picked one up and thrust it toward her. For a moment she could not take it in. Then she saw. It was a tiny, shriveled, human head. A shrunken head. Moray was dangling it by its hair like a grotesquely comic toy. Discolored and wizened as the face was, there was no mistaking its features. They were her own. Moray, laughing, lobbed it toward her. She dodged and it tumbled by her, scattering with all the others.

The staircase in all directions was now alive with heads. They rolled and careened everywhere. Wildly, Devane struggled to collect them and replace them in the suitcase. He scrambled this way and that, scooping them up by the armful, dropping most. His life's work.

The members of the audience stood on all sides, watching his futile efforts, jeering. They kicked the heads out of his reach. Devane, rushing on hands and knees among them, looked like a baggy-pants clown in a circus act. "Be careful, head shrinker!" Moray was shouting. "They bite."

At the words, Devane let out a wail. One of the heads had fastened on the flesh of his forearm. He fought to shake it loose, but its bite was deep. Alarmed, he turned and began to race away down the stairs. Moray took off after him, crying, "Too late, head shrinker. It's poison."

Deirdre watched after them, saw Devane trip and sprawl, bumping down the stairs into the darkness below. *Toward Bedlam,* she thought. *Toward hell. Toward worse.*

It was time to dispel the dream. She would do that and let Moray know he could not have his way. Where was he now? Somewhere below, pursuing Devane, hounding him. She followed Devane into the yawning depths of the dream, into the nothingness that made his terror, his humiliation meaningless. Then she was alongside him, keeping pace. Behind, at his heels, the heads were following like a pack of pursuing furies. His face was a horror. He was wild with fear, plunging forward, fighting for breath, not finding it. If only she could break through his frenzy and calm him. Instead, his headlong descent was dragging her farther down. She reached to take hold of him. As she did so, he turned to her.

The dream stopped. Froze.

His face, locked in an expression of amazement, began to smear across the dirty light. His image was shredding like tissue paper stirred in water. Nothingness showed through him. And then she was alone in a darkness that was not the darkness of sleep, but an abyss that sucked and consumed.

She was in the mouth of something about to swallow.

* * *

Moray was awake. He looked up to see Costello hovering over him, his face eager.

"She's in the dream?" Costello shot the question to Moray as soon as his eyes flickered open.

"Yeah. She's there," Moray answered. "Do it now. She's with him. *Now!*"

Costello moved swiftly to the bed where Devane lay in fitful sleep. He reached down to the hypodermic syringe that lay taped to Devane's forearm and pressed the plunger. The needle jabbed, just at the place where, in his dream, Devane felt the shrunken head bite and hold fast.

The yellow fluid in the syringe vanished into Devane's arm. There was a small shudder as his lungs fought for breath. Then surrender.

*   *   *

The dream was over. She should have been awake, back in her bed, beside Ripley. Her body was there. And when her mind was like this—cleared of dreams—it should be with her body. It wasn't. Instead, her mind floated, wrapped in darkness, a darkness she had never experienced. It seemed alive and voracious. It was folding upon itself, constantly inward. Folding and folding. And as it folded, she was being squeezed down. The sense was not that of falling. She could not fall. She was held solid. She was contracting under pressure of the dark. The lightlessness all about her was not that of light shut out, but of a place where light had never been, could never be. Darkness congealed, made solid, thrusting the light away, allowing no motion. She had come to a place of absolute stillness.

This was not the space of dreams. There was nothing here of illusion or false imagery. This place was *real.* She was fully wakeful within it, her attention keen. She was somewhere beyond the place where dreams happened. Where dreams stopped, where unconsciousness ended, this place began. The mind could wake up here, no longer a part of the world where the body lived.

And she was not alone.

There was a living presence here. She could recognize it as surely as if it had a face upon it. Devane. Clinging to her. A fierce embrace, needy and despotic. Devane's mind held her with the grip of a drowning man clutching a timber in rolling seas.

Beyond Devane—others, silently there. There were many minds here. She sensed them as a blind person might sense objects in a room, not seeing them, but feeling at a distance how they filled the emptiness. Minds were near her, surrounding her. Numberless, but all sounding to a single pitch, a single feeling.

Sorrow.

She was intensely aware of sorrow. A grief so fathomless that its cause could not be imagined. The sorrow hurt. It hurt more than she could bear. And she knew it would never stop hurting.

Never.

*   *   *

At the moment Aaron Devane died, Deirdre's sleeping body went rigid in a hard spasm. A choked moan rattled in her throat. Ripley, disturbed, woke and turned to take her in his arms. He felt her stiffen against him, then go wholly slack.

"Deirdre?" he whispered.

He turned her toward him, calling her name over and over, finally shaking her. She gave no response. Her flesh, naked against his own, was cool and moist. He could not hear her breathing. Frantically, he reached to switch on the light, then looked back.

She lay beside him, as lifeless as a figure shaped of wax.

28

"It seemed worth a try," Costello explained. "Two birds with one stone."

"But what gave you the idea?" Shawsing asked. He had arrived at the Clinic the evening before to lay plans for its transition to new hands. Costello had arranged a working breakfast in his office, but so far only the coffee had been delivered.

"Arthur Goldschmidt. You don't recognize the name?" Shawsing didn't. "No, that would have been before you joined us. Well, he holds a landmark position in the brief history of dreamwatching. He was the first. Devane's original discovery. The son of a Korean War vet Devane was working with at Bethesda. He might have become one of our best instruments. Young, but very promising. Devane brought him out of autism, trained him carefully. When he was ready, Home Office put him to work right away. He did extremely well with several targets, Devane's first major assignments. Then we put him on a Soviet military attaché. Unfortunately, this time we pushed things a little too hard. We concocted a course of nightmares for the Russian that succeeded in scaring the man to death—literally. Apparently, he had a weak heart. These days that's something we'd check out before we got started. Trouble was: when the target died, poor Arty was still in the man's dreams. Do you follow me? The watcher got trapped in a dying mind."

"Which means . . . ?"

"God knows. But whatever it means, it doesn't mean coming back in one psychological piece. Maybe it's like falling into a black hole. The effect was devastating." Costello switched on his intercom. "Laura, we're ready for some food. What's holding things up?"

His secretary's voice came back. "Just arriving. I'll send it in."

"What happened to the watcher?" Shawsing asked.

"What happened to him *observably* was that he went into shock, then into a deep coma. Without intensive care, he would never have survived. There was one period of nearly forty-eight hours when he was registering as clinically dead. The doctors gave up on him. Devane didn't. Somehow he managed to resuscitate our man. Even so, he was on life-support systems for a full month afterward. Absolute vegetable."

The door opened and a mobile buffet was wheeled in by the brooding attendant Shawsing had seen several times before. In his usual stiff and unspeaking way, Smitty went about placing cups and dishes on Costello's desk. Inwardly, Shawsing gave a small shudder of disgust as he watched the man's robotlike movements, the blank face. "How do you interpret what happened?" he asked.

Costello settled back and gave a weighty sigh. "Ultimately, all this dreamwatching has some neurophysiological basis. Aaron and I used to disagree about that, of course. The Freudian versus the behaviorist and so on. But I'm sure that, eventually, we'll have the physical mechanics of it worked out. The watcher gains access to the dreamer's cortical centers—just like bugging a telephone. Two brains sharing the same circuitry. In this case, the target was stressed to the point of electrochemical overload while the watcher was integrated into the nervous system. The result was mutual burn-out. A total miscalculation on our part. It lost us a first-class instrument."

"The watcher died?"

"His brain died. Or at least the major cortical areas. We tested him extensively. Speech centers, coordination, logic, spatial perception—all cooked. But the autonomic functions survived."

"Did he come out of the coma?"

"In time. But he remained in a semicatatonic state for months. Devane worked on him like a Trojan. Understandably, he was attached to Arty—sentimentally. It was an absolute waste of time. Years of effort, but the man was never more than a half-wit. I suppose it was a mistake to put someone that young on such a heavyweight assignment in the first place. He was only about twenty years old at the time. Rather delicate boy. It was more than he could handle. That's one of the problems we haven't solved yet. Most of the watchers can only be drawn out of their autism by unlimited coddling and stroking. Our staff budget for professional TLC is sky-high."

"TLC?"

"Tender loving care. Endless amounts of it. But, of course, what we train them to do is a total change of pace. We want them to be real nasties. Sadists, perverts, killers. The reversal is a murderous strain.

Too many of them break." He glanced at Smitty, who stood gazing with unfocused eyes out the terrace windows. "Smitty," he called. Smitty did not respond. "Smitty," he snapped again. "What about the rolls? The rolls." Costello pointed. The man understood and rushed to offer him a plate of pastry, in his awkward haste dropping a sugary bun on the floor. "Well, pick it up!" Costello ordered, while he handed Shawsing the plate. Smitty hunkered down and busied himself picking every crumb off the carpet. Shawsing tried tactfully to mask his revulsion as the man began to crawl around the desk examining the floor.

"But this only happened once?" he asked. "How could you be certain things would go the same way with Mrs. Vale?"

"I couldn't. It was a gamble. But once Devane became dispensable, what was there to lose by trying? We had to liquidate the man anyway. Why not try to give Mrs. Vale a good scare at the same time? If it worked, we had her blocked out for good. If it didn't, well, we had a backup plan to neutralize her. The daughter. Moray had her prepared as a target, a sort of psychic hostage to keep Mrs. Vale out of our way. So we gave it a shot. When we knew she was in Devane's dream—and I mean well in, determined to take control—Moray simply pulled out and we put Devane under. One hundred milliequivalents of potassium chloride. Instant blackout."

"With what result for Mrs. Vale?"

"Complete success, so it would seem. She's been in Queen of Angels Hospital in a deep coma for the past two days. We've had her under surveillance since she left the Clinic. She moved in with the priest, incidentally; the theology of liberation makes convenient bedfellows. They were together the night Devane died—unfortunately for us. It may have been Ripley's efforts at resuscitation that kept her alive long enough for the ambulance to arrive. Even so, we understand the prognosis is not good."

"So that clears the decks, I gather. Do we proceed with Mother Constancia?"

"Why not? There'll be no obstacles now."

"You realize there's not much time. A few weeks at most."

"We won't try anything very subtle. We've got one button to push. We'll push it hard until something gives."

"The spiders, you mean?"

"The spiders."

"You're sure they'll do the job?"

"As sure as we ever are of anything about these assignments. We don't exactly know *why* spiders. But even a saint can have her accountable phobias. In this case, there seem to be strong religious overtones. The spiders figure in Constancia's fantasies as a diabolical symbol. Devane's dreams never came through clearly on that score, but we gather this is some part of the native lore in Constancia's region of Central America. Possibly she's carrying around a lot more of the old pagan superstitions than she'd care to admit. In any case, we intend to make the most of the phobia. Moray will get started on her tonight. No time to lose."

Shawsing finished his coffee and reached to pour more. "We'll need a successor for Devane."

"No rush. I can hold down the fort for the time being. I've made up a short list of candidates for Home Office to consider. Mainly senior staff from the Clinic." He handed Shawsing a stack of personnel files. "Lichtman would be a good choice, I think. Young, bright, cooperative. I've been clueing him in on our applied research over the past few months. Also, we'll need an obituary for Devane. You'll understand if I leave that in your hands. I'm sure you can do the great man more justice than I can."

Smitty, still on his hands and knees lint-picking the rug for crumbs, had begun to work his way between Shawsing's shoes. Shawsing, nodding toward the man, directed a pleading glance at Costello. "Please. May we . . . ?"

"All right, Smitty," Costello said, amused by Shawsing's annoyance. "That will do. That's very good. *Good.* You can go now."

Smitty rose, frowning with incomprehension.

"You can go," Costello repeated, gesturing toward the door. "Come back later for the dishes. Later. That's right. Good-bye, Smitty."

Costello waved him toward the door. Smitty, still clutching a mangled sugar bun, slouched away. At the door, he turned and held out the bready mess in his hand, a questioning look in his eyes.

"That's for you," Costello told him. "Go ahead. Eat."

Smitty studied the bun for a moment, then thrust it into his mouth, showering crumbs down his shirt. Chewing fiercely, he left the room.

"You know, Bob," Shawsing said when Smitty was gone, "I do think the Clinic could budget somewhat more competent coffee service. Must you continue with this occupational therapy?"

Costello grinned. "Sorry, I do intend to retire Smitty. He was Devane's pet. But I thought you might want to meet the man himself."

"The man himself?"

"Arthur Goldschmidt. Or what's left of him. Smitty to his friends."

"That . . . ?"

"Um-hm. Devane was rather proud of bringing him along far enough to sweep and clean and bring in the coffee. But that looks like his upper limit."

"Poor man."

"Yes, though actually a miraculous improvement, considering where he started. Aaron made a heroic effort to salvage the boy."

"As a matter of conscience, I suppose."

"Yes, but not wholly. The motivation was much more a matter of professional curiosity on Aaron's part. He thought Smitty might have an interesting story to tell."

"What story would that be?"

"Where his mind went—after his brain died."

29

Nothing about Deirdre's condition made sense. The doctors attending her could find no cause for her coma, no reason for the unfamiliar electrical vibrations with which her nearly quiescent brain was teasing their monitors.

"We would have concluded that she had suffered brain death as soon as we examined her," the physician in charge explained to Ripley and to Deirdre's sister Meg. "Except for the unusual ocular readings we picked up."

"Ocular readings?" Meg asked.

"Eye movements. Quite extraordinary. When people dream, their eyes move in a characteristic way—usually in short bursts for several seconds at a time. That's how we can tell they're dreaming. Mrs. Vale's eyes are registering constant movement. One of our technicians noticed that, quite by accident during the examination. We put sensors on her eyelids and, sure enough, there was movement. Not rapid movement, but a steady visual scanning. It's absolutely regular and it never stops. That's not what you'd expect in a coma. Then, just this afternoon, when we were checking further, we picked up auditory response readings. Very slight, but definitely there. Mrs. Vale is *hearing* something. Not from outside; we cut her off from all external stimuli. She's registering sound—a constant and steady stimulus."

"What does that mean?" Meg asked.

"Your sister is dreaming. That's unique for a patient in her condition. It means her brain isn't dead. She isn't comatose; she's in some exotic state of consciousness for which we frankly have no name."

"But Deirdre doesn't dream," Ripley said, not knowing how he would explain the remark. "Isn't that so?" he asked Meg, groping awkwardly.

Meg looked back warily. How much did this man know about her sister? Reluctant to confirm what he said, she went blank and gave a noncommittal shrug. "As far as I know, she has dreams. Doesn't everybody . . . ?"

"Well, she's certainly dreaming now," the doctor insisted. "Though, frankly, it's like no dream any of us have ever seen our equipment record. Somewhere in her coma, her brain is very much alive. But I don't think there's an expert anywhere who could tell you what she's experiencing."

*   *   *

Moray wasted no time. He struck the next night, as soon as he was certain that Deirdre would present no obstacle to him.

When she had returned to *Casa Libertad* from the Clinic, Constancia reverted to spending as much of each night in meditation as possible. Distrusting sleep more than ever, she ensconced herself in the fortresslike security of her trance. It was Deirdre who prevailed upon her to set her fears aside, promising to guard her sleep. But there seemed to be no need for the precaution. Constancia's nights passed without incident. She grew more confident about sleeping. She needed the rest. With her staff, she was in the midst of busy plans. The Christmas Mobilization was constantly in her thoughts. She frequently found its image in her sleep as well; it was there the night her ordeal began.

She dreamed she was kneeling on the steps of a large familiar building. The White House. Behind her, beyond the gates, she was aware of a vast throng of people gathered to support and cheer her on. She could hear their bustle and murmur like the surge of the sea. She concentrated her thoughts and prayed more fervently, one solitary figure pitted against the powers of the nation.

Then the front door of the White House swung open and a man emerged carrying a large American flag. It was the President. He strode up to Constancia, smiled, and spoke with resonant authority. "Your prayers have been answered," he proclaimed. "I shall do justice to your people."

From the crowd, a great shout went up. Orating to the people outside the gates, the President made a long speech that promised peace and plenty. Most of what he said flowed together into incomprehensible dream speech and was drowned in cheers. When he was finished, he turned and gave his hand to Constancia. With the utmost courtesy, he escorted her toward the door. She accepted his invitation graciously, suddenly feeling young and buoyant and victorious. She noticed too that the President looked very much younger than she would have expected. Younger and oddly familiar. When they were inside, he said, "Before we sit down to dinner, we must free all the political prisoners, don't you agree?"

Overwhelmed by her success, Constancia felt hot tears welling up in her eyes. She followed where he led. They entered a plushly upholstered elevator and began to descend. "I had this especially installed," the President explained. "It will take us directly to the dungeons."

He pointed proudly to the control panel. "*Yanqui* ingenuity," he boasted. The panel was a tiny map. All the Central American nations were there, each equipped with a button. If she looked closely, she could see each country, models of tiny cities, highways, villages, houses. There were even people—tiny people positioned on the map, going about their work. In her own country, she could make out her own village and see people she knew at work in the fields.

"That is the new Guatemala," the President said. "I hope you approve of our design. We will rebuild the country from the ground up. No expense will be spared."

The elevator seemed to be descending for hours. Soothing music filtered into the little air-conditioned cubicle. All the way down, the President apologized for the mistakes he had made. Constancia's heart warmed with gratitude. Finally, they reached the bottom. The air and the light were much heavier here, a viscous substance that clung to the skin. The door opened and Constancia saw a corridor lined with metal doors. It was lit with a harsh, acid-yellow neon glare and stretched away until it was out of sight.

"Shall we begin?" the President asked. And together they threw open door after door. From inside, wretched, emaciated prisoners emerged. Faces Constancia recognized. Old friends. Political allies. Coworkers she thought were dead. They embraced and gave thanks.

"Our prayers have been answered," Constancia announced. "You must thank the President."

Soon the narrow corridor was thronging with happy, chattering people. The space became close and musty. Above the clamor, the President called out, "The Pope has invited you all to dinner." A thunderous cheer went up.

But where was he leading them? Down farther, along a sloping tunnel. The light grew dimmer and heavier; the walls were rough, damp stone.

"Are you sure this is the way?" Constancia asked with some trepidation.

"Of course," the President replied. "His Holiness thought you would like to dine in your native habitat."

She did not understand his answer, but she continued to follow. Behind her, the heavy shuffle of the prisoners filled the crooked tunnel. She heard moans of complaint and distress. "I hope they will be patient," she said to herself. At last, they reached a cavernous grotto lit by hundreds of dripping candles. The air was thick and unpleasant, mixed bitterly with smoke. At the center of the space, there was a long table neatly set with glassware and china; at the far end sat the Pope on a high, glittering throne, wearing the triple tiara.

"Welcome," the Pope called out and gestured to the chair beside him at his right hand. Constancia approached reverently and kissed the ringed finger he held out to her. She was puzzled to see that the insignia on the ring was not a cross, but a skull and crossbones. She settled into the seat assigned to her; the President sat across from her. At once the table was besieged by the prisoners she had brought, now looking more vile than ever. Their faces were hollow with hunger, their eyes goggled idiotically. They fought to find chairs. "No need to fight, my children," said the Pope. "At the banquet of life, there is room for all." But there was no food in sight. Only dusty plates, cobwebbed cups. The prisoners gazed greedily along the table, waiting. Constancia tried to avoid their eyes.

"You look troubled, my child," the Pope said.

Timidly, Constancia confessed, "I do not like caves." She gestured about her toward the grotto that was growing closer and mustier all the time.

"Nonsense," the Pope said. "You must remember the Church began in the catacombs."

Yes, that is true, Constancia thought and was somewhat comforted. But the eager, thrusting presence of the prisoners still oppressed her. "They are very hungry," she said, appealing in their behalf.

"But first," the Pope insisted, "we must serve our guest of honor." He raised a covered silver serving dish from the table and held it out to Constancia. She felt guilty to be eating first, but the Pope urged her to do so. She thanked him, noticing as she did so that he too looked elusively familiar.

She lifted the cover. From underneath, a gleaming black gelatin slid suddenly out onto her plate and into her lap. It was not food. It was not food at all.

It was a compacted mass of spiders.

Freed from under the cover, they scattered in all directions, racing over the table, across her robe. Constancia went faint. She stumbled backward out of her chair, her mind blurring with terror. The spiders were on her. She flailed at them, wanting to scream for help. But the cry died in her throat. She looked pleadingly at the Pope and the President. They had changed. The Pope was not the Pope. He was Archbishop McCaffrey, his face frozen cold with contempt. And the President was not the President. He was Moray.

Help me, she tried to cry to her friends. But now she recognized no one in the cave. The crowd at the table was a sea of empty, imbecilic faces. They were swatting the spiders, catching them, eating them.

Constancia reeled away, looking for escape. Her robes were cruelly weighted with a cargo of spiders. She could feel them under her clothes, on her flesh. They were on her neck, her cheek. Not knowing where to run, she ran, lurching along a tunnel that led down and down. She was sick with panic, but still unable to scream. Far in the distance, she saw a dancing light. Was it the mouth of the cave? The light became a liquid tangle of colors, growing larger, then a burning whirlpool. At its center, darkly silhouetted, she saw the form of a woman.

It was Doña Rosaura, her arms widely outspread, in each hand a torch.

The swirling light coiled up from a stone bowl suspended above a small smudgy fire at her feet. She stood in the rainbow smoke, solid and impassive as a rock.

Constancia remembered. She remembered this image. It came from long, long ago. A memory that trembled with dread.

Forbidden.

Unclean.

"Save me, Tia Rosaura!" Constancia croaked, clinging to her aunt's skirt, hiding her eyes. It was coming back. The cave. The fire. And she was the little girl Ixta again, unwilling apprentice to the great *sabia* Rosaura.

"Stand up, sobrinita!" her aunt roared. She forced the child Ixta to her feet and placed the torches in her hands, then spun her around to look back down into the cave. Something moved there, coming forward. "Stand! Defy him!" her aunt commanded. Doña Rosaura, hovering vastly over her, began to chant. The old dialect. Words Constancia had not heard in more than half a century.

Says: I belong to the sisterhood of pure water.
Says: I am a woman of the flowing water.
Says: I am the woman who defends.
Says: I am the woman chosen of Kulkulcan.

The old words renewed themselves in Constancia's mouth. She joined in the chant, standing in the acrid smoke, breathing the colors of the fire, the drunken power of the Sainted Children.

"Blasphemy!" part of her cried out. These were unclean rites. Forbidden.

"Idolotria."

But she clung to the words in fear, for the words were power, the only power she possessed.

The cave before her was filled with a predatory black presence, moving forward. Shape of a man. He—it—advanced into the light of the leaping fire.

"Stand!" Doña Rosaura shouted.

Constancia remembered. Long ago. In the far recesses of the cave, she and Tia Rosaura together, gathering the spiders from the sweating walls, bringing them to the fire, burning them in the stone bowl.

"They are his allies," Tia Rosaura had taught her. *"Evil ones. Enemies."*

The burning spiders held close to her, their odor mixed with the fumes of the Sainted Children. Tia Rosaura had gripped her, refusing to let her hide her eyes. *"See them burn,"* she commanded.

She had seen. She was certain she could hear their tiny cries. Could hear them now, squealing.

He—it—was no more than inches away. A man's body, wrapped in a dark blanket. But not a man. Where his head should be, there was no head. There was a crouching spider, large as a cat, staring with its many red eyes. Jaws like horns worked, pinching the air.

Leaped.

Too swift to follow.

It was upon Tia Rosaura, taking her down. The child Ixta watched, horror-stricken, while the spider struggled above her aunt's fallen form. The abdominal bulb swayed and pumped methodically. There was the wet clicking sound of mouthparts working.

When the beast was finished, it left behind a motionless gray lump, a mute mummy wrapped in a shroud of silk. It turned. It was man-faced upon eight legs.

Moray's face.

Moray. Faustino. The Evil One. After all these years. Returned.

The child Ixta wanted to run. Couldn't. Held fast. The headless body was there, behind her, holding her for the beast.

"Lord Jesus, defend me!"

She knew as she spoke, these words possessed no power in this place. Her will did not fill these words. They died on the dark air. He— it—was coming for her. She must have words. Madly frightened, the child Ixta did as she had learned long ago.

Stood, straddling the rainbow fire, breathing the Sainted Children, the power of their colors.

Held the torches forward. Swordlike. Fangs of the serpent. Talons of the quetzal.

Spoke.

> *Says: I am a woman who gives life.*
> *Says: I am the Holy Star woman.*
> *Says: I am the woman wise in herbs.*
> *Says: I am a woman of the light.*

Finally, a great shout, drawing the words up from the deep womb of the earth:

> *Says: I am a woman of the sacred colors that strike.*
> *Strike!*

And the colors swelled. Whirled. A terrific blow. A small star exploding, cleansing the darkness. The beast was blasted back. Gone.

She stood alone. Safe.

"Lord Jesus!" She turned, calling.

But the smoke of the Sainted Children was whirling her around, down into a deep hole of the universe where Lord Jesus would not find her. And the hole was sinking deeper.

She wailed.

*   *   *

Moray woke, his head exploding with pain. He had been struck a savage blow. Stupidly, he flung his arms across his face to defend, as if he were under attack.

But there was no one. He was alone in the dimly lit guest suite of the Clinic, his new base of operations. What had happened?

For a long while, he lay on the bed like a man who had taken a beating, his body soaked with sweat, throbbing. His recollection of

Constancia's dream lay shattered, in pieces. Slowly, as the night waned, he gathered the fragments and examined them. The chanted words in a language he did not understand. The torches. The many-colored fire. He did not understand these images. But he remembered vividly the little girl Constancia's fear. And then, with a shudder, he recalled her protecting power. He had encountered a devastating force that had flung him back into dizzy wakefulness. Constancia's mind was ringed about by a defense he could never penetrate.

But he remembered one thing more. How she had refused to take up that defense until the last possible moment, when the fear had driven her to the threshold of hysteria. Only then. And he recalled how she had wailed when she did. The sound of her wailing was still in his ears. There was no mistaking its meaning. Shame. Horror and shame. She had used the power, loathing it, loathing herself.

Moray, still shaken by the experience of the night, was nevertheless amused by the delicious irony of the matter. Constancia had the power to thwart him. But her power was her weakness. She could not touch it without contaminating herself. He did not have to break her. She would do the job herself.

30

Let the bastard squirm awhile, Moray was thinking. Costello, the man of ice. It was a rare sight to see him badly rattled. Moray was enjoying it.

"How many times has this happened?" Costello wanted to know.

"Three times since I started with her last week," Moray answered. "Every time I play spiderman, wham! She lets me have it. Right between the eyes." He was teasing, exaggerating the unexpected resistance he had encountered in Mother Constancia's dreams.

"Something's wrong here," Costello insisted. Obviously shaken, he rose and began to pace the office. He whipped a handkerchief out of his pocket and used it to dry his palms. "There's every reason to believe your probes are breaking her down—just as we planned. We've got her under surveillance. Report is: she's gone into seclusion. Canceled all her appointments, won't leave her room. Yesterday she pulled out of an important speaking engagement. Excuse was: she's sick."

"Yeah, well, let me tell you—what she hit me with is a psychic H-bomb. First time she tried it, I thought my brain must have exploded."

Under his breath, an infuriated Costello growled savage curses. Moray was telling him that he was thwarted; with only a few weeks left to complete the assignment, Mother Constancia was slipping away. "I thought you could handle this," he scowled. "One feeble old lady. What's so damn funny about it?"

Moray, grinning mischievously, decided to relent. "Okay, relax, Costello. She's by no means feeble, but don't worry. We've lucked out. I've got her right where I want her." Costello stopped his pacing and fixed him with a stern gaze, waiting for an explanation. "She's got a defense, a damn good one. But here's the kicker. It *costs* her."

"What do you mean?"

"Every time she uses it, it does her more damage than I could ever do siccing the spiders on her. This mumbo-jumbo she throws at me—

the chanting, the fire, the spooky colors—she hates it. I don't know what it's all about, but I know she's ashamed to have anything to do with it. And I mean ashamed. Absolutely defiled. That gives me something better than the spiders to use on her. Guilt. That's always better than fear—especially with religious types. Fact is: I never got into the head of anybody so guilty."

Suddenly delighted, Costello flashed on the connection. "Of course! *Blasphemy.* She's a devout Catholic—or pretends to be. She's a nun. But what she's using to defend with is some kind of witchcraft. It's perfect."

"Right. She can't go either way. She's scared shitless of the spiders. So she defends. What else can she do? Then she wakes up guilty as hell because she used the old black magic to save her ass."

Costello's admiration was greater than he was willing to show. Moray had trapped Constancia in a classic double bind. He savored the fact for a long, appreciative moment. But then asked: "You say she's hitting you hard. How much of that can you take?"

Moray gave a dismissive shrug. "The first time, she caught me off guard. I didn't see it coming. As long as I know what to expect, I can skip out before she gives it to me full blast." Smugly, he displayed his usual bravado. "Hell, it's a kick. Puts some sport in it."

"That's *not* a prime consideration here," Costello instructed him. "I want this wrapped up fast. You take no chances, understand?"

Moray, clowning, imitated a punchy boxer. "She never laid a glove on me, boss," Then, sobering, turning mean: "She's grinding herself to pieces. I give her another week at the outside."

*   *   *

"She refuses to admit she's dreaming," Sister Charlotte was telling Ripley. "But I know she is. She's been talking in her sleep."

"What does she say?"

"I can't pick up much. But I know it isn't Spanish."

It was obvious to everyone at *Casa Libertad.* Constancia was in great distress. She spent her days secluded, sunk in constant prayer. Her world was shrinking. It became one darkened room she would not leave, where she would meet no one but a few of the sisters. Visitors came and went without seeing her. Scheduled events slipped by unattended. Even with those closest to her, she became morose and snappish. By turns, she would lash out angrily, then fall into profuse apologies, begging forgiveness, reviling herself. Ripley recognized what was happening. Deirdre had told him about Peter's experience just before his death. It was the same. Constancia was dreaming dreams she could not recall; she was suffering nightmares from which she could not awaken. Her attention was wandering, her thoughts splintering into a hundred doubts and anxieties. Somewhere at the root of her mind, the black dreams were eroding her sanity.

The morning after Deirdre went into coma, the newspapers carried a brief report of Aaron Devane's death. Heart failure, the papers said.

Devane's death. Deirdre's coma. Constancia's black dreams.

On the surface, three separate events. But Ripley knew they made a pattern. There was some subterranean connection between them. And it led back to the Clinic. Deirdre could have told him what that connection was. But Deirdre lay like a breathing corpse, her mind locked in a vault of silence.

Each day for hours, he sat at her bedside in the hospital, aching with his sense of helplessness. "Stay with her," her doctor told him. "Hold her hand. Talk to her. There's no telling what might get through to her."

Not hopefully, he followed instructions. It was all he could find to do.

At the end of Constancia's first week of nightmares, he visited *Casa Libertad* late in the day. Sister Charlotte met him, sober and white-faced, with a troubling report. That morning, the day-care group had baked cakes. The children decorated one for Constancia, who, they understood, was sick, then asked Sister Concepcion: might they bring it to her as a get-well present? Sister Concepcion led them up the stairs to Constancia's room, where Sister Charlotte, guarding the door, decided: *Yes, it might cheer Mother to meet the children.* She invited Constancia away from her prayers for just a few minutes. Grumbling, Constancia came, stood unspeaking, staring at the children's gift with lightless eyes. A long moment passed. Crookedly scrawled in a frosted sugar ribbon across the cake's top were the words *"Vaya con Dios, Madre Constancia."*

Never looking up, she reached out to the word *"Dios"* and rubbed her finger through the sugared script, erasing it. Again and again, back and forth, harder and harder, until the little girl holding the cake could not balance it any longer. It fell, splattering at her feet. The children, frightened, drew back, while Constancia looked down stupidly at the ruined gift on the floor. Then turned and went back to her room.

"It might have been another person, a total stranger," Sister Charlotte told Ripley. "She didn't seem to recognize anybody. I don't think she knew what she was doing."

Sister Charlotte had something more to add. She brought a miniature tape recorder out of her pocket and laid it on the table between them. She often used it to record Constancia's conversations: part of her personal archives for the biography she would one day write. Hesitantly, she reached across to switch the tiny machine on. Ripley listened. The voice was faint, the words garbled. But he could recognize that it was Constancia speaking.

"I've been recording at her bedside," Sister Charlotte said, looking deeply ashamed. They listened for several minutes. The voice on the tape fell in and out of an odd guttural cadence.

"What is it?" Ripley asked. "I can't understand a word."

"It's Kanjobal. She's chanting in the old dialect. It goes on like this for hours."

"What do you make of it?"

"She's defending herself."

"From what?"

"From whatever's in the dreams. As long as she chants, she sleeps calmly. When she stops, she begins showing signs of distress. Then she chants again."

"Can you understand any of it?"

"Not much. I can pick up the words: 'woman' . . . 'children' . . . 'save' . . . 'light' . . . 'enemy.' Just fragments like that. It's a defensive incantation. I'm sure I've heard the name 'Faustino.' " They listened awhile longer. Then Charlotte made a guilty admission. "I played it for her. This afternoon."

"And?"

"It was a mistake." Charlotte turned her face to the side and drew back the hair she had let fall across her left cheek. There was a red welt just below the cheekbone. "With her cane."

Ripley was astonished. He had never seen Constancia come close to a violent act.

"I should have known better," Charlotte said. "She's eaten up with shame. She calls herself unclean. All day long, she prays for forgiveness. But when she dreams, she goes back to the old magic. She hates what she's doing to defend herself, but it's all she knows how to do. She's tearing herself apart."

Then Ripley knew. He had to act.

31

Ripley never admitted to himself why he kept the gun. About a year ago, soon after he and Constancia had settled in Los Angeles, a Chicano boy had brought it with him into *Casa Libertad.* It was a violent neighborhood; many of the boys carried weapons. But that was strictly forbidden in the House. Sister Monica, spotting the gun in the boy's belt, reported it to Ripley. He promptly confiscated it. But he did not dispose of it. He took it to his apartment, cleaned it, oiled it, placed it in a drawer under his shirts. He did not forget it, but filed its existence away at the back of his mind. He liked knowing the gun was there. Recently used when he took charge of it, it still held four bullets.

If he had focused his thoughts on the matter, he would have confessed that keeping the gun was not merely a matter of negligence. In Guatemala, he had grown accustomed to living with weapons, had kept a gun, had used it. Soberly, after long thought, he had reached the conclusion that there were evils in the world that can only be overcome by violence; there was killing that had to be done. As much as his faith had once needed a crucifix, his passion for justice now needed an emblem of righteous violence. He had taken up his first gun after he had witnessed his first atrocity. Cristina had given it to him; she showed him how to care for it. How to break it down, clean it, prepare it for use. He had studied the structure of the gun the way he had once studied the complexities of a theological argument. He practiced the use of it, until the movements became as smooth as the movements of the Mass. When he came with Constancia to *Casa Libertad,* he left his weapon behind. And then missed it. The little .22-caliber pistol he confiscated from the boy gave him the chance to close that gap in his life. He took it.

The gun lay beside him now on the floor of the car as he drove north along the ocean. It was wrapped in a newspaper. He had no idea how he would use it when he reached the Clinic. Perhaps he would not even take it from the car. Nevertheless, it was there to remind him how far he must be ready to go.

. . . *evils that can only be overcome by violence.*

There was such an evil quartered at the Clinic. Devane had been one of its lesser agents; behind him there were others, no doubt a long chain of others. The man Costello was surely part of that chain. Ripley had met him only a few times while he was at the Clinic, but he knew from Deirdre how important Costello was. Very likely, he was the Clinic's connection with official power. Someone endorsing Archbishop McCaffrey's politics had ordered Costello to destroy Constancia. He was succeeding, using a kind of violence upon her that could never be traced or demonstrated. If Ripley could track the evil to its source, he had no doubt that the path would lead him to Guatemala City, to Washington, perhaps to Rome. He knew he had no chance of reaching that far. But he could get to Costello—and perhaps through Costello he could find Moray. He could break the chain there. He was determined to do that much. Constancia must not suffer another night of black dreams.

Ripley had no clear plan in mind. He was doing his best to ignore that worrying fact. He had no reason to believe he would find Costello at the Clinic when he got there. He knew nothing of the man's schedule or his movements. He scarcely understood Costello's function. But if he met him, he wanted it to be at the end of the day, when his office staff would be gone. They should be alone. He would confront Costello, then go where the next step required. He would make trouble— as much as he could. He had no illusions about how far he could expect to get with a small pistol and four bullets. The fury he carried within him was no substitute for real power. But it was all he had.

Costello's secretary was straightening her desk when Ripley entered. "You may remember me," he said, giving his name. "I was here with . . ."

"Yes, of course. Father Ripley. Have you an appointment with Mr. Costello?"

"No, but it's urgent."

She announced him on the intercom. There was a long pause before Costello asked to have him sent in. "Will you want anything more?" she asked.

"No, you can leave," the voice came back.

"Father Ripley," Costello greeted him, unsmiling but with a firm handshake. Routinely, he offered a drink. It was refused; he took none himself. "I'm afraid I don't have much time. If I had known you were coming . . ."

"I only need a few minutes." Ripley decided to be blunt. He did not control enough information to be subtle. "I've come about Mother Constancia."

"I hope she's well."

"I think you know she isn't." Costello gave no answer. Waited. Eyes growing chill. "She's having nightmares."

"Sorry to hear that. Possibly she left the Clinic too soon. She's free to return. I'm sure Archbishop McCaffrey would agree to that. Though, of course, just now we have no one here of Dr. Devane's stature. Sad to say. However, I believe Dr. Lichtman . . ."

Ripley cut him short. "I know where the nightmares come from. I'm here to put a stop to them. I want you to call off Moray."

"Moray . . . should I know who that is?" Costello was testing him.

"Your dreamwatcher. Call him off."

"Dreamwatcher . . ." Still testing.

"Take me seriously, Costello!" Ripley let the anger show in his eyes. "Devane told Deirdre everything about the Clinic. I know about the watchers, about Moray—what he did to Peter Vale, what he's doing to Mother Constancia."

"I take you seriously, Father Ripley. But what we have to decide is: who else would? Let's see how it stacks up. Dr. Devane told Mrs. Vale a story. But Dr. Devane is deceased. Mrs. Vale passed the story along to you. But Mrs. Vale is . . . I understand she's in the hospital, in a coma. As for the person you mention—Moray: do we know who he is, where he is? Let's say we don't. That leaves you, a priest, not in the best repute, a political malcontent. A third-hand source for a rather bizarre story. Something about dreamwatching that you say you learned from one of our former patients. People watching other people's dreams. All part of a grand government conspiracy, run by . . . whom shall we choose? FBI, CIA, Secret Service? Sounds like a classic paranoid fantasy. Of course, I'm sure you can find someone in the journalistic breadline hungry enough to publish what you have to say. May I recommend *The National Enquirer?*"

Outside the open window of Costello's office, the sound of cars starting up, driving away, could be heard from the parking lot below. The staff on its way home.

"Let me add it up another way," Ripley suggested. "Devane ran the Clinic. You ran Devane. Who runs you? Probably some set of paramilitary mandarins in Washington the taxpaying public has never heard of. All right, Devane is dead. And I haven't got the ghost of a chance of getting to the mandarins. So that leaves *you*—right here and now. I do, incidentally, have Devane's notebooks and tapes—the things he recorded with Mother Constancia. I won't pretend that proves much. But then I didn't come here to take you to court, Costello. I came here to threaten your life, for whatever good that might do. Maybe you're nothing but a junior flunky, easily replaced. Or maybe you're important enough, so that if I harm you, I can scare somebody up the line. Or maybe all I can do is get it out of my system. Here's what I want you to take seriously: I'm mad, I'm desperate, and I'm *here*. I don't intend to go back to Los Angeles and watch people I love washed down the drain. I'll kill you first."

"Not very priestly of you," Costello remarked.

"Think of it this way," Ripley answered. "I'm as much of a priest as McCaffrey is. The only difference is our politics."

Costello's face, smooth and expressionless, might have been carved from marble. But behind the cool surface his mind was ticking over at maximum efficiency. After a long moment, he said, "You want to protect Mother Constancia. I can think of a way for you to do that. It would be as simple and as clean as telling the truth. All you really need to . . ."

For the first time since Ripley had entered the office, Costello lost his self-possession. Only for a moment. A twitch of authentic surprise tugged sharply at his face. At the far end of the room, behind Ripley, the door had swung open. Ripley spun around in his chair. As he did so, he made a slight but telling movement with his right hand—toward the gun he carried under his jacket. He was sure Costello's trained eye had caught it. The man was warned.

At the door, entering backward as he pulled a mobile serving table behind him, was the white-jacketed Smitty. Mute and zombielike, he wheeled his little table awkwardly around and started for the terrace, not even glancing at the two men in the room.

"Not now, Smitty," Costello snapped, clearly vexed by the intrusion. Smitty continued across the room, not hearing. "Smitty. Smitty!" The last call—sharp and mean—was as close as Costello would let himself come to a shout. Smitty stopped, jerked around toward Costello, stared stupidly. *"Not now,"* Costello repeated.

Smitty's confusion was painful to see. He looked from Costello to the terrace. Outside, Ripley could see a table piled with dishes, remnants of an afternoon snack. Above the remains of a coffee cake, a few flies buzzed and hovered. Smitty started again toward the terrace.

"Smitty!" Costello barked once more. The man stopped, turned again, then pointed toward the dishes. His face toiled through a succession of questioning frowns and grimaces. He teetered indecisively, like a robot whose programming had been interrupted. At last, yielding with marked exasperation, Costello growled, "Oh, all right. Go ahead. Be quick. Go ahead, I said."

Smitty, back on automatic, trudged heavily on to the terrace and began transferring the dishes to his server.

"Don't mind him," Costello said to Ripley. "He's . . ." He gestured toward his head, a rocking, floating movement of the hand. *"Non compos mentis."*

"Yes, I know," Ripley said.

"My secretary must have rung to have things cleared away." With pronounced irritation, he swiveled in his chair to eye Smitty on the terrace behind him. "Actually, I took him off this job two, three days ago. There must have been . . ."

Impatiently, Ripley brought him back to the business at hand. "You were saying something about the truth."

"Yes," Costello turned back to him, picking up smoothly. "Suppose you were to call a press conference at *Casa Libertad.* Suppose you used it to tell the world what Mother Constancia is really up to."

"Meaning?"

"That she's a Marxist revolutionary. That she supports the guerrilla movements in Guatemala, El Salvador, Honduras, the Sandinista regime in Nicaraugua. The whole works."

Almost naïvely, Ripley answered, "That wouldn't be true."

Costello shrugged. "It's true enough, isn't it? With a few minor qualifications. Maybe she agonizes over it, but she supports the People's War. Certainly *you* do."

"Perhaps. But I can't speak for Constancia."

"It seems to me you speak for her every chance you get. And it always comes out of your mouth sounding the same. Full endorsement of the revolutionary movements. Come on, Ripley—just tell the truth. You're not part of the Church. You don't give a damn about any church. You believe in the revolution. You believe in its ends and its means. You've carried guns for the cause. You've killed for it. You're not ashamed of what you've done, are you?"

"But I'm not Constancia."

"You're her right-hand man. Her chief political adviser. Her personal confessor. That's got to mean something."

"She and I have real disagreements about the use of violence. She's never condoned it, which is why she has more critics in the revolutionary movement than you seem to be aware of. And she's not a Marxist. Nor am I."

"It doesn't come out sounding that way. I can't recall that she ever condemned the revolutionaries."

"She has. Sometimes against my advice, sometimes with it."

"It doesn't filter through very clearly."

"The press doesn't always play fair with us. In any case, I can't speak for her."

"All right, then leave her out of it and speak for yourself. And for all the other *compañeros* who believe what you do. Just come clean. *Casa Libertad* is riddled through with leftist revolutionaries. It's a secular political operation. It's working for radical, social change. Admit it and let the public judge Constancia by the company she keeps."

"Revolution isn't incompatible with a Christian commitment."

"And a lot you care, Ripley, about Christian compatibility. What's it worth to you?"

"You know what would happen if I made a public statement like that. It would discredit Constancia in the eyes of millions of Catholics. The Church would disown her."

"Possibly. But it would also save her life."

"That's what this is all about? You simply want to smear her reputation?"

"You wouldn't regard that as a 'smear,' would you? Letting the world know you're a revolutionary? I should think you'd be proud to say so. It might even ease your conscience. How much longer do you want to keep pretending you're a priest?"

"That's it? That's what you want?"

"You say it, loud and clear and soon, within the next two days, I guarantee Mother Constancia can look forward to sweet sleep and pleasant dreams."

"What about Deirdre?"

"That's another matter. I'm not sure what the Clinic can do for her. We can try to help. We know something about her condition."

"Why is she in a coma?"

"That's hard to explain. If they keep her alive long enough, she may come out of it. I can't promise anything."

The proposition was demonically clever. It tempted Ripley with a truth he was eager to speak. But he had no right to burden Constancia with his commitments. He was being asked to end her career in the Church. No question but McCaffrey would seize upon his admission immediately as an excuse to condemn, very likely excommunicate her. Agitated, he rose, walked around his chair once, twice, pondering. Then sat. "I can't do it. I have my politics. Constancia has hers. We . . ."

On the desk in front of Costello, lying flat on its side, Costello's hand discreetly covering it, was an automatic pistol. "What else did you think you could arrange?" Costello asked. His eyes were dead cold. "You see, Ripley, the offer I'm making you requires that you leave here alive. It ensures your survival. And Constancia's. Maybe Mrs. Vale's. You lose the prize, but you live to fight another day."

"Prize . . . ?"

"But what's that worth to Mother Constancia anyway? What does she care for these wordly honors? On the other hand, the rather quaint scheme you have in mind—a personal threat at gunpoint—now why wouldn't that be the world's best justification for making you dead? Everything you've said since you came into the room has been recorded. With a bit of editing, you'd be condemned out of your own mouth. Wild threats, paranoid fantasies, irrational violence. The local police are very friendly. I wouldn't have to answer many questions. Think it over. Do you really have any . . . ?"

It happened too suddenly for Ripley to follow. As if the scene before him were on film and had skipped several frames. Costello's body stiffened as if with an electric shock. His eyes went from icy calm to frantic, nearly exploding out of his face. His words stopped and his jaw gaped in astonishment. A small, comic clucking sounded at the back of his throat.

What had happened just before that seemed to have no connection with the expression of nauseated amazement that was now engraved on Costello's face. One moment, Smitty, finishing on the terrace, had been backing into the room with his loaded server. There was a faint rattle of china as he stepped backward toward Costello. Then—another moment—he turned full around. That was all. He stood there now, behind Costello's back, mute and unmoving. His eyes were on Ripley. He raised one hand, his finger to the lips, signaling for silence. Then, letting the other hand ease down slowly, he used the handle of the knife to lever Costello's body forward until it folded over the desk, his forehead pressed against the gun that still lay there. By then, the entire back of his coat was a scarlet stain spreading from where the long bread knife had been inserted, very precisely, into his heart with one swift thrust.

Smitty, quite calm and looking not the least bit confused, said in a whisper, "Not safe yet. Still one more to kill."

32

The room writhed with bodies. They coiled and braided in fantastic sexual contortions. Rock music, brutally loud, pounded the walls like giant fists. A swirl of colored lights played garishly across an undulating sea of oiled flesh, singling out image, image, image. On a waterbed: two mind-blown women, joined head to tail, mouthing one another voraciously. Suspended from exercise bars: a giggling fat lady servicing two men at once. A snaky black girl, raised high by four beefy bodybuilders, lowering herself, legs spread, on the greedy face of a cadaverous old man. A succession of disembodied penises, caught close up in the throes of ejaculation, pumping slow-motion fountains of white foam.

The movie left Moray cold. He had seen it before. Last week? The week before? He could not remember. Since coming to Santa Barbara at the beginning of the summer, he had consumed all the hard-core fare he could find in the nearby beach towns and was working his way through second and third helpings. After a time, all the films congealed into one greasy stew. Strung-out misfits forcing orgasms, faking sexual frenzy. He sat sullenly in the nearly empty theater, draining a slender ration of arousal from the erotic labors that muscled their way gracelessly across the screen. His appetite craved stronger stuff. Cruelty, humiliation, pain. He sat through hours of routine pornography, waiting for the few flashes of sadistic elation he needed, usually not finding it.

The assignments had done this. They calloused the sensibilities, stifled feeling. It had begun a few years back, at first with his eyes and his powers of touch, then worked slowly through the web of his senses, deadening sensation and response. Compared to the nightmares he engineered—the extremes of terror and anguish—the experiences of his waking life became remote and muted. Movies like this were no longer much help; they were not abrasive enough to keep his mind alert for more than brief intervals. When the images faded from memory, he began to sense something like death seeping through him.

Leaving the theater, standing in the open air, Moray felt like a sea slug forced out from under a rock. The daylight seemed alien, threatening. Not his natural habitat. He shuddered with discomfort. He was no sooner out on the streets than he wanted the sheltering darkness again, so much more like the world of black dreams. He had sat through the entire double bill and it was still only three in the afternoon. Easily six or eight hours before he was due to return to Mother Constancia's dreams. Too much time to kill. It made him edgy.

Down the street from the theater, there was an adult book store. It did not offer much scope for browsing. Moray had been through the place several times and had bought everything that interested him. He tried it again. After a brief search, he turned up a video cassette that looked promising. *High School Concubines.* He would keep that for tonight—in case Mother Constancia failed to dream.

Then he was back on the streets again, hunting. Santa Barbara's abbreviated and antiseptic version of a Tenderloin had little to offer. A few blocks this way, a few blocks that. Pawn shops, liquor stores, tacky lunch counters. There were some brothels he knew of, near the beach. The whores—mainly Mexican girls, new and skittish at their trade—used a few old hotels there. They worked quickly and furtively, offering minimal services, always on the lookout for the police. Santa Barbara was like that. Tame, buttoned-down. It oppressed him with a sense of moral claustrophobia. He decided to head south toward Ventura, a half hour's drive along the coast highway. He had found some hookers working out of a trailer court there who were a bit more accommodating. It would not be much, but it passed the time. He loitered along the way to his car until he caught sight of the man who had followed him out of the movie. Costello's agent, shadowing him, not even trying hard to disguise the fact. Moray didn't mind any longer. It made him feel secure, knowing there was someone looking after him. It was almost presidential, having a bodyguard.

He spent a semisatisfying hour with a black hooker named Annie whose trailer was so close to the freeway the walls vibrated to the traffic. For a price, Annie was willing to play along with his fantasies. She was reasonably good at faking pain. Even so, she was strict about how far he could go. "No real knots," she insisted. "And don't leave me no marks." Moray sometimes pressed a little beyond the limit, but it never worked. She broke off fast when she tired of the act and made him pay high for the extras.

As he was leaving this time, she remarked, "I sure wish I could bill you for what you gettin' off me in my dreams. Hoo! You been beatin' me to mashed potatoes. I don't know why I'm dreamin' 'bout a kinky boy like you. Sure don't do nothin' for me." Moray smiled and left an extra twenty-dollar tip. "That's to cover the dreams," he said.

On the way back, Devane entered his thoughts—a long rambling revery. It angered Moray that, for the first time since Devane's death, he was experiencing a twinge of guilt. Was his hatred beginning to thaw? That must not happen. He had a right to hate. Devane had betrayed him, had let him be used for vile and destructive purposes, then abandoned him without a word of explanation or apology. Moray's mind wandered back across the years to his earliest memories of Devane. The big, fatherly man who had spent so much time soothing him out of his autistic withdrawal, bringing him back to language and to trust. Behind Moray's guarding wall of silence, Devane had discerned a lively mind, a depth of sensitivity. Slowly, he had erased the fears that once locked Moray away from the world. Together they began to explore the dreams of Devane's patients. Moray had worked hard at that: many times Devane complimented him for his daring, his insight. But then, one day, he was asked to do something quite different, something that seemed mean and dirty. It was his first target.

Moray, remembering, felt the fury surge into his mind. It had been his initial experience with sadistic fantasies and he was painfully confused by what was expected of him. Wasn't it wrong? he asked again and again. But he was only seventeen at the time, still totally dependent on Devane and eager, so eager to please. Devane, letting him know that only total compliance would please, had led him through the assignment step by step, instructing and encouraging. With clinical precision, Devane had taught him the ABCs of depravity, insisting that the exercise was only a joke, a prank. Like playing bogeyman.

The target had been a Libyan embassy official with whom a meeting was arranged at an East Coast beach resort. Moray's assignment was to draw the man into dreams of bizarre perversion, letting himself be used as the masochistic love object. Under Devane's tutelage, he was encouraged to take on submissive, effeminate roles, sometimes to become a woman, to wear a transvestite caricature of a woman's body. That became frequent in his assignments, almost all of which involved men who were being tempted and manipulated. To please Devane,

Moray became adept at strange forms of homosexual love: giving pain, taking it, inviting humiliation, playing upon the deeply buried desires of his targets. By the time he had done several more stints of that kind, his sexual tastes had taken on a permanent warp. He came to like—or at least crave—the sick things with which he filled the dreams of his targets, the things which Devane praised and rewarded. Meanwhile, his homosexual tendencies, strengthened and expanded by constant exercise, reached out toward Devane, loving him, needing him. And were rejected bluntly. Devane was very good at playing doctor, drawing a screen of icy objectivity around himself. Exiling.

More than once, Moray had tried to slip into Devane's dreams and there bring him the love he was forbidden to display in their waking relationship. But Devane had trained himself carefully. His dreams were well-defended and he punished severely for such transgressions. So severely that for years Moray scrupulously avoided Devane's sleep. Then, quite suddenly—some two years ago—Moray found himself being moved out of the Clinic, located away from Santa Barbara in a succession of new places—hospitals and military installations mainly— where his assignments began to grow even more grueling. Now it was Costello, whom he had never liked, who gave him his instructions. He asked when he would see Devane again and he was told "Soon." But it did not happen. And then he knew it would never happen. Devane had discarded him. A damaged instrument.

His outrage made him daring. He tried again to infiltrate Devane's dreams. To his surprise, this time he succeeded. Partly because his own powers had become keener, subtler than Devane realized. But partly too because something in Devane had weakened—his alertness, his intellectual edge. He had gone soft with age, with drink, with self-pity. Discovering that, Moray came to despise the man he had once idolized. He freely entered Devane's sleep and there observed dreams as filled with follies, petty anxieties, and ordinary desires as any he had ever seen. Nothing special. Nothing exalted.

And then he discovered Deirdre. She was there, in Devane's sleeping mind.

It was the woman he remembered from Peter Vale's dreams, the watcher who had nearly thwarted him in that assignment. Devane had taken pity on her, had protected and favored her. He had not allowed Costello to use her against his targets. He cared for her, loved her. No, *lusted* for her. For her woman's body. Moray loathed women's bodies, the female softness and smoothness he was so often forced to simulate in dreams. The female form meant humiliation to him. He longed to scar and deface the bodies of women. He wished he could have done that to Deirdre or one day to her smart-ass daughter. It was a fantasy he frequently rehearsed.

He knew there were other watchers who had gone through this same mortification of the sensibilities. Devane called it "burning out." But that was just a name for it; Devane never really understood the strange hell he had created for the watchers he trained, never really cared. He addicted them to extremes, then let the numbness come and eat them alive. They went dark; their minds turned to ashes. Moray was holding out against that. He was stronger than the others. But more and more often, even his will was beginning to go slack; he could feel his existence being erased. With each passing month, it was becoming more difficult to appease his hunger for sexual violence. He was only fully alive now when that craving lit his mind. But the fantasies were no longer enough to ward off the numbness. He was like a man freezing to death, feeling himself go dead in all his limbs as his blood chilled to ice, needing to chafe and beat his moribund flesh in order to know he was there, alive. Moray had reached the point of needing real waking violence, violence that left a lasting mark on the flesh. Costello did not know how busy his mind had become with planning acts of that kind. Like now, with Annie. Nigger slut! When this assignment was finished, when he was ready to move on, he would get his money's worth from her. He was flirting with it, teasing himself with it—the moment he would make the make-believe knots real and not stop when she ordered him to.

Back in Santa Barbara, he spent the early evening on the beach, scripting the girls he saw there into more favorite of his fantasies. He imagined the places where he might meet them alone, imagined how he might follow them to their homes or lure them away to deserted places. He loitered until the sun had set and the sky gone dark. Then he started for the Clinic. He was staying there now, in the guest suite. Costello had moved him in when they started working on Devane. "More comfortable," Costello had said. The suite was luxurious, with sumptuous furnishings and a panoramic view of the Pacific. But Moray knew he was no guest of honor. Costello simply wanted to keep him close and well-observed.

He began to anticipate the night's work with Mother Constancia. He knew he had his hook in her now. He could turn the slightest flutter of her sleeping mind into a black dream. She was a tough old lady,

holding out better than he would have expected. She had become a
tantalizing challenge. He remembered the nights when she had begun
doing something in her dreams with a chant and colored fire. It had
thrown him for a loss and nerved her mightily against the spiderman.
But what she did also filled her with an insupportable guilt. Moray
could feel that guilt building in her dreams. It was close now, the
moment when her will would disintegrate and she would accept any
command he planted in her defenseless mind. Costello had given him
some statements—about God, the Pope, the Church—which he was to
instill in her at the critical juncture. It might be tonight. He hoped it
would be. He wanted to be finished with the Clinic, with Santa Barbara,
with Costello. Moray had projects of his own in mind.

He pulled into the Clinic grounds, parked, and entered at the front
door. Except for the night staff, the main building was empty. The
security guard at a desk in the lobby nodded him by. Moray went up the
stairs to his suite, locked his door, and flopped wearily across the king-
sized bed.

That was when the closet door opened and the man stepped forward. In the still unlit room, Moray could not tell who it was, but he saw
the gun swing into position, so close he could have touched the muz-
zle. His cry of surprise was only halfway up his throat when the bullets
struck.

The head. The neck. The chest. Three blows merging into one
battering thrust. A door slamming against his life.

Then nothingness.

33

"You're a priest, Father Ripley. You should know better than any doctor where the soul goes after the body dies. In your religion, isn't there a place where the damned go, where there is nothing but sadness? Sadness that never ends. The dead end of the universe. That's where I was. That's where Mrs. Vale is. Both of us—we're the living dead."

Smitty's voice was a rusty tool, unused for fifteen years. Perversely, it kept sliding out of control, cracking and squeaking as he haltingly maneuvered his way around words and phrases. Resurrected from stubborn silence, it functioned as awkwardly as his body. Smitty's movements were as wooden as ever, his face as impassive. Yet everything about the man had changed. He was no longer a zombie. Intelligence illuminated his presence. His mind was alive.

"And you pretended for all these years to be . . . ." Ripley groped for a word that would not hurt.

"An idiot?" Smitty suggested. "Yes. It was how I survived. After a time, an idiot becomes a nonentity. Nobody notices. Nobody cares. He has . . . peace."

"How could you do it—for all these years?"

"Time means very little after you live through hell. A thousand years, a split second—they both mean the same. Zero. Nothing. When you know what life comes to in the end, it's comfortable to be an idiot. No decisions. No goals. You just drift. You don't even have to decide if you should go on living."

All the while they talked, Ripley sensed he was in the presence of an alien being. Smitty spoke calmly, sensibly. But he had traveled where no one was meant to travel. He had shared another man's death, another man's damnation. There was a mute knowledge in him that made him either more or less than human.

"But you've taken it all in?" Ripley asked. "Everything around you—what you've heard and seen?"

"Not right away. Not for—I can't say, perhaps for years. But then I begin to make sense of things. It's like I'm on a high mountain, far away. I'm watching—even myself—from that great distance. People are just little strange animals—far off. I see, I hear. But I don't . . . can't care. Because it's so remote. Myself—I'm remote. And—this is strangest of all—there's no *time*. There's one minute, then another minute. But no connection between. You understand? There's just *now*, and *now*, and *now*. Fragments. I live in these little fragments, little islands of time. And in between—nothing. An ocean of nothing."

Ripley had noticed that Smitty's grasp of time was insecure. He could not recollect time intervals; he struggled with tenses when he spoke, never too clear about past, present, future. For him, time gave no direction to action. "Will it be like that for Deirdre—when she comes back?" Ripley asked, wondering if he really wanted to have the question answered.

Smitty shrugged, confessing ignorance. "Impossible to say. I think it depends on how long Devane holds her."

"Devane?"

"Devane's mind . . . whatever it is that remains of him. You see, the dead cling. Devane is clinging to her. The mind I died with—it held me. It wanted my life. It wanted to drain me. I could feel that, how it sucked at me, until it grows weak and surrenders. Then I came back. But for me, there was nothing. Nothing to live for. Or die for. My life, you see, was only the dirty things Devane gives me to do. I am . . . I was an instrument. Not really human. Much easier for me to become Smitty the robot. Not to think, not to feel. Mrs. Vale . . . with her, it's different. She has her daughter. She has you and Mother Constancia. Show her kindness. Don't give up. Remember—finally, I did *this*."

A light, something like pride, came into Smitty's eyes as he gestured stiffly toward the far end of the room where Costello's body still lay draped over his desk, the knife handle protruding from his back like the switch on a mechanical toy.

"Yes, but why?" Ripley asked. "Why did you . . . bother?"

"I'll tell you. For a long time after my . . . death, I understood nothing. My memory is gone . . . full of holes. I don't know myself, don't know anyone around me. Then, I can't say when, but sometime, pieces of my life begin to come together. They make pictures. Memories. There are things I hear Devane saying about me, things I remember. And then, one day, when I remember enough, I discover something inside of me. Hate. For Devane, for Costello, for the Clinic. And I take hold of this hate—because it's all there is of me. Of *me*. It's painful to hate so much, but this is a *good* pain. It's life. I'm coming back to life. I *want* something. One thing. Nothing else. I want to *punish*. Everything begins to come together around this hate. You see? It's hate that brings me back. Because it gives me this one thing to do. I know that someday I'm going to kill. I have *that* to live for. Maybe Mrs. Vale will have something to live for too—something better than killing."

"But why did you choose to kill Costello now?"

"I heard them talking about how they killed Devane and made Mrs. Vale like me—one of the living dead."

"Devane was murdered?"

"Yes. His dreams were a trap for Mrs. Vale. They trapped her the way I was trapped. They want her removed."

"You heard *who* talking about this?"

"Costello. Shawsing."

"Shawsing? Who is he?"

"I don't know. He comes sometimes. From Washington. From the Head Office. He decides things—with Costello."

"Is he here now?"

"No. Gone. He and Costello talk as if I don't understand. But I hear it all. I understand. I hear that Costello wants to send me away. He doesn't care about me. He wants me gone. Then I knew I must punish him soon."

Nearly an hour had passed since Smitty had "punished" Costello. The Clinic had become quiet, deserted. Smitty, with his cloudy sense of time, seemed content to sit relating his story forever. The minutes weighed more tellingly on Ripley. He glanced nervously at the body across the room.

"Smitty—suppose someone comes."

"Yes. There's a guard who comes around."

"When?"

"When? Not yet. Very late. There's . . . time. I have to find the other one."

"You mean Moray?"

"Yes."

"You know him?"

"When he came to the Clinic, I knew him. Just a boy. I was here while he was being trained."

"You intend to kill him?"

"Yes. He trapped Mrs. Vale. He makes nightmares for Mother Constancia. They're kind people. Kind to me. Moray hurts them."

"Maybe there's another way to deal with him."

Smitty dismissed the words impatiently. "He's evil. Like me. He does the same things I did."

"I know."

"Like me. An instrument. The last one."

"The last one?"

"The last watcher—besides Mrs. Vale. When he's gone, the evil will be gone."

"You know where he is?"

"Yes. Costello brought him here. He's staying in the other wing. The guest suite. I can be in his room when he comes. Nobody notices me. I'm like a ghost here. I'll wait. When he comes back . . ."

"When will that be?"

"When . . ." Smitty puzzled over the word. "Soon. I should go to his room soon—before dark. I can hide and wait." Then, frowning deeply, "But I need . . . something." He gazed down into his empty hands.

Ripley understood. He took the pistol he carried out of his belt. "We have this."

Smitty eyed the gun dubiously. "I don't know how . . ."

"I do. Leave this to me."

Smitty shook his head angrily. "No! This is for me to do. You show me how to use it."

Ripley began to protest. "It would be better if . . ."

"Show me!" Smitty insisted. "You can't go to his room. You can't move here like me. What can you do?"

He was right. There was no way Ripley could imagine gaining access to Moray without drawing attention. There was also the nagging doubt in his mind that, confronting Moray, he would not be able to go through with the killing. He had used a gun in combat against armed men, against government forces in Nicaragua and Guatemala that he despised both in person and in principle. It would be very different facing an unarmed man up close, someone as sick, as pathetic as Moray. On the other hand, Smitty was clearly capable of murder; he was already guilty of one death. And there was the stored hatred of many years in him. Hesitantly, Ripley agreed to show him the use of the gun. He showed him once, then again, then again. He showed him how to stand, how to grip with both hands, how to aim and fire. He showed him how to come in close for a final shot when his man was down. He did not rush. Teaching Smitty was his vicarious experience of the act. Animated by a cold, matured fury, Smitty learned quickly and well. When he was certain Smitty could do the job, Ripley asked, "Do you want me to stay near you until it's done?"

Smitty shook his head sternly no. "I think you should know," Ripley told him, "I came here today mad enough to kill. Maybe I would have. I'm willing to stay and share the responsibility, if that's what you want."

Again, angrily, Smitty shook him off. "*My* killing. You stay out." Then, more gently, he added, "Others need you. Mrs. Vale. Mother Constancia. You go back to them."

"But how do I stay out of this, Smitty? Even if I leave now, the police will know I was here when Costello died. That makes me some kind of accomplice. What do I say about that?"

Smitty fell into a long frowning moment of thought. It was difficult for Ripley to trust that the mind behind his impassive face was a reliably functioning instrument. He grew edgy. But when Smitty spoke, it was with a commanding decisiveness. Gesturing toward Costello's body, he said, "He has keys. Get them."

Ripley went to the desk and fished in Costello's trousers. In a hip pocket he found a chain and—on it—a ring of keys. He removed them. At the same time, he took the gun out from under Costello's head and placed it out of sight in a desk drawer. The bloodstain on Costello's back had thickened into a brown crust; against the blue of his jacket, it looked like the map of an unnamed continent.

Ripley brought the keys to Smitty, who had gone to a small alcove beside the terrace windows. "One key unlocks this," he said, his hand upon a narrow metal door. "I've seen him open it many times. Not secret. Just fireproof." Ripley tested a number of keys, found the right one, and unlocked the door. It slid heavily to one side and settled with a solid metallic chunk. He reached inside and flipped on a light switch. The interior was a compact storage room, not big enough for more than three people to stand in. The windowless walls were stacked high with files on metal shelves. The room was densely built out of steel with a tile floor. Sunk deep into the ceiling was an air vent and a tiny fan that started when the lights were switched on.

"Say it was open when you came," Smitty said. "Say I used the gun to make you go inside. Nobody can hear you in there, unless they're in the room. When the guard comes, make noise."

Ripley tested the door. It would lock when it was slammed shut. He went back to Costello's body and slipped the key ring back on the chain. Then he quickly sorted through the story he and Smitty were concocting. He could explain his presence at the Clinic well enough: something about Mother Constancia's further care. That was even reasonably close to the truth. Once he got to the point of Smitty's attack on Costello, no one would expect him to supply sane reasons for anything that happened. There was nothing to link him to Smitty. The gun he had given him could not be traced.

"Why will they think you did this?" Ripley asked.

For the first time, a smile brushed across Smitty's lips. "Crazy," he said simply. "Nobody asks why a crazyman does things."

"You're sure you want it like this?"

Smitty nodded.

"What will you do afterward?"

Afterward. The word clearly had no meaning for Smitty. The killings were the single focus of his thought. After that, time stopped for him.

"I mean when the police come," Ripley explained. "What will you tell them about me?"

"Smitty doesn't talk. Who's going to try getting anything out of him? After I lock this, Father Ripley, *this* Smitty is gone. He has no life. There is just the other Smitty. The zombie. What can they do to a zombie?"

"They can put him away. Somewhere. For a long time."

A long time. But Smitty was looking back at him with the eyes of a man who had already lived a thousand weary years.

Ripley stepped into the little vault. He turned and reached back for a last handshake. There was unmistakable gratitude in the gesture. He said, "When you do it, Smitty, stand as close as you can get. Use all the bullets."

Smitty nodded. The door slid shut with a heavy click.

*   *   *

Three hours later, Moray lay dead on the floor of the Clinic's guest suite. Knowing the shots would bring the security guard, Smitty unlocked the door and left it ajar. When the guard rushed in, gun drawn, he found Smitty waiting calmly beside the body.

"What the hell's going on here?" the guard shouted.

To the man's surprise, Smitty's mouth opened and words came out.

"Punishing," Smitty answered. "Punishing Mr. Costello and Father Ripley too. One more punishment."

Smitty had used three of his bullets on Moray. He had saved the last for himself. He did not have to. When the nervous guard saw his gun lift, he fired, point-blank.

34

It's over.

The thought blazed at the center of Ripley's mind like a bonfire lit to celebrate a great victory. All the while he talked to the police, he struggled to fight down the shameless elation that bubbled inside him. *Smitty did it. It's over.*

Meanwhile, as sober as he could keep, he was telling the police, "We were discussing Mother Constancia's condition, when Smitty came up behind Mr. Costello and . . . stabbed him. I didn't even see the knife, it happened so quickly. Before I could decide what to do, he had a gun out. He forced me into the storage room and locked it. That's all I know until the guard found the body and let me out. No, Smitty never said a word. I can't think of why he did it. From what I knew of him, he was very gentle, quite harmless. Maybe Dr. Devane's death had some unbalancing effect."

Nobody expected Ripley to make sense of a senseless killing. That night he told his story once, twice, three times; he answered the same questions over and over. Finally, he signed a statement. The police dealt courteously with him; he did not discourage them from calling him "Father Ripley"—though he did not sign himself on paper as a Jesuit. By late morning he was on his way back to Los Angeles. The law was finished with him. His conscience was not.

He tried to console himself that he had come to the Clinic ready to do murder and was going home having done nothing worse than lying. But he knew that was not true. Whatever the police might believe, he was Smitty's accomplice. He had planned Moray's death and assented to Costello's. Not that his complicity in the murders troubled him. Somewhat to his surprise, he felt no guilt whatever for that. He was convinced that killing Costello and Moray was part of the war he had long been fighting at Mother Constancia's side. They were enemies, forces of irreconcilable evil for whose destruction he would not permit himself to feel remorse. Constancia might condemn what he had done, but his own sense of vindication was unshakable. Yet there was something else that gnawed at him: the way he had let Smitty act as the weapon of his own murderous fury. He might have guessed Smitty would not come out of the matter alive. He half-suspected, despite the security guard's story, that Smitty's death was really suicide. He had let that happen and now felt exhilarated to be bringing news of the killings back to Los Angeles.

There were three deaths behind him and he was coming home happy.

* * *

At *Casa Libertad*, he repeated the same story he had told the police in Santa Barbara. There was no point in saying anything different; nobody would have understood the truth except Constancia. But he would spare her that until she was strong enough to take it in. He told her only that her ordeal was over. Moray was dead; she would be free of the dreams. He told her again and again because she was desperate to hear the words. As he spoke to her, he found in her haggard face all the justification he needed for what he had done. Fearing what the night might bring, Constancia had neither slept nor meditated since her last nightmare. Her exhaustion was extreme. She lay on her bed, a wasting wraith of herself. Worst of all were her eyes. The black dreams lingered there, a shadowed horror that would never leave her. Ripley could not know that the darkness he saw there was the remembered darkness of the Cuchumatán caves; he could not understand the shame she felt for the ancient sorcery she had practiced in her dreams in order to ward off the evil. But he could see with searing clarity that she stood at the outer limit of sanity. Moray had broken her; she could not have endured much more. Saving her, Ripley told himself, was worth the lies, the violence. He would make himself believe that.

* * *

Four days after the killings, Deirdre's eyes opened—as naturally as if she were waking from an afternoon nap. Ripley was there, the first to see. He had resumed spending his days beside her, softly repeating her name, stroking her brow, her hand. In his surprise, he was caught staring speechlessly at her. And it was Deirdre who spoke first.

"Aaron," she said in a whisper. "I was with Aaron. I don't know where. He let me go. He let me come back."

Ripley bent to kiss her. Her lips met his coldly, as if she did not understand the gesture. After a long pause, she said, "Aaron's dead," and looked to him for confirmation. He nodded. "And I was with him. I was . . . *with* him." She listened to her own words as if they were spoken by another person and wondered what they meant.

He held her close, comforting her, all the while sensing she had locked out his comfort. She was not allowing his love to enter and ease her mind. In time, when he thought it might help, he told her that Moray and Costello were dead, that Constancia was safe. "It's over, Deirdre," he said. He said it many times, trying to work it into her awareness. But she showed no response. He felt he was talking to her over a great distance, so far that his words grew faint and died along the way. He remembered: Smitty had told him of the remoteness he brought back from the dead. The opaqueness he had seen in Smitty's face now filled Deirdre's eyes. Eyes of marble, a statue's eyes. She was awake and well; the doctors were satisfied with her recovery. But there was nothing glad or triumphant in her awakening. Some vital part of her had not returned from the darkness. Or perhaps, Ripley thought, some portion of the darkness clung to her, an indelible grief that had stained her mind. Its mark was permanently upon her for all to see. While she lay in coma, an ashen stripe had appeared in her dark hair just above her left brow. A psychic scar made visible.

People visited. Meg, Sister Charlotte, others from *Casa Libertad*. They assumed Deirdre wanted to be filled in on things. They were eager to tell her all that had happened during the fifteen days of her life she had lost. They brought her magazines, newspapers. They passed along gossip and news of the world. Deirdre listened, understanding and yet not understanding. She understood their words, but not the importance of what they said. Her face seemed to reply, *But why does that matter? Why bother to tell me?* Worse, in the withering vacuum of her gaze, they felt their own words losing significance. Often, Deirdre's visitors broke off in midsentence, as if there were no point in continuing.

It was only when Meg brought Laney to her that Deirdre showed signs of warming to life. Her face brightened noticeably and she made the effort to talk—about school, about friends, about any of the ephemeral things that filled her daughter's life. She questioned Laney closely, watched her intently. She acted with Laney as if she knew she ought to care, but her manner was that of someone behind a wall of glass, trying to reach through, failing. Again and again, she asked, "Are you all right? Is everything all right? You're sure?"

"Sure, Mom," Laney always answered. "Everything's fine." But later, with Ripley, she asked, "What's wrong with my mother? When will she get better?"

Ripley did his best to explain without arousing memories of her father's tragedy. "Your mother suffered a sort of nervous breakdown. Dr. Devane's death caused it. She'll take a while to recover. We have to stay close to her and try not to worry her."

"But why does she look like . . . like that?" Laney had no words to describe the desolation she saw in Deirdre's face.

"She'll be all right," Ripley assured her. "She needs time. Let's be as cheerful with her as we can."

Each day after Deirdre had been brought back to *Casa Libertad,* Mother Constancia sat with her. It was more like a vigil than a meeting. The two women rarely spoke, but there was a bond between them that needed no words. They had shared the black dreams; they had passed through an abyss of the mind that Deirdre remembered as being "Bedlam, hell, and worse." The experience had brought neither of them wisdom, only resignation. Ripley, watching them, understood that they were huddling together for consolation. He could tell that Constancia was praying for Deirdre. All the while they sat together, Constancia's hand fingered the rosary of brown beads beneath her robe. But there was no sign the prayers were taking effect.

Then, one day toward the end of October, Sister Monica bustled in while Constancia sat with Deirdre and Ripley. "Mother," she said, a puzzled frown on her face, "there's a phone call for you. Long-distance. Oslo. Norway." Her eyes went to Ripley, questioning. "The Nobel Committee . . . ?"

Constancia and Ripley were gone for more than half an hour. When they returned, Ripley's face shone with delighted amazement. He knelt and took Deirdre's hands, then carefully told her the news. He spoke slowly, as if she would have to read his lips to understand. "Mother's been awarded the Peace Prize. The Nobel Peace Prize. Do you understand what that means?"

Deirdre stared back, nodded.

"That was a call from the chairman of the committee. Mother will have to go there. Oslo. That's where they award the Peace Prize. She'll be asked to speak at the ceremonies. Deirdre, do you see? That's what it was all about—at the Clinic. Costello, Devane, McCaffrey—they knew about this. Remember the entries in Devane's notebook—the ones we couldn't understand? 'NP.' That meant Nobel Prize. They had inside information. They wanted to break her, discredit her before the award was made. Deirdre, do you see? We've won."

She nodded, understanding his words. But her eyes said, *Why does that matter?*

35

By the next morning, the congratulations were flooding in. The mayor called; the governor called; the President called. From the capitals of the world, telegrams arrived, authored by functionaries who were licensed to transmit the same effulgent platitudes their governments had sent to last year's prizewinner. The press and television besieged *Casa Libertad,* grumbling at the meager facilities they found there for their purposes. The world felt obliged to be at Mother Constancia's doorstep, shabby and uncomfortable as it was. But as for Mother Constancia herself, she would have given years of her life for a good place to hide.

She knew what lay ahead of her and, despite the brimming exuberance of her associates, expected to loathe every living minute of it, beginning with the airports (which made her sick) and the airplanes (which made her both sick and frightened). Beyond the rigors of travel, she could see nothing in store for her that she did not abominate. On the way to Oslo, there was going to be a triumphal tour of American and European cities. That meant a dizzy, exhausting round of press conferences, where she would have to repeat the same things over and over like a parrot; it meant official receptions crowded with self-important dignitaries; it meant state dinners where she would be served nothing she could digest and where people would feel offended when she refused their champagne. She would have to endure being lionized by pompous luminaries who cared nothing for her work. She would have to listen politely while she was toasted and acclaimed by cynical political leaders who would contribute nothing to her efforts but their windy words and empty good wishes.

She had experienced more than enough of this elegant hypocrisy since coming to the United States, where, to her astonished dismay, the media had decided she possessed "star quality." In America, she seemed to be functioning more and more often as a political celebrity, appearing at rallies and demonstrations to do nothing more than show herself, speaking to be quoted, performing to be filmed. Ripley, along with the others who advised her, insisted that the publicity she gained was worth the demeaning things one did to receive it. They said it would allow her to influence public opinion.

She let herself be guided by their advice, but in her heart Constancia did not believe in public opinion. She could not form a picture in her imagination of this many-headed figment called "the public" whose approval one was supposed to coax and court and whose favor was able, so she was assured, to heal the wrongs of the world. She suspected "the public" was an illusion conjured up by the people who owned the newspapers and the television cameras in order to inflate their own importance. Acts of charity, she knew, were not won from "the public" the way one gained applause upon the stage from an audience of strangers. The good things that got done were done by single human beings who had been strengthened by God in their love and courage. Their deeds arose from the secret travail of the conscience and were freely offered without hope of success or congratulations. She had seen anonymous *campesinos* die the deaths of heroes and go down to unmarked graves. These were the human beauties of life, unseen by men but pleasing to God and somehow sowing mysteriously the seeds of justice and decency. Such acts counted for more than all the grand declarations of the politicians and opinion makers.

The Nobel award frankly embarrassed her. It belonged to a world of heady power and high prestige where she saw no place for herself. She was a poorly educated, often confused, not very articulate old woman. Not even a well-trained nun. She was at home in the villages of the banana forests, working face-to-face with the wretched people from whom she sprang. There had always been sweat stains on her habit and dirt beneath her fingernails from hoeing her own garden. Her only gift seemed to be that of arousing people's dignity, giving hope, inspiring resistance to injustice. Why this happened in her presence, she could not say. She had never uttered an eloquent word; she had never announced a new idea or a memorable teaching. In truth, she often did not understand what people described to her as "issues." Even her own followers bewildered her when they talked about "forces" and "necessities" and "programs."

She guessed that most of what she had become in people's eyes was there because people, in their desperation, had projected it upon her. They wanted a wise and godly person to lead them. They wanted a

saint to march behind or—more often—hide behind. They burdened
her with these expectations. She bore them. That was all. It was nothing that deserved prizes. She was troubled enough that she had been
forced to live so far away from the suffering of her people and the evil
of their oppressors. Now her forthcoming trip to Europe would take
her still farther away and no doubt keep her globetrotting for months
to come. It seemed very stupid, very wrong.

And on another, more personal level, it was frightening. She would
have to make a speech in Oslo. The world would be listening, judging
her people and her cause by the elegance of her words. When she
learned of that, she froze with fear. She dreaded speaking to vast,
faceless audiences. It was worse than self-flagellation. And so very
empty. For the words never truly expressed the suffering or the injustice.

Well, John would take care of the speech. He wrote with power and
sincerity. She would speak his words. But she would speak them in
Spanish! No matter what the television people wanted.

At last, she consoled herself that there was something more to be
gained than acclaim for undergoing this ordeal. There would be *money*.
A great deal of money. And Constancia valued money with a hard-
bitten peasant covetousness. Because with money she could buy food
and medicine and tools for her people. The money would fill bellies
and heal wounds. It would repair roofs and plant the soil. These were
things she could see and grasp clearly. It was actually not until somebody had mentioned the money that she had made up her mind to
accept the prize.

Normally, Constancia was the resident workhorse at *Casa Libertad*,
the first to rise, the last to lie down. But the endless, intricate planning
for her journey that now filled her days tired her more than a day's
labor in the fields. By the second week after the prize had been announced, she was, for the first time anyone could recall, retiring early.
She yearned for the contemplative calm she could find only in her
solitary room at night. She wanted her sustaining vision of the fire-
bright garden, the shielding peace that would hide her from the intrusive fatuity of the world—and especially from the demands of her
overeager followers.

She was now only some thirty-six hours away from the flight that
would begin her tour of America and Europe. But weary as she was, on
this night, she could not find the rest she sought. In her room, she
kneeled by her bed, waiting in vain for her mind to clear and grow

quiet. There was a nagging distraction. Somewhere in the House, a child was whining, wanting attention. It was a familiar enough sound in *Casa Libertad*, but this time it was strangely abrasive. And it went on and on. Why didn't somebody attend to it? The noise seemed to have been there for hours; it was making her head throb. She would have to ask one of the sisters to quiet the child.

She rose from her bedside on unsteady legs, her head pulsing miserably, and made her way along the corridor outside her room, then across to the staircase. The House was still, except for the whine of the child. There was no one in sight, not upstairs or down.

Clinging to the bannister, she followed the child's crying down into the entrance hall, where she would have expected to find someone on duty. She had never known *Casa Libertad* to be so quiet and deserted. It was as if the entire staff had departed. The women's shelter and emergency nursery were dark; no one stirring. She could hear nothing from the kitchen, where there was always someone at work, even in the small hours of the night.

The child, she now realized, was not in the House, but in the street outside. She went through the front door and hobbled down the stairs to the sidewalk. To her surprise, the street was as deserted as the House. There were no lights in the shops or the windows of the houses. She could not see a single car moving. But now she spotted the child. A little girl, seated under the streetlight on the curb across from the doorway of *Casa Libertad*. She was sobbing in deep distress, her face buried in her skirt. Constancia, her head hammering with pain, approached the child. She realized how very tired she was; the effort was straining her tremendously. She could not catch her breath; her chest labored and ached. A spearpoint of fatigue dug into her lungs. But now she was at the child's side, asking what the trouble was. She lifted the girl's head. The little face was tear-stained and twisted with fear, but Constancia recognized her at once. *"Niña, niña, por qué lloras?"* she asked. "Why do you cry?"

She bent to comfort the girl. As she did so, the pressure of the headache suddenly turned needle-sharp—just above her eyes. She struggled to ignore the pain, but it was impossible. It was too much and growing worse, drilling into her forehead. She was becoming faint, losing her balance. She reached to take hold of the frightened child.

And then she was awake. Fully, brightly awake. In her bedroom, kneeling beside her bed, her face against the sheets. The crying was gone. There was only a tightly knotted stillness in the dark room. But her head, her chest were bursting with pain. She groped for the light on her bedside table, found it, switched it on. And saw.

*   *   *

Ripley, up late making plans, had only just stretched out and begun to doze when the phone in his apartment blasted through the thin membrane of his sleep. It was Sister Charlotte, sounding frantic, telling him to come at once. The clock at his bedside read: 3:30 A.M. He threw on his clothes, jammed his bare feet in his shoes, and left, running the two blocks down darkened streets to *Casa Libertad.* When he reached Constancia's bedroom, Sister Charlotte and Sister Concepcion were outside the door waiting. "She won't talk to anyone but you," Charlotte said, her voice and her face lined tight with anxiety. "Why is it happening? Why?"

Ripley clattered through the door and rushed to Constancia's side. She lay on the bed, stretched rigid, her eyes gazing up at him like those of a cornered animal. The bedclothes beneath her were stained hot scarlet. Someone had bandaged her, but from the never-healing wounds in her forehead and breast the blood was streaming again freely.

There was a word on her lips, a frail whisper. Ripley bent to hear it.

"Laney . . . Laney . . ."

36

"Let's try to be as cheerful as we can," Ripley had told her. And Laney had been trying her very best.

She knew she must not burden her mother, who was having—she guessed—some kind of nervous breakdown. Whenever she was with Deirdre, she willed herself to be as bright and chatty as she could be. Just all froth and giggles. Like an airhead teenager in a Coke commercial. But sometimes the way her mother looked at her—with keen, frowning eyes—it was as if she could tell Laney was pretending. And secretly Laney hoped she could.

Because she was certainly going to have to tell somebody about these dreams.

They had started ten days before—on the night the killings had happened at the Clinic in Santa Barbara. Nobody at *Casa Libertad* or at Aunt Meg's house where Laney was staying would tell her much about that. They thought they were protecting her. Some secret! It was all over the newspapers and the television: how Smitty—poor Smitty!— had gone crazy and killed two people, then was shot himself trying to kill a security guard. She read it, but she didn't believe it. Not what it said about Smitty being a homicidal maniac. She had liked Smitty, had always felt he was a lot smarter than people thought. At the Clinic, he used to bring the mail to their bungalow; once she had caught him shuffling through a stack of envelopes as if he could read the addresses. And then there was the raccoon. The rule at the Clinic was: no pets. But one day, Laney found a hurt baby raccoon in the garden. And Smitty had brought it food and showed her where they could hide it in the tool shed. He had helped her nurse it along until it got well. How could he do something as terrible as the papers said?

But there was a greater shock still. The newspapers carried pictures. A picture of Smitty. Another of Mr. Costello. And one more. The name under it was "Richard Moray." *Her* Richard. There he was, identified as a "staff member" of the Clinic. Laney could not make sense of it. Nobody at the Clinic ever mentioned Richard; she had never seen him there. He was just this guy she bumped into at the beach. But now she was dreaming of him every night. As if he were somebody that mattered to her. And they weren't nice dreams, not nice at all. They were dreams that made her afraid to sleep.

She needed to ask questions. But of whom? Not of her mother. Not now. She had tried to talk to Aunt Meg. She had started out—tactfully, as she thought—by asking, "Do you ever have any really bad dreams?" To her surprise, Aunt Meg had given her a sharp, startled look and had lashed out, "I don't care to talk about dreams, if you don't mind. There's nothing wrong with my dreams." Aunt Meg had been acting like that—skittish and abrasive—ever since Deirdre had fallen ill. Later, apologizing, she had taken Laney aside and asked, "Why did you want to know about my dreams? Is there something wrong?" But she was asking too nervously, as if she really did not want to talk about the matter. That had scared Laney into silence and she had begged off. After that, as the dreams grew worse, she felt ashamed to speak of them to her aunt.

She would have been willing to talk to John—or maybe Mother Constancia, who was being very caring with her. But there was no chance for that. Everybody at *Casa Libertad* was too busy. They were making plans for Mother's trip to Oslo. It was a big, important thing to win the Peace Prize. Laney understood that. She had seen Mother Constancia and John being interviewed about it on television; she had read the front page stories in the papers. Mother was going to make a speech to the whole world. It was going to be about lots of big words. Like "justice" and "freedom" and "revolution." Laney's dreams were pretty minor in comparison. But that didn't make it any easier for her to get to sleep at night.

Bravely, Laney resigned herself to silence. She had no one to turn to. She would have to wait for the dreams to go away by themselves. But they didn't. They were getting worse, lasting longer.

Improvising desperately, she looked for a way to stave off sleep. She knew there were pills people took to stay awake. At a drugstore near Aunt Meg's house, she found some—not for sale to children. She slipped them into her purse—the first time she had stolen anything. With their help, she managed to get through one sleepness night. But then, dosing too heavily the next, she made herself sick. It was while she was retching in the bathroom that Aunt Meg found the pills.

* * *

When Ripley phoned the next morning, he was not sure what to say. "Is everything all right with Laney?" he asked.

Meg's voice, answering, was strung tight with worry. "God, I'm glad you called, John. I didn't want to trouble you with this. I know how busy you are just now."

"Tell me all about it, Meg."

"She was really sick last night. I found these pills in her room. She won't admit she took them, but . . ."

"Amphetamines?" Ripley asked, thinking he understood.

"No. They're No Doz tablets. You know, stay-awake stuff."

"Is that the latest high with the kids?"

"No no. This isn't about drugs. It's about nightmares. Laney's having nightmares—every night. She took the pills because she's afraid to sleep. I don't know what to do. She's running herself down something terrible."

Ripley saved the rest of his questions until he got to Meg's house. It took him over an hour to fight his way to Santa Monica through the early morning commute. When he arrived, Meg led him to the kitchen and closed the door, not wanting Laney to hear them from her upstairs bedroom.

"How long has this been going on?" Ripley asked.

"Several days. She's been trying to keep it to herself—but that isn't easy when you wake up screaming. That started about ten, twelve days ago. Woke up the whole house. Now, this last week, she's stopped screaming. And that's even worse."

"What do you mean?"

"Because she's *still* dreaming. I can tell. I go in to check at night and she's moaning and fretting in her sleep. She goes completely rigid, sweats like mad. She's scared stiff. It's terrible to watch. But she doesn't wake up. She can't. She's too deeply asleep. I have to make an effort to wake her. Poor kid."

Ripley, recognizing the symptoms, chilled at her words. "Has she told you what she's dreaming about?"

Meg shook her head. "She's as tight as a clam. She won't even admit she's dreaming. It's because she doesn't want to worry Deirdre." She paused, swallowed hard, and felt her way forward hesitantly. "Probably you don't know about this, but Peter—Laney's father—had some problem about dreams, just before he went off his head. I don't know what it was. Something . . . very bad. I think Deirdre's been afraid Laney might inherit it. Should I take her to a doctor?"

In less than thirty-two hours, he and Constancia were scheduled to be aboard a plane headed for New York, the beginning of the tour that would take them to Oslo. But Ripley knew he had no choice. Even if it meant he had to cancel his flight, he must talk to Laney. "Take me to her," he told Meg.

*   *   *

Laney could not look him in the eye. Shamefacedly, she was evading him, yet he could tell she wanted help, wanted to be forced to talk. She was drawn with fatigue but as tense as a frightened cat. Not far below the surface, hysteria simmered.

"Tell me about the dreams," Ripley said with no preliminaries.

Her face went stiff with surprise. "What dreams?"

"Tell me about them, Laney."

"I don't have any dreams to tell you about."

"I know you do. Tell me. Now!"

She bit her lip hard, held back, then let it come, riding on a high wave of tears. "I don't want to have these dreams! I'm not like that."

"Like what?"

"Kinky. Dirty. I'm not like that."

"Of course you're not."

"*He* makes me do those things. I hate it. I want him to *stop!*" She was shouting now, the blocked anxiety breaking loose, rushing out in a torrent. Ripley hugged her close.

"Who? Who's doing these things?"

"Richard. Why am I dreaming about Richard? That creep. That weirdo. That son-of-a-bitch prick. Get him out of my head!"

Her frail little body was convulsing wildly, vomiting up the words from her belly in great spastic gulps. But Ripley did not want her to stop. He wanted the story to keep coming. "Who's Richard? Tell me."

"The guy from the Clinic who died. Smitty shot him. The dead guy."

"Richard Moray?"

"That creep! I hate him."

"How do you know him? Did you ever meet him?"

"On the beach. This summer. A couple times."

"You met him on the beach? In Santa Barbara?"

"Yeah. Why am I dreaming about him? I don't care about him."

"Tell me about the dreams, Laney. Don't be afraid. Or ashamed. Tell me."

She told him. Not much at first. She could not bring herself to tell him much. But slowly, slowly he coaxed enough out of her to understand the torment she was experiencing. The obscenities that filled her dreams were nothing a twelve-year-old child could invent.

"He *makes* me do it!" Laney howled, burning with shame.

"How does he make you?"

"The sewer babies. He says I have to do what he wants or he'll give me to the sewer babies."

"The sewer babies . . . ?"

"There. That." She was pointing over his shoulder across the room. He turned to look. There was a heavy bureau against one wall. "Behind that," Laney whined. He tried to move the piece of furniture. It was not easy. Finally, he angled it away from the wall. Behind it, he found the torn and crumpled remnants of a paperback book. When he brought it back to the bed, Laney grabbed it from him. *"He* gave me this. God damn book. Damn!" And she tried to shred it further.

Ripley rescued the ruined heap of pulp paper from her hands and studied it. *"The Blood Club . . . ?"* Then he saw the inscription.

"He says if I don't do what he wants, he'll let the sewer babies get me. In the basement. I wouldn't dream that. That isn't me. It's *him.* He's doing it. Fucker! Rotten, damn fucker!"

"But he's dead," Ripley said, more to himself than to her.

"Not in my head, he isn't. He's *alive!"* She spat out the words with disgust. "And he's inside my head. I know. Oh . . . oh . . . I must be crazy."

He folded her into his arms again. Her hands clawed into his shirt. "Laney, try hard to remember. When did these dreams begin?"

"Back when he gave me the book, I had some dreams about it, about the things in the book."

"And was Richard in the dreams?"

"No. They were just, you know, regular dreams. I didn't like them. But they didn't really make me scared. They weren't dirty. Not like later, when he came."

"Later *when?* When did you begin seeing Richard in your dreams? Can you remember?"

"Yes."

"When?"

"That night he was killed. When Smitty killed him."

"How could you know he was killed?"

"I didn't. Not when I dreamed about him. I found out the next day, when I saw it on the TV—about what Smitty did. But it was that night I dreamed about him. He broke in. I remember. It scared me."

"Broke in?"

"Like—he was just there in the dream. Just like that. He didn't belong, but he was there. I was dreaming about that book. And all of a sudden, Richard came."

"In your dream?"

"Yeah. He was there. And he said, 'Help me!' And he looked terrible, like he was sick. And real scared. More scared than me. It was crazy. Because I thought: 'This is so real, he must be in my room.' So I woke up. But he wasn't there. He was only in the dream."

"And after that?"

"He's always there. When I dream. He's waiting for me. And he makes me do dirty things I hate."

"But he's dead. He's not anywhere, Laney. It's just a dream."

"It isn't! It isn't! He's really there. And he says he's *always* going to be there. He says I should tell my mother—that as long as I live, I'm always going to have to do what he wants. Why? Why is he there?"

"I don't know, Laney."

"Can't you do something? Can't you pray or something? Or Mother Constancia? Can she do a miracle and make him go away?"

"We'll think of something. I promise you."

"But you have to go away. To the Nobel thing."

"No, I don't. Mother Constancia does. But not me. I'll stay with you."

She clung to him gratefully, her trembling body finally calming in his arms. "But you can't stop the dreams from coming. You can't be inside my head where he is."

"No, Laney, I can't. But there's someone who can."

37

The shots that killed Smitty were the last sounds of this world that Richard Moray heard. They came to him like drumbeats, faint and fading, echoing down the tunnel of his waning consciousness. Dead, but not quite dead, he lay crumpled on the floor of his room, feeling himself spreading thin in a black vacuum. Coming apart, becoming little scattered points of light, each flickering out.

There was a thought in his mind. It bobbed and floated gently there. He fished it out and studied it. The thought was *I'm dead.* But he did not feel his death. His wounds were not reporting in. A wall of numbness held them back. The wall was advancing, subtracting his life.

I don't want to be dead, he thought.

"It's time to be dead." It was a voice speaking from within him, calm and magisterial.

Not yet, Moray insisted. He did not want the numbness to win. He would not let it have him. His will coiled itself.

"Time to be dead," the voice repeated. *"Now!"*

But Moray refused to obey. Inside him, a tiny ember of rebellion flared hot, fueling itself on the last tremor of his pulse, the last flutter of his breath, blindly striving.

To do what?

Launch his mind out across the darkness, a collapsing bridge of light, an escape route.

But there had to be a dream to anchor the far-swaying end of that bridge. He must have a connection.

Hurry! Find it, he thought. For the bridge was weakening, falling into oblivion.

Hurry! Escape!

Where?

A tiny signal. *There!* A dream, looming faintly. *Reach for it. Connect. Hold.*

He held.

Behind him, suddenly, there was nothing. Cold. Dark. Empty. There could be no return. His brain had become dead meat. Behind him lay Moray the corpse.

But the bridge of his consciousness had held secure—just long enough. He crossed. Moray—the remnant of him—lived, a mind within a mind. The watcher sheltered in the dream he had invaded.

But whose dream?

He was in a room, luxuriously furnished with plush carpets. One wall —all glass—presented a sweeping view of gleaming high-rise towers in the night.

He spun around. There were people . . . dream figments. Blank white faces, cadaverous expressions. But the room vibrated with a strange erotic heat.

Then he spotted what he was looking for. A small face, startled, staring at him from a far corner. Laney. It was Laney's dream.

"Help me!" he cried, dizzy from the effort of his escape.

But she was gone, fleeing.

The room closed upon him, became a protecting darkness, a shelter. *Still here,* Moray's mind thought. He could wait for her return, when she dreamed again.

He was *safe.*

Alive.

Home.

Moray had taken possession.

38

Locked away with Laney in her room, Ripley felt like a professional torturer. Each time she nodded off, he would prod her awake and press her to tell him more. The child was achingly tired, in spite of the caffeine overdose that was still sparking her nervous system, but Ripley would not let her rest. Not until she had wept and cursed and raged her way through every detail of her dreams. She had been run through a gauntlet of humiliations. Ripley listened, wavering between pity and blinding anger, allowing himself time for neither. Provisionally, he was accepting Laney's perception that Moray was "really" there, an alien presence in her dreams. That meant he needed to know everything that might help him understand the man's state of being, his motivations and designs. Finally, as the afternoon came on, he let her nod off, but only for a brief nap. When she did sleep that night, he wanted it to be deep and long.

While Laney dozed, Ripley returned to the book Moray had given her, checking her reports against what he found there. It was not much to work with, but the novel seemed to function as the main point of contact between Laney's mind and whatever survived of Moray. Her dreams were mostly embroidered around its repulsive images and incidents.

The Blood Club. It was meant to be a chic variation on the old Gothic theme, with the vampire host updated to jet-set New York. The inane plot threaded its way, none too coherently, through the glittery world of modeling agencies and *haute couture.* The moldering Transylvanian castle had become a swank Park Avenue condo; the midnight rituals in the crypt had become exclusive penthouse orgies. There were unsavory hints of an alliance between the insatiable bloodsuckers and an accommodating network of high-society abortionists. This connected with the feature that did most to season Laney's dreams with terror, the shadowy sewer babies, a contingent of half-formed humanoid beasties who inhabited the inevitable dark basement. The book seemed to touch all the requisite bases for the genre: languid female victims, sensational gore, ghoulish sex, mayhem, eviscerations, decapitation, castration. . . .

"Soon to be a major motion picture," Ripley had no doubt.

The book was kid's stuff. But Laney, after all, was a kid. And for her, so young and vulnerable, it carried a palpable terror, especially in the vicious nightmares Moray had designed for her. There was one thing more, something more chilling for Ripley to hear than any of the horrors Laney reported. The *Nothing*. The all-devouring emptiness that Deirdre had told him came with the black dreams. Laney had felt it, though she could not match words to the experience. "I feel so lonely, where he takes me," she told Ripley. "It's so far away that it makes me feel lost forever. And that makes everything worse. Because nobody could ever know I was there." He remembered the way Mother Constancia had put it: ". . . as if God has turned his face from me." This—more so than any fear or obscenity—was nothing a child should know.

Downstairs, while Laney napped, Ripley pressed Meg for permission to take the girl back to *Casa Libertad* with him. Meg struggled over the idea of letting Laney be taken out of her hands. "I shouldn't. She's my responsibility. I know that Deirdre . . ." And then, breaking into wrenching sobs, she confessed to Ripley, "Laney wanted to tell me about her dreams. I didn't give her the chance. I didn't listen."

"Why not?"

"I was afraid. It makes me afraid."

"What makes you afraid?"

"I don't know. That's why I'm afraid. Not of Laney. Of *Deirdre*. Ever since we were kids. It's crazy I know, but I used to think . . . she was in my dreams. That scared me. It scared all of us. My father, my mother . . . we all knew she wasn't right. She was autistic, you know, for four or five years. Completely out of it. Just like a ghost. With those eyes . . . as if she could look right through you. Sometimes she still. . . . And then there was what happened to Peter. He was having some kind of nightmares, terrible nightmares. Now . . . Laney. I can't help it. I think something about Deirdre is . . . wrong. Jinxed. The way she is now. The way she stares at you . . . I hate it! What happened to her? Why is she like this?"

Ripley had no answers for her, nothing he could tell her that might not frighten her still more. He promised he would have a doctor see

Laney at *Casa Libertad*. He also told her it was his intention to bring Laney and Deirdre together; he was gambling that it would do them both a great deal of good.

By midafternoon, Laney had been moved into Sister Monica's room, next door to Mother Constancia. There Father Paul, the House physician, visited to check her over. He found no physical problem beyond exhaustion. He suggested a mild sedative for the night, but Ripley judged she would not need it. It was proving nearly impossible to keep her awake.

In the course of the day, Ripley stubbornly blocked out everything that had to do with the upcoming trip, dumping the lot into the hands of an overworked but uncomplaining Sister Charlotte. She soldiered on bravely into the evening, uncertain now that anybody would be going anywhere. Mother Constancia had recovered from last night's crisis; the troublesome wounds had been successfully staunched or, their warning given, had stopped bleeding on their own. But she had been heard to say she would not leave *Casa Libertad*. Not until Laney was safe. That was a problem only Ripley could handle. At last, he met with her and told her all he knew about Laney's condition. As he suspected, she seized upon the occasion as an excuse for canceling the tour. Ripley knew better than to oppose her head-on when her mind was made up. Constancia could be fiercely stubborn. He settled for asking one important concession from her. She must wait to see what Deirdre would do.

"Deirdre? But she is in no condition . . ." Constancia protested.

"Not now, I agree. But later. Tomorrow morning. Let it wait until then. If Deirdre comes around, if she says she wants your help . . ."

Constancia agreed.

*   *   *

There was a hand at her shoulder, rocking her awake. Deirdre turned to find Ripley beside her in the darkened bedroom. When he bent to kiss her, she received his lips without response. He had come to her like this once or twice before in recent days, seeking to revive the warmth that had once existed between them. As Ripley expected, it was not there to be rekindled, not a dying coal of it.

"Come with me," he said in a low voice. She dressed and followed him where he led across the darkened building. It was nearly midnight and *Casa Libertad* was as quiet as it ever became. From downstairs, there was the faint sound of voices and the clatter of dishes in the kitchen.

One of the sisters was talking to a distraught woman with a child in the front hallway. Ripley had still said nothing when they entered Sister Monica's bedroom, where a dim night-light burned. On the bed in the corner, Laney lay asleep but not at rest. Her body was knotted with tension, her face fiery red and streaming with sweat. Deirdre stared down, observing the sleeping girl's anguish. There was only the faintest hint of concern in her features as she looked to Ripley for an explanation. He told her nothing.

"What's wrong?" she asked finally. But he gave no answer, only kept his eyes fixed on Laney, forcing Deirdre to turn back and gaze at her daughter twisting and curling on the bed. Seconds that weighed like hours passed while they watched. Ripley was determined: before he spoke, he wanted Laney's suffering to pierce the shell of ice that encased her mother's feelings. He waited stubbornly, finally detecting the signs of honest distress. Deirdre's breath caught, her throat worked. Her fingers gripped and braided. He told himself: *This is as much for her as it is for Laney.*

At last, as if a mask of wax had melted from Deirdre's face, grief, then alarm began to show through. "Tell me!" she said and repeated the words, shouting. It was the first time since she had emerged from her coma that she had felt such a human turbulence inside herself. "What's wrong? Tell me!" She seemed ready to fly at him in her frustration.

Still silent, he led her to one side, holding tightly to her hands, welcoming the way she gripped back—angrily, wanting to hurt. As blunt as a blow to the face, he told her, "It's Moray."

She was shocked enough to give a quick, sharp whine. *Good,* he thought. He remembered how Smitty had spoken of the *good* pain, the pain that restores life. But he would make her fight to find out more—for every crumb of information.

"Moray's dead," she said.

"Yes, he's dead. But he's in her dreams."

"How could that be?"

He left her waiting for his reply until she had to ask again, her annoyance edging rapidly closer to vehemence. *Reach for it,* he said silently. *Show that you care, God damn it!* To her, he said, "He's been in her dreams for days now. Ever since the night Smitty killed him."

"That can't be so."

"Look at her, Deirdre. You know what's happening. It's a black dream. She can't wake up. It will go on like this all night. Every night."

"No."

"It will. It has—for the last two weeks."

"But if he's dead . . ."

"He *is* dead. So is Devane. But Devane held you while he died. You—some part of you—died with him, right? It's the same now with Moray. He died. But before he did, he connected with Laney. He got into her dreams. He used this—like a bridge between them." He dropped the crumpled paperback into her lap. "It's a book he gave Laney this summer. Their point of contact, like the magazines he gave Peter. Laney was being set up for him to use. Smitty killed him, but the watching part of him survived. He's there—like some rotten parasite in her brain. He's eating her up inside."

It was too much for her to take in. He saw her retreating, looking for a way to hide from her anguish. *Block her,* he told himself. *Don't let her defend. Make her feel this.*

"Do you know what he's doing to her? I do. Laney told me. She didn't want to tell you because she didn't think you cared. He's forcing her to do every filthy, vile, sick thing he can think of. He's making her into his own private, psychic whore."

Every word was scoring, just the way he wanted. Pity, fear, rage were crowding into her mind. Above all, there was her love for Laney, coming alive explosively, giving her the power of desperation. But he wanted still one more thing from her—the emotion that would drive her to act—cruelly, if necessary.

"He told Laney to let you know he's there. He's using Laney to mock you. He despises you, Deirdre. He told Laney you're a stupid, cowardly cunt."

He saw the muscles in her jaw twist hard. It was what he wanted. Hatred. All the hatred he could muster. "He thinks you can't do anything about it. Nothing. You couldn't stop him in Peter's dreams—or in Devane's. He beat you both times. He took your husband and your children from you. Now he's going to beat you again. He's taking Laney. He's turning her into garbage."

There was a trembling all through her. He felt it in her hands. Her head arched far back. Behind her clenched teeth a caged cry was fighting for release.

"Go ahead!" he snapped at her. "Let it come!"

It was not a scream but a roar. Rising, then cut short. She wrenched loose of his grip, stumbled across the room to the small sink in one corner, and finished the outburst choking on her own vomit. For several moments she hung above the sink, wracked by spasms of sickness.

Ripley stood behind her, watching her narrow shoulders quiver. When she turned back to him, though her cheeks were hollowed, her face was no longer that of a corpse. She had come alive, noisily enough to wake the house, but Ripley did not care. She had broken through.

39

But she did nothing that night, except to keep by Laney's side, cradling her close, comforting her as she submerged and resurfaced in a sea of nightmares. Deirdre's inaction puzzled Ripley. He had no idea what she might do, but he expected her response to be immediate. Toward three in the morning, when she took a break from Laney's bedside, he asked, "Don't you intend to do something?"

"Oh yes," she answered. Her resolution was unmistakable.

"When?"

"When everything's ready."

Ripley waited to hear more. She said nothing. But he could see: her hatred for Moray had been tempered by cunning. Her mind was at work.

"We do have to decide something about Constancia," he told her. "Her plane takes off in four hours. She's refusing to leave."

"Yes. I'll talk to her," Deirdre said, as if she had already decided the matter. "But I need to know something. While I was recovering, what happened in her dreams?"

Ripley told her all he could. "Except for what we can conclude from the chanting we heard, we have no idea what she experienced. But my guess is that it came close to accomplishing what Costello wanted. The dreams took a terrific toll of her. Charlotte was right about one thing. The old pagan lore has deeper roots in Constancia than she's ever wanted to admit. She knows that now. She doesn't like it. I'm not sure how she's going to come to terms with what she's learned about herself in the past few weeks."

Deirdre, tired and troubled, gave his words a long, silent moment of thought. Then she said, "Take me to her."

*   *   *

The last time Constancia talked with her, Deirdre had been the withered husk of a woman, ashen and desolate. Now, as she stepped into Constancia's room, the transformation that had come over her in the course of the night was startling to see. It was more than a matter of vitality regained. At once, Constancia recognized the presence of an empowering authority. When the two women had first met, her intuition had prompted her to identify Deirdre as a *sabia,* a woman of knowledge. Since then, she had learned that Deirdre possessed an exceptional gift. But only now did she sense that the gift had summoned up a power that stood poised for battle. Deirdre had become a warrior. Constancia responded to her with a deference Ripley had not seen her offer before, not even to the Pope.

"I don't want you to stay," Deirdre told her at once with quiet but immovable firmness. "I have so much to thank you for. You heard Laney calling for help when I couldn't. But I don't need you here now. You have important things to do. I want you to do them."

Constancia began to protest, but Deirdre, continuing without a pause, caught her by surprise. "Constancia, there *is* something I want from you. More important than your presence. Something it will be harder for you to give me."

Constancia was puzzled. "Anything I can . . ."

"I want this." Deirdre's hand reached boldly into the old woman's robe and took proprietary hold of the necklace of brown beads. "Will you leave this with me?"

At once, Constancia's hands went defensively to the beads. "But why?"

"I want them for Laney." Her tone had modulated from a request to a demand.

"It is . . . it is . . ."

"I know what it is. I know what it means to you. It's from Doña Rosaura, isn't it?"

"Yes." There was a note of embarrassment in the admission. Constancia glanced at Ripley with apologetic confusion, as if she had spoken a guilty secret never mentioned to her confessor.

"That's why I want it," Deirdre said.

Ripley could see that Deirdre had shaken Constancia. He also saw that this was a clever move. Deirdre was outflanking Constancia's insistence on staying. She was challenging her to offer a greater sacrifice than giving up her European trip. But he also wondered: *Is the request anything more than a ploy? Does Deirdre truly value the beads?*

As if it were a great testing, Constancia removed the necklace. It might have been a part of her very flesh she was cutting away. "From my dreams you know of this?" she asked.

"Yes."

"It has never been off my body. No one has ever seen . . ."

Deirdre, taking the beads in her palm, fingered the silver crucifix that was suspended from them. "This was attached later, wasn't it?"

"Yes," Constancia admitted. "In the convent."

"I won't need it. May I take it off?"

After a troubled pause, Constancia gave a nearly imperceptible nod. It was only a slight inflection of the head, but it wiped away more than half a century of shaming silence. She was admitting a forbidden allegiance.

Deirdre handed the necklace to Ripley. "John, can you get the cross off this?"

Ripley took the beads and examined the clasp that held the cross in place. "You're sure it's all right?" he asked Constancia. Again, the small, rigid nod. He used his pocket knife to undo the crucifix. It came away easily. "It wasn't on very securely," he remarked as he handed it back to Constancia. Without looking at it, she thrust it into a pocket of her robe. Ripley could now see that the cross had lain over a flat black stone the size of a fifty-cent piece. There was a design carved upon the stone, but he could not make it out. He returned the beads to Deirdre, who held them under the light.

"You understand what it means?" Constancia said.

"A little," Deirdre answered. "I want you to tell me more. Teach me how to use this—the way you used it against the devil that was in your dreams."

Constancia's face went slack with amazement. "No, I cannot do this."

"I want to know the *words*," Deirdre insisted. "Tell me."

The old woman shook off her demand. "No. This I must never do." In a whisper, she added, "*¡No es cristiano!*"

Deirdre took hold of Constancia's hands and gazed commandingly into her face. "We're doing this to drive off the evil. To save Laney. You do believe that God wants to see her saved?"

"Yes. But there are other ways. We must do as God wills. We must pray."

Deirdre's voice swelled up; it was crisp with angered urgency. She held the necklace out like a weapon before her. "Constancia, *this works*. I want this."

"*Querida, querida,* there are things God does not permit us to touch. Unclean things. We are not strong enough."

"Look at me, Constancia," Deirdre ordered her. "You see—I'm strong enough. I understand your fear. But I don't share it. I think, if there is good in us, we can use all powers for good."

Constancia's expression was knotted with moral anguish. "The things I learned from Doña Rosaura—they come from long ago, when the people could not tell the good from the evil. They are . . . *revuelto.*" She looked to Ripley for the English.

"Mixed. Mixed up."

"*Sí.* Mixed. That is why God has forbidden us to use these powers."

"Not God," Ripley corrected. "The *Church* forbids it. That means men like McCaffrey forbid it. *Men,* Constancia, who teach that the powers women use are powers of evil. You know better than to believe them."

The old woman lowered her head in a deep gesture of shame. "I have been taught . . . this is blasphemy."

"You may be right," Deirdre said. "I don't know. But to save Laney, I would do anything, even if it was forbidden by God." She held up the necklace. "I'm going to use this. I'm going to use everything I have. I don't ask you to stay and approve. If you stayed, I think your shame would get in my way. It would be an obstacle. I can't be weakened like that. But I want you to teach me this power before you leave."

"The power is not in the words. It is not in the beads," Constancia said.

"I know that. It's in *you.* I want what you have inside. Something your mind does with the words that takes away fear. I need your conviction. You must show me how to look the devil in the face."

Constancia locked into Deirdre's gaze; there was an authority there she could not deny. At last, she nodded her acquiescence. But her eyes told Ripley he must not be present. She was drawing an invisible tent of secrecy around Deirdre and herself where no man would be welcome. He withdrew. For the remainder of the night, the two women were huddled together, locked away. Between them, remnants of a teaching older than the Christ of the Conquistadors were exchanged. Not much, just enough. A chant, a gesture that carried something of Doña Rosaura's defiance. When they emerged from the room, dawn was in the sky. Constancia, submitting to Deirdre's insistence that she leave, pressed a kiss on her pupil's cheek. "*Voy a rogar por ti.* You will be in my prayers," she said. Then she signaled Ripley that she was ready to go.

*　　　*　　　*

Later that morning, after Ripley had put Constancia and her entourage aboard the plane and seen them off, Deirdre asked him to find her a quiet place, well away from *Casa Libertad* and the city. She wanted to take Laney into seclusion for the next few days. He knew of a retreat the Dominicans maintained in the San Gabriel Mountains north of the city. It was a liberal establishment; he had some good friends there. He phoned and made the arrangements quickly. It was a two-hour drive. Along the way, Deirdre let Laney doze against her shoulder. The girl was frazzled, but she had recognized the change in Deirdre as soon as she woke and had brightened at once to have her mother's attentions. Even asleep, she held tight to Deirdre and would not, when they reached the retreat, let her out of sight.

In the afternoon, the three of them sat together in a thickly shaded courtyard beside a tiled pool. Deirdre brought out a book.

"Laney," she asked, "do you remember *The Lord of the Rings?*"

Of course she did. The Tolkien fantasy was one of the few remnants of childhood that Laney, in her assertive adolescence, would still admit to enjoying. She had read it several times.

"Do you remember," Deirdre went on, "how Frodo had to carry the ring through the Mines of Moria? It was very frightening, wasn't it? And very dangerous. Let's see—he had to deal with orcs . . ."

"And a Balrog," Laney added. She could recall all the story's characters, especially the monsters and villains.

"That's right. But Frodo was brave and clever. And he made it—out of the Mines back into the light. Your dreams are like that. A dark underground place filled with terrible things. And Richard, in your dreams, is like the Dark Lord. He's powerful and he's evil. And we're going to have to beat him, just the way Frodo did."

She was playing upon a vivid and familiar imagery, something Laney could cling to in her anguished confusion.

"But I'm all alone," Laney protested. "Frodo had all his friends with him."

"You're going to have friends, too. You won't be alone tonight."

"But it's a dream. How can anybody be there but me?"

Deirdre took Laney's face between her hands and gazed soberly into her eyes. "I promise you, baby—if you want it enough, I'll be there."

"Oh yes, I want it."

"Then I'll be right with you—as real as I am right now."

"I didn't know anybody could do that. How can you do that?"

"I can. I know a way. Dr. Devane taught it to me. It's like . . . mental telepathy."

"Really?"

"Really. Just believe me." Laney was baffled, but she clutched at the fragile strand of hope Deirdre held out to her. "And it won't just be me who'll be there. We can have others. All the others you want. I'll bring them with me. It'll be our own expedition through the Mines of Moria. Tell me: who do you want to take along?"

"I think John. John should be there," Laney said, slipping uncertainly into the spirit of the game her mother was playing.

Ripley gave Laney a curt salute. "Right. I'll be there."

"Of course, in the story there was a wizard," Laney observed, trying to sound too grown up to let anyone suspect she might wish she had a wizard on her side. "We wouldn't have anybody like Gandalf to lead the way."

"Do you think we might find a substitute?" Deirdre asked.

"Well, maybe Mother Constancia," Laney suggested hopefully. "She might be better than a wizard. She's a saint."

"Then she'll be there," Deirdre promised.

"And Sister Charlotte—because she's so smart . . ."

And suddenly Laney was into it without constraint, caught up in the excitement of acting out a favorite story. The terror she carried inside her was taking the shape of an adventure and she was becoming its hero, no longer its victim. The exercise was more than morale boosting. Deirdre knew: all the while they talked, Laney was gleaning the raw materials of that night's dream. With Deirdre's help, the people, the imagery Laney conjured out of her imagination would fill her sleep.

"And Alma. I want Alma there too. She'll get scared, but I'll look after her. And Smitty. Definitely Smitty. Because he must hate Richard as much as I do. And he knows how to kill him. And I don't think Smitty was a maniac—like they said on TV."

"All right. Smitty will be there. It's going to be quite an expedition."

"I could have anybody, couldn't I? In a dream, I could have Luke Skywalker . . . and Han Solo."

"Sure. But I think we have more than enough. We're going to be a really great little brigade. The Dark Lord won't stand a chance."

"So I won't be alone tonight?"

"No. I won't ever let you be alone again. But it's going to be rough, sweetheart. Because we're going all the way to the end of the story. Remember the end? How Frodo had to take the ring to Mordor?"

"To Mount Doom."

"To the Chambers of Fire. Remember how dangerous that was? And how frightened he was? But he did it. He went right to the edge."

"The abyss."

"The abyss."

"Do we have a magic ring to take with us?"

"We have something better." Deirdre reached into her pocket and brought out a fisted hand. In it was a jumble of brown beads. "Mother Constancia left this with me. For good luck. She's worn it all her life." She let the crude little necklace unfold and sway in front of Laney's eyes. "Doesn't look like much maybe, but she was given this when she was about your age. By her aunt—who was sort of a wizard."

"A wizard?"

"Mother Constancia comes from a long line of wizards."

"It didn't say so in *Time* magazine."

"Even *Time* magazine doesn't know about that. It's top secret."

Laney reached out to heft the beads in her hand. "A rosary, huh?"

"She uses it as a rosary," Deirdre explained. "But it isn't. See here." She held the flat black stone in her palm for Laney to see. It was worn smooth with being fingered over the years. The shape that was carved there was barely visible.

"There's a bird . . . or something."

"A sort of bird."

"It's got a tail."

"It's a serpent with wings."

Laney frowned uncertainly. She wasn't sure she liked the sound of that.

"Where Mother Constancia comes from, the serpent bird is powerful good luck. It's on our side. And there's something more about it. A special secret. Remember how sometimes Mother Constancia has these ecstasies? John told us about that."

"Sure."

"When that happens, she fills up with light. Everything around her becomes like diamond and crystal. It's as beautiful as you can imagine."

"Yeah? How do you know?"

"She told me about it. And this is where all the light comes from—

this bird. It gets as bright as the sun. And there's no darkness anywhere it can't light up. And when it does that, it drives off everything evil."

Laney, frowning thoughtfully, looked to Ripley to confirm Deirdre's words.

"Really," Ripley said.

"Really," Deirdre said as she spread the necklace and looped it over Laney's head. "So now we have our own talisman to keep us safe."

Laney's lively young mind was already hard at work elaborating the pictures her mother was skillfully storing within her. That was what Deirdre wanted. Laney's imagination must act, must make its own dreams. If she entered sleep with a timid, vacant mind, Moray would fill the vacuum.

"Now I just want you to rest and listen. And enjoy yourself," Deirdre said. She hugged Laney close and began to read sections from *The Lord of the Rings.* She read for the rest of the afternoon and into the evening: well-remembered passages that dealt with elves and dwarves and trolls, with feats of magic and great daring. And finally, as night came on, Deirdre read of the Dark Lord's defeat by the gentle little creatures called hobbits. " 'The Ring-bearer has fulfilled his Quest.' And as the Captains gazed south to the Land of Mordor . . . there rose a huge shape of shadow . . . terrible but impotent: for even as it leaned over them, a great wind took it, and it was all blown away, and passed; and then a hush fell."

Laney was deeply comforted. She could remember when Deirdre had first read the story to her. And she remembered something else that she had forced out of her mind. Her father had been there, every evening, listening with her, holding her beside him, sometimes sharing the reading. When he read, he liked to act out the characters. A crackly old voice for the wizard; a deep bass voice for the Dark Lord. The memory, censored and thickly veiled, now seemed as remote as a story read in a book, not part of her life at all. But it had happened only a few years before, when they had all been together, a family bound by love and loyalty. She was grateful to have the recollection back, to have the chance to be that little kid again, guarded by wise and trusted grown-ups. The vulnerability she suffered in her dreams left her craving for a dependence that would bring others to her defense. When the reading was finished, she went promptly to sleep in the bed she and Deirdre would share, holding tight to the bead necklace.

"It was her favorite book," Deirdre explained when she returned to spend a final hour with Ripley. "I first read it to her when she was eight.

I think it taught her everything she knows about good and evil. And about nobility and heroism and honor . . . and whatever else there is that's supposed to make the world decent enough for the kids we bring into it."

"You're lucky you have that much to work with," Ripley commented. "I don't know what images of nobility you could find in the fantasy lives of most grown-ups. There's plenty to scare and degrade us. Not much to edify ourselves with, is there? Maybe that's why Moray has it so easy."

Deirdre pondered his words. "I think you're right. Laney's just on the borderline now. A young woman, really—but not quite so much so that she can't allow herself to be babied a little. Another year or so and she'll probably be out of reach of these fairy tales." She gave a small guilty laugh. "I *am* babying her, I know. She needs it. But maybe I need it even more. Last chance to play all-knowing mother. I didn't get to do much of that with my other kids."

"What happens now?" Ripley asked.

"She sleeps. We dream."

"You've planned this out very carefully."

"Every time I've met him in the past, it's been on *his* terms. I've had to deal with *his* images—morbid, ugly things. That's what he knows how to do—find everything we carry around inside that makes us ashamed and afraid. That's how the black dreams work. They blot out the light. They make us forget what there is to love about ourselves. Even Mother Constancia. He broke her spirit too. She had the power to stand against him, but he made her ashamed to use it. Aaron did such a good job of training him. He really is a superb instrument. But Aaron taught me something too. That dreams can heal as well as destroy."

"The Mount Doom part. What's that about?"

"I thought everybody knew the story. That's where we finish off the Dark Lord."

"What does that mean?"

"I'm not sure I know."

"Will Laney be able to put it all together . . . the fairy tale, the talisman, all the rest?"

"She doesn't have to. Dreams have their own way of weaving things together. All she needs are images—as many and as bright as possible. The important thing is: she's got to dream for herself. If she does, her dreams will be as fine and as gentle as she is."

"How can I help?"

"Pray." She said it quite seriously, an honest request.

"To whom? The god on the cross? The plumed serpent? The elves and the hobbits? Or maybe Dr. Freud?"

"To everyone you can think of."

*   *   *

Alone in his room at the retreat, Ripley's thoughts strayed across a continent, across an ocean. He had wanted with every fiber of his being to accompany Mother Constancia on her tour of American and European cities: Washington, New York, London, Paris—finally Oslo. The journey she detested, he hungered for. Eagerly, he had scheduled meetings with political allies; he had prepared for press conferences that would invite the support of the world for the Latin American revolutions. He had been elated to see his struggle for justice—so long pursued in obscurity and against cruel odds in remote banana forests and mountain villages—breaking through to a new, high level of visibility. The Nobel award had brought with it the bracing taste of power. It was a once-in-a-lifetime moment of vindication. Two days ago, he would have given the blood in his veins to be at Constancia's side, speaking for the cause, denouncing the infamy of those who had butchered the people he loved.

But he would not be there, perhaps not even to hear Constancia deliver the address he had written for her at the award ceremonies. Instead, he was as far from the arena of public acclaim as he could be, hidden away in a mountain retreat, waiting for morning to hear about a young girl's dreams. He was astonished at how little he resented the sacrifice. Why? Perhaps because Laney's suffering was so very real, so palpable. He was coming to know something about himself. He was not a man who navigated securely among words, ideas, symbols; he had no taste for political rhetoric. He trusted his choices most when he was working close to the flesh and blood. When he held a frightened child in his arms, he had no doubt about the right and wrong of things. Then he could act with a sure, swift impulse. He craved that order of moral clarity in his life.

But there was something more that made him willing to be where he was. The world might never know it, but this tiny private battleground on which he was camped—one child's tortured dreams—was the front line of the struggle. The terror that stalked Laney's sleep was as toxic a distillation of human evil as he would ever face. Devane, Costello,

Shawsing—the forces they worked for—had taken the great healing gift of the dreamwatchers and had deliberately distorted it into something far worse than a bomb or a rocket. They had devised a psychic weapon, a force that could tyrannize the secret recesses of the personality. Hard-faced, political men had gotten a purchase on the power of damnation and had used it to rot the souls of their victims, even of a child.

If there was a Dark Lord at work in the world, this was as close to his empire as Ripley was apt to come.

40

Oh no no no! Laney thought.

Because it was happening again. The bad dream, sweeping through her sleeping mind, taking her, an undertow she could not fight.

There were hands, mopping greedily across her body, molding her young, shapeless frame. By the time the scene came fully into focus, she was enormously breasted, two great cones of jellied flesh rising from her chest. In another dream, at another time, she might have enjoyed the voluptuous exaggeration, but these were Moray's hands—and what Moray wanted of her, she was ashamed to give.

His face swam into view close up, pressing at her cheek. There was a fevered shine in his eyes. They burned darkly against his ghost-white skin. "Hello, sweet stuff," he said. "Come join the party."

Fighting against it, not wanting this dream, Laney felt herself being sucked into Moray's fantasy. It was always the same fantasy: her dream, but dominated by his will. The dimly lit, sultry room, heavily draped and richly furnished. People languishing on all sides on great silken cushions, elegantly dressed, but with hard, bloodlessly pallid faces. The scene came from the book Moray had given her. A vampire gathering. And at its center, one naked figure: Laney, who was their victim, this night and every night.

Moray's hand was at work along her thighs now, sculpturing lush female curves. And then between her legs, shaping an oversized, thickly furred sex organ. Laney wanted to hide the ugly thing, a blood-red tangle of flesh, mushy as rotted fruit. It was a humiliating caricature of a woman's body Moray inflicted upon her, the shape of a life-sized inflatable doll. A joke. Burning with embarrassment, Laney tried to lock her legs together. But other hands were holding her open, stroking and probing—not gently. She knew what came next. Moray would give her to his guests, the men and the women alike. One by one, in endless succession, they would feast upon her body while he watched. That was mostly what Moray did. Watched. Like a puppet master supervising his dolls, dancing them through the same depraved repertoire. The obsessive repetition was becoming tedious for Laney; it depressed her with its maniacal sameness. But when he noticed her attention slipping away, he made it hurt more. He could do that. And he did.

"If your mother could see you now," he teased as the dream guests went for that other blood she was mortified to have taken—her own, but made to feel unclean by their contaminating touch.

Suddenly, at his words, her dulled mind brightened. Remembering. A promise from another world. *Her mother.* Where was her mother? She looked around—and found her. She was there, just as she had said she would be. She was stepping forward from the shadowed edge of the room. But Laney had never seen her mother's eyes like this. They were as feverish and unpitying as Moray's—but Moray was their object and he shrank from their gaze. For a moment, the two of them—Deirdre and Moray—studied one another, watchers making sure each was "really" there. It was Moray who flinched, registering confusion, then unease. Swiftly, Deirdre moved to her daughter. With her finger, she traced a circle around Laney's neck. "Remember?" she asked. And the bead necklace appeared, reminding Laney. "Remember who we are? Let's show Richard who we really are."

It was as much as Deirdre would let herself do. The rest was up to Laney. She had to act, to take possession of her dream from Moray. *Come on, baby,* Deirdre secretly appealed, as fervently as if the words were a prayer. *Show him what you've got.*

At first slowly, then more rapidly, the lewd female form that Moray had willed upon Laney began to melt away. It shimmered like a reflection on water and was gone. Deirdre could not be sure what her daughter would choose to replace it. She expected something childishly obvious. Perhaps, remembering the tale of the Rings, Laney would now emerge as the brave and stalwart Frodo, the hero of the quest. But Deirdre misjudged. Laney had outgrown that little girl's perception of the story. Greater forces moved within her. Where Moray's helpless victim had once lain at the center of the nightmare, a different figure stood, tall and majestic in a gown of glimmering silver. Deirdre recognized at once the choice her daughter had made. It was the Lady Galadriel, the great elven queen of the story.

But Deirdre was astonished to see how the image came through. The Galadriel that Laney imagined herself to be had nothing of fairy-tale whimsy about her. Rather, she was gloriously shaped of flesh and blood: warm, womanly, and charged with a startling erotic power. It was Laney's own bright young idea of sexuality, at once both mysteriously potent and joyously innocent. Goddesslike in her dreaming mind, she stood commanding her ground, fighting back Moray's influence. The protecting talisman at her neck glowed fiercely, surrounding her with its bright aura. Feeling its power, she moved toward Moray. One hesitant step . . . then another.

That's it, baby! Deirdre silently wished her on. *Drive him off. You can do it. Oh, baby, you're magnificent!*

Moray, suddenly disoriented, backed off at once. He had designed a dream for a timid and troubled child whom he could effortlessly intimidate. But the Laney who stood before him now was a woman, sensual and unashamed. Her unexpected self-possession was thwarting him. And not that alone. There was something more that was disrupting his concentration. Deirdre. Though she did not move or speak, her presence seemed to second her daughter's strength. The two of them, mother and daughter, were more than he dared to take on. Hastily, he drew off, seeking shelter somewhere deeper in Laney's dreaming mind. She, turning to survey the room he had abandoned, was delighted by what she saw. For *yes,* her friends were there. As soon as she remembered, they appeared. Ripley, and Mother Constancia, and Alma, and Smitty . . . each was busy with Moray's guests, quite simply collapsing them to dust with a clap of their hands. The vampire host was nothing. A collection of puffballs, that was all. Laney laughed to see how they exploded into air. She wanted to join the fun. In a far corner, two chalk-faced ghouls cowered, trying to avoid the sun that was flooding in the room. Sister Charlotte was throwing open the curtains, exposing the guests to the cleansing light of day. Laney moved with regal grace toward the couple she had spotted. She raised her arm to point a righteously destroying finger at them: they popped like bubbles. Laughing with relief and pure delight, she returned to embrace Deirdre. "I love you, baby," her mother whispered at her ear, though she knew this was no child she held against her now, but her daughter's dream ideal of womanhood. Laney's proud resistance had exhausted her; she trembled in Deirdre's arms. Her mother let her slide gently into secure sleep for the first time in days.

When she woke, she found Deirdre, still in bedclothes, at her side, her head propped on a supporting hand. Laney remembered some of the dream, enough of its emotional tone to know it had taken a triumphant turn. She rolled over in the bed and gave her mother a loving bear hug.

"Is that it? It's over?" Laney asked.

Deirdre, smiling encouragement, shook her head. "Uh-uh. That was the semifinals. Remember, we have to go to the end of the story."

Laney frowned uncertainly, not understanding. "Where's that?"

"Deeper."

*   *   *

"Last night was fun and games," Deirdre told Ripley when they were alone, loitering over breakfast in the refectory of the retreat. "I think that part is over. We took him by surprise this time. Laney loved it. It was a grand romp for her. She needed that. But he's been warned. Now it gets a lot harder."

She looked pleasantly tousled. He could tell she felt good about last night, but he could also catch the nervous tautness in her voice. He asked, "He's definitely there? I mean he's not 'just' a dream?"

"Yes, he's there. The way a watcher is there. The same way I was there. The difference is, when Laney wakes up, I wake up too. I have a life, a body to come back to. He hasn't. He's got no place to be but her nightmares. That's all the life he has left. He won't give that up easily."

She paused to revolve a dark judgment. "He's quite insane. The way he looked, the things he wants Laney to do . . . whatever part of him survived, the scrap of him that's in there—it's crazy. I suppose you might say he's a ghost. A crazy ghost. And Laney's dreams are his haunted house. He's dug in there, hiding. He's going to be damn mean."

"You plan to go looking for him?"

"I have to. Last night, we just scared him off. But the poison is still there. I have to cauterize the wound."

"But how do you 'look for him'?"

She gave a thoughtful smile. "It's not easy to explain what it's like to be inside someone's head, inside their dreams. Aaron's the only person I ever talked to about it. It isn't like being in a physical place, of course. But there is a kind of geography to it. There are two important directions. Up and down. *Up* toward the light—that's being awake. Or, like in Constancia's trance dream, *more* than awake. And then there's *down* toward the dark. Those are just figures of speech, but that's how you have to think about it. You have to use images like that to find your way. The images are unreal, but the directions aren't. They exist . . .

somehow, somewhere. I learned all that working with Aaron. He was quite brilliant, you know. He taught me that it isn't just *what* people dream that's important, but how *deep* they dream it. 'Deep,' meaning *down.* Meaning how far they get from where we are right now, awake, talking, thinking. It's the deep dreams that matter most. That's where people hide their big secrets.''

Ripley listened with growing fascination while she told him of a world he could never know, the veiled landscape of the unconscious mind. She talked to him with the self-assurance of an experienced traveler. He could sense the pride she took in her skill; despite the dangers, there was even a note of exhilaration in her voice as she talked about the adventure at hand. Her courage was almost enough to quiet his fears for her.

"Right now, you see," she went on, "we're awake. We're up here in the world where it's full of light. Some dreams happen close to the surface, but they don't tell you much. Black dreams—those are the other extreme. They happen as far away from the light as you can get. Once you go beyond that, there's . . . Well, Aaron didn't think you could ever go beyond that—not and stay alive and human. He had an idea: that the mind is connected way down deep with something that never wanted to be alive, never wanted to think or feel. Some dead, ancient stuff that's pure nothingness. Against life. Hating it. The closer you get to that, the closer you get to suicide. Which is exactly the way Aaron used black dreams: to make people will death. It was like pulling a plug and flooding the mind with negativity.''

"Devane was a Freudian, wasn't he?" Ripley asked.

"Yes."

"Because Freud had much the same notion."

Deirdre was impressed to learn that. "Did he?"

"He called it 'Thanatos'—that dead, ancient stuff.''

"I once heard Aaron use that term."

"Greek for 'death.' The physical foundation of the brain. Rock bottom."

"He said we had that inside of us?"

"At the core of the mind. Freud was a pretty grim customer. He didn't believe life was at home in the universe. It was a sort of rebellion against the natural dead state of things."

Deirdre was pondering the word with fascination: "Thanatos."

"The old enemy."

"Black dreams take you close to that, close enough to wipe out the

will to live. Aaron used to think that's where we get all our ideas about
devils and demons—the dark things that attack life. That's where I
think Moray is hiding, as deep as he can get. Like an ogre at the bottom
of the sea. Where he thinks I'd never dare to come looking."

"You're sure you're up to this?" Ripley asked. It was a feeble question, a gesture of concern that carried no advice with it. She did not
need to answer. Her hand on the coffee mug she held turned dead
white at the knuckles. It tightened until, fearing she might shatter the
cup in her grip, he reached across to take it from her.

She said, "Do you know how much I hate him?"

He did. He had brought her to that hate, hoping it could become her
weapon. Now he realized he had released a force in her he could not
contain or direct. It would run its course down into the obliterating
abyss of the mind. And beyond that—if there was anything beyond—
even she could not be sure where her pursuit would take her.

41

There was a sound. A scraping. A creaking. Sharp and metallic. It had a rhythm.

It was the next night and Laney lay once more in troubled sleep. Deirdre strained to see into the compacted shadows of her daughter's dream. Her eyes adjusted to the faint glow that filled the space before her. She could just make out Laney's form. The girl was lying stretched on her stomach, face down, fiercely intent. She seemed to be wedged into a narrow horizontal crack, barely large enough to admit Deirdre as she tried to draw close.

The dream was happening so deep, Deirdre had struggled a long while bringing it into focus. She entered cautiously, trying to orient herself without disturbing her daughter. She inched quietly forward, squeezing herself into the low, cramped opening where Laney seemed to be hiding.

The sound grew louder. It was nearby. Overhead. *Creak-squeak. Creak-squeak.* A slow, rocking tempo. Oddly familiar. Deirdre knew the sound. It floated just off the edge of recognition, a sound so often heard that one ceased to hear it. When she drew close to Laney, she could tell the girl was rigid with anxiety. Just above her in the darkness, there was a slight movement, a bulky oscillation that accompanied the sound. Inches above her head, there was a rough, gauzy texture. It was crisscrossed by a pattern of hard circles that carried a springy vibration. Deirdre, feeling across it, was again struck by its elusive familiarity. Then it came to her. It was the underside of a bed. Laney was hiding under a bed, pressed down tight against the floor, scared stiff of detection.

Suddenly. Intruded into the darkness. A face. Moray's face, twisted by a cruel smile. "Caught you!" he screamed. "One, two, three for Laney!"

And then the bed was rolling, being yanked away. Moray was shoving it aside, revealing Laney. Deirdre, watching, saw two entangled figures on the bed. Naked, sweated bodies overlapping, merged. She recognized them at once, even in the dismal light that Moray was permitting to enter the scene. Herself and Peter, making love. Peter was still locked into her body, his belly tight up between her spread legs. In the dream, she and Peter were gazing at Laney with shocked faces. Her own dream face was distorted hideously, blackening with rage. Still coupled to Peter, she pointed down at Laney, who was cowering in her pajamas, a cruelly isolated target on the floor. "She saw us. Kill her! Kill her! The dirty little spy."

Deirdre, watching, recognized the room Laney was dreaming. It was their bedroom—hers and Peter's. And the tell-tale sound—it was still there, now loud, growing louder, becoming the raw cry of a bird of prey circling. *Screech—screech—screech.* She remembered. The bedspring that had so often softly groaned beneath them, timed to the rhythm of their love.

"Kill her!" the dream Deirdre was shouting. "She saw! She saw!" And Deirdre, watching, could feel her daughter's anguished embarrassment turning to fear. Had Laney ever really done it—hidden under their bed, eavesdropped upon her parents' lovemaking? Had Moray found a real memory or only a wish, a shameful fantasy sequestered in the dark closet of Laney's mind? In either case, he had staged the crime of the primal scene with shattering power. *Poor thing, poor thing,* Deirdre wanted to say to Laney, carrying the foolish, needless guilt of it for so long. Deirdre rushed to take hold of her daughter, to tell her "It doesn't matter."

But Moray was moving the dream too rapidly in another, more ominous direction. Peter, crudely wrenching free of the dream Deirdre's body, rose from the bed, naked, his alert penis thrust before him, a grotesque weapon, jutting. He was stalking Laney. The knife was again in his one hand and in his other, her dead baby brother, limply hanging, a bloodied remnant. It was Laney's final remembered picture of her father. The blank eyes, the zombie tread, his hands filled with murder. And behind him, sprawled obscenely on the bed, her sex gaping like an angry mouth, the dream Deirdre goading him on. "Kill her! You're mine, not hers! Kill her! Kill all the little fuckers!"

In an instant, Deirdre grasped what Moray was doing. He had linked two terrifying memories. Laney, hiding under the bed, violating her parents' sexual privacy. Laney, fleeing from Peter that murderous night. The two recollections now merged to become Peter wildly slaughtering his children in punishment for Laney's transgression.

On the floor of the bedroom, in a paroxysm of terror, Laney screamed and screamed before her father's approach. Deirdre moved forward to take her, calm her.

It was the wrong move.

Laney, in her panic, could not tell the real from the dream Deirdre. The two had become one menacing identity. Moray had counted on that, was using it to break the protecting bond that held mother to daughter in Laney's dreams. Howling with fear, Laney fought free of Deirdre's embrace, bolted blindly away. Moray rushed to lead the way for her. He opened an endlessly long, blank corridor. Laney ran along it, disappearing. Peter, in pursuit, entered behind her.

Keep your head, Deirdre thought as the dream began to fragment around her. Moray was maneuvering Laney away from her, shifting the dream to a still lower level. He was clever and willing to run high risks. She would have to search deeper.

*　　　　　　*　　　　　　*

Deirdre could not know, in her sleep, that she was watched over. Beside her, Ripley sat in the darkened room, studying her face and Laney's, looking for signs, clues. He felt unbearably helpless. Somewhere inside the bone capsule of her skull, fine sparks of nervous energy shot across the billion-stranded web of her brain. Electrical juices too fine to be measured squirted through synaptic channels. And from this subtle chemistry, a secret universe arose whose imagery was a skewed reflection of what people call the "real" world. How deep, how dark would this night's dreams become? Ripley could not know. He was locked out, left to imagine, and imagined the worst. He thought he saw faint traces of surprise, hurt, despair in her face; and in Laney's face, the evidence of terror.

Cautiously reaching across the bed, he slipped his hand under Deirdre's limp fingers, gave a tiny pressure. She gripped back in her sleep, held him tight. It was an anxious gesture. He left his hand in hers, trying in vain to link himself to her adventures.

*　　　　　　*　　　　　　*

"Quick! Quick!" Moray commanded, holding open a narrow door.

Laney, racing breathlessly forward, stopped short, but there was no way to turn. Behind her in the confining hall, her father was still coming on, shambling after her. She looked around, caught sight of his terrible nakedness, his dead eyes. That was worse than Moray. She dodged into the offered door. It slid shut behind her and the room—it was an elevator—began to descend smoothly and swiftly. "You're safe," Moray said. "I saved you, sweetie pie. Be grateful. Your daddy would have carved you into hamburger. Parents hate spying, prying little brats who interrupt their fucking. Especially that mother of yours. De—eir—dre. She's some hot piece. A world-class nympho. She was glad to see your brother and sister get chopped. Gave her more time for screwing. She screws every guy who comes along. Did you know that? Dr. Devane—she screwed him. Father John—him too. Every night. She doesn't want you around. You're a pain in the ass to her."

Laney, trembling with shame and dread, could not look at him. She tried to edge as far away as she could get. But the elevator was shrinking, forcing them together. Moray was making that happen. And now she was up against him. His hands were on her, feeling down her belly, wanting breasts on her unformed chest. Vaguely, at the edge of her attention, other images tugged at her, reminding her of another, prouder adventure, of friends who should be with her. It had to do with her mother. But her mother—Moray kept saying—could not be trusted. "I said, 'Be grateful,' you little twat," Moray shouted. "Otherwise, I'll show you what happens. Next stop—all the way down. The bargain basement. Remember what we keep down there?"

He reached to push a button on the control panel. The button was a great, piercing eyeball. It moved this way and that. The eye of the Dark Lord, looking for her. She shrank back, trying in vain to hide. But the eye was on her steadily.

Endless descent, pressed close to Moray, enduring his violating touch. The air, the light were growing so thick they were like a smothering jelly. At last, the elevator door opened. "End of the line," Moray announced. Laney tried to dart away through the open door, then froze. There was nothing she could see beyond it—only a yawning black void. But there was a stench that hit her like a fist. "You want out?" Moray snapped. "Then *out!*" And he shoved her forward. She stumbled out and down, landing on hands and knees in reeking water. There was a hollow burbling sound; she felt a tide of muck rising rapidly about her. Knee-deep in it and sinking, she groped her way back toward the open door of the elevator, now hovering just out of reach. "Didn't I tell you what would happen if you were difficult?" Moray shouted. "This is it, sweetie pie. See how you like it."

Around her in the fetid darkness, there were moving shapes, softly stirring in the sludgy waste. They made little squeaking speech sounds. She could hear something like her name being called. *"Lan-ey! Lan-ey! Lan-ey!"* The word was not being formed by human lips. She knew who was calling. She remembered from the book. The sewer babies. He had thrown her to them. *"Lan-ey! Lan-ey! Lan-ey . . ."* she heard from all corners of the cellar. Their dark eyes shone like oily bubbles around her. Moist, tendril-like fingers brushed across her legs. And then she felt a gummy little sucking just above the knees.

"Take me back!" Laney pleaded to Moray. "Oh please!"

"Don't beg him!" a voice commanded. Laney spun around, searching. In a far corner of the basement, there was a faintly phosphorescent figure. *"Remember the necklace,"* the voice said. And Laney did. She felt for it at her throat. At once it began to shimmer, to come alive with light. A bright circle formed around her, driving back the filth, making a clean space. Now she could see—at the far end of the chamber, it was Mother Constancia. She was striding slowly in her long robe just above the surface of the foul waters. Where she stepped, the shapeless, human-featured vermin with which Moray had populated the black dream shrank back, dissolving. Laney gave a cry and rushed toward the advancing figure, embraced her fiercely. "Help me! Help me! Help me!" she cried.

"Stand and face him!" Mother Constancia gave the order almost fiercely, her voice like the lash of a whip. "You have nothing to fear from him." She was closer now, gliding into the ring of light that had spread from where Laney stood. "Make the room bright," she commanded. And Laney did, taking hold of the bead necklace for all she was worth, squeezing radiance from it. The shadows of the deep basement were gathering up and receding, vanishing in a rapid swirl down a hole in the corner. Vibrant light was sweeping through the stale air. It streamed from a white-hot center just above Laney's head. A burning cloud. And in it, she could discern in hazy outline the serpent-tailed bird that was carved on the black stone of the necklace. No longer a carving, it had become a living thing that whipped and fluttered in the air. It was a fearful presence. But Laney understood: it was a guardian. *Her* guardian, as savage as the evil it must fight. And its gaze, unpitying and predatory, was directed at Moray. Brightness issued from it like a rain of spears, driving him back.

Moray, suffering the light, struggled to steady his will and make it felt. But his concentration was flaking away, yielding. Why? Then he realized. *Words.* There were words all about him. He did not know their language, but their brutal cadence hammered at him, strong as an angry wind, tearing his thoughts from him like leaves from a tree. He had heard these words before. They belonged to Mother Constancia. In her dreams—the black dreams he had created for her—the same ritual chant, rasping and guttural like the growling of an infuriated animal, had served to focus her defiance against him, had become an explosive force. But *those* were Constancia's dreams and in those dreams, Constancia had burned with shame to use these words. *This* dream was Laney's. Why were the words here—and this time battering him without any inhibiting trace of shame? It was more than he could grasp, more than he could stand against. Each rhythmed intonation that Constancia uttered slashed at him cruelly, as if the bright fangs of the serpent bird that hovered over her were devouring his mind.

Retreating in the face of her defending sorcery, he felt himself being forced toward the yawning hole where the sewer babies had disappeared from sight. He was shrinking. He was already as small as a bug being washed down a drain.

"You see," Mother Constancia said, "he is nothing to be afraid of." Laney, looking up into her face, saw it framed by a blazing halo. The fiery bird sailed above them, drawing them up and up, a swift, dizzy ascent from the pit of the black dream. Soon there was only the gloriously bright sky overhead. And then Laney saw: it wasn't Mother Constancia—not quite Mother Constancia. The face she saw was mixed with her mother's. She strained to remember . . . something Moray had said. Wasn't she supposed to be afraid of her mother? A small discordant memory lingered in the corner of her mind, but she could not draw it into focus. Then it was gone and she was in Deirdre's arms, holding close.

They were someplace open and benign. A garden clustered with glowing trees. It resembled the courtyard of the retreat house, but filled with a gemlike radiance wherever she looked. The air was crisp with sunlight.

"Is this Mother Constancia's garden?" Laney asked.

"Well, not quite," Deirdre answered. "I'm not exactly up to that standard. But it's as close as you or I may ever get. Do you like it?"

"Oh yes."

"It's always here, whenever you need it."

"How long can we stay?"

"As long as we care to. It belongs to you. You can come here whenever you like. You just have to remember it's here."

"I'll remember."

"But you have to remember something else too."

"What?"

"The other place. Where you were before. Where Richard took you. Down below. Do you remember, baby?" Laney did not wish to answer. She hid her eyes. "Tell me," Deirdre insisted, raising her face. She was smiling, inviting courage. "You can't remember this place without remembering the other."

"It was a horrible place. The basement. I don't want to remember."

"I'll show you where you were. Look." Deirdre reached down into the glistening grass. She searched with her finger, combing through the silvery blades, until she picked up something. It lay in her hand, a black dot. Laney could hardly see it. It kept getting lost in the glare of the day. "Here, take it. Look close," Deirdre said.

On the tip of one finger, Laney held the tiny dark piece of grit. It seemed to be a minute fragment of glass. As she studied it, she discovered she could see it more clearly. It had a shape. Pointed—like a pyramid. And it was transparent. If she put her eyes very close, she could see movement inside. A dark vapor, slowly circulating. The longer she stared at it, the more details she could pick out. There was a figure . . . Richard, moving along the inside of the pyramid, feeling his way, as if he were looking for a way out. She could see him well enough to recognize the anxiety in his face. And surrounding him, churning and whirling in the black cloud, were all the things with which he had filled her nightmares. The vampires and the sewer babies were there. The dream Deirdre was there too, ugly and menacing. And Laney herself as the bloated, sexual caricature Moray had wanted to make of her. It was no longer frightening to see, but it was ugly. Still, Deirdre would not let her take her eyes away. Close at Laney's ear, she whispered, "See what Richard turned us into—you and me? Hideous things. He did that to your father too." And in the pyramid, Peter Vale appeared, the terrible knife-wielding killer with the blank eyes. "Richard made him that way," Deirdre was telling her. "He was nothing like that, baby. Remember that. Always."

But that was too sad, too woundingly sad for Laney to hold in her mind. She turned away, flinching from the sight. As she did, suddenly, the things in the glass spire seemed to loom big, an expanding shadow reaching out to envelop her. But Deirdre took the pyramid away and the fearful forms shrank out of sight. Resting again in Deirdre's palm, no larger than the head of a pin, it became harmlessly insignificant. A speck. Laney felt safe to touch it with her finger.

"Mount Doom," Deirdre said.

"This . . . ?"

"That's it. That's the size of it. If you don't forget how much bigger the world is, it's next to nothing. Not quite nothing. But next to it."

Fascinated, Laney studied the tiny object in her mother's hand for a long while. Finally, Deirdre asked, "Do you think we're ready to let him out?"

"Who?"

"Richard."

Laney was astonished. "No. Never."

"It's safe here. As long as you know: This is *your* world, not his. You're in charge of things here."

"I'm . . . I'm afraid of him."

"That's why we have to let him out. So you can learn that you don't have to be afraid. Remember—that's what he wants. He wants you to be scared to death of him. Because as long as you're scared, you can't hurt him. You can't hurt him even by hating him. You know how we can hurt him most?"

"How?"

"By letting him out in all this light. I think it'll hurt so much we'll feel sorry for him. And he'll hate that even more."

"I'm not sorry for him. Are you?"

"No, not just now. I feel the way you do. Maybe even stronger. But I think I might feel sorry for him by the time we're finished."

The statement amazed Laney, even troubled her. It sounded faintly treacherous. "Why would anybody be sorry for a stinking creep like him?"

Before she answered, Deirdre considered: how much of this would Laney bring back from her dreams? It was a subdued conversation, a quiet, sweet time. This was very likely the closest she and Laney would ever be in all their lives. But Laney was not apt to remember much of what they said—not clearly. She would only take away the feel of the dream. Deirdre answered her question: "Because I was the same kind of kid he was—once. He wasn't born evil. He was born . . . gifted. What they did to him, they might have done to me."

She stood up, tousling Laney's hair. "Now be strong, baby. Show me how bright you can keep things." Quite casually, she flipped the tiny glass pyramid onto the lawn and stepped down on it where it fell. A small black fume rose from the grass and vanished almost too soon to be noticed. Where it had been, Moray stood, bewildered and frightened, blinking at the assaulting light. Laney shied off at his presence. As she did, the light that surrounded Moray wavered slightly like a candle flame in a puff of breeze. "Keep it bright," Deirdre instructed her sharply. "There, don't you see? You're holding him. He can't do anything. This place is *yours.*"

It was true. Moray was suffering the cleansing brightness of Laney's dream. It wrapped around him punishingly like an alien element, an air he could not breathe. *"Don't be here,"* Moray's raging mind told him. But there was no place else to be. Laney's dreaming mind was his last, crumbling margin of life. Beyond it, there lay a boundary he must not cross.

Something moved near him. He squinted against the light to take it in. His vision was too stunned to recognize that it was Deirdre. What he saw—what she made him see—was the figure of a woman, simply there, naked, offering comfort. It was a kindness, but the sight of it was a horror to him. He had never touched a woman's body but with a secret wish to violate it. This body could not be taken like that. It was armed with pity. Nakedly vulnerable, it nevertheless resisted his fantasies of defilement.

"Richard," Deirdre's voice said, "it's bedtime. Time to sleep." She spoke to him the way she had talked to the autistic children she cared for—strong and calm, giving gentle commands. And came closer. Moray saw the woman shape make a movement. He looked hard. She was stretching her arms toward him, asking to hold him. It might have been a gesture of love, but Deirdre, reaching for him, knew she was inviting what he could not give, something more hideous than annihilation. Automatically, he drew back, as she expected he would. But there was no place to receive him. This was the edge and he was tilting toward the darkness that was greater than any black dream.

For Laney, looking on, keeping the garden as lucidly bright as she could, Moray had already become a vacant form. It was as if some clever artist had found a way to draw pictures in smoke upon the air, a transient outline that quickly thinned, dissipated. She recalled the words of the book, the demise of the Dark Lord: ". . . a huge shape of shadow . . . terrible but impotent . . . a great wind took it, and it was all blown away. . . ."

It seemed a peaceful departure. Laney could relax into its sense of finality. But for Moray, it was an exquisite anguish. The lingering, minimal substance of him was dissolving in the light. And he, clinging stubbornly to the only existence he had, was a man trying to stay alive while he watched himself burn to ashes. The last of it was only his to know. Deirdre never saw how his vanishing mind met the uprushing darkness. Something like the shutter of a camera fanned open around him, at the same time both fast and slow in its action. In that strangely prolonged instant, he was swallowed down toward another shutter that blinked and then toward another, opening within opening. And then, below him, there was a black expanding vacancy, like the pupil of an eye that winked, consumed a morsel of the light, and would forget at once what it had seen, preferring the undisturbed darkness.

At the end, Deirdre pressed as close to his disintegrating form as she dared, wanting her face to be the last thing he saw. She could not know if he recognized who had brought him to the abyss. If he did, it would have been no more than a moment's revenge. But she wanted it all the same.

42

For the next several nights, Deirdre carefully orchestrated a run of gentle dreams for Laney, innocent amusements that calmed the last of her anxieties. Rapidly, the black dreams faded from her memory; only a few blurred fragments of her final encounters with Moray survived, enough to remind her of great danger surmounted, evil overcome. Enough to assure her of her own power. The sense and substance of the adventure stayed with her; the details, as Deirdre intended, slipped away into a merciful amnesia. At some secret level of her being, Laney had learned to own her dreams. When Deirdre was sure of that, she withdrew from her daughter's sleep—the last time, so she hoped, that she would ever stand vigil over Laney's dreams.

By then, Mother Constancia, brimming with complaints and discomforts, had returned with her retinue from Europe. She brought the great prize home with her the way a peasant woman might lug an especially heavy load of washing to the river; not as a trophy but as a burden. Ripley took satisfaction in knowing that her speech—his speech—had been universally regarded as the most politically provocative address delivered at the Nobel ceremonies within living memory: a tough, eloquent appeal for the justice without which peace is a sham. All the appropriate people had been offended, all his allies inspired. But he was soon heard to observe, sharing Constancia's misgivings, that the prize was going to make *Casa Libertad* a very different place. It brought with it a lifelong, inescapable spotlight.

"Do you mind that?" Deirdre asked.

"I guess I do," he said. "We used to be a small circle of friends. A family, free to have our quarrels, speak our minds, make our mistakes. We did some good that way. Now we have the attention I always wanted and that makes us a well-lighted target. You can just feel everybody weighing their words before they speak. There's been serious talk about not taking in any more political refugees. The House is just too much in the public eye for that. I suppose it takes something like the Nobel Prize to teach you: not everything worthwhile happens where the spotlight shines."

He was talking more and more often of returning to Central America, to one or another of the troubled places where the revolution continued. As he once wanted, Deirdre had found a place for herself in Mother Constancia's world. She ran the day-care program, one of the less political activities at *Casa Libertad*. She suspected it was only her presence in the House that kept Ripley from leaving. But even that might not hold him much longer. She felt certain that someday soon he would ask her to come with him. She had no idea what her answer would be. She had not turned the least bit more political, but Ripley had raised an interesting possibility. She thought about it often. He was certain that her powers as a dreamwatcher and a healer would have the chance to flourish in that distant and obscure corner of the world. In the mountain and forest villages where so many of the old ways continued, she would not be seen as either an instrument or a freak; she would be accepted as the *sabia* she now knew herself to be. She might come as a disciple of Mother Constancia, someone who wished to heal and to serve in secrecy.

"You could do a lot of good there," Ripley assured her.

She had to admit—she was tempted.

      *   *   *

And then one day—it was in the early spring following Constancia's return—Laney asked, "Did Daddy ever wear a white suit?"

It was the first time she had mentioned Peter in . . . Deirdre could not remember how long. Years, it seemed. Deirdre knew she had dreamed of her father many times in the past, especially in the first few weeks after his death. Unhappy dreams, fearful dreams. Dreams she did not want to talk about. There was an unspoken agreement between them: nothing would be said of Peter unless Laney asked about him. Now she was asking and Deirdre felt a little worried. "No," she answered, "I don't recall a white suit."

"Oh."

"Why?"

"Because I dreamed about him last night and he was wearing a white suit." Catching the look of concern that passed across her mother's face, she was quick to add, "It was a real nice dream. He was all dressed in white. White tie, white shoes. He looked just great."

Laney was growing up fast. By leaps and giant strides. In just the last year—it seemed like overnight—she had become quite the attractive and self-possessed young woman. Her stick-thin frame had begun to round and fill; her tastes had matured into the oh-so-very-adult airs of a thirteen-year-old. But there were cast-off remnants of her life still waiting to be reclaimed—and this was the most important.

"I wonder why he was dressed in white," Deirdre said. Meaning, *Why did you choose to dress him in white?*

"I asked him about that. Guess what he said. He said, 'Because this is our first communion.' "

"Communion?"

"Yeah. Like the Catholic kids do, you know."

"Yes, I know."

"Daddy wasn't Catholic, was he, ever?"

"No."

"Well, anyway, that's what he said. 'This is *our* communion.' I remember that. And then there was this big party—for the communion. Lots of people were there—everybody we know, just about. It was in a big, beautiful, sunny park—like, remember, that garden at the Dominican place? Like that. But really huge. And Daddy was giving this, like, picnic. There was just endless food. Tables and tables of it. And you were there, and you said, 'There isn't enough time to finish all this. It'll spoil.' But Daddy wasn't worried. He just laughed and said, 'We'll throw away the spoiled part. There's lots more.' And he took out this tablecloth, this white paper tablecloth. It didn't look very big, but when he shook it out, it turned into a long white carpet. And it rolled and rolled, farther than you could see, all the way to the horizon. And then, he picked me up—all of a sudden, I was just a little girl—and put me on his shoulders. And we started walking down the carpet. Just Daddy and me. And the people who were watching, they started applauding. I was very proud of him, the way he looked, so handsome. Very . . . proud. And he said, 'We'll make the good things last and last. We'll have parties all along the way.' And I could see up ahead, all these parties that we were going to have. They were like little cities filled with people and with bright lights and towers—one after another all the way down along the carpet." After a pause, she added reassuringly, "I wasn't afraid of him. I wanted to be with him. I had this feeling—that he wouldn't hurt anybody, not if he was really himself. Do you know what I mean?"

"Yes, I do."

"He looked so good in that white suit. He looked just right."

A few days later, on her way out the door with some friends, Laney rushed back to thrust something into Deirdre's hands. The gesture was hasty and offhanded, but deliberately so. "Hey, shouldn't we give this back before it gets lost?" she asked. "We don't need it anymore . . . do we?"

It was Mother Constancia's necklace. As far as Deirdre knew, Laney had been wearing it day and night since it had been given to her as a talisman.

*   *   *

Mother Constancia had never asked about the beads. She had been anxious to know that Laney was safe and well and, during her travels, had phoned more than once from Europe to make certain of that. But she never asked about Laney's dreams. Deirdre had been waiting for months for a question from her; finally she decided it would not come.

One evening at *Casa Libertad*, when she found a quiet moment at bedtime, she visited Constancia's room, bringing the beads with her. "I know you must want these back," she said.

For a long moment, Constancia did not reach to take them. "You are sure you have no further need?"

"Yes."

"They were . . . useful?"

"Yes."

"I am glad to know." She took the beads and poured them thoughtfully back and forth through her fingers. "I was very selfish not to help you."

"But you did help. You couldn't have done more."

"It was true what you said about the shame. When I was a child in the convent, the sisters could not make me forget what I learned from my aunt, but they made me ashamed to remember. It was cruel to do this, but they taught me as they had been taught. Perhaps Sister Charlotte is right—that God has many names. Still, for me, it must be like so." She had fished the little silver crucifix out of her pocket and was trying to attach it again to the string of beads. Her arthritic fingers could not quite manage the task. Deirdre reached to help, finally clipping the cross upon the black stone. Constancia thanked her, then slipped the beads over her head and hid them away beneath her robe. "Two gods here at my heart."

"Two gods," Deirdre said. "One necklace."